LOVE COLLIDED

HOLLOWS GARAGE
BOOK 4

KATE CREW

For the ones who are told they are too sensitive, too emotional,
or too much:
You're not too much; they're too weak.
Sensitivity isn't a flaw; it's a superpower.

CONTENT WARNINGS

Sexual content (Consensual), acts and references to domestic violence, references to car wrecks, violence, & explicit language.

LOVE COLLIDED PLAYLIST

Gorgeous - Taylor Swift
Party Crasher - Buddy
Chalk Outlines - Ren, CHINCHILLA
Wishing You Hell - Taylor Acorn
he never will - Alexander Stewart
Devil Doesn't Bargain - Alec Benjamin
I Think He Knows - Taylor Swift
Heartbroken - Diplo, Jessie Murph, Polo G
Wish on an Eyelash, Pt. 2 - Mallard, The Chainsmokers
Minefield - Nic D
Friends - Emma Lov, Loote, JORDY
Shoot Me Dead - Cameron Whitcomb
Look What You Made Me Do - Taylor Swift
Killa - Brennan
you should see me in a crown - Billie Eilish
HONEY (ARE U COMING?) - Maneskin

Wild Ones - Jessie Murph, Jelly Roll
Different Kind of Beautiful - Alec Benjamin
Superfan - Bones
Beautiful Things - Benson Boone

Cover Designer: Books and Moods at booksandmoods.com

Editor: The Author Buddy at theauthorbuddy.com

CONTENTS

ONE

SCOUT

THE COLD ASPHALT under my hands was a harsh contrast to the warm blood trickling down my face. They had come up from behind, pushing me hard into my car before I fell to the ground.

The brute who had knocked into me was talking and I tried to sit up to focus, but fell back again. I leaned back until I could feel the cool metal of my door against my head, and looked up, finally getting my bearings again.

"We need the money," he said.

"I have like fifty dollars on me. Go ahead and take it, but ask a lady before throwing her to the ground." I wasn't sure what kind of mugger *asked* for the money, but I guess it was better than hitting me more.

He gave a harsh laugh before kicking at me again. I jumped, tucking my legs up and out of reach.

"Fifty dollars isn't going to cover the ten thousand dollar payment we are expecting."

My stomach dropped as I tried to piece together what he was droning on about. "Ten thousand dollars? For what? I don't have any debts."

"Your next of kin does and says you're the one to help pay. So, congratulations, now you do."

"I don't have ten thousand dollars to just hand over! Do you think I keep a stack of money in my purse?"

"I think based on your car and the garage you work at, you have something to spare," he said, the toothy grin making my lip curl.

"The garage?" I couldn't hide the panic in my voice. He said next of kin, which could only mean my dad, and if he was mentioning the garage, it meant my dad had told them about the crew too.

"Business seems fine. Plus, it's hard to spend money when you share the living costs with several friends."

My dad, his debts, my friends. My stomach clenched, threatening to throw up everything I had eaten today.

They knew everything about me.

"My dad said I would pay his debts?" I asked, not quite believing the answer I already knew was coming.

"He said you're good for the money because he's out. And I think he was right. You have two weeks and then he's out of time."

"And what happens when he's out of time?"

"We will first do our...due diligence with you and your friends to get the money. *Of course*, this is simply a polite reminder. After that, he's out."

"Out of what?"

"Money, time, life," he drawled. "You name it, he's out. Either way, you'll be paying up. Two weeks," he said, stepping back towards the black SUV parked behind him.

I stayed frozen, watching the tail lights light up bright red in the dark night. They became the only thing I could focus on as my thoughts spiraled. I watched until the fuzzy red color disappeared and there was nothing but black.

My dad sold me out. He told them everything about me so I would pay his debts.

I couldn't move, my fingers freezing and every inch of me starting to shake in the cold night air.

As though I didn't have enough to think about, now this? I don't know how long I sat there before I finally got up, brushing off dirt and rocks and getting in my car.

Ten grand had to only be the start of what he needed, and there was no way I would be able to get that, unnoticed, in two weeks. Even if we had it in the garage savings, I wouldn't be able to take that much out without endless questions from the crew. It didn't matter what reasons I had, none of them would ever agree to letting me do this. They knew my dad and his issues, they would try to stop me even if they were in danger.

There was also no way I would be able to come up with so much money in such a short time.

I turned the car over, but let it idle, trying to warm up along with the engine. Everyday I seemed to wake up to find my life getting messier. The worst part was I couldn't figure out how to clean any of it up.

Two Days Later

The stress of trying to come up with ten grand had turned me into a sleep-deprived snarky goblin, and at this point, I couldn't even hide it. According to the crew, I was a little more *annoyed* than usual, but that was their way of politely telling me to knock off the attitude without causing a fight. Not that I didn't agree, but it was getting more frustrating not to tell them what was going on.

On top of hurrying to get the money, my car kept acting up, making it nearly impossible to make extra cash with racing.

I needed a new car, and I needed to find a way to tell the guys that I was done with this one.

I groaned at the thought.

Almost five years ago, I had been brought down to the garage on my sixteenth birthday to find this car, a gift from the guys that I never expected. It made it special. I would never get over how lucky I got to have them in my life. Now, I was having a hard time coming to terms with telling them it wasn't in great enough shape to keep racing, and my heart broke at the thought of retiring it. Not that they would be mad, they had all updated their cars over the years, but I wasn't great with change. At least not with something like my car.

The biggest problem with getting a new car was now the cost. I first needed to make the money to deal with my dad, and tonight's races could have secured it for me, but not with my car acting up.

I knew they were giving me two weeks to find money for my dads debts, but in the meantime, I couldn't let anyone else here find out where my money would be going. Hopefully, I could borrow a car to quietly race for extra cash.

I slammed my hood closed, the roar of the crew's engines coming my way, and making me groan again. They were on their way to pick me, and my car, up to go out racing tonight.

There would be five in their own cars tonight for racing.

They all lined up in front of the garage. Ransom and Quinn in his RX7, Fox with his Supra, Ash with her Aston Martin, Jax and Carly in the Charger, and Kye with his 350Z. The colorful lineup always made me smile, and now it was making me sad I wouldn't be joining the line-up tonight.

The engines shut off and I could hear my phone buzzing now.

JESSE

I'll be late. Meet you at the races?

SCOUT

Serious? Your shop has been closed for hours.

JESSE

Yeah, well, I have some things to catch up on.
I will meet up with you later.

SCOUT

Fine.

We were coming up to a year of dating, but each month we seemed to see less and less of each other. Now, he wasn't even making an effort to show up for race night? It had become the one constant for us, but that was crumbling now, too.

One more thing that kept falling apart no matter how much I tried to piece it back together.

I had even asked him to help me practice my driving more often since Holt Racing was now giving me the chance to be on their drag racing team with Ash. Since Holt hadn't seen me race enough, he was giving me the chance to show off what I could do in a few upcoming races, and how well I did in those would determine if my future was going to be in racing or in working at the garage.

Fox and Ash walked in, laughing about something Kye had done.

"What are you working on?" Fox asked, looking at the wrench in my hand.

"Just checking it over before tonight," I said, forcing a smile.

"And? How's it running?" Ash asked.

I blew out a breath, looking at the car. The neon green Supra had been my pride and joy.

"Not great," I finally said. "At this point I'm not sure what I can do to make it run right again."

Fox laughed, throwing an arm around me. "If you are still hinting at wanting a new engine, we can figure something out."

"Oh, yeah? You think we, the people who own this garage, could figure out how to put a better engine into my car?"

He grinned, messing up my hair. "I know. We are *so* generous. Are you driving it tonight or do you want to take one of ours?"

"One of ours?" Ash scoffed, her eyebrows shooting up. "You think I'm giving up my car to race tonight?" Fox only groaned and pulled out his keys.

"No babe, I think I'm giving up mine," he said to Ash before turning back to me. "But we'll get your car fixed up this week so you're ready to go next time."

"Thanks." I leaned over, hugging him as Ransom and Quinn walked in.

"Let's go," Kye yelled from his car. "If we don't get there early I'm going to miss my first race and will already be out thousands."

"Maybe don't bet all your money before you even show up," Jax yelled back with a laugh as he walked in with Carly.

Kye turned, the wicked grin on his face letting me know exactly what type of parking lot fight would break out if I didn't stop them now. And while it was all for fun, the minute these guys started fighting, it would take forever to stop them. I was with Kye on this, I needed money and I needed to actually make it to the races for that to happen.

"Before this entire place erupts into chaos," I said. "Let's go please."

For once, everyone listened, heading to their cars as I went to Fox's new yellow Supra. He had always had a yellow Supra, but upgraded it over the years. I'm pretty sure he had demanded to buy me mine so we would match, which only made it harder to think about retiring it.

My phone buzzed again, but I ignored it. I wasn't ready to face the fact that Jesse might not show up at all. Every part of my life was getting overwhelming, even the parts that used to make me feel calm and happy were now only bringing me anxiety.

I hated it.

And when it came to Jesse, it felt like all I did anymore was ask to spend more time together, while he spent all his time explaining how I needed to be the cool girlfriend and not complain so much. I really didn't want to spend another night of my life playing that game with him.

Whether he showed up or not, I needed to focus on the races tonight. I needed to win enough money to put this mess with my dad behind me, and move on with my life. I had more important things to worry about.

I hit the gas, the car taking off with ease, and I moved through the gears. If there was one thing I could do to take my mind off of all my problems, it was go for a drive. And lucky for me, all I needed to do tonight was drive.

TWO
CHASE

THIS EVENT SUCKED.

They were keeping the alcohol to a minimum, and smoking was out of the question. The things I would give to get high right now just to make it through this thing were reaching desperate levels.

Instead, I had to sit here, almost completely sober, and listen to another one of my dad's long winded speeches. Not only that, but I had my mother next to me, criticizing my every move while setting me up on a date in the same damn breath.

I stifled a groan when my dad went on a side rant, putting down all the people he had stepped on over the years so he could get ahead.

Yet, I managed to be the problem in our family. They had planned for me to be the golden child, but their dreams were crushed the day I came home drunk from the Ivy League of high schools, and explained how I only planned to do it again. Or maybe it was the day I crashed the Porsche into the house.

Honestly, who knows.

"Chase Williams Parker, sit up, stop frowning, and at least *pretend* you aren't miserable," my mother snapped.

I listened, knowing she would repeat herself until I did. The woman could say the same thing for hours, a skill I assume she mastered raising me.

"I'm getting another drink. Do you need anything?"

"Wine," she said, already knowing I knew her order.

The driest red wine they had. I tasted it once, and immediately had to spit it out. It was now a day my mother could never forget. The red wine and the *white* dress she wore to my sister's wedding looked great together. My sister cried tears of joy, my mother screamed until her face turned as red as the wine.

"Refills on these please," I said to the bartender, holding up the wine glass, and my glass with the big ridiculous ice ball barely melted.

Square ice cubes were beneath us now? It's like they went out of their way to be as pretentious as possible, and somehow, this ice felt exactly like that.

I would still take any drink they would give me, but I was pretty sure my mother told them to cut me off at three because the bartender looked weary handing me the next glass.

It's not like I was going to cause a scene, this event was just boring. Another expensive party so old male lawyers could pat themselves on the back for getting old male *scammers* off the hook for another year. I don't care if you were ripping people off a hundred dollars or a hundred thousand; you're a scammer. But when you have the hundreds of thousands of dollars you stole, you can afford a pretty good lawyer. It also means you get to be called a CEO, not a scammer.

The irony that I was here seething about this while my dad stood at the podium behind me congratulating everyone on doing this was not lost to me.

I threw back the next glass of whiskey and set it on the bar top. The bartender only shook his head, letting me know I was right. My mother had cut me off before I had even started.

I headed back to the table with her wine, resisting the urge to empty the glass before setting it down and placing a careful hand on her shoulder.

"I have to go. I have exams all next week and planned to study tonight," I said.

"Of course. You will be at dinner on Saturday?" she asked. The lack of emotion in her voice was nothing new to me, but each time it still grated on my nerves.

"Yes, I will." I tried not to let my face show how little I was looking forward to that.

She only nodded, it was enough of an acknowledgment that I took the opening to leave quickly.

I nodded to a few of the other lawyers' kids on my way out, each one of them was in the same position in life. We were to go to law school, and one day, take over the business our fathers started all those years ago. A family business we had no say in, but were now expected to be loyal to.

Unlike me, some of them were happy about it.

I hit the key fob, unlocking my Porsche, while ripping off my suit jacket and the tie that was currently choking the life out of me. The 918 Spyder, sadly, had become the only thing that meant anything to me lately.

There were two options tonight.

Go to a party at Justin's lake house, and get drunk out of my mind.

Or I could go to the races and try to drive away this endless, anxious buzzing that seemed to keep me right on the edge of blowing up. Nothing calmed me down, but nothing made me explode, it was just endless dread I couldn't stop.

Most days, I couldn't even find a reason for it. I had every-thing I wanted. I could buy anything I wanted, go on any vacation. I had friends who invited me to every party, and every event. I was the life of those parties, too, and people bent over backwards to do whatever I needed. But the high of it all had lost its edge and now I was searching for something that would make me feel…anything.

I turned right out of the parking lot. There was no way more alcohol was going to make me feel anything at this point, and somehow, a party was the furthest thing from my mind right this second. Plus, I could always still make it to the party after, and maybe then I would be in the mood to forget everything.

Thirty minutes later I pulled into the parking lot that was already overflowing with cars. I already knew the line to race would be long, but I didn't feel like waiting so I idled my way through the crowd to the front.

I grabbed a hundred from the side pocket of my console and put the window down.

"A hundred bucks for you if I can take the next race," I said to the guy running this informal shit-show. I had paid him off plenty of times to skip the line, and I already knew he would take it.

He snatched the hundred. "This one was betting a thousand."

"No problem. I'm in." He waved me forward, bringing me up to the made up line next to a yellow Supra. The windows on it were tinted out black like mine, leaving both of us unable to see each other.

The yellow car revved and I revved mine back. Adrenaline shot through me, the first small taste of excitement I'd felt in days.

I had become numb to my life, looking for anything to give me some semblance of feeling, and tonight, it would come in the form of racing.

THREE
SCOUT

I ROLLED my eyes at the dark Porsche pulling up next to me. For how much cash I needed, this guy cutting in was perfect. These rich guys drove up all the time and expected to win based on the cost of their car alone.

Taking a deep breath, I revved Fox's car, waiting for the girl flagging the race to move us up to the line. After a few seconds, she finally raised her arm and hit the light, the Porsche taking off just before the light turned on.

I took off after him but I had to be twice as fast to catch up and win. Our cars stayed close, racing through the mix of shadows and lights until we moved around the first sharp turn. I gained a slight edge, the Supra better at handling the turns but the Porsche let out a burst of power on the straight stretch, passing me by inches.

Adrenaline pumped through me, my heart beating faster as we came up to the next turn. The Supra managed better around the turn again, but he seemed hellbent on trying to make it around the corner faster, almost turning into me.

I pushed the Supra harder, the whine of the engine letting me know it had nothing left to give. He was fast, his car staying a second ahead of mine when we crossed the finish line, but he had already lost by my rules.

I swung my car, cutting the guy off before he could leave the makeshift track. There is no way I was going to owe him money when he left before the light.

He jumped, which in the rules around here, meant you lost the race.

And while I came to bet money, I had none to lose, so him winning after he cheated wasn't going to work for me.

I stomped over as his door opened, already prepared for a fight about this, but one glimpse of him was making me trip over my own feet.

I had been around a lot of good looking men, but none of them so...*perfectly handsome*. His dark hair laid flawlessly, complementing his tall and visibly well-muscled frame. The crisp, unwrinkled button-up stretched just right, rolled up to reveal toned forearms. With the top two buttons undone, his broad chest was on display, creating an absolutely flawless image.

I wanted to ruffle up his hair or add a smear of grease some-where on him, anything to make him look more normal when the perfection seemed to come so easy.

Even his face was perfect, a sharp jaw, high cheekbones, an arrogant gleam in his dark eyes, and each sure step he took towards me only made me more nervous.

This wasn't a reckless confidence, it was wildly contained, and I wasn't sure what to do with that.

A storm of emotions rolled through me, but I shoved them down. Now wasn't a time to swoon over a hot man. I could do that later.

Maybe when I saw Jesse again. My boyfriend.

My mouth fell open at the sight of his pants."You wore dress pants, and those shiny dumb shoes to a night of street racing? Do rich boys not have jeans and a T-shirt?"

He glanced down at his clothes like he had forgotten what he had on before his eyes roamed over me.

"I didn't realize there's a dress code. Next time I will wear leggings and, apparently, a dirty old hoodie," he said. He was calm, and I didn't like the way he so easily bit back. There was no way he would be able to know I was self-conscious about my clothes ever since I had been bullied back in high school, but somehow, people like him always knew what to go after to cut you wide open.

This was the exact type to bully me – rich, perfect, and ridiculously *unbullyable*.

I had been wearing this hoodie when I fixed my car, the dirt stains making that obvious. Unlike him though, my outfit was a little more appropriate for a race night.

It didn't stop me from feeling as small and poor as I used to feel when people commented on my less than expensive clothes. And even though I could afford better clothes now, I didn't need to show up at a race night in my best dress.

"Can you buy these pre-dirtied now?" I asked, pulling at my hoodie. "Maybe you could get one for yourself. A thousand dollars and you could look like you worked on a car one day in your life."

The words were clipped, and rude. I tried not to be mean to anyone but something about him brought me right back to those days when I was younger and couldn't find my voice. Between that and everything else I was dealing with, no part of me felt like giving him the benefit of the doubt.

His eyebrows shot up. "Oh, a temper." The smile that came over his face unnerved me. It was wicked and perfect, like the rest of him. "Did you cut me off to insult me, or did you want to pay up now?"

My mouth fell back open. *"Pay?* I'm not paying you for cheating." My heartbeat thundered in my ears, drowning out the rest of the cars around us. I couldn't pay him. I couldn't lose money when I came here to *find* money.

Not when they were threatening to come for me and the crew if I didn't settle my dad's debts in less than two weeks.

"I don't cheat," he said, the deep tone and unwavering confidence making my temper flare more. I could bet he was so confident because he always got what he wanted in life, and now, he wanted to win this race.

"You jumped off the line before she clicked the light, you cheated."

He smirked, the curve of his lips bringing out a dimple on one side.

"Just because you're too slow, doesn't mean you can call me a cheater."

"You jumped. That's an automatic loss for you. And there is no way I am too slow. You jumped and I still caught up to you," I said, pleased there was no way he could deny that. My hands went on my hips, trying to stand tall and wait for an answer, but he only rolled his eyes.

"If you don't have the money, I honestly don't care. I just want to go race again."

"No, you want to go cut in line to cheat again. I have the money," I lied. "But I prefer getting paid when I win."

I could see the crew noticing the commotion now, and they headed this way.

Good. Maybe they would scare him, and he would pay up.

"Admit you lost and we won't have any problems," I said, pulling my shoulders back and mustering up more of my own confidence as I looked up at him.

"Problems? Now you're threatening me?" he asked, his lips twitched with a smile again as he stepped closer, his body towering over mine. It was a little intimidating, but I knew the guys were coming over. "What are you going to do? Beat me up?" His eyes burned into me as he took me in. "I'm shaking in my shiny shoes."

The crew finally made their way to us, Fox looking the guy over. "What's up, Scout?" he asked. "Everything okay?"

"Scout? You're here giving me shit, calling me rich boy, and your name is *Scout*?"

"You dick," I said. "You're just mad you were beaten by a girl."

"I don't give a fuck who you are. I'm mad you're calling me a cheater." Now I could hear the slightest amount of anger, but his tone was still calm, every bit of him still under a tight control.

Somehow that made me more angry.

Fox moved to my side as Kye and Ransom moved around the guy's car. Jax stood with Carly, Quinn, and Ash, all of them curious, but probably hoping this wasn't going to escalate.

"What's going on? You two raced, he won. What happened?"

"See, even he agrees I won," the guy said.

"He agrees because he didn't see you jumped the light," I said.

"Well, if you jumped, you know that disqualifies you for this one," Fox said.

Ash stepped forward, peering around Fox to look at the guy, her eyebrows furrowed.

"Chase?" she asked, stepping closer towards him. His head whipped to her, taking her in before a genuine smile grew.

"Ashton?"

Her smile matched his as she ran over and threw her arms around him. "What are you doing here?"

I rolled my eyes, of course they knew each other. I loved Ash, but knew this was the type of rich jerk she grew up around.

"I *was* trying to race, but your ankle-biter here is pissed at me."

I charged forward, moving past Ash and Fox. My hands went up, intending to hit his chest, but he was so tall I ended up against a firm stomach, pushing him back hard.

"Ankle-biter? What the hell is your problem?"

He stumbled back and Fox's arms wrapped around me.

"Calm down," Fox said, spinning me and blocking the guy, Chase, from my view. "What are you doing? Why are you so pissed off? We deal with this all the time."

"Because the rich boy wants to cheat and take my money. What? Like he needs it? He's being a jerk."

"Well, now you are, too. Calm down," Fox said, apparently surprised at my sudden attitude. I wanted nothing more than to hug him and tell him why I couldn't calm down, but this definitely wasn't the time or place for that. I don't think there would ever be a time or place to tell him I needed money, and why I needed it. I'm on my own in this. On my own for the first time in a long time, and I needed to handle that better.

Maybe, I was already a little pissed off about the money thing. Or the Jesse thing. Or *maybe*, I just didn't like this guy.

"Fine. But I'm not paying him."

Fox shook his head, turning back to where Ash was talking with Chase. The crew stood around, listening but not joining in.

"Alright," Fox said, interrupting them. "She thinks you jumped, you think you didn't. Would you rather call it even and no one pay or go back and work it out with another race?"

Chase's arrogant smile wasn't lost on me. "I'm good. I don't need money or a fight tonight." He looked around Fox to me. "At least not a fight with her. I'm pretty sure I know the outcome already."

"Don't be too sure of yourself with her," Jax said. "She could probably kick your ass."

Chase laughed, his eyes going heavy when looked me over again. "I would be curious to see how that works."

Heat flooded me, followed by shock. I never had someone look at me with so much... blatant interest.

The heat filled my face, my cheeks probably turning red already. This rich jerk was looking at me like he had a chance to win me over even for a minute.

"I don't want his money. I would prefer to just agree that I never have to see him again."

He smiled, his lips curving up on one side, and making the dimple appear one more time.

"I can agree to that."

"Fine, then. We are done here," I said, pushing past them all and getting in the car.

Jesse, the money, now Chase.

Tears were threatening, the stress of the entire week boiling over. This night was going to hell, and I think it was about time to give up on it. Maybe I could drive for a while and get my mind off of everything.

Jesse's car pulled up next to the crew's line of cars and I didn't hide my groan.

I couldn't run off now.

The truth was here to smack me in the face. My problems were inescapable, relentlessly closing in on me at every turn.

I was starting to worry I wasn't fast enough to outrun any of them.

FOUR

CHASE

ONE WEEK LATER

I rolled over, hitting the bed next to me. The cool rush of relief came over me when I didn't feel another body there. I hadn't brought anyone home with me, and while going home alone had been the plan, I never knew what drunk me was going to do.

It was already two in the afternoon, meaning I almost managed to sleep another day away.

Lucky me.

One less day to deal with, it was Saturday anyway. No classes, no pretend job at my dad's law offices. Nothing but endless, empty time.

My phone buzzed with texts. The first few useless updates about things that happened last night at a party which hadn't seemed to end.

I was twenty-four years old, in law school, and partying like I was in high school. It had brought me some sort of purpose before. Being the life of the party, all eyes on me, but somewhere along the line, that lost its appeal, too. Now each party felt like one more thing to get through.

Every single fucking thing in my life felt like one more chore.

I got up and got dressed, figuring I could at least go grab myself some breakfast down the street.

The Porsche sat in the back of the garage connected to my condo, the dark green paint looking black in the dim garage, but I knew it would shine the minute I pulled into the sun.

The car purred as I pulled out, the sound of the engine keeping me calm.

It didn't last long, though, the engine's purrs quickly turning into a high pitched whine.

"Shit," I said, slamming the steering wheel. I had known something was starting to go wrong, but kept putting off bringing it to the shop. Now, I had no faith that I would be able to make it all the way across town to the dealership.

I pulled out my phone texting Fox to see if he was around the garage to look at it. Ash had stuck around catching up with me after the races the other week and Fox was quick to see if I wanted to hang out with them that weekend. One night out with the guys and they all seemed more than happy to ask me to go out again later this month.

A few minutes went by before I got a reply.

FOX

I'll be there in about 30 minutes. Head over now and I can take a look at it then.

I punched in the directions to Hollows Garage. Ten minutes later I was pulling up to the old brick building. The exterior wall was painted with a mural of their name.

I walked in and knew I was in the right place when I saw the bright green Supra car in one of the bays. I headed over, looking the car over, and growing even more impressed by their work. Not only had endless modifications been done, but the engine bay was almost a work of art. Everything was color coordinated and there wasn't a wire out of place.

A head moved over an engine of a WRX in the next bay over, the red hair catching my eye.

"Well, if it isn't the ankle-biter," I said, not missing the way her hand tightened on the wrench.

A strange feeling bloomed in my chest and I realized it was the semblance of being excited. I could see the recognition in her eyes, and wasn't surprised when she scowled.

"What are you doing here?" she asked. Her arms were covered in dirt and grease, she crossed them over her chest, but the small black tank top wasn't hiding anything. Two locks of her red hair had escaped, framing her lightly-freckled face. Despite her size, there was an undeniable strength in the set of her jaw, the cute, sharp nose, and the way she held her head up high. Bright, hazel eyes stared back at me, and it took me a few seconds to remember what we were talking about.

"I'm waiting for Fox and Ash."

"They aren't here right now. You can leave your car if they are looking over it or I'll tell them to call you. Quinn's in the office, she'll take the keys." Her words were so clipped, but the annoyance was bubbling. I didn't know what it was, but getting under her skin was quickly becoming a favorite hobby of mine.

"I know they're not here. That's why I said '*waiting.* '"

She gave a hard eye roll but looked back down at the car. "Well there is a designated waiting area," she said pointing again, the scowl on her face deepening. "*In the office.*"

She was trying so hard to be polite, professional even, and I wanted to see how easy it would be to make her break.

"I can wait out here. Mind if I look over the cars?"

"I do mind. We don't like snoops. I don't like cheaters, either."

I moved around the car, closing the distance more. "And why is that? Bad ex-boyfriend? Cheating current boyfriend? Why are you so quick to brand me a cheater?"

She gave a harsh laugh and reached over the engine, grabbing a different wrench. "How exactly would you like to be branded then?"

I had made it to her side, and leaned down. "Usually just nails down my back, but I'm open to suggestions."

Her nostrils flared and eyes went wide. The wrench slammed down onto the car and she spun to face me, her body only inches from mine.

"Did you come here to make lame attempts at flirting or were you actually waiting for Ash and Fox?" She tried to keep her face calm, but the deadly look in her eyes gave her away.

I still wanted to push her more. I reached up, winding one of those stray locks of hair around my finger. "Oh, I'm actually waiting for them, but this is a lot more fun than a waiting room."

"You know what is even more fun?" she asked, stepping back. "Waiting in a Porsche."

"The Porsche is why I'm here. I need it fixed."

"Couldn't figure out how to change a tire?"

I flashed another grin, grabbing a wrench off the car and flipping it around. "I can change a tire. What I can't do is diagnose a Porsche's engine without a code reader. Sorry to disappoint you."

"Not disappointed. Just busy, so why don't you get going?"

"And how would I get my car fixed if I leave exactly?" That got to her, her nostrils flaring again.

"What is your problem?" she asked.

"I don't have a problem. You're the one who seems less than happy about my being here. What is your problem?"

"My problem is that I don't particularly like you, you cheated during our race, and now you won't leave me alone."

"Apologies. I'm used to women falling all over me, being more easy to please. I'm not sure what to do with one so full of thorns."

For some reason that's what finally made her smile.

"What you do is you leave her alone because you're incapable of handling her," she said, her voice as sweet as the smile she gave me.

The sound of an engine turning into the parking lot cut me off before I even had a chance to respond. We both looked out the open garage door, the dark Aston Martin flashing when it pulled in and parked beside my car. Scout didn't waste any time stalking outside to the parking lot as Fox opened his door.

"You have a friend here waiting and he's bothering me," she said while they all walked back inside with her.

"Everyone has been bothering you lately, Scout. I can't kick all their asses," Fox said.

"You absolutely can."

She glared at me. I couldn't figure out why she hated me right from the start, but I also didn't blame her. I would think I'm fairly easy to hate.

"Alright, *grumpy gills*, don't go biting his head off, too," Fox said. We both watched her stalk back into the garage.

"So I was right in the ankle-biter comments?" I asked.

"Maybe, but probably stop saying it to her face," he said with a laugh, quiet enough so she couldn't hear as we headed over to my car. "She's usually Little Miss Sunshine so I don't know what you do to her, but don't do it again."

I didn't think Scout knew I had been hanging out with Fox and Ash, at least not based on her dislike for me, but I was starting to think Fox was cool with me being around. He and Ash had invited me out to catch up more after the race night. And then he invited me out again for what I guess they considered a guys night, where they brought me out to find street races and hang out. It was surprisingly one of the better nights I've had in awhile.

I looked back at Scout as Fox started messing with the engine. She was inside, ignoring me. Maybe my reputation precedes me.

It probably should.

I could almost bet Ash let her know all my dirty, public secrets. Most of them weren't pretty or flattering, even if I was a little proud of them. It would make sense why a girl Fox would call Little Miss Sunshine would be so pissed right from the start at someone like me if she knew about my past.

The things I've done are usually *why* certain people liked me. Why they hung all over me, vying for my attention, my money, my time. They all wanted some part of me, but yet there she was, turning her back to me.

It seemed Little Miss Sunshine didn't like my brand of trouble.

"Hey," Ash said, stepping in front of me, and waving her hands in my face. I looked away from Scout, letting Ash come into focus.

"Hey," I replied.

"Do you want to stay and hang out? We have a cookout on the first Saturday of the month, which is tonight. Just food and relax type of thing."

"A party? *Obviously* I'll stay for that," I said, grinning when she smiled back.

"Not a party, a hangout. Nothing crazy."

"You think I can't convince any one of these guys to do something crazy and make this a party?"

She groaned. "Don't make me regret inviting you."

I looked past her to Scout, who glanced out and met my eye.

"You wouldn't be alone in that regret at least," I said, laughing quietly as Scout turned her back to us.

Fox stood back up from leaning over the engine. "And stop staring at Scout. She doesn't want you bothering her, and I don't keep friends around who try to sleep with my little sister."

"You're related?"

"Not by blood, but I promise it doesn't matter."

"Hey," I said, throwing my hands up in surrender. "I was trying to figure out why she hates me, not how to sleep with her."

"How about you stop pushing her buttons and solve both of the problems?"

"I promise I will stop trying to purposefully push her buttons. I can't promise it won't happen by accident. I think I could say hello and it piss her off."

He nodded, going back to work on the car and Ash came over to help him.

I just liked to annoy her, he had nothing to worry about at all.

Scout stood up after crawling under her car, looking way too hot for a girl covered in dirt. There was no reason I couldn't stay away from her. I was here to hang out with Ash and Fox, maybe the rest of the crew, annoying her was only an added bonus.

There should be nothing about Scout that caught my attention.

FIVE

SCOUT

I STAYED focused on the car, losing myself in what I knew. One bolt and part after another, until this car ran better than ever.

By the time I looked up again, darkness had fallen and Chase's car was still sitting outside.

Quinn walked in the back door, the cocked eyebrow letting me know they had all noticed my absence.

"Have you really been in here the entire time?"

"Yes."

"Why?" she asked, her hands on her hips now.

"Because I see Chase's car is still here, and I didn't notice anyone leave to take him home yet."

"He is back there, but I'm confused. Since when are you not the life of the party that loves everyone? You're the one we have to drag away from a cookout, not drag to it."

"And I always will be except when we invite stuck up rich boys." She smiled, the slow curve of her lips making me nervous. "What is the smile about?"

"Just funny to see you so rattled. Did he do something terrible to you?"

"Besides cheat and call me ankle biter? If that doesn't tell you what you need to know, I don't know what will."

She shrugged. "You are a mean little thing when you need to be. I wouldn't go so far as *ankle-biter*," she said, smiling again. "But feisty enough to talk back if you need and I'm sure you could race him again."

"And what happens when he's a jerk again?" I turned back to the engine. "Why do the hot ones have to act like that?"

"Is that what this is about? You think he's hot?"

"No, I think he is just like those guys in high school that would give me shit for trying to dress up or look nice. You know how much I dealt with it back then, and it was usually from guys like him."

"I honestly don't know how anybody bullied you. You have a knife on you at all times and a group of men who will pull up to any fight for you. But we aren't in high school. He isn't here to make your life miserable. He's here to hang out with some friends."

"I think he is already making my life miserable," I said with a small smile. "And don't even tell me someone like him doesn't have plenty of friends."

"Maybe he doesn't have a lot of good friends and you already know we are the best of the best." Quinn's smile dropped and she crossed her arms. "So really what I'm hearing is you think he's hot and he's just like those guys in high school that you had crushes on, but were jerks to you, and that's pissing you off before you even give him a chance."

"A chance to what? Hurt my feelings?"

"A chance to see if he's actually a jerk like they were."

"Ankle biter, Quinn, he's calling me ankle biter."

She tried to hide her laugh, but failed. "Interesting that you didn't deny anything I said."

"I don't have a crush on him, and I'm with Jesse. The guy

who is a lot more like me. He's a mechanic, and likes cars, and isn't stuck up. Did I like the popular guys in high school? Of course, who didn't."

Quinn raised her hand. "Me."

"Only because you and Ransom are meant to be together."

"And I didn't think I should be with someone like him, but I still had a crush on him. Just because Jesse feels like the person you *should* be with, doesn't mean you should ignore if you like other types."

"Are you suggesting I should cheat on Jesse and go for Chase?"

"Don't even get an attitude with me or I'm going to start calling you ankle biter, too. All I'm saying is learn that lesson from me, what you *think* you need, isn't always what you actually need."

"If I go out there, can this conversation be over?"

She laughed again. "Yes, but only if you play nice with that hot-as-sin man and not be rude."

"There is no way I would agree to that. I will say that I will try to be nicer if he stops getting under my skin."

"Come on," she said, pouting out her bottom lip, "let's go see if the hot man is really as bad as you say he is."

I followed her back out, catching Chase's head of dark hair as he was talking with the guys, not missing Kye laughing at something he said.

He was in jeans and a hoodie tonight instead of the dressed up look he had at the races. Every part of him was relaxed and so different from what I saw the night of the races. Then he had been perfect, every hair in line, shoes shined, and suit pants pressed.

Now he looked a little more like the guys. There was still a difference to his edge though. Where the guys seemed feral and reckless, Chase was sharp and calculated. Even the way he was looking at me now didn't feel fun and wild, it felt like he was watching my every move, waiting for a chance to make his move.

Normally, I would know exactly what that move would be, but I wasn't sure with him. Would he hit on me? Or just insult me? Or maybe something worse.

Our eyes locked, and a sly smirk spread over his face before I turned away, following Quinn to join the girls huddled around the fire.

"You okay?" Carly asked.

"Fine."

"*Right* because you usually hide away and look all pissed off when we're all together."

"Someone has an issue with the newcomer," Quinn said, grabbing a drink from Carly and sitting closer to the fire.

"Chase?" Ash asked. "Why, because of the racing thing? I thought it was all resolved."

"It was," I said, "but I'm still not a fan."

"I mean, he's a bit of a partier, kind of a playboy, too, but he's fun, and from everything I know, not a terrible guy."

"What *do* you know exactly?" Quinn asked.

"His family were the lawyers for Holt until there was some sort of falling out with him and my dad. They are still cordial, and work around each other. I know Chase is going to law school, and will become a lawyer for his dad's firm after. He parties a lot, more so now than before even, which is surprising. He was pretty much the party house when we were in high school, and I thought he would grow out of that, but never did, apparently."

"And relationships?" Carly asked, her lips pursing with a smile.

"He had a few girlfriends throughout high school, but they

weren't serious. They probably didn't last more than a month. After that, I don't know. Nothing I've heard about."

"Interesting," Quinn said.

"Why? Looking for a new man?" I asked, the snark not hidden.

"Not even a little bit," she said, kicking out her boot at me.

"Speak of the devil," Ash said, making me look over my shoulder to see Chase only a few feet behind me.

"Probably an appropriate nickname," I said, his eyes moving over each one of the girls until they landed on me.

Carly clicked her tongue. "Watch out, Scout, you're sounding more like me every day."

I leaned back, trying to ignore him, but he decided to sit down next to me, giving me a front row seat to the clean musky cologne he had on.

The girls were quick to scatter, mumbling things about the guys and needing to get another drink, leaving me alone with Chase.

I didn't know what they thought they were doing, I had a boyfriend, and that wasn't going to change because of some random guy showing up. It didn't exactly help that Jesse wasn't here with me.

"Where's your boyfriend tonight? Too busy to come to your party?"

My eyes snapped to him, wondering how he knew what I had been thinking about.

I hated that Jesse was once again finding a way to embarrass me. He was probably out at a party tonight, just one more wild than this.

"Where's your girlfriend tonight? Can't find one who wants to be around you that long?"

He smirked. "Something like that. Still hating me?"

"I'm not sure how to like anyone who cheats at a race."

"For the hundredth time, I did not cheat. Stop being so mad I won. Who would have thought the tough little racer girl was such a sore loser?"

"You couldn't beat me at a race without cheating."

Somehow all the crew had a radar, and at the word "race," they headed our way.

"We can take it out front and race, if you think you could beat me fairly," he said, laughing. Like traitors, the rest of the crew laughed along with him.

His stupid charming face had won them over enough to laugh at me now.

"You don't even have a car, and mine is waiting on a part."

"I'm sure your friends wouldn't mind lending us two. You all know I'm good for the money if I break anything."

Kye walked over, slapping his keys into Chase's hands. "Pay back damages with interest because I've had my eyes on a new set of seats."

"Perfect. What do you say Fox? Would you let Scout use your car again to try and kick my ass?"

Fox beamed and handed me his keys. "Always. Actually kick his ass this time, Scout. His ego needs to be knocked down because he also beat me the other day."

"What happened the other day?"

"Fox was nice enough to invite me out with them the other night," Chase replied, the smug smile on his face making my hands tighten on the keys. "I kicked his ass and he's a little salty about it, too."

A burn of jealousy moved through me. Now he was hanging out with my friends, and they weren't telling me? And not only that, but the guys were purposefully inviting him out to their guys' night?

"To be clear, you may be friends with them, but you aren't friends with me. Let's race."

He laughed and nodded, following me out to the cars. The entire crew filed out behind us, ready for the show.

The one I was going to win.

TWENTY MINUTES LATER, WE WERE BOTH PULLED UP TO THE LINE. The warm engines rumbled next to each other, the sound echoing around us. The garage was in a more industrial area, leaving us alone on the road and making it easy to race down to where Kye was parked.

I looked over, both the windows tinted so I saw nothing, but I suddenly wished I could. I wanted to know if he was smiling at me, if this was secretly as fun for him as it was becoming for me.

Jesse never wanted to race me, I don't think he wanted to risk losing against his girlfriend. Looking back now, I was almost glad, because I'm not sure I wouldn't just let him win so an argument wouldn't start. With Chase though, even if he was mad if I won, I wouldn't care.

Chase had seemed high on the idea of racing me again. When we were getting in the cars, he had looked me over once, and winked before disappearing into Kye's car. I glanced over at the dark window again before facing forward. I needed to focus on this race, not dark eyes that swallowed me whole.

I revved the car again, the rumble of the engine bringing me back.

Ransom walked to the front of the cars, making sure we were both ready before raising a light and hitting it on.

Tires screeched against the pavement, both cars shooting forward. I hit through the gears fast, lucky that I was already so familiar with Fox's car. It was a short race, from one block to the next, enough we could gain speed, but not enough to overtake him if I didn't get ahead immediately. Kye's car was a blur next to mine, and I kept my focus forward. I couldn't lose to him. There was no cheating this time, I think Chase even made sure to leave a half second after the light, but I should still be able to beat him with ease.

The engines screamed when we made it to the halfway mark, both of us taking the last few seconds of the race to push the cars to the limit.

Everyone but Ransom stood by Jax's car at the finish line. Eyes glued on us, as we reached the finish line. We were still so close, and there was no way I was going to look over and check if he was winning. I could do it, though. I could get the smallest amount ahead of him, and maybe it would be enough of a win for Chase to not even want to come around again. In one blink of an eye, we passed everyone and slowed the cars.

I could tell the outcome the second I saw the crew. Their faces ranged from pursed lips to not even looking at me.

I couldn't believe it.

I had lost to him again.

I shifted, moving past them back to the garage without even stopping to talk.

When I looked back, Chase was right behind me, following along as I parked the car in front of the garage.

He got out, the big cocky smile on his face making me want to slap it off.

"You look ready to bite my ankles," he said. "Are you going to try and accuse me of cheating again?"

"No," I said, slamming my door. "I don't know how you won, and I don't care."

"You do care. I didn't cheat, and I'm going to need to hear those words right from your lips," he said.

My gaze dropped to his lips before I snapped them back up, a rush of heat washing over me.

"It's not that big of a deal." I went to stomp away but he

grabbed my arm, spinning me to face him. His other hand reached up, cupping my chin and forcing me to look at him. A thrill shot through me when I met his dark gaze.

"It's a very big deal considering I haven't heard the end of you telling me I cheated. So I want to hear the words directly from your mouth." He made the smallest step closer. "Right now," he whispered.

"You did not cheat," I finally said.

"And?"

"And you won," I said, gritting my teeth.

He flashed a smile, dropping his hands from me and leaning back against the car. "I feel like we have all the evidence we need now. Verdict is in, ankle biter, I'm a better driver than you."

I didn't hide my shock. "Excuse me? You think you win one race and you're a better driver than me?"

"Should we ask the jury? They have been there for both of our races."

"Verdict? Jury? Do you always talk like an uptight lawyer?"

"I'm in law school so you're pretty fucking close. Not a lawyer yet, though."

"That's your life then? Be rich and perfect and gorgeous and go to law school to stay that way?"

"Don't forget becoming a partner at my father's law firm and taking over one day."

My lip curled. I was probably being rude, but I hated everything about it. Even more, I hated that I noticed the sadness in his tone when he said it.

Nope.

No.

I wasn't going to ask more about it.

I didn't think he didn't care about my life. Why should I care about his?

A sleek, modified car slowed as it reached the garage. I

almost thought it was turning in until it took off, shooting down towards the crew instead.

"Who was that? Finally your boyfriend possibly showing up?"

"No, that wasn't him. And he isn't going to come tonight. Does a couple always have to be together?"

"Not at all, but with a girl like you, I would assume a guy would want to be with his girl on a Saturday night. Unless you didn't invite him here."

"This isn't one of your fancy galas. I don't send out formal invites. He could stop by if he had the time."

I looked down the road, hearing the engine of Jax's Charger start up.

"Interesting. And you didn't want to go with him wherever he was going?"

"No, he likes to go to clubs and parties, I don't, so I stay behind. Problem solved."

He cocked an eyebrow, apparently expecting me to say more, but I wasn't going to continue talking about Jesse.

"What about you? No girlfriend to hang out with?"

"Not a chance of me having a girlfriend. I understand that I can't, and won't, be spending all of my time with one girl. And unlike your boyfriend, I don't have the heart to lead a girl on."

"Rich boys don't have hearts," I said, smiling.

He smiled back, pushing off the car as the Charger came closer. He leaned down until his forehead was nearly resting on mine. "It looks like we finally agree on something."

For a moment we stood there, neither of us moving until the crew was about to pull in. I stepped back, taking a deep gulp of cool air, not daring to look at him again.

A HALF HOUR LATER, WE WERE GATHERED AROUND THE FIRE behind the garage. Chase was still there, sitting next to me without a word, and so far, I hadn't said a word to him.

I took a long sip of my drink. The cocktails Ash made were always strong, and normally I didn't drink too much but tonight, I didn't care.

"So," Fox said, leaning forward. "Now that you two are getting along, this might be a good time to let you know you're going to have to be the one to work on his car," he said, looking at me.

"What? Why me?"

"Because we are all booked up and you're the only one with some free time. I know you have your races with Holt to worry about, but Chase has agreed to be flexible on when it gets done."

"Are you serious?"

"Yes, and one more thing."

"What?"

"He wants to help. He asked to learn more about the mechanics part and I already agreed before I realized I didn't have enough time."

"Fox!"

"Scout!" he yelled back with a small laugh. "You can handle one guy asking questions about a car for a week or two while you show him a few things. I already told him not to bother you or purposefully try to piss you off, and that he has to listen to what you say. Think of it as a win in your favor. Now you get to be all high and mighty because you know what you are doing and he doesn't."

"But I would also have to deal with him for weeks. Not days, Fox. *Weeks.*"

"I'm sorry. I know you're going to be a little upset about this, but we need the help Scout. With Jax gone for the charity half the time, me trying to keep up with Ash, Holt, and her racing, and all of us picking up more with you needing to be preparing for your races at Holt, we really need the help."

I sighed, staring into the fire. A few weeks ago, Ash let me know that Holt would consider me for their team, there was no hesitation that everyone was going to pick up my slack so I could race more along with helping me at the track when I was there, so I had no room to complain about one car repair. I looked over at Chase who was leaning back on the trunk of the Charger with a beer in his hand.

I wasn't sure why everyone seemed to find Chase so... delightful. Apparently, the guys even liked him enough to invite him to guys' night.

This was the guy they needed me to deal with for a week or two while I fixed his car.

This stupidly gorgeous, annoying guy.

I had to do it.

"Of course I'll do it. Sorry for even suggesting I wouldn't."

Fox smiled, the scar on his face showing more clearly as his lips tightened, but he didn't care about it anymore.

"Don't worry, I will promise for him that he will be on his best behavior."

I looked at Chase again, a bit of his hair breaking free to fall down across his forehead. The tousled look only enhanced his gorgeous face.

That wasn't exactly what I was worried about, but I had no idea *what* I was worried about. There wasn't anything I could do though, if any of them needed my help, I was going to do it.

SIX

CHASE

IT'S NOT like my father barging into my apartment and screaming at me was a new thing, but now he was here at 9 AM on·a Sunday, and I had to admit I was a little thrown off.

"You are sitting here not even dressed, probably hungover, instead of ready to go to the company outing."

"I barely work there. I'm more of a volunteer than anything anymore. I don't even get paid. Why would I need to go to the company outing today?"

He walked around the island in the kitchen, and ripped open my fridge, pulling out a bottle of water and shoving it in my direction.

"Because you get plenty of money to live on and you need to prove that you bring some value to the company. Which, I think you've made it obvious that you're adding nothing lately, but you should at least attempt."

I sipped the water as he glared at me. Despite being in his sixties, my dad took great care of himself. He was about my height, still pretty slim, and worked out regularly. He was gray- ing, and the wrinkles made his age obvious, but overall, he looked good. I almost wondered if he could kick my ass if he wanted to right now.

"Wow, what a way to motivate a man to work harder. Tell him his hard work isn't worth anything," I said, rolling my eyes and pouring a cup of coffee.

"You know damn well you aren't doing your best there. I would assume you aren't doing your best *anywhere*. Now get dressed, the outing starts in an hour and like hell will we be late. I'm supposed to set an example, and by now some employees are already there. Your mother is waiting in the car and expects you to look your best. Claire will be at the outing today, too, so actually look your best."

"Claire?"

"The girl your mother has picked for you."

I suppress my gag and turn to him. "Picked for me? Are we in the 1800s? Do I get a wife chosen for me now?"

"Considering your taste in women has historically been a less than desirable girl for one night at a time? Yes, I think we're done waiting for you to choose."

"First of all, disgusting of you to say that. Second, I'm twenty-four, not quite the end of marrying age. I think that counts even for men in the 1800s."

"I think for an up and coming lawyer who is set to take over my firm, you're well past the age to settle down. You're sloppy drunk half the time, and party like you're still in college. I don't know that you have any responsibilities outside of law school, and I still have to question if you even take that seriously. I've given you the chance to find yourself a girl who can help you take on this life. Now I'm out of options. Hopefully, a nice girl like Claire can help you get on track and take this all more seriously. Your mother helped me when I was starting this business. I think Claire will help you focus on taking it over."

"I am in college. Why would I be focused on taking over your business already?"

"You're in law school, Chase! Law school isn't for partying. Law school is for focusing on becoming a lawyer while you learn the ins and outs of my company. And you can't get ahead in this business without a suitable woman on your arm to show that you are serious and reliable. One who will act appropriately at work functions, who will handle this lifestyle. Claire is beautiful, well educated, knows the family, and is ready to find a husband. Luckily, I have one for her."

"And when is the wedding?" I asked sarcastically, sipping on my coffee that I suddenly wished had whiskey in it, if only to help my mind drown him out.

"Two years. The fall after you graduate as a lawyer would work nicely. And a respectable time to date and be engaged."

"Wow, so generous with my time."

"Knock off the dramatics, Chase. We've given you time to grow up and you refuse, so it's time for us to step in. You're twenty-four years old, and you can barely get out of bed by noon. At your age, I was getting up to work before going to law school, and then worked again after. You want my money, this lifestyle, and connections? Get your ass dressed, nicely, so we can go."

I only nodded, not having it in me to fight him more as I headed into my room to change.

At first, there was no question I wanted his money and connections. But now? The care I had for any part of this life-style was getting smaller every day.

I changed into a dark casual suit, not taking a tie, and walked back out to see him digging through my desk drawers.

"I don't know what you think you are going to find in there, but they don't print out report cards in law school."

"No? Then why don't you show me your grades?"

"Couldn't you call your friend *the Dean* and make him tell you?"

He huffed, fixing his suit and looking me over.

"He won't tell me. He said you're doing fine and I shouldn't worry, but I think he's being kind. Where is your tie?"

"I seemed to have lost all of them."

"Are you kidding? So your idea of dressing up nice is an open collar?"

"I thought it gave me a nice edge." I said, turning to hide my grin as I grabbed my keys.

"What are you doing?"

"Leaving?"

"I mean, why did you grab your keys? I told you your mother is downstairs waiting. Your sister came, too. We drove."

"And I'll drive myself."

"So you can run out the second Claire turns around?"

"Am I that predictable?"

"Yes. Now put those back. We are driving you and I swear if you upset your mother and don't talk to Claire all night like a gentleman, you're losing the Porsche and any other ridiculous car you may have bought recently."

"Are you serious?" I asked, coming to a hard stop and letting the door slam shut behind me.

"You're damn right I'm serious. Either you take this life seriously, or I'm no longer serious about supporting you."

"Fucking hell," I mumbled, following him to the car. "Hello, Mother," I said, sliding into the back seat, surprised my sister was back there, too.

"You got roped into this too? Are we off to find you a husband, old maid?"

Sophie gave a grim smile as she glanced up from her phone. She was only a year and a half older than me, but by my parents' standards that had to count as a spinster at this point. Our oldest sister, Emma, had married last year and quickly moved across the country. She rarely came home, and neither Sophie nor I blamed her. I wasn't sure what was stopping me from moving across the country, but it would be good to start considering the options.

"Are we both being sold off today?"

"Apparently," I muttered, zoning out when my mother started to scold us both. My sister wasn't like me, in the best way. She was determined, smart, and ready to graduate as a lawyer next year. Even more unlike me, she *wanted* to go to law school, and unlike our dad, she wanted to do good things with that degree, not help scummy rich men. She should be the pride and joy of the family, yet my father seemed to believe that should fall on my shoulders no matter what.

I stayed silent on the ride, clicking my phone one too many times to see if any of the crew had texted. Even Scout, although the idea she would text me should probably be laughable. She had agreed to fix my car, and even though I knew she wanted to protest more, she had agreed to me being there to help. I would rather learn a fraction of what they knew so maybe I could do more than change a tire.

I was hoping that me suddenly wanting to be a mechanic had nothing to do with Scout's smug look when she told me I couldn't do anything more.

We pulled up to the valet, and I reached back, helping my sister out of the SUV.

"Thanks. Getting out of lower cars is hard enough in a dress, but having to gracefully *jump* out of a car is almost impossible," she said.

The entire country club was made up of other lawyers at my dad's firm or his clients, and they were all here for the company outing today. I swear this company had more get-togethers than a frat house.

By the time I made it inside the packed building, I needed a drink, but I assumed it would be out of the question considering it was the middle of the afternoon and my mother was already glaring at me.

I looked over the crowd, a crown of red hair catching my eye, the wave of excitement hitting me first, followed by a nervous feeling settling into my gut. I messed with the rings on my fingers, spinning each one as I watched the red head of hair move through the crowd.

The excitement surged and then quickly deflated. She wasn't Scout, and I had no idea why I would think she would be here. I didn't know which one was more ridiculous, her being at an event like this, or me being excited about it.

Maybe it was the races or the attitude, but every time I saw her it gave me a rush. It was a feeling I had been looking for day after day, but it was getting harder to find. Things I loved seemed to dull the more I did them, and until two weeks ago, racing had almost become one of those things.

That was until the little ankle biter got out and came at me like an attack dog. I smirked at the nickname she hated so much.

Five minutes had barely gone by before I was surrounded by friends.

"Hey. Drinks?" Justin asked.

"Are there any? I was beginning to think this was a dry party."

"For us it is, but ours are now hidden in the back. Apparently, our parents are requesting that we don't drink tonight."

"Let's go," I said, grinning as I slid the chair back and started following after him, making it about ten feet before my dad stepped in front of me.

"What are you doing?"

"Going to grab a drink," I said, technically not lying.

"For you and Claire?"

"It's like you read my mind," I said, smiling and not hiding an ounce of my sarcasm.

"Chase, this isn't a joke."

"I wasn't laughing. I do need to go get those drinks, though."

"You have five minutes, and if I don't see you with Claire, I will be calling for that Porsche to be picked up before you can even make it home."

A car.

A fucking car.

He found the *one* thing I cared about and immediately used it as a bargaining chip. A way to threaten me into doing what he wanted me, too.

I knew I had to listen, though. That was the problem.

I had to do what he wanted me to do, or else he would follow through. Although, with the Porsche broken down, I wasn't sure why he would care to pick it up.

I wasn't about to test him now, so I headed over, grabbing two drinks and heading back over to him. Claire, my forced bride, stood next to my parents, all of them waiting for me.

"Hello," she said, her smile pleasant and kind.

"Hey. How are you?" I asked.

"I've been better. Your dad tells me we will be hanging out more tonight."

"I believe my dad thinks we will be hanging out forever."

"Yeah, I did hear the plans for us. I guess that's how these things go, though." She didn't look as defeated as I would have guessed, but then again, we both grew up in this life. We knew when to hide our emotions.

I've known Claire for a while now. I knew she was a nice person, seemingly kind to everyone. She never made a scene or raised her voice in these settings. She didn't drink excessively, and I would bet my car that she wasn't going out racing anytime soon. There really wasn't anything wrong with her. On top of her personality, she was beautiful. There was no way to deny it, but it didn't seem to matter.

My heart didn't race any faster, my stomach didn't flip around until I was nauseous. There was no spark of emotion, and definitely not the full on tidal wave of emotions that hit me when Scout was around.

At this point, though, I wasn't sure if feeling all of that was a good thing or not.

We talked a little longer until my dad waved me over to him. For once, I was fine with having a reason to excuse myself and head over to him.

"Behaving?" he asked.

"Obviously."

"Does this mean we are good? Things are still on track?"

"Was it ever not?"

"I wasn't sure," he said. "That's all for now. You and Claire can continue enjoying your night." He dismissed me right away, waving a hand as he turned and disappeared into the crowd.

My lip curled as I watched him go. Claire was back in conversation with her friends, and I had no need to go over there again. I turned away, heading over to Justin and waving for him to come with me.

I made it to the back room and sat down at one of the makeshift poker tables, a few of the other guys already surrounding us to pass around a joint.

I was king of a castle here, or at least they made me feel that way, but it wasn't a celebration. It was a hollow feeling that seemed to stretch on forever. I could feel the emptiness seeping into my bones the moment I stepped into this place, the moment I woke up. Every minute of the day.

A picture of Scout flashed across my mind unprompted, but I shook it away.

"Make it quick," I said. "I apparently have a date waiting out there, and if I don't entertain it, my car will be gone."

Justin took a hit and passed it to me. "Didn't realize you had dates."

"I don't. This was apparently a surprise blind date," I said, shaking my head immediately as I sucked smoke into my lungs. "No, actually, it was apparently a blind proposal. According to my dad, I'm engaged."

A roar of laughter and sarcastic congratulations went around the room.

"No shit? You know what that means?" Justin said, lifting the bottle of tequila like he was giving a toast. "Time for a party!"

I should have guessed that would be his reaction. It would take a few hours, but he would turn my family's lake house into chaos tonight.

I didn't care.

I would have a party any night of the week if it kept my mind off of all of this bullshit. Even if the party tonight wasn't exactly what I wanted, it might be exactly what I needed.

SEVEN

SCOUT

ON ONE HAND, I had managed to come up with three thousand dollars, get my car running again, and go out with Jesse tonight. On the other hand, it still wasn't enough money, my car didn't seem to want to go over seventy miles an hour, and Jesse was currently bitching about us being out because we weren't going where he wanted to go.

It wasn't even completely my decision. I agreed to go out with the crew before I knew where we were going, and didn't realize we'd be going to Chase's house tonight for a party until it was too late. Apparently, he had set up a huge, last-minute party tonight and invited us all to come.

By the time I walked around the back of the house, I already knew I wanted to leave.

Who had this much money for a random party? It wasn't even a party for something, it was only because they were bored.

The entire backyard was covered in colored lights, balloons, and the pool was even filled with hundreds of light up floating balls. It was all over the top and everyone seemed to think that was normal. Someone yelled out, catching our attention as we turned towards the back of the house.

Chase was on the second-story balcony shirtless and yelling something out.

"Is he about to jump into the pool?" Quinn asked, apparently as surprised as me. No one answered, watching him step onto the ledge.

The guys didn't have the same concerns, cheering him on with the rest of the crowd. Chase handed his beer to the girl next to him and then jumped.

Water splashed over all of us, bringing the familiar irritation that always seemed to happen when Chase was around right back to me.

"What the hell, Chase?" Ash yelled, stepping back while Fox laughed.

Jesse leaned into me, holding me closer. "Are we really here for this guy?"

"Yeah, it's Fox and Ash's friend," I whispered back.

"And it makes us need to be here? I know other parties going on which are less pretentious and a hell of a lot more fun."

"We are already here. Can you not find a way to have fun here for an hour?"

He groaned, watching Chase climb out of the pool, throwing water onto every one again. "Fine. I'll go find us some drinks," Jesse said, disappearing into the crowd before I could say anything.

Chase got out, shaking the guys' hands and acting all sweet with the girls. Then he got to me.

"Quite the party. Is the money bonfire around here some-where or does that start later?" I asked, not hiding any hint of snark.

"Money bonfire?" he asked with a smirk. "Is this all not enough of a waste for you that I need to throw away more?

While I appreciate your style, I'm a little surprised to hear it coming from you."

I rolled my eyes, trying not to look at his bare chest.

I never thought I would like a man so...wet.

"Don't worry, the money bonfire will start soon. I'm going to change now so I don't miss it. Feel free to head inside for drinks and whatever food is still there after this crowd."

"Have a golden suit to slip into?" I asked, trying to calm my snark down and failing.

His smile grew, and he leaned down closer to me.

Too close.

"No, but thanks for the suggestion. I think I would look good in all gold." He winked and walked away, Jesse curling a lip at him when he went past.

"How the fuck are you friends with him?" Jesse asked, turning to Fox while handing me a drink.

"What's wrong? Hate anyone who has a personality?" Fox asked. "He's cool and I would prefer if you're going to talk shit about my friends, you say it to their face."

Jesse rolled his eyes. "All I'm saying is he's some rich, privileged asshole. Anyone from this background isn't worth a damn in my life."

The crew went silent. No one dared to move as we waited for Fox's reply.

"I was almost offended because my girlfriend comes from a background like his, but I don't actually want her in your life so, problem solved," Fox said, pulling Ash close to him. She patted his chest in response, almost giving me an apologetic smile. I tried to give one back. This wasn't the first time Jesse and Fox had butted heads.

"Can you two knock it off for tonight?" I asked, wishing for once they would get along. There was nothing worse than Fox not liking someone I was dating, and these two never seemed to stop this type of bickering. Every time I thought they were moving on and becoming friends, something like this happened.

"Let's go see what food he has inside," Jax said, burying his head against Carly to whisper to her as we all headed for the back door. I knew they were talking about Jesse and I which only made me feel worse about bringing him tonight.

Jesse pulled me aside. "I went inside to grab drinks for us because I wanted to stay outside, not go right back in."

"Okay, but I want to go see what there is to eat. We can come back out in a few minutes." I was trying to sweeten my voice, to sound like the person I usually always was, but the words still came out clipped.

His lips pursed together, and I already knew what he was about to say. "I'll wait out here for you."

"Fine," I growled, ripping away from him.

I didn't understand it. The guys couldn't get enough of Quinn, Ash, and Carly. They hung on them constantly. If they were going inside, the guys were going unless told not to. Even Ransom had changed the moment he started dating Quinn and couldn't get enough of her, but Jesse never did with me. He seemed content if we didn't touch all night.

I caught up to Kye, walking alongside him. "Do you think if you get a girlfriend, you would want to touch her all the time?"

I knew Kye was the one to ask. Between never having a girlfriend before, recoiling when people touched him, and looking less approachable than almost anyone in the crew, he would give me an honest answer, not clouded in already being in love.

"No, but that's exactly why I'm not getting a girlfriend. They all want touchy feely shit and I don't. I don't think it would ever change for me. Trouble in paradise?"

"More like confusion in paradise. He seems like he could take it or leave it with all that, but none of these guys are like that."

"Some people aren't big on the touching. Some people are just assholes. I guess it's up to you to figure out which one he is."

I nodded, trying to think it over as we looked at the ridiculous amount of food in the kitchen. The table led us to the living room where Chase sat, the center of attention once again.

"Hey ankle-biter. Come here," he said, waving me over with a cocky grin before motioning for me to sit on his lap. I could feel the heat rise in my face, and my nostrils flared as I stomped over.

"If you call me that one more damn time, I'm *going* to kick your ass."

"Damn, I would love to see that. I was only inviting you over for the money bonfire," he said. The sinister smirk on his face was unsettling as he pulled a hundred out of his pocket. He laid it out on the table, moving some weed onto it and rolling it up.

"You are not serious," I said, not sure if I was more disgusted at the blatant waste of a hundred dollars, or inhaling burnt money.

He pulled the rolled up bill to his lips and brought the lighter up, burning one end until it caught on fire and died out. He inhaled once before handing it over to me.

The intensity of the anger I felt made me shake as I smacked his hand, the bill and weed flying onto the floor, where someone stomped it out.

"You're disgusting," I said, turning on my heel and heading to the back of the house. Jesse was right. We didn't need to be here.

I could hear Chase laughing behind me. "Hey wait, ankle — I mean Scout. Hold on." He caught up to me, grabbing my arm and pulling me into a small room along the back of the house before I could stop him. Two large glass doors ran along the back wall. They were closed now, but could open up to the pool and patio. A bar ran along the opposite wall. If the doors were open, it would be the perfect walk up bar for a party.

"I thought it would be funny after your money bonfire comment," he laughed, leaning back against a bar top that ran along one wall, every other wall was covered in windows. "Obviously, you're not the humorous type."

"Oh, I love humor. But that wasn't funny."

"It was a little funny."

"To waste money someone could use? Money that could feed a child for a week? You're right. I'm doubled over in laughter," I said.

"And here I thought the fiery little ankle-biter would be the life of the party now, but now she's determined to ruin it all." His eyes got heavy as he leaned his head back. "Are you not having a good time?"

"Why would I be? Are you? Based on the fake smile that you're struggling to keep on your face, and the desperate need to get everyone's eyes on you, I would guess that you aren't. And I'm allowed to be annoyed at something you did without ruining your entire party." I looked him over, my body reacting the exact way it had the night of the races. "And why the hell do you not have a shirt on?"

His head snapped back up, looking past me to the pool, but I didn't turn around. "Because drunk me might want to go for another swim. And what do you mean, I'm not having a good time? It's my party."

"And yet you look like a zombie walking around here. I don't know about you, but I'm usually having the best time when I throw a party with my friends, not walking around looking like I would rather launch myself off a roof and drown"

"I think you're the only one who would argue I'm not having fun. My friends seem to think I'm having the time of my life."

"Then you need better friends. Making new ones might be easier if you stopped walking around like a pretentious jerk."

"Bold of you to say I'm a jerk when you're dating a bigger one than me. Honestly, that's saying something."

"Jesse is not always a jerk."

"No? Just half the time or something?"

I hated that my first reaction was to agree with him, but I forced myself to shake my head. "Not always."

He took another step closer, caging me in as his hands pressed against the window behind me.

"Are you completely sure? Because from where I'm standing, he is openly staring at those girls in their bikinis. Seems like he likes other boobs a little too much, no?"

He smiled down at me, making me lose track of what he was saying, his dark hair and eyes only inches from me, and I couldn't figure out how he smelled so good. It should only be chlorine, but somehow it was still that clean musky scent that made me get a little too lost to the world around me. I was a little to lost to it all until he grabbed my chin, gently turning me around.

I looked out over the pool, the lights from it shining enough to see Jesse on the other side. Chase was right. Jesse wasn't hiding how much he was staring at a girl in a small bikini, her big boobs nearly spilling out. Not only was he staring at her boobs, but he seemed more engrossed in their conversation than he had with me in months.

It made me mad the first thing I did was look down, noticing how small mine were in comparison. It's not like it was the first time I've seen Jesse noticing other women, but it was the first time someone else had called him out for it to my face. The fact that Chase was the one seeing how much my boyfriend liked other women made this so much worse.

"It's not like I'm one to talk when I'm in here alone with you," I said.

"Is being alone in a room with a man really crossing a line in your relationship?" he asked.

"I don't know. Maybe. I may have my issues with Jesse, but those are none of your business."

"No," he said, shrugging, as his lips curved into a devious smile. "But you seemed pretty high up on your fucking horse, so I thought I would help you down. Plus, I can't figure out how the guy has you. If he wants to fuck around, why have a girlfriend like you?"

I couldn't catch my breath. The way he made it sound like I was worth so much more made my chest tighten until it ached.

"Why do you think?"

He shrugged again. "I'm guessing it's a 'have his cake and eat it too' type of situation, which leads me to one conclusion."

"Which is?"

"I may be a wasteful jerk, but he's one of those tried and true jerks. At least I don't date a girl only to cheat on her."

"He's not cheating on me," I said. The word 'yet' hung unspoken in the air between us. "And it doesn't matter what, or who, he is. You're a jerk who wasted money someone in this world needs."

He rolled his eyes and leaned back towards me. "When I sober up, I'll donate a hundred dollars in your honor to some food for kids' organization."

"Three hundred," I said, making him stop and stalk back over to me.

"Excuse me?"

"Donate three hundred. One for my wasted one you burned, one for wasting my time, and one to convince me you *might* be a step above Jesse on the being a jerk scale."

He stepped back, his jeans falling a little lower on his hips.

"Fine, damn, I called it when I called you a downer. Bringing me down so far, I need to remember to wake up and donate money to some charity."

"And send me proof. Maybe then I'll keep helping you with your car."

"You drive a very hard bargain, and you should be thankful I'm drunk enough not to fight back. As an almost-lawyer, it's pretty much my nature to negotiate, but I'm giving you this one."

"Good. That means you will leave me alone for the night. Go off and find another girl to bother."

"It only means I would rather go get a beer than watch you go fawn and cry all over your boyfriend about how mean I am. Why would I need to find another girl when I already found one that is *so* much fun?" He pulled on my braid, my head going back as his nose ran up my neck.

Heat and pleasure moved up my spine, my thighs clenching together.

"Pretty sure you're crossing a line now," I said, using every ounce of sternness I had in my tone.

His chest rumbled, and the heat of his breath on my neck made me shudder. "I like crossing lines. According to you, I like crossing lines before I'm supposed to. Isn't that all this is?"

"No, this is you being a rich jerk, and thinking you can do whatever you want."

"And yet, you're not telling me to back up."

The heat of him was conflicting with the slight chill from the window behind me, and it wasn't doing anything to help convince me to tell him to back up. If anything, it was making me want to lean in and steal the warmth.

Finally, I caught my breath, my hands meeting hard stomach as I pushed him back.

"Okay then, back up."

He listened, smiling as he stepped back.

"Now go back to your party and stop bothering me."

He gave another slow laugh and headed to the door, the drunken grin on his face falling when he turned back to me.

"Fine. Fine, but for what my opinion is worth," he said, leaning against the door and looking me over. "Which, based on your face, is probably nothing." The heat filled his gaze again, making a shiver run down my spine. "He's an idiot for not having you in this room doing exactly what I would like to be doing to you."

I lost all words, trying to come up with any comeback, but I couldn't think of anything as I watched him walk out.

Nothing but wondering what he had on his mind.

I turned back to look at Jesse, who was still talking to the girl, but he wasn't touching her. Could I say anything to him when Chase had almost been on top of me a minute ago? Especially when I had liked the feel of Chase against me.

I didn't have anything to say. To him, to the crew, to Chase. I stayed in the room for a few more minutes before heading out to Jesse, barely saying a word the entire rest of the night.

EIGHT

SCOUT

JESSE PULLED the car into Haven, the fanciest restaurant we had in town, and one I rarely stepped inside of. The small street was lined with little stores and restaurants the crew would come to once in a while, but we had only been to this restaurant once. I had asked to go out somewhere nice for my birthday, and he was trying to deliver. There was nothing wrong with the food. The atmosphere was romantic and calming, but something about him was rubbing me the wrong way tonight.

He parked and huffed for the thousandth time since getting in the car.

"We can go to the diner if this is bothering you," I said again.

"I told you it's fine. You said I had to do better. So, here I am, doing better."

I nodded, getting out and meeting him at the front of the car. He really had insisted, and for the first time in a long time, it almost felt like he wanted to act like my boyfriend, but that was short-lived.

"Alright, come on. Go spend all of my money on one

dinner," he mumbled, clumsily taking my hand and pulling me close.

"Like I keep saying, we don't have to go in. You're the one who suggested it."

He mumbled again, but this time I couldn't make out the words when he turned away and pulled open the door. The low lights and music surrounded me, the effect immediately calming. Jesse's hand moved to my lower back, making me jump at the touch. I wanted to feel calm and at ease with him. I wanted to take it all in and enjoy the feel of his hand on my back. I wanted a small sliver of this life with a guy who was crazy about me, but I knew no matter what he was saying, he wasn't happy to be here. My chest ached at the thought. My mind always went back to one thing, I don't think there was anywhere in the world the guys wouldn't want to be if the girls were there.

This was exactly the type of place Ransom would hate going, but he would be there with Quinn in a heartbeat, and even be happy about it.

I would bet all the money I currently had sitting in my purse that Jesse would rather be at the bar down the street to celebrate my birthday. The loud music, and crush of dancing bodies was more his style than a fancy, sit-down restaurant. I don't know if it was Quinn's insistence we go out to nice places once in a while or just the need to grow up, but I would rather be here than at any packed bar tonight.

I loved dancing and having fun more than anyone, but somehow lately, I always ended up standing at the side, watching Jesse have the time of his life. There was no room for me to relax and have fun when I was always worried about what argument he might start next.

The hostess walked us over to two small seats that surrounded an even smaller table. I wasn't even sure how my plate and a drink would fit at this thing. The last time we came, we had reserved the biggest table here for all of us to come out. This was pathetically tiny, but I sat down and took the rest of the restaurant in. I don't know what would make me want a bigger table when it was only the two of us.

"Impressed enough?" he asked, a small, forced smile on his lips.

"I wasn't asking to come out to make you impress me. I wanted to come out and have a nice night without blaring music and cheap beer."

Although, now, I was regretting asking him to take me out at all. I wanted to open up to Jesse, but every part of me held back. And now I couldn't talk to him about the things happening with my dad. The things that were piling up more than going away, and I wasn't sure how to talk to him about the fact that I had five grand in my purse, waiting for a text to go pay off my dad's debts.

Jesse knew about my dad, but hated him. *I* should hate him enough to not do this, but the nagging feeling I had to help my only blood relative was too much for me to ignore.

The waitress came over, Jesse's eyes lingering a little too long on her top while she took our drink order.

"Do you just have beer or are you too good for that?" he asked.

She gave a tight smile. "No, we have a few options."

He picked one out with a huff and I ordered some fancy cocktail after. If there was one thing I loved, it was the fancy drinks. I can get mediocre beer at the garage if I wanted.

"Are you coming to my race at Holt Racing in two weeks?" I asked, hoping if I reminded him now, there would be no missing it.

"What day?"

"Friday afternoon. I'll be there all day, though."

There was no missing the small way his lips tightened or how he looked away from me before answering. "Yeah, I'll be there. Are you trying to win and move into the nationals?"

My eyebrows furrowed. "Why else would I be driving in a qualifying race if I wasn't trying to win and move into more professional races? I'm trying to make this a career."

"You race down random streets. You aren't suddenly professional because Holt asked you to try out for his team."

"No, but I have the potential to be. Ash agrees. Her dad agrees I could do it. Why wouldn't I try?"

"I just think it's dumb. You already work at the garage. Why change it now? Are things not going too good there?"

"Yeah, they are going great, but there's enough of us that I can step away a little more to work on these races. Everyone is fine with it, and I'll still be there to work every chance I can."

He nodded, but I looked past him, the man walking through the front door catching my eye immediately.

The dark hair and dark hazel eyes. Eyes which seemed to burn into me. My heart beat picked up and I willed it to stop. He looked good tonight, wearing a more simple suit than the one he had on at the races, and he seemed a little more disheveled tonight. There was even one perfect curl of hair that fell over his forehead, completely out of place and making me lose my train of thought.

It made the urge to run my hands through his hair and mess it up more almost unbearable.

Chase.

His eyes roamed over everyone in the restaurant, stopping at me. His eyebrows jumped up, probably surprised I could be at such a nice place.

I shook my head, silently hoping he would get the hint to *not* come over here. Jesse didn't know he was coming around the garage and I didn't think he would like finding out.

Not that I was doing anything wrong. I was helping a customer. It's not like I was trying to hang out with him.

Of course, Chase didn't get the hint and rounded the corner to us, smiling when he saw Jesse.

"This was the last place I was expecting to see you," Chase said, the deep tone making me give him my attention as he sidled up to the table. His eyes ran over me and I felt like I could read his thoughts.

What was a girl like me doing in such a nice dress in such a nice restaurant?

Or maybe I was jumping to conclusions.

Chase was calm when he looked over at Jesse, the run-in nothing to him, but I knew Jesse was already sizing him up.

"Yeah, out for a date for my birthday," I said, grabbing my water and taking a nervous sip. "Jesse, you remember Chase? And Chase, my boyfriend Jesse."

"Oh yeah," Chase said. "I remember you from my party."

"Really?" Jesse asked. "I'm surprised you remember anything from that night."

Chase smiled down at me. "Oh, I remember *every* detail."

Jesse stood up, the chair sliding back. "What does that mean?"

Chase didn't step back, his smile not even faltering. "Exactly what I said. While I was drunk, I'm aware of all of it. I was glad to finally meet you, though. The crew talks about you so much, but you never appeared. I was starting to wonder if they'd all made you up, or if Scout just preferred hiding you." There was an innocence in his tone now, but I was too busy turning red to intervene.

The air charged, and I was about to push between them when Jesse finally took a step back.

"She wasn't hiding me," Jesse said, sitting back down. "Some of us work for a living."

"Don't worry, I know she calls me rich boy. You can say it to my face."

Jesse looked at me, the anger burning in his eyes, and I knew what came next when Jesse got like this. He would take whatever chance he could to start a fight with someone, and my face was already hot at the thought of how embarrassing that would be.

"We kind of need to get back to dinner. *Thanks* for stopping over," I said, nodding my head, my eyes wide, to let him know he should keep going.

"Of course. And I'll see you tomorrow? First day of fixing my car?" The smirk on his face made it obvious he knew exactly what he was doing.

"Yes," I said through gritted teeth. "See you then." I looked away from him completely, knowing if my gaze lingered too much longer, I wouldn't be looking away again.

Why was this clean cut, dressed up guy having any effect on me?

He finally left, leaving us both speechless with the soft music playing around us.

"What the *fuck* is he talking about, Scout? Why would he be there while you fix his car?"

"He asked us to fix the car, but also show him a few things while we did. He's only there to learn."

"Learn the car or learn about you?"

I ground my teeth together, trying not to snap. "About the car. He has no interest in me. I was the only one who didn't have a line of cars to work on already this week."

"So Fox is taking over his car soon?"

"No? I am finishing it."

"Great. So not only are you hanging around all those guys at the garage, but now you're adding one rich, entitled fuck who probably thinks he can have whatever girl he wants."

"Hold on. Did you just say all those guys at the garage? Do you mean my friends? Now you're pissed about them?"

"I'm pissed about all of this, Scout. You're telling me you have never wanted to get with any of them, and none of them have ever wanted to get with you? I don't buy it."

I shook my head, not quite believing what was happening.

"I can tell you that no, none of us have ever wanted a sexual relationship with each other. That's disgusting considering I've made it clear I consider them my brothers."

"Yeah? Is Chase your brother now, too?"

"No, but I'm also fixing his car, not trying to jump into bed with him."

He only shook his head, and before I could respond, my phone went off.

UNKNOWN

Here's the address. Be there at 9pm with the money. Then this will be done.

It was the one stupid text I had been waiting for and it had to come at the worst time. It was a little after 8 PM now, which gave me less than an hour to get over to the warehouses where the address was. Luckily, they were only about thirty minutes from here. Not enough time to run home and change, but enough time to get my car, get there and scope it out.

"I need to cut this date short," I said, not sugar-coating it after his attitude.

"Excuse me?" he asked, eyebrows shooting up.

"I have somewhere to be and need to get back to my car."

My words were firm. Final. And he seemed to hate that.

"Are you fucking kidding me? I take you out to this nice

restaurant, and then that fucking guy shows up and sends you one text and you want to run out of here?"

"He isn't who texted me. Someone needs me, and I need to go help them. That's what I do. It has nothing to do with him. And I love you brought me here. I was hoping to have a nice night tonight, but something came up and I'm sorry. I have to take care of this."

"Take care of what?" he asked.

"I can't tell you," I said. How was I supposed to tell him the man I hated more than anyone needed me to bail him out of his own mess and I was going to do it? No one would understand that.

He stood up, the chair pushing back into the one behind him.

"This is fucking ridiculous, Scout. I'm done. I'm done with all this shit. I take you to this stupid expensive restaurant you begged for, and this is what you do? I'm leaving."

I grabbed my purse, moving to slide the chair back, but he shook his head.

"No, *I'm* leaving. Whoever you were running off with can give you a ride. Happy fucking birthday."

"Jesse, wait!" I said, standing up to grab for him.

"No, I didn't even want to be at this stupid fucking place, anyway. There's a bar down the street with cheaper drinks, better music, and girls who would kill to hang out with me." He threw up a hand, walking out.

I stared at the door shutting behind him.

There was a part of me that always thought Jesse would cheat on me if he hadn't already. That he enjoyed other girls' company over mine, but I always told myself it was my own insecurities coming out. Then, every time we fought, he made sure to let me know there was a line of women waiting to hang out with him. I stepped back, my purse falling from where I set it on my chair.

Of course, when I turned to pick it up, it was Chase's dark eyes on me.

I just needed him to stop looking at me.

Why did he suddenly show up everywhere in my life?

He leaned back, an older man and woman across from him, with a beautiful woman by his side.

She didn't seem to be a mess. I bet she wasn't heading to a creepy warehouse tonight to pay off her deadbeat father's debts, because he used her as a pawn in his life.

No.

She would be enjoying food at this beautiful place, maybe going out with gorgeous Chase after, and probably not worrying for a second about her dad's finances. If anything, her dad would be funding her entire night.

I sat down, turning my back to Chase and hoping he would get the hint I didn't want him over here.

I had hoped but I wasn't even surprised when he sat down in the seat where Jesse had been.

"Trouble in bad boy paradise?"

"Yes. Must be trouble in rich boy paradise, too. What are you doing over here? Get back to your date and leave me alone."

He gave me a cocky grin, leaning back and getting comfortable.

"My date? I don't know how things work where you are from, but I usually don't go on dates with my sister. I also don't do double dates with my parents. I appreciate the jealousy I could be on a date here, though. Your boyfriend ran out. I had to assume that was your signal I join you."

"You assumed wrong. Get back to your family."

"No thanks," he said, leaning onto the table, his watch and rings flashing in the glow of lights. "I'd rather hear more about this rich boy paradise. What exactly happens there?" A devilish smirk grew on his face. "I mean, I have a few suggestions, but ladies first."

I rolled my eyes. "What do you want, Chase?"

"To know what happened to your boyfriend."

"He left. Obviously." His eyes were still trained on me. The unwavering attention made me look away.

"Why?"

I only shrugged and looked out over the restaurant, not wanting to chance meeting his eyes. It was embarrassing enough to have your boyfriend act like this, but to have Chase witness it all only added to it.

"I wasn't coming over here to be a jerk. I was going to offer you a ride home. But I also have to say, if I found out my girl-friend is spending time with a hot, rich guy who doesn't have a fragile male ego, I sure as hell wouldn't be running out on a date."

"Yeah, I guess so."

He shook his head, but didn't add to it. "I can give you a ride, or Fox and Ash are nearby at Holt tonight. I'm sure they could pick you up," he said, shrugging as though him suddenly being friends with anyone in the crew was normal. I shouldn't be surprised. We had welcomed the girls into our group with no problem. I loved them being around now. Quinn felt like my first true girl friend, Ash quickly followed, and even Carly had finally opened up and became one of my best friends, too.

I thought when Jesse came around it would be the same, that the crew would welcome him in and there would be no prob-lems, but it hadn't been the case.

The guys tried to hang out with Jesse, but it went downhill every time. Probably only for my sake. They had tried to invite him out with them, but he always blew them off. Now there was no trying from either side, just endless passive aggressive comments and glares.

He wasn't their friend, but now Chase was?

I met his eye, realizing Chase wasn't *my* friend.

"I can't call them for a ride. I need to go somewhere they can't know about, but I don't care if you know. And now, I've wasted another ten minutes, and I don't have enough time to get back to my car."

"While sneaking around with you sounds hot," he said with a wink. "I won't be bringing you somewhere you shouldn't be."

"Oh come on. What does it matter to you? I have to go either way. I'm only asking for a ride."

I held my breath, waiting. It was a stupid hope, but he was one person that could go with me and it didn't matter if he was upset about what I was doing.

"What do I get out of it?"

I quickly looked away, trying not to panic. I really had nothing to offer. Money wouldn't help, parts weren't a problem with him. I ran through anything I had to offer and came up with nothing.

"I don't know. I can't think of anything I could offer you."

"How about you agree to be at the races this Thursday to race me, and we will call it even?"

"How is that a trade?"

He shrugged. "A ride for a race. Seems fair enough. You did say you just need a ride there. Do we have a deal or not?"

"If you won't tell Fox and Ash, or any of the crew, about this, then yeah, we have a deal."

He gave a sharp nod. "Head out to my car. I borrowed my dad's blue Audi tonight. Can't miss it," he said, sliding me the keys. "I have to go tell the tyrants over there that I have to go."

I assumed this meant he didn't want me to be seen leaving with him, which would only help me. I didn't want anyone knowing who I was, where I was going, or who I was with. I grabbed the keys, glancing back at him and the table he was headed to. The older man, his dad, looked pissed. The deep crease between his eyebrows only grew stronger as Chase walked over.

I smiled when I saw the Audi sitting out front, the car beeping when I hit the unlock button and slid behind the wheel.

It was time to pay off some of my dad's debt and, hopefully, it would be enough to get him out of my life for good.

NINE

CHASE

IT HAD BEEN a few days since Scout had walked into my party and looked at me like I was no better than the mud on the bottom of her boots.

Now she was asking me for a favor.

And somehow, with one look at her, I was doing it. I was even fine with it as long as it was clear that I might be scum of the Earth to her, but I was still better than her deadweight boyfriend. Every time I saw him, the overwhelming urge to punch him in the face almost got the best of me.

Why I felt like she needed to see me be better than him wasn't a thought I was going to linger on tonight.

At least now I could spend my week looking forward to racing her again. She raced with every ounce of herself. The pure focus she had was unmatched, and I wanted to feel that again.

I walked out five minutes later. A fight was already brewing between my dad and me, but I couldn't find it in myself to care when I walked out and saw a mane of red hair in my driver's seat.

"You honestly think I'm letting you drive my car?" I asked, smiling as I leaned down against the open window.

"You handed me the keys. Was that not an invitation?"

I shook my head. "Out, ankle-biter. I'm driving tonight. This car is on loan and will be the one I'm racing next Thursday. I can't trust you won't learn something about it to win."

She rolled her eyes, but got out and headed to the passenger seat. "I should have guessed, but I was hoping you weren't one of those macho, fragile ego men, too."

I slid behind the wheel, not missing how she pulled her long hair over one shoulder and leaned back.

"Oh, I'm not worried about you being able to drive. I'm worried about you somehow figuring this car out more and using it to beat me on Thursday. And what do you mean, *too*? Have someone else in mind like that?"

She threw me a pointed glare before instructing me to take a left out of the parking lot. "Why would your only stipulation be we race on Thursday?" She asked.

I shrugged, pulling out onto the dark street. "I like racing you. You're a good opponent to have, and I want to beat you again. I like how mad you get when I win. It makes me feel like a god among men, and it's getting harder and harder to feel that way these days."

"Because everyone treats you like a god already. Do you really need another instance to feed your ego?"

"Yes. Obviously," I said, smirking when she glared at me.

I navigated the dark streets, a light mist of rain starting to fall as we wound through the small town, and she kept directing me until we were in an area filled with manufacturing buildings.

"Right here." She pointed to an older, almost run down ware-house mixed in with the nicer ones.

"You think I'm dropping you off here?"

"Yes."

"No, absolutely not. What the hell are you doing at a place like this? You were willing to leave the nice restaurant to come here?"

"Yeah, I did, and I'm here on business. Business I don't need your approval for. I asked for a ride, you gave me one. I'll see you at the races on Thursday."

"You will, but in the meantime, I'm sure as hell not letting you go in there alone."

I shut the car off and got out, not giving her a chance to protest. There was no way I was going to let her walk into this place by herself. I couldn't imagine what she could need here and I worried if I asked too many questions, I would be literally hauling her ass out of here. I went around the car, pulling her door open and holding out my hand.

"Are you meeting someone here? Buying drugs? Buying stolen cars?"

She rolled her eyes and ignored my hand, struggling to get out of the low car.

"I also assumed you would appreciate the assistance in that dress."

"Funny you choose here to suddenly be a gentleman."

"Well, it seems to only be us, so I thought it was safe."

She tried not to smile, but failed, the small curve of her lips making me wonder why I hadn't been nicer sooner. While it was fun to have Scout angry and rabid at me, making her smile seemed to pull at something in my chest. Her hand intertwined with mine as I helped her out of the car, and she brushed her dress down, shivering from the onset of the cold, misty rain.

"You weren't actually planning to come here, were you?" I asked, grabbing a hoodie out of the back of the car and handing it to her. She took it without a word, pulling it over her head until it engulfed her.

"Not exactly. It was a last-minute thing."

"A last-minute thing which was so important you had to leave for it in the middle of your fancy date, and piss off your boyfriend? Or is it ex-boyfriend now?"

"Yes, it was that important," she said, her eyebrows furrowing a little too hard. "And yeah, I didn't even think about it, but I guess it has to be ex-boyfriend."

"You didn't even think about it? Shouldn't you be a mess of tears that your boyfriend just walked out on your date?"

The way her big hazel eyes looked up to meet mine made me want to fall over. "I think if I dwell on the fact that my boyfriend ditched me at my own birthday dinner, I might not get through this, so I think I will have to deal with it all later."

My jaw tightened until my teeth pressed so hard together that it felt like they would break. He ditched her on her birthday? I could see her shoulders straighten, and I knew I couldn't ask more about it. She needed to get through whatever this was, and me asking more about her less-than-stellar boyfriend wasn't going to help. I only nodded, wondering how Jesse had ever had a chance with her.

"Is there a problem?" she asked, one eyebrow arched.

"A few, yes," I said, looking around the old warehouse. There was one creepy main door, a roll up garage door which was so rusted I didn't think it would work anymore, and the rest of the building was a faded blue color, but was so overgrown I couldn't even make out the logo that had once been there. "The first one being, what are we doing here? Who are you meeting?"

"Someone for my dad, and I have some money to give him. The rest is not your business."

"Is your dad in some sort of trouble or are you…in business with him somehow?"

"I think that falls into the *not your business* category. I need to go inside. I'm waiting for someone. You can stay in the car."

"Not a chance would I let you walk into that building alone."

"How chivalrous. Then come on and please keep your mouth shut. Not only tonight, but keep your mouth shut about this forever. No one else is allowed to know we were here."

"Yeah, I got that. You don't have to worry. I tend to keep my mouth shut about any illegal things I do."

We reached the door, and she rolled her eyes. Rather than making any effort to open it herself, she chose to stand there, waiting for me to open it for her.

"So I take it you like my gentleman act now?" I asked, pulling it open.

"My hands are frozen. I figured if you were offering, I'll accept."

"Suddenly finding your value now?"

She stopped, spinning to face me, her face etched with anger.

"What is that supposed to mean?"

"Nothing," I said, waving her forward. I wasn't going to explain the irony that I should be the one holding open doors, but her boyfriend could treat her like shit and get away with it.

Her phone pinged, and she looked down at it. I could see the number wasn't saved, and it put me more on alert. We obviously weren't meeting friends. "He said he will be here in ten minutes."

I only nodded, walking down the long hallway and looking in each room. There was one office at the end that I waved her over to.

"This one has two doors and two large windows. Let's wait here."

"Why?"

"In case we need to leave quickly, we have some options."

"Seriously? I don't think I'm here meeting a mob boss. They just want to be paid."

"Paid for what?" I asked, crossing my arms and doing my

best to intimidate her into telling me. It didn't seem to be working at first, but she finally blew out a long breath.

"Gambling debts."

My arms dropped as my eyebrows shot up.

"Are you and your dad big gamblers?"

"My dad is."

"So you're here paying off his debt?"

"Unfortunately, yes."

"But you don't seem happy about that. Is it his money?"

"Wow, so observant. No, it's not his money, so I'm not happy about it. Would you be?"

I rubbed at the back of my neck, looking out over the parking lot. The rain was coming down harder now, which was to be expected this time of year, but it wasn't helping the stress of her wanting to be here to meet up with some random gambling broker.

I roped myself into coming here, and now I was roping myself into feeling responsible for her safety.

Before I knew it, I was walking laps around her, the nervous energy leaving me restless. I already knew I hated waiting for anything, but I couldn't figure out the tightening in my chest or why I had the nagging feeling I needed to get her out of here.

"Where is he?" I asked. Ten minutes had gone by and I hadn't stopped pacing, my steps now silent on the cement floor.

"I don't know. This is where I was told to meet him. I didn't get his itinerary. He told me ten minutes."

"And it has been fifteen."

"Can you stop?" She asked. "All your nervous energy is making me nervous."

"Are you not already nervous?"

"No? I'm only handing someone money?"

"In a dark, run down warehouse that would be better suited for a horror movie than a girl like you in a dress like that."

"What's that supposed to mean? If you're trying to bully me again, please just don't. I'm not in the mood and I've heard it all before, anyway."

"Bully you? I meant you look fucking incredible and should be sitting at a dumb restaurant waiting for some over the top birthday dessert rather than here. And to add to that, your stupid boyfriend was going to let you come here alone?"

"He doesn't *let* me do anything. I do whatever I want."

"You know damn well what I meant." I stopped, taking her in. She did look incredible, and I couldn't understand what anyone would have to bully her about. "Do you think I bully you?"

"Considering the ankle biter comments, yes, but I've taken to bullying you back, so I guess we are even."

I smiled and turned back to look out the window. She had been giving it back as much as she took it, but I was surprised she actually thought I was actually trying to be mean to her.

"Why don't you wait in the car, and I'll hand the money over?"

"Why don't you try to understand you are not in charge here, and all I asked from you is a ride?"

"And you call me the bully?" I asked, smiling again. "Come on. Do you honestly want to keep waiting here?" I asked, hating how much my heart raced. I had been in plenty of fucked up situations, and never cared this much.

"They probably got stuck in traffic. Why are you freaking out?"

"Traffic? Really, that's your reasoning? And I'm freaking out because Fox is going to kill me if something happens to you while we're out together."

"We aren't *out* together. You gave me a ride. You're essentially my Uber."

"You think you call an Uber and an Audi rolls up? You better leave a big tip."

"The only tip I have for you is to not offer rides to places you can't handle going."

"Do you think I would knowingly have you come here alone? Fuck, Fox would kill me for that, too."

"You're awfully worried about Fox killing you."

"Fox has made it clear his friends are not people that find his sister attractive or put her in danger. I think that's practicing self preservation and keeping a friendship I actually enjoy."

"You do know we aren't technically related, right?"

"Because of blood. I think for every other point that matters, you are his little sister. I'm the asshole he wants to make clear is not going after you or harming you in any way. Which, based on the looks of this place, I have already failed at one."

"But at least we know you will only be failing at one of those things," she said.

"I think this can technically count as putting you in harm's way, so I would say I would be failing at both.

She leaned back on an old desk and I stepped in front of her. Her mane of hair was loose tonight. No braid, no bun, nothing but wild red hair. Her eyes narrowed, and I could see she was trying not to react to my comment.

"We are not crossing any lines tonight."

"Really? I thought we were having fun crossing them the other night."

I leaned in, running my hand through her hair, shock shooting through me as blood rushed to my groin, my cock twitching as she looked up at me with big hazel eyes.

"What made you think I was having fun?"

"I can show you," I said, grabbing a handful of her hair and pulling her head back. I moved to her neck, moving my nose along the delicate skin. I wouldn't kiss her, I wouldn't put my lips on her at all until there was a clear breakup for her, but I would push the boundary of that until she snapped.

She sucked in a hard breath, moving her head back and giving me more access to her neck. The small gesture made every part of me respond, and took every ounce of willpower not to sink my teeth into her.

"Nope," she breathed. "No fun."

I went to respond, but a bang echoed throughout the warehouse.

"No, *abso-fucking-lutely* not," I said, grabbing her to throw her over my shoulder before she could even attempt to stop me.

Her scream echoed in the empty room, and all the way down the hallway.

"Chase, put me down right now!"

"No. We are sitting around waiting to be ambushed by someone you don't even know. You're getting in the car and staying there."

"I can't!" She shrieked. "I have to give them the money or they are going to hurt someone!"

She kept yelling, her fists slamming on my back as I made it to the car and pushed her inside.

"Who are they going to hurt?" I asked, blocking her from getting back out.

Her nostrils flared, her ragged breathing making her chest heave. "Any one of us. They want this payment tonight or they are threatening to come after me or the crew."

"And the crew doesn't know about this?"

"No. My dad is a terrible person. If they knew I was paying off his debts, they would stop me. Even if it meant putting themselves in danger."

A black SUV pulled in, and I groaned, leaning down and grabbing her arm.

"Stay in the fucking car. I mean it, Scout. You look like a

damn princess and in this car, they aren't going to believe you don't have more money. *Stay in the car.*"

I checked she was in and slammed the door shut.

How I managed to get from the nicest place in town to the shittiest in a matter of one hour was almost laughable. How I got here with Scout was even more ridiculous.

Lucky for her, I dealt with rich, uptight assholes every week, every day, if you included my dad. I could handle this without an issue.

That was as long as Scout stayed in the car.

TEN

SCOUT

MY LEG BOUNCED as Chase stepped in front of his car. The black SUV had come to a stop and three guys got out.

Maybe he had been a *little* right about not coming here alone.

And I was feeling a bit better that he was out there taking care of this.

That was until the older guy stepped forward, flashing a gun at his hip. Chase didn't flinch. His body relaxed while they talked, but mine wasn't.

I couldn't let him get hurt because of me and my dad. This wasn't even his fight.

Without hesitation, I was pushing open the door, making every single one of them jump.

"Scout," Chase growled, his eyes darkening when he looked at me. "What the hell are you doing?"

"While I love meeting new people, I have somewhere else to be. I'll take the money and be leaving," the main brute said.

Chase nodded, handing over the envelope of cash I had brought. The guy flipped through it. "All the money?"

"No," I said. "I could only get five grand. But I counted it over and every dollar of that is in there."

The guy's eyebrows shot up, looking me over and then Chase.

"You're giving me five grand because you couldn't come up with the ten I originally wanted?"

Chase's eyes whipped to me, but I didn't dare look back. I could already imagine they were already burning with anger.

"I'm still trying to get the rest. I hoped you would agree this would be enough, and I could have two weeks for the rest."

"It might have been. Until you rolled up in this car, both of you dressed like that. It seems like you're trying to insult me now. You don't play poor very well."

"None of this is mine," I said quickly. "This dress included. I don't have any more money to give you tonight."

The guy turned to Chase. "But I think he does."

"He's just my ride. He has nothing to do with this."

"So? He's here. He obviously must have some care about what's going on. Another five thousand right now, or I will double the original price."

"Double? Come on, I'm fighting to get another five thousand. How would I manage to find another ten?"

He didn't care what I said, not looking away from Chase.

"You had to get out of the car, didn't you?" Chase said, shaking his head and pulling his watch off. "Here. This is a vintage Rolex. It's older, but it should get you five at least. It will more than cover what she needs."

The guy looked over the watch, apparently impressed. "I usually don't collect items for payment, but I like this one. I think it will look nice on me." The goons next to him nodded along as he slid it on his wrist. "This will hold me over for now. I'll contact you if your father fails to pay the rest."

"The rest?" Chase asked, and the guy laughed.

"This was a payment to keep her friends out of it. Her father is still deep in his own trouble. If he figures it out, you won't hear from me again."

Chase shook his head. "We both know that isn't how this works. What happens when he doesn't figure out his own mess?"

"I like to text now. You'll hear from me when that happens."

I was frozen, watching the guys get back into their car. Chase stayed at the front of the car while they pulled out before coming over to me.

"Come on. You're getting soaked." Chase's hand moved to my lower back, leading me to the passenger side and pulling open the door for me to slide inside.

I could only stare at his empty wrist as he turned the car on, blasting the heat and making sure my vents were open.

He pulled out without a word, and I could feel myself cracking. Emotions boiling up faster than I could handle.

"I'm sorry," I said, my voice breaking, the small sob betraying me.

He didn't turn, didn't say anything as he shifted and sped up.

In the glow of the dashboard, I could see his jaw tighten, his hands flexing on the wheel. Chase had been nice enough, but I knew there was a more wild side to him. I just didn't know what that wild side did when he was angry.

"Chase?" I asked, carefully reaching out, my fingers moving along his forearm.

He looked down at where my hand rested on his arm. "Yes?"

"I said, I'm sorry."

"I heard."

I pulled away, assuming that meant exactly what I thought it did.

He was pissed, and he had every right to be, but the thought cut through me like a knife.

"What do you want? Do you want me to pay you back or buy a new watch?"

He gave a harsh laugh. "You couldn't get five thousand more, but you're going to buy me a ten thousand dollar watch?"

My heart flipped and my stomach churned. "You were wearing a ten thousand dollar watch?" I tried to swallow my shock. It didn't matter what it had cost, I owed him now. "But yes, if that's what it takes, then I will. I'm the one who messed that up. I'll fix it."

"That's not what it takes, but I want to know how much he owes. Are they going to leave you alone now?"

I checked my texts again, wondering if my dad had answered. I had texted and called him a few times over the past week without any response.

"I have no idea. I tried to talk to him, but he is either ignoring me or doesn't have his phone anymore."

"What is he up to? Why tell them about you?"

"Because they are threatening him, and he doesn't want to be held responsible. He thinks I'm loaded because the garage is doing well, so he told them I would help pay it. Then, they started threatening me and the crew, so I decided to go along with it until I could figure out how to make them leave me alone. I wasn't expecting you to hand over your watch like that, though. I would hope that was enough that they will give me a longer deadline for whatever else they want."

"You can't just keep giving them money, Scout. If your dad told them about you, and you pay off his debts in return, he is going to treat you like his own little bank."

"I know, but I'm not really sure what to do to make it stop. I was hoping this was going to be a one-time thing. I wasn't even thinking about him using me for more."

He was quiet for a few miles, lost in thought, before he finally looked over at me.

"Keep texting him. We need to know the actual amount that he owes, and he needs to understand you won't be helping a second time."

"I'll keep trying. I don't know what to do in the meantime."

"Well, you've had a pretty ridiculous night. How about you keep my now-bare wrist company and we figure this out more tomorrow?"

My fingertips moved along his arm, the muscles flexing under my touch. I reached his wrist, laying my hand overtop.

I tried to feel casual about it, tried to remind myself this wouldn't be weird with any of the guys, but I knew I was lying to myself. This was different.

The air in the car charged, putting me closer to an edge I didn't know existed. I was trying hard to force my hand to stop before my fingers started to move in lazy circles along his wrist.

I looked up at him, nothing on his face giving away that it was affecting him at all, let alone the same way. Which was probably better. It didn't need to be going to both of our heads.

He stayed quiet through the ride, not moving away when my hand stayed on top of his. We finally pulled up to our apartments, and he stopped right in front of our door.

"Try to make it up to bed without pissing off any more boyfriends, wandering into any run-down buildings, or losing people's belongings."

"I am sorry."

"It's fine, Scout. I can go get another one. Maybe after we work on my car."

"You still want to do that?"

He didn't move, waiting while I pulled off my seatbelt and pushed the door open.

"Yeah," he said, the deep, husky tone spending a shiver down my spine. "I still want to do that."

It reminded me that I was still wrapped in his hoodie.

"Here," I said, starting to pull it off. "I guess I shouldn't steal all of your things tonight."

"It's fine. You can bring it to me tomorrow. No point in getting wet now."

I wasn't sure what it was, but everything out of his mouth now sounded dirty. Touching him the entire ride home was making my entire body hum with wanting more.

How was wrist touching now basically foreplay for me? Was I that desperate for human contact?

"Alright," I finally squeaked the words out. "I'll see you tomorrow then."

He didn't respond, waiting while I headed inside before I heard the tires spin, the wet pavement making the tires screech in the silent night.

Hopefully, no one looked out the window and saw the car. They all still thought I was out with Jesse, and it wouldn't take them long to connect this car to Chase.

I headed up to my apartment, kicking off the heels I had worn to make it quietly past everyone's apartments.

My door shut behind me and I pulled off my dress, pulling the straps off under the hoodie and letting it fall to the floor before crawling into bed and passing out.

"*HONEY*, I'M HERE," CHASE'S VOICE RANG OUT AROUND ME, making me jump underneath the car.

I had come to the garage early this morning, deciding to get my mind off of everything with a few hours of work before Chase showed up.

A hand wrapped around my ankle, pulling me on my crawler out from underneath the car until I was looking up at Chase.

"Did you just call me honey?" I asked.

"Relax, it was a joke," he said, pushing me back under the car. "You're not nearly as sweet as honey."

"Hey! I'm plenty sweet, just not to you."

His hand clamped around my ankle again, pulling me back out. He crouched down, his eyes raking over me. I had to be a mess at this point, but I resisted the urge to fix my hair, hoping the two long braids stayed reasonably in place.

"Yeah? And why is that?" he asked.

I shrugged, still laying there looking at him. "Maybe the ankle biter nickname, maybe the burning of the money —"

"Maybe the giving up of my watch?" he asked. The smile on his face got to me, making me smile back.

"Okay," I hissed, pulling myself up and looking around. I pushed him further into the garage, trying to move between the cars so no one would overhear us. "*Maybe* I could be nicer because of that, but don't talk about that here. I know I owe you, but *please*, I still don't want anyone here to know yet."

He looked down, my hands still on his chest, his dark lashes getting heavy. "Alright. Then you better hurry up and get me a new watch so I forget it ever happened."

The words rumbled under my fingers, and I think my fingertips pressed harder against him, wanting to feel it again.

"Why does that sound so threatening?"

"Because you're currently touching me and I think I *like* it," he said through gritted teeth. Each word sounded like he was in pain.

"Chase," I hissed, ripping my hand away and looked around to see if any of the crew had noticed.

"Scout."

"Why are you making things sound worse than they are?"

"I'm not. Do you not like honesty?"

"No, I prefer it, but that's not honesty."

"No? Interesting. And here I thought I was being more

honest than ever. If we are being honest right now, then I am going to need you to tell me why you don't want anyone here to know what's going on? I thought you were all one big group and have each other's back type of group. Why hide it?"

"Because," I said, the shame of it turning my neck hot, "I know they won't approve of it. I know they will tell me not to pay, not to help him, and worst of all, not to worry about them. They won't care if those guys come after them. They will all say we will take care of it."

"And? Everyone here seems more than capable of taking care of themselves."

"I've always been the one they take care of. I'm the youngest, their little sister, the one they never want in danger. They have taken care of me in every way possible from day one. Why would I turn around and put them in danger in return? How can I tell them I'm not able to handle this, so now they might have to suffer? It doesn't matter anyway. It's taken care of."

"*For now*. Don't let your guard down and think that's the end of it. You need to get a hold of your dad, and actually figure out what the amount they are after."

"I am. I mean, I'm trying at least. He still hasn't picked up."

"Just stay alert and keep me updated. I'll keep your secret for now as long as you tell me what's going on. Now come on, show me how to fix this damn car."

He turned away, heading back to his car and pulling open the door to pop the hood.

Fox and I had already looked over the car, and I knew where to start. There were two parts already waiting in the office with more on the way.

We got started, both of us working and only talking when it had to do with the car. It was nice, and before I knew it, two hours had gone by. I was apparently too busy enjoying seeing Chase fight with the wrenches and then fight with the parts. His arms were now streaked with grease and sweat and I was having a hard time ignoring them.

"I think your hands work a lot better at holding that wrench without the watch weighing you down, *rich boy*," I said, leaning down and pulling at the wrench to try to loosen the last bolt, but it wasn't budging.

He leaned down at my side, running his fingers along my arm until his hand enveloped mine, then he pulled back with me, the bolt breaking loose immediately.

His lips were at my ear and that dark, threatening tone was back. "Call me rich boy all you want, that heavy watch bailed your ass out." He pressed into my side, the heat of him making me lean in more. "And honestly, my poor wrist is so light I can barely function."

"Then fix the car and I will go buy you a new watch. Not a ridiculous Rolex, but *a* watch."

"And here I thought I would always end up being the sugar daddy. I should have guessed you would try taking that title from me, too," he said, smirking when he stepped back and I grabbed the next part.

"If you're going to be my sugar daddy, maybe you could start by having someone else fix your car, or just buy a new one I could drive."

"Yeah? What kind of car should I be buying you?"

"A neon green Hellcat," I said, smiling harder when his eyebrows shot up.

"Wow, you are not a cheap date. Fine, why don't you be a good girl and get your sugar daddy some water, and then maybe we can talk about getting a car."

My mouth dropped open at his audacity. I was almost angry until I realized I could do exactly what he asked.

I was going to get him plenty of water.

I grabbed a bucket, filling it as heavy as I could with cold water from the hose, before heading back to where he was bent over.

Kye and Jax walked out from a garage bay, watching with quiet laughs when I brought the bucket up and tipped it over his head. Cold water splashed back onto me as it crashed over him, and I bit my lip, suppressing a shriek. I wasn't sure how he would react, but I didn't really care with the guys here. It's not like he would get away with much.

He was still bent over, shaking water from his hair before standing up and turning to me.

Without a word, he charged forward, wrapping his arms under my ass and lifting, pinning my legs and stomach against him.

"Chase!" I yelled, the cold water already seeping through my clothes.

"Yes?" he asked with a laugh, lowering me until we were almost face to face.

"Put me down!"

"Why? It's only fair that I get you just as wet," he said, laughing so hard my body shook along with his.

I only stared for a second. I wasn't sure how everything he said sounded so dirty, but it seemed to shoot a thrill for me each time.

"Put me down *right* now."

"You threw a bucket of water on me. You have no authority to boss me around."

"You were trying to boss me around first!"

"Only because I like when you get all angry and flustered. I didn't actually think you were going to listen. Then again, you seemed to take your own interpretation of what I said. I'll be more clear in the future."

"Put. Me. Down."

He finally set me down, waiting until my feet touched the

ground before stepping back. I thought I would be relieved, but it didn't help when I noticed his shirt was now clinging to him. The wet t-shirt left nothing to the imagination.

He shot me a winning smile. "You got me there. Maybe I should go get a Hellcat. Honestly, that might be pretty fun. Want to go out racing tonight? Maybe you could race me and try to win the car."

"I'm busy."

"Too busy to race?"

"They are having the first round of qualifying races at Holt tomorrow. I don't want to be out all night messing around street racing when I have to focus. Tomorrow will determine if I move on or not, so we will be there all day and either celebrating or drinking my emotions away after."

"Interesting that you failed to mention it all day. I guess if you win at these races, I should expect you to kick my ass finally?"

"I think you could expect me to kick your ass the next time we race no matter what."

Kye yelled to Chase that he was leaving as he headed out to his car.

"That's my ride home today since Fox picked me up." The shirt still clung to him and his hair fell in a damp mess, those few stray pieces falling across his forehead. It was becoming pathetic how much I liked seeing them there.

"Kye?"

"Yeah, problem?"

"No," I said, wondering how he had gotten on Kye's good side, too. "But I would suggest putting on the harness imme-diately."

"Worried about my safety now?"

"Worried about Kye going to jail if you get hurt, Mr.

Lawyer." He smirked, taking a small step forward before thinking better of coming any closer.

"Since you'll be busy this week, I guess I'll be seeing more of you next week for the car?"

"I would say so."

"The worst news I've heard all week," he said, his eyes dropping to my lips. "You'll do fine at your races. Just imagine me in the other cars, fueling your hate and attempting to finally win against me.

"That's actually a great idea."

Kye honked again.

"Good luck tomorrow, ankle-biter. I'm sure you'll do amazing."

He headed towards Kye's car, and my heart flipped again when he turned back, shooting me a smile and waving as he slid into the passenger seat.

I had spent my first full day with Chase and somehow, I felt lighter than I had felt in weeks.

What worried me, though, was how much I was looking forward to that feeling again.

ELEVEN

SCOUT

THE NEXT MORNING I woke up nearly shaking in anticipation for the races. By the time I got dressed and headed down to Fox's apartment, the entire crew was there waiting.

"Hey," Ash said, smiling as she handed me a cup of coffee, "you ready for today?"

"No. I suddenly feel like I haven't driven a car a day in my life," I said, the panic bubbling up again.

Ash was the only one here who had raced in any professional races, so I knew she would understand the most.

"You'll be fine. Treat it like any other race, on any other day, and you're going to be okay. Remember, you don't need number one, you need top ten today, which will be easy for you considering you beat us all half the time."

The races were going to have four different race days, and each time I would have to place in the top ten, five, or three to continue on. It sounded so easy, but you never knew what would happen once you were actually out there racing. It wasn't like our street races, if I messed up, I couldn't turn around and race again or lose a few dollars. If I messed up in these races, I was out, and I didn't know if Holt would give me another chance to prove myself or not.

"It sounds easy, but the thought of actually doing it? That part sounds a lot harder, and I can't even beat Chase right now. How do I manage to race some of the top guys in the country when I can't beat one jerk in a Porsche?"

She laughed. "You can't underestimate him. Chase never got into sports or things like that. He was at the track with us constantly, and besides partying, all he did was race around. And do you think there could maybe be a possibility you psych yourself out when you race him?"

Quinn and Carly walked over, grabbing their own cups of coffee.

"Are you insinuating I've been letting him win?" I asked.

"No, not at all. I'm suggesting this one good looking man in particular is a little too distracting for you," Ash said, her lips pursing hard as she tried not to laugh.

Quinn and Carly's heads dropped together, both laughing along with her.

"You guys suck. That is not what is happening. I think calling him so good looking that I can't handle racing him is giving him way too much credit. And it doesn't matter, I'm dating Jesse. Why would I be thinking of Chase like that?"

I didn't actually know if I was still dating Jesse, but I hadn't told them about the night at the restaurant. I hid my groan. It was so embarrassing. It was already embarrassing enough to face the fact that I had let him give me the bare minimum for so long. Now I had to tell every one of my friends how he walked out on my birthday dinner.

"You're still dating him?" Fox asked, no hint of humor on his face.

"Um, yeah? Why wouldn't I be?"

"Chase said he saw you two get into a fight when he was out with his family. I guess we all assumed it was over," Ash said.

"So now he's gossiping about me to my friends?"

"It's not gossip. I was texting him about the races today and he asked if Jesse was coming. When I asked why, he said he thought you two were fighting," Fox said.

Heat filled my cheeks, and I knew they would be turning red. "I should have guessed you would be the one gossiping."

"Am I not allowed to know what's going on in your life now?" Fox asked. "How else would I know? You were about to walk in here and act like everything was fine. I'm sure Jesse would show up and pretend nothing ever happened."

"What does it matter if we get into a fight? You and Ash do it, and I don't need you to tell me every detail," I said.

The crew watched us in silence. I knew they had a million things to add, but it seems Fox had been appointed the spokesperson for this.

"That's different."

"How?"

I didn't know what he was about to say, but I figured it wouldn't be good based on the way his lips pursed together.

"I think that's enough today, Fox. She has more important things to worry about," Quinn said, before turning to me. "This is your career, and all of us are here to support you today. No one else. Let's forget about all the gossip and fights. We need to get to the track."

I stayed still, glaring at the floor as a lump formed in my throat. I hated keeping so much from them, but it felt like my only choice right now.

"Come on," Fox said. "I wasn't trying to start anything, but you've been a little out of it lately, and I'm worried. We all know Jesse isn't always that great. If you're out in public fighting *and* not talking to us, then we are going to start asking questions."

I sighed, looking around at them all. "Okay, when you put it like that, it's fair of you to ask. Everything is okay, though, and today has nothing to do with Jesse. I would prefer to not worry about it, and attempt to get my nerves calmed down enough to actually race."

Ash jumped up, throwing her arms around me. "Then we're dropping it for now. Right, Fox?"

His jaw tightened, but he nodded in agreement. It was enough of a confirmation for Ash, who turned back to me. "You got this. None of us would be here if you didn't. Everyone, including my dad, saw how good you are. Now believe it or you are going to go out there and suck. Come on, we still have to get there, set up, and test the car, so you have a few more hours to freak out."

"Perfect. Exactly what I was hoping for," I said, groaning as she handed me another cup of coffee and waved me out the door and to the car.

———

Four hours later, we were set up and ready, the races starting soon.

I grabbed my helmet and walked out to the car where the entire crew was gathered around it. I already knew they were looking over every inch, making sure it was ready to go for me.

There were so many times in my life I was grateful for them. Their endless support and concern for me still astounded me to this day. While I had been rude about it this morning, I was already grateful again that they were all here for me.

I hadn't exactly lied to Chase that it seemed Jesse was my ex now. And I hadn't exactly lied to the crew that everything was fine. Jesse had texted me a few times since the night at the restaurant. Once to apologize, once to defend himself, and once to tell me that he had only been upset that I had wanted to leave in the middle of dinner.

He wasn't totally wrong about the last one. The fact that I had tried to leave in the middle of a nice dinner was rude. There wasn't a great way for me to be mad at him when I had done that.

So I had let him know if he really wanted to move on, he could show up and help today. It felt like an ultimatum, like if he showed up, maybe I could believe that we were meant to be together.

I looked around, noticing that he still hadn't shown up.

"Jesse isn't here?" I asked them, hating I even had to bring it up after this morning's confrontation.

Kye looked up from the driver's seat. "Haven't seen him. Did he say he was coming?"

"Yeah, he said he was like ten minutes away, but that was over twenty minutes ago."

They all looked at each other, and then back at the car.

"Don't worry, I won't let it get to me," I said, trying to hold back tears. I didn't even know what I was upset about. I hadn't exactly needed Jesse here, but I wanted that person. The person that wanted to be there for me, wanted to support me on one of the biggest days of my career. I watched all the guys, the way they always supported the girls. The way Fox was at every single race with Ash, every day of training, he even went with her to check on the cars when she needed to. Even Jax supported Carly and everything to do with her cooking business without a second thought.

I just wanted that person today.

Arms circled around me from behind, picking me up and spinning me once.

Relief flooded me. I wasn't going to be alone in this.

He was here.

My feet hit the ground again, and I turned with a smile, coming face to face with Chase.

"What are you doing here?"

"Hello to you, too. I'm here to watch you race," he said, looking effortlessly hot in sunglasses and an easy smile.

"I didn't invite you."

He smiled harder, a smug laugh escaping him. "I know, Fox did. Am I not allowed to watch you race now?"

"You can do whatever you want. I just wasn't expecting you," I said. For not even racing yet, I already felt defeated by this day.

"You look ready to cry. Why so pissed off already? It's your first qualifying race. Isn't this one of the best days of your life right now?"

"It should be," I grumbled, turning away and heading to the car.

"Jesse isn't here," Fox said. I could hear the eye roll in his voice, making me grind my teeth together.

"Wow, thanks. Like that's any of his business." It was already embarrassing enough to admit to the crew. I hated admitting to Chase that my boyfriend didn't even care enough to show up.

Chase's hand wrapped around my bicep, pulling me away from everyone.

"Why isn't he here? Or better yet, why is he supposed to be?"

"I don't know. He said he was on his way, but he should have been here already. And I technically told him he could show up and we could try to fix things."

The crew turned back to the car, apparently done with worrying about Jesse.

Chase pulled me further back until we were out of earshot from everyone.

"Why?"

"Because he pointed out that I wasn't exactly acting the best at the restaurant either, and I was the one who messed up the night first."

"Yeah, because you didn't even trust him enough to ask to go with you. That isn't a you problem, that's a him problem. You should trust your boyfriend with something like that."

"But that's on me because I didn't."

"No, that's on him because he didn't make you feel like you could trust him."

I only shrugged, my thoughts at war with themselves. Me blowing him off hadn't been nice, but Chase was right. I should have no problem trusting my boyfriend with something like that.

"You don't need him here."

"But I wanted him to want to be here."

"Why? To tell you how much better of a driver he is? To stare at some boobs? Piss off Fox? I can fill in if you need," he said, smirking.

"Wow, aren't you a true support system? That's not what he would do to help."

"Fine, what does he do?"

I shrugged, embarrassed I couldn't think of anything big. "I don't know. Kiss me, tell me good luck. Make me feel ready to race."

"You're lying."

"No, I'm not."

"Yes, you are. You can't even look me in the eye and say those things. I'm literally getting a degree in bullshit. You think that pathetic attempt is going to get past me?"

"I can't look you in the eye because you're wearing sunglasses." He shook his head, pulling them off.

"Jesse doesn't have it in him to make you feel good about doing something like this. Doing something better than him.

Between what I've seen and what Fox has told me, the guy's a rat who makes you feel bad for being so fucking amazing."

I pushed away, but he grabbed my arm, pulling me back in. There was a hint of anger in his face, but I didn't know why. He didn't need to take it upon himself to make me feel bad about Jesse, too.

The sadness of Jesse not thinking those things about me enough to show up tore through me, and I was worried I was going to lose control of all of my emotions. There were too many of them, and they were all coming to the surface at once.

"If he hasn't already figured out what he has, he's never going to."

When I looked up again, Chase's eyes had that dark gaze to them, so focused on me I couldn't breathe. He stepped a little closer, his gaze dropping to my lips.

"What are you doing?" I asked, shoving my helmet into his stomach with a satisfying grunt.

"I'm not sure, maybe the right thing for once."

"Telling me how terrible my boyfriend has been lately is the right thing?"

"I'm not telling you. I'm reminding you. You're just pretending you don't already know it. I'm telling you to remember you're here doing something thousands of other people would kill to do. If you're standing around crying about him, they are going to take it from you. It's up to you and how much you want it to decide if you're going to sit down and let them."

Tears brimmed my eyes. He was right, and I hated that. Every single person here today was fighting for a place on a racing team, and I was here nearly in tears over someone who didn't even show up.

"I wasn't crying for him."

"Then why the sad look?"

"I wanted him to step up and be this person. How does he know me for so long and not think I'm worth it?"

"Because he's not worth it and not willing to get better to match your worth."

I could only scoff, my mouth dropping open as I looked at him.

"You're going after what you want," he continued. "You're going after something huge that he should have made time for. If he doesn't make time for it, then he isn't the person for you. You said it yourself, these guys would never miss a day like this for any of these girls. If he was right, he would show."

"I guess there could be some truth to that."

"Would it help if I take over his job duties and kiss you?" He asked, the quiet, playful whisper sending a shiver through me.

"No."

"Are you sure? I think me kissing you could probably make you forget Jesse even exists."

"I doubt that," I said, still trying to catch my breath. He was so close now, I could feel the light press of his body against me and part of me really wanted to lean in and test out his theory.

"I don't. I wouldn't stop kissing you until it worked. Until you couldn't even remember whose air you were breathing."

"I think that would take a while."

"Who said I had a time limit?"

He leaned in closer, and I was starting to think I was leaning in too, but then a car started. The engine revving so loud the ground shook, and I jumped back.

Chase's smile fell as he looked past me to the crew. "You have something more important to focus on, and he is not worth you messing this up."

"I'm not going to mess this up."

"Based on how upset you look, I would bet I could beat you out there today."

"You wish."

"You already know I could," he said, a hand reaching up to move a stray lock of hair through his fingers. "I've already beat you twice and I would bet my car I could do it again. I guess if you are too upset, I could take your place today."

"That's not going to happen."

"I don't know. If you're going to let some stupid man ruin your race, might as well let a different stupid man step in and win this thing for you."

"Chase."

"Yes?"

"You're fucking with me, aren't you?"

"Absolutely. Now, go focus on your race. If you let any one of these guys beat you at this race today, I'm kicking Jesse's ass."

"How is that fair?"

"Because there are at least twenty people here who know damn well, you can win this, and if you don't, my only assumption will be that it's his fault."

"Chase, you better—"

"*You* better go get your ass in the car and get ready."

I spun on my heel, heading back to my car because I knew he was right. I needed to focus, and he was quickly becoming a distraction. He was quick to catch up, falling into step next to me.

"You look pretty hot in your racing suit, by the way. I've never been so attracted to a girl so heavily clothed."

He looked me over, taking his time checking me out with a grin.

"You are the worst."

"Not the worst. For once, I can think of one person who is worse than me. Now go."

TWELVE

CHASE

I SAT BACK, watching the crew finish preparing everything for Scout's race. She was in the car now, lined up and ready while they ran around finishing every last second item they could.

It was chaos and excitement like I had never seen before, and I was loving every second of it. Ash let me know there were ten rounds of races, with Scout needing to win at least six of them to place in the top ten.

Ash had done this years ago, and I remember coming to one of her races. I had been too drunk to remember most of it, but I had been there. This time, though, I was enjoying myself instead of searching for any substance to drown out my own thoughts.

Ransom and Kye finally pulled back, coming to stand next to me as Fox and Jax lined Scout's car up. Quinn and Carly were beside the track on Ransom's car. Everyone was somehow relaxed, but I wondered if it was only for Scout's sake.

I knew Scout couldn't see me, but I was dying to see her. I could watch her do this all day. She would walk around with her race suit pulled down, the arms tied at her waist. Or when it was fully zipped up with her helmet on, two long braids the only indication of the girl underneath.

She was a fucking dream come true in a race suit. I hadn't been lying when I said I'd never been so attracted to someone so fully clothed. A race suit that covered her neck to feet, but I couldn't look away. She was smiling again, all her worries from earlier apparently lost to the excitement of her race, and I tried not to give myself some of the credit for that.

The light moved through its steps, snapping green, and as if Scout counted down the seconds, she was gone. Her car roared when she took off, the one next to her a half a second to slow. Before I could even take a full breath, it was over, and Scout had won.

Of course she had.

The day moved fast, and what felt like minutes later, the last race had finished. Scout had made it to the number five spot, which meant she had placed high enough to move on and put her one more step closer to professionally racing for Holt.

She idled the car over to us, parking it and getting out to the crew surrounding her with cheers and hugs.

Then she looked back at me with a genuine smile on her face, and this time it didn't fall when it reached me.

She was fucking beautiful.

I weaved through the dispersing crew, their hands busy with the task of packing things up. When I finally reached her, I wrapped my arms around her while she laughed.

"You did great," I whispered, my lips against her ear, trying not to be obvious about how much I wanted to touch her. I didn't know why I was suddenly dying to be near her, why I was fighting the urge to lean in and kiss her. "You placed high enough to move on. And looked so fucking good doing it. I couldn't look away."

"Chase," she said, pushing me back the smallest amount.

"What?"

"I don't know what you're doing."

I didn't even know how to tell her that I didn't either. It's not like I could do anything with her. Messing around was out of the question when she kind of still had a boyfriend, and Fox made it clear it wouldn't be okay with him since we were friends now. And it's not like I was going to date her. I wasn't lying when I said I wouldn't be a good boyfriend, but now I also didn't want her dating Jesse. She could do a hell of a lot better than him.

None of that led me to a reason on why I was so close and only wanted to be closer.

For how much of a mess my life was, for how much I couldn't decide on what I wanted, being close to her seemed like an easy decision.

"Congratulating you."

"It feels like more than that."

"Does it? Maybe you're just finally warming up to me."

Fox yelled behind us and I let her go. "He said we need to go," I said, quietly.

"Go where?"

"It's a surprise, as far as I understand. Do you want to ride with me?"

"I don't think I should."

"That's why I asked. I thought it would be more fun."

She bit at her bottom lip, and for one breathless heartbeat I thought she might consider it. There was no way she was going to trust being alone with me in the car right now, though. I don't know what happened over the past few days, but it had led me to this moment, standing in front of Scout, ready to rip her race suit off and learn every inch of what was underneath. I reached out, hooking my finger on the zipper that was pulled down to her stomach now.

How could something be close enough to touch, but I still

wasn't allowed.

"I'll see you there," she finally said.

"I wouldn't miss it." I said, making her scowl. It wasn't that I was trying to take jabs at Jesse on purpose, not completely, but he made it so damn easy.

She spun on her heel, heading towards the cars as Fox yelled to me.

"You coming?"

"Meet you there," I said, needing to make one stop before getting to the restaurant.

AN HOUR LATER, I PULLED UP TO THE RESTAURANT FOX TOLD ME to meet them at. The line of modified cars in a bright array of colors confirming I was in the right place.

I grabbed the box I had stopped for off my seat and headed inside. The restaurant wasn't packed, but the back room was filled with the crew and a few people from the track I recognized.

I could see Scout set at the head of the table, smiling and laughing with Quinn next to her.

The moment I walked into the room, Scout's smile faded, her gaze shifting from me to the person on her right. Fox waved me next to him and Ash, the open seat apparently reserved for me even if I had been hoping for the one next to Scout.

As soon as I sat down and looked over, I knew why that seat hadn't been empty for me.

"Did Jesse seriously show up to this after missing the races?" I asked Fox.

Fox curled a lip, a look that seemed ten times more intimidating with the giant scar on his face.

"Yeah. He somehow made it here right when we did. Weird

how he can time out free food and drinks, but not several hours at the track."

"And she let him stay?"

"I wanted to tell him to get the fuck out, but she asked me to let her handle it. Scout's tough and all, but I think she's been avoiding the conflict."

I rolled my shoulders, stretching back in the chair to look at Jesse. "I personally don't mind some conflict."

"We don't either," Jax said, grinning.

The waitress came over, taking our orders and interrupting my making Jesse leave.

"Let's eat first and then I have something that might…help."

Thirty minutes later, I pushed my chair back, picking up the box I brought and heading towards Scout.

Her eyes went wide, and she looked down, trying not to meet my eye when I crouched down next to her. With my height I was almost at eye level with her, but she still didn't look my way.

Jesse did, though.

From everything she told me earlier, he was trying to make it all out to be her fault, and I hoped she wasn't falling for it now.

"Here, Hellcat. I picked this up. Consider it a belated birthday present you never got, and congratulations for today."

She glanced over at me from the corner of her eye, and I knew she wanted to ask about the nickname. Her attention moved back to the box, slowly opening it, but Jesse groaned.

"Why are you calling her that? And why are you getting *my* girlfriend gifts?"

"Because she mentioned it's her favorite car, and she proved how fast she was today. A Hellcat in her own right today, but I guess you wouldn't know that," I said, not taking my eyes off Scout. "And the gift is because it seemed you missed out on dessert the other day, and you killed it today. Overall, pretty well deserved."

"A cake?" Scout said, all eyes turning back to her.

"I thought you might like one tonight since you didn't get one the other day." It was a jab. No, not just a jab. It was a full on knife to the chest aimed right at Jesse. The guy had run out on her birthday dinner, and now everybody knew it.

A smile broke across her face as she looked at the box filled with a huge chocolate cake.

Finally, she looked over, the smile staying there. "Thank you."

"Anytime."

"Trying to buy her presents to get in her pants?" He mumbled, quiet enough that only I could hear him over the noise of the restaurant. The crew's eyes were on us, but I stopped.

"Excuse me?"

He looked past me to Scout. "You're seriously going to take a bribe from him?"

"What exactly is he bribing me for, Jesse?" Scout asked, and I tried not to feel a little pride in the edge to her tone.

"He's trying to buy you, Scout. He thinks he can buy you a few stupid things and get in your pants."

This time, it was loud enough for the table to hear.

"What did you say?" she asked, a sharp edge to her tone.

"I said he's trying to fucking buy you. He wants in your fucking pants and thinks he can flaunt some money and get everything he wants. You think he cares? He cares about one damn thing, and every guy at this table knows what that is."

The room went silent before Scout's chair screeched back, and I stepped a little closer to her as she stood.

"You think *he* doesn't care? The guy who showed up today is the one who doesn't care? He sat with us all damn day while I raced and you were nowhere to be found until the free booze was involved," she yelled. He scowled, and stood up, towering over her, but it didn't matter. Everyone else in the room stood up, too. This girl had her own army, and Jesse knew it.

"Oh, did you think nobody noticed you weren't around until now? You think you care about me because you showed up to the party after all the hard work? Fuck you, Jesse," she said.

Scout pushed past him, stomping out the door. I thought Jesse was going to immediately run after her, maybe fall to his knees begging for forgiveness, but he only turned to me.

"You fucking asshole. You've been in her head, telling her I'm no good, all because you want her. Fuck you," he said, turning and heading out after her.

The crew went to move, but I stopped them.

"I think this one might be on me since I knew I was going to piss him off. I'll take care of it."

"Fine, he's just going to run off, and she's going to be upset. We will wait here, but bring her back inside," Fox said.

"Got it," I nodded, heading out.

I pushed open the door, hearing Jesse yelling something. It wasn't until I was closer before I could finally hear what he was ranting about.

"...so what? You are trying to fuck him? One new guy comes around and you can't control yourself? I knew it! I knew you wanted all those guys, and this proves it."

There had been so many times in my life I had been angry.

So many times I wanted to tell my dad off, fight people at school, punch and hit until my knuckles bled.

There had only been a few times I had actually acted on it, though, being told from a young age to bury every emotion I had.

This wasn't going to be one of those times I buried it, though.

I passed Scout, not listening to anything else Jesse had to say as I punched him in the face.

THIRTEEN

SCOUT

I DIDN'T SEE Chase at first. My brain was trying to catch up with every nasty thing Jesse was throwing at me. I had missed the noise behind me until Chase was a blur going past me.

Blood splattered across the ground, Chase's fist connecting with Jesse's nose. I stayed frozen, wondering if the rings Chase wore made it hurt worse.

Jesse had been standing there, looking me right in the eye and telling me horrible things about myself. Every bad thought I had about myself being verbalized. And I froze, letting it all seep in because it didn't matter who was saying the terrible things, it mattered that it was all said. The words were out in the world and it felt like everyone could hear. I should have punched him, or at least yelled back, but all I could think of was the 'maybes'.

Maybe it was me, maybe I was the problem. Maybe I was bad in bed, so that's why he had to go sleep with other people. Maybe I wasn't good enough to be a girlfriend. Maybe he was right and I should have been the 'cool' girlfriend that I apparently made people think I would be.

Jesse was doubled over, grabbing his nose and trying to stand up straight without his nose gushing more blood.

Chase stepped to my side, and they kept yelling. I was trying to pay attention, but my mind kept going back to what he said.

Apparently, there wasn't any more time to think about what he said because Jesse hurled a can of beer at Chase. It missed him, though, and instead hit me square in the chest.

Beer spilled down my chest, soaking my shirt and making me gag at the foul smell.

"Shit, Scout, that was meant for him. Are you okay?"

Chase stepped between us, his face murderous when Jesse tried to get closer.

"Move. She needs help," Jesse said.

"Yeah, and it sure as hell isn't coming from you. Get the fuck out of here."

"She's my girlfriend, you dumb fucking rich boy."

"And if you touch her, I might actually kill you."

"You don't have a chance with her, so move on."

"No," I said, loud enough that they both turned.

"No, what, Scout?" Chase asked, the edge to his voice only giving me more confidence.

"I mean, no Jesse, I'm not your girlfriend anymore. How dare you even think that would be a possibility after what you said to me? And how dare you treat me like you have been? I don't think I've been your girlfriend for a while now, but now it's officially done."

"Are you seriously breaking up with me because of this guy?"

"No, I'm breaking up with you because of you. Because I know there's better and I'm finally done trying to convince myself that you are better."

"Better than what? Him?"

"No. No, not even better than him, just better. The bar I set for you was even lower than the one I set for him, and you still managed not to hit it. The only reason you can be mad at him is for pointing it out."

He shook his head, a harsh laugh escaping. "Who would have thought one rich boy comes around and you immediately turn into one slutty fucking bitch for him?"

"Scout, go inside. Now," Chase said, already stepping towards Jesse again. I wrapped my fingers into his shirt, pulling him back as hard as I could as Jesse turned and ran to his car.

"Fuck you both," he said, the door slamming shut, but I didn't let go of Chase.

It wasn't until Jesse's car peeled out that Chase turned to me, his hands moving up my arms to my face.

"Scout," Chase said. The soft whisper of my name made tears well.

"Chase."

"I'm not apologizing for hitting him."

"I didn't expect you to," I said, catching my breath. I finally unwound my hand from his shirt, realizing my own was wet, cold and stuck to my body.

Not to mention, it smelled so bad I was nearly gagging. I hated the smell of fresh beer, but the smell turned stale to me so quickly that I was going to throw up if I didn't change.

He reached out, a large warm hand running along my jaw. "Are you okay?"

"Yeah. I think I'm fine."

"After what he said?"

I nodded, not moving away, his hand still holding my jaw. It was warm, steady, and calming, letting my mind finally quiet.

"There was no ending to that which was going to be pretty. I wasn't expecting the beer, though, and I don't have my car here for something to put on, so I think my night is done."

He scoffed, but smiled and reached into the car. He pulled

out a hoodie and held it out to me. "You never even returned the first hoodie I lent you and now you want another one?" He asked. "Come on. Get in my car, take that off, and put this on. You should still have a good night after all of your hard work today."

"Back to being a gentleman, then?"

"With you? When did I stop?"

I got in, sliding into the dark backseat and pulling my shirt off, before wrapping myself in another one of his soft hoodies.

I would steal every single one of them if they all felt like this.

Minutes went by before Chase pulled the door open and leaned down.

"I'm not trying to be a creep, but it is taking you a very long time to change a shirt."

"I'm done. But I don't think I want to get back out."

"Why not?"

"What am I supposed to do? Go back in and hear everyone celebrate me breaking up with Jesse? Tell them what happened? Explain how I lost my shirt and am in yours? None of that sounds fun."

"Because you're upset about the breakup?"

"Because I'm embarrassed. They've all made it clear I should have done that months ago, and I didn't. I put it off because I knew breaking up was going to suck and it did."

"Suck because you're going to miss him or because he said all those things?"

I thought it over. "There's nothing to miss, but yeah, it kind of sucked hearing all of that."

"Come on," he said, sliding into the driver's seat and pointing at the passenger seat before starting the car.

"What? You think me leaving with you is going to help? Sure, let me go tell Fox that I just broke up with my boyfriend after his good friend Chase punched him, and now I'm going home with said friend. Sure, that will go over *so* well."

"Your options are go back in there and tell everyone, or leave with me. I guess I could be nice and give you my car, but we might have even more questions if you take off, and I have to get a ride from someone else. Pick your poison, Hellcat, because you're not getting out of this one unscathed."

I groaned, throwing my head back and closing my eyes. "Right now, my choice is that I don't move from the backseat and maybe all my problems disappear."

The car rocked, and when I opened my eyes, Chase's face was inches from mine.

"What are you doing?"

"Joining you, but the backseats are a little small, so hold on." He shifted around until he was sitting next to me, his knees pressed against my legs. "Alright, way smaller than I thought it would be."

"Don't spend much time in backseats?"

"I, surprisingly, prefer beds over tiny backseats. The more expensive the car, the smaller they get, it seems."

I rolled my eyes. "What a subtle brag, rich boy."

He flashed a bright smile. "No subtlety about it. This is my loaner, and the backseat is at least usable."

"As soon as I start to like you, you talk like that and we are right back at square one."

"If I can make you like me for even a minute, I could do it again, so I'm not too worried. You get five minutes back here and then I'll be dragging you back into the restaurant."

I groaned. "What if I don't want to go?"

"You know I won't hesitate to throw you over my shoulder, so that's your choice."

"Why are you insisting that I go back in? Can't I just sit here and pout over this?"

"After those races? Not a chance. He's really not worth another second of your time."

"And let me guess, you are?"

"*Fuck* no. I've spent enough time with you to not be that delusional."

I groaned, throwing my head back again. "I can't believe you're the one with some semblance of sense."

"I can't believe you're unashamed in agreeing that you're too good for me, and here I thought we were about to have some heart to heart about self-worth for you. Apparently, I need to have it with myself."

I smiled. "Sorry, I've just dealt with guys like you in my life. I know what type of girls you tend to go for, and they are nothing like me."

A rumble came from his chest and I could make out his eyes growing heavy. "I don't know where you got the idea that I don't like girls like you, but that's not even a little true. What's not to like?"

My breath hitched, and I fisted my hand into the hoodie, the warmth spreading over me, and making me want to move closer to him. I could barely believe that Chase was sitting here telling me that he liked anything about me.

"Everything," I breathed, having trouble finding anything that was worth a damn about myself at this moment.

"I would say that's exactly what I do like about you."

I don't know if this is what they consider a rebound or if it's the strange way that Chase has been there for me, but I leaned closer, moving across the seat until we were an inch apart.

It didn't matter if I did this. Chase would be around to get his car fixed, and would probably stop hanging around us soon after that. I couldn't imagine him not wanting to get back to his life and his friends.

And right now, I didn't see a reason why I shouldn't kiss him.

I leaned into him, nervous as my lips pressed to his.

Seconds passed with both of us hesitating. Then, he took over, grabbing my hips, and dragging me over his lap until I was straddled over him. His lips were soft at first, but grew demanding. Heat pooled as his hands ran down my arms and circled my waist, pulling me against him. I could feel him already growing hard underneath me, and I moved my hips, rocking once against him before his fingers dug into my hips.

"*Fuck*," he mumbled against my lips, making me shutter.

I pulled back, gasping for air, but his hands held me in place.

"I officially like back seats. Might have to start spending more time in them," he whispered.

"Good luck with that."

"You won't be joining me?"

"I'm pretty sure this will need to be a one-time situation."

He smiled, wrapping his arms around my lower back until I was pressed against him again. "It could be a two or three time thing."

I slipped out of his arms and slid into the front seat, never looking away from him as his head tilted back, and he closed his eyes. It was exactly what I had been doing when he came back there with me, and I wondered why he looked so hot doing it. Like he was ready and waiting for me to climb over him again.

"Thanks for the hoodie. And for…." My voice trailed off, not sure how to say it.

How was I supposed to say thank you for helping me break up with my boyfriend, or thank you for being such a jerk that I saw that he was a bigger one? Or maybe thank you for letting me kiss you?

None of them sounded all that great.

"Just thanks, I guess."

"Ready to go back in?"

"To face the entire crew?"

"To get a drink and have a party. If we aren't staying in this backseat with you on top of me, then I am sure as hell going to need a drink."

That made me smile, and I nodded. "Yeah, I'm ready for that. And no throwing over the shoulder will be necessary."

FOURTEEN
CHASE

OVER A WEEK HAD GONE by and I hadn't seen or heard from Scout except when she canceled our planned time to work on my car. She didn't text me back, and apparently, wasn't thinking about me the same way I had been thinking about her.

The girl crawled in my fucking lap to kiss me and then ghosted me.

It was honestly a first. Usually, I was the one dodging calls and texts, but suddenly I'm interested in doing that again with her and she's the one to ditch me.

The way the world was turning around to bite me in the ass for all the times I had done that to someone was almost rude. Now I'm the one left wondering, and waiting, for her to respond.

Every day that passed was starting to eat at me more. I don't know when I became so worried about Scout, but now I couldn't stop thinking about her. Classes, parties, and working didn't seem to take my mind off of her. The one thing I usually did to clear my mind was race, and that only made me think of her more. The worst part of it all was the thought that she wasn't responding to me because she was back with Jesse.

I was so annoyed about it all, I finally texted Fox to ask if they were at the garage because I needed to get things done on my car.

Luckily, he responded quick, and twenty minutes later I was pulling up to the garage.

Scout was out front, her red hair braided into the two long braids again, giving me a full view of her face. The sharp slant to her jaw, the small nose, and the cute way her eyebrows furrowed as she fought to pull a large box out of her car. She was dressed in jeans and a tight Holt Racing shirt, and fuck if I couldn't sit here all day watching her. I assumed the Uber driver wouldn't love that. After I gave back the Audi, I hadn't decided on a new car to buy, and decided coming in an Uber might give me a good excuse to ask Scout for a ride back home.

I hopped out, and her face fell when she turned to see it was me. I hoped it wasn't as bad as I thought, but I was already trying to decide if I was going to hold my tongue or cuss her out if she told me she was back with Jesse.

I didn't know why she was mad this time, but I was pretty confident that I was going to pry it out of her. The girl was a tidal wave of emotions, and I didn't think she was going to be able to hold back from me for long. If the first night we met was an indication, I was going to have to wait all of five seconds before she exploded.

"Hey Hellcat. You've been avoiding me."

"Yes, and?"

"And I've run out of patience waiting for you to be done avoiding me."

"That sounds vaguely threatening."

I smiled, watching as she slammed her passenger door closed, and walked around to me.

"It was meant to be a little threatening," I said, smiling.

"And where is the Audi you had?"

"Returned it. It was boring."

"And why exactly are you showing up here to threaten me?" she asked, a hint of a smile gracing her lips.

"Because I've missed my little ankle-biter."

Her hands pushed against my chest, forcing me back with a laugh.

"I told you don't call me that anymore."

"You didn't call me at all, so what does it matter what I call you?" I asked. She wasn't obligated to call me, yet here I was, pissed off that she kissed me and disappeared.

Her scowl deepened, and my heart rate picked up. The fact that I was nervous to ask this wasn't a good sign, but I forced the question out, anyway.

"Are you back with Jesse?" I asked, thankful I didn't sound as panicked as I felt.

"Why would you think that?"

"I assumed that's why you haven't responded to me, and keep canceling our time to work on the car."

She blew out a harsh laugh and pulled the driver's door open. "And you think I was supposed to break up with Jesse and immediately fall all over you? Maybe I needed a break from men."

I stepped closer, blocking her in. "You didn't answer me."

"And you need to take about five steps back before one of the guys walks out and sees you this close to me."

"Do you really think they would be that mad if they found out we made out *once*?" I asked, smirking as she looked from me to the garage before pushing me back again.

"First of all, no, I'm not back with Jesse. Second, yes, I think if you want to be invited to any more guys' nights, then stay away from me, and don't bring up the make out thing again. And third, I'm leaving, so have a good day. I probably won't text you because I don't even know where to begin with everything I need to say to you."

"Where are you going?"

"To get a part for your car that I've spent all week trying to find. Lucky for me, Quinn found one, but they won't ship. You drive a ridiculous, uncommon car, so now I have to drive five hours away to pick it up. Thanks. We can work on the car later this week."

She got in, slamming the door shut before I could respond, but I ran around, jumping into the passenger seat as she shifted into gear.

Her mouth dropped open as she watched me slam the door closed.

"What are you doing?"

"Going with you. If it's for my car, I'm obligated to assist," I said.

"No thanks. I would rather be alone today."

"Why? I'll even be nice and let you choose the music."

"You'll *let* me choose the music in my own car? How generous." She rolled her eyes, turning her head away from me with a smile. "And we're listening to true crime, not music."

"So you are sweet and smiley to the world, but a murderous little killer underneath. I like it."

She didn't say anything, a range of expressions crossing her face until she was staring blankly at the road.

We made it almost an hour out of town before she pulled into a gas station and shut off the car.

"I don't know what game you think you're playing with me, but I'm not okay with it. Stop teasing me," she said. Her words were angry and upset, her hands tightening on the steering wheel.

"Teasing you? Are you already turned on?"

"I meant teasing me like you seem to be playing this weird

game of flirting and making comments about liking me. Just knock it off. I don't have the time or energy for it."

"I feel the need to point out that you're the one that kissed me, and while I couldn't exactly say this is a game, it is fun. Do you not like men spending time with you and telling you they like you? I can't say I'm the best at this, but I thought I was doing okay."

I couldn't remember the last time I had this much fun flirting with any girl, or the last time I was thinking about the same girl over and over.

The last time I felt this obsessed with kissing someone again.

"I'm sorry. I shouldn't have kissed you," she said as I leaned over and grabbed her braid to run it through my hands. It was so long that I grabbed it again, twisting it around my knuckles and tugging it. She was forced to look over at me, her lips parting and eyes wide.

"Don't apologize for that. *Never* apologize for that."

"It wasn't right, though. I don't know if I was using you for comfort or thanking you for the help, but either way, kissing you wasn't right."

I slid my hands down her neck, wrapping it around the back until I could pull her closer. Damn, I wanted to kiss her again. I wanted her to crawl onto my lap one more time, wanted her to kiss me like she had the last time, like she needed me to give her the air from my damn lungs.

"Don't ever apologize for kissing me," I finally said, the words strained. "It's almost literally all I've been thinking about for a week now. I don't care why you did it."

"I don't usually go around making out with people for the wrong reasons."

"You can kiss me anywhere, anytime and for any reason, and it wouldn't be wrong. Kiss me to make Jesse jealous, kiss me when you need someone, you could kiss me at your own fucking wedding because you need the comfort and I would gladly participate. There is no wrong reason to kiss me."

She smirked. "All of those are exact examples of wrong reasons to kiss someone."

"No, Scout, kissing you could never be wrong."

"It is if one of us gets hurt."

"If you're doing exactly what you want, you won't be getting hurt."

"The other party would be the one to get hurt, then. Whether it's you or apparently, my future fiancé."

"A price most people would be willing to pay."

She shook her head with a laugh.

"You're saying that it could be my wedding day and I tell you *Chase, I'm getting married but come make out with me first*, and you would?"

"Yes, although if we are making a plan now, future me would also like to add in more than just a makeout session."

She gave me a dramatic eye roll but didn't turn away.

"And you don't think cheating on my currently made up fiancé would be a problem?"

I leaned over further, the conversation doing nothing to change my need to feel her lips against mine again.

"No, I'll tell him ahead of time that we already have an agreement. How mad could he be with a prior arrangement made between friends?"

"I think he could be pretty mad."

"I guess we will deal with that mess on your wedding day. But how about for now you kiss me again? What wrong reason do you have today?"

"Or you can show off your gentleman-like attitude and fill the car up with gas."

I leaned in further, her lips so close to mine that if she moved even an inch, I would be touching her.

She reached over to me, her hands moving along my stomach to my jeans and for a moment, I couldn't breathe as her fingers roamed. This was it. She wanted this, too. She needed to touch me as badly as I needed to touch her. I leaned in again, my forehead falling against hers. I wanted her to push for this. I wanted her to make any move so I could break this hold she had on me, and make a move, too.

Suddenly, her hands were doing more of a patting motion than feeling me up.

"What are you doing?"

"Trying to find your wallet, rich boy. The gas for this car isn't cheap, and it's a long drive," she said, smiling as she patted me down more.

The groan that came from me was agonizing.

"You better be glad that you're fucking cute. Sit your ass here, and I'll fill up the car."

"Thank you. I'm going for snacks," she said, the winning smile still plastered on her face. It was probably well deserved because I was pretty sure she was winning.

I looked around at the creepy gas station. Even in broad daylight, it seemed a little to run down. The sky was dark, leaving everything coated in an eerie gray color.

"I think I'll get those, too. Just stay here. Figure out whatever murder story you want next."

"I can handle a gas station, Chase."

"I'm sure, but there's no point when I'm here. Plus, I've been listening to people going missing, and this is about what I'm picturing when they describe it, so I got it."

She let out a long huff and looked around. "Maybe you're a little right, but I hope you know that I will be judging you based on the snacks you get us."

I clicked my tongue, paying for the gas before filling up the car. "Always looking for a way to intimidate me," I said, leaning down to her through the open window. "I bet it's infuriating that it never works." I smiled, heading inside before she could yell at me.

Being stuck in a car for seven more hours never sounded like so much fun.

FIFTEEN

SCOUT

A FEW HOURS LATER, we were back on the road after picking up the part, and I was trying to ignore the tiredness that kept threatening to take over.

It had been a week of restless sleep. Between Jesse, Chase, my dad, the races—I couldn't keep anything straight and it was keeping me up at all hours.

Now Chase was here, handing me snacks, filling up the car, opening my drink. One minute he was quietly listening to the podcast and the next he was going on a rant about whatever theory the podcasters had.

The only problem I had with it was how much I liked it. He was somehow the most infuriating man I've ever met, but still calming. Every moment with him came easy. Easier than it ever did with Jesse.

I yawned again, the dark skies moving in earlier than normal as a storm moved our way.

"I do know how to drive, Scout. I've quite literally beat you racing. A few times. I can drive the rest of the way."

"No, it's fine, and stop reminding me about that. I don't know how you managed to beat me, but I will figure it out."

He gave a deep rumble of a laugh, the sound filling the car and making me lean back into the seat more, a warm, comforting feeling overwhelming me.

"Come on, pull over and I'll drive. You're obviously tired."

I shook my head and went to protest more, but the sky opened up, rain coming down on us like a thick blanket.

"Alright," he said without a hint of humor, "pull over now, Scout. We are not driving in this with you half asleep."

"Maybe it will pass," I said, not even able to see an exit off the highway.

"Scout," he warned. "Get off the road now."

"Fine, *fine*. I'm looking for the exit now. Stop yelling about it and help me."

His hand came down over mine on the shifter, resting there as he directed me off the next exit and into a motel parking lot.

"So now what? We sit here until the rain passes? I can't sleep in the car."

"No, we go inside and sleep until the rain passes, and your stubborn ass rests enough to drive again."

"Hey! I'm not being stubborn. I just don't want you to drive my car."

"I think you're worried I will be able to drive it better than you." He had that cocky grin again that made me want to smack him.

So I did.

His leg at least, but he moved fast, grabbing my arms, and pulling me over the console until I was hard against his chest. My heart stopped, his lips inches from mine.

"Nice try. Let's go inside and get a few hours of sleep, and then we will be on our way first thing in the morning."

"Before sunrise," I demanded, trying to force myself to stay still. I couldn't let myself kiss him again, even if I wanted to. I had to remember that Ash made it clear that Chase wasn't the type to date, and only messing around with someone who was friends with them wasn't a good idea.

"Come on, we are just sleeping, unless, of course, you change your mind about that. Now, let's get going."

I followed him around the car, the rain pouring down on us now. He went to grab my hand, but changed his mind, throwing an arm around me instead, trying to shield me from the rain.

"What are you doing? I won't melt," I said, even if I liked the way he thought about my needs.

"I didn't think you would, but why risk it?"

His arm stayed around me as we stepped inside. Ahead, a man, who I assumed was drunk based on the half-closed eyes and swaying step, was checking into a room in front of us.

He finally moved aside and Chase stepped forward, pulling me with him. His arm tightened around me, but this time I leaned into it, feeling safer tucked under his arm than standing off on my own.

"A room please," Chase said, pulling a hundred out of his wallet.

"One? Why not two?" I hissed.

"Why would I leave you in your own room in a strange place? We can get a room with two beds."

He looked at the guy behind the desk, who nodded in agreement.

"I'm capable of sleeping in a room by myself."

"And you're also a pretty, rather small, woman that will have me up all night worrying if anyone else noticed that. I don't care how scrappy you are. If you're here with me, I won't be risking one red hair on your beautiful, annoying head."

"You just think I can't handle myself alone in a room all night?"

"It's okay, Scout. All we're doing is getting some sleep and leaving first thing in the morning. I'm sure you've slept next to your other friends all night, and it wasn't weird. And he said the room has two beds, so you will have plenty of room between us."

I rolled my eyes, but stayed tucked against him as we walked to the room. He wasn't wrong. I've slept next to all the guys at some point. I've cuddled up to all of them at some point to either stay warm or even watch a movie, and it never crossed my mind to be weird, but this was different.

"I don't think we can count ourselves as friends," I said.

"No? And here I thought this little road trip was going well."

A cold shiver ran through me as he opened the door and he ushered me in. Between being wet from the rain and the room feeling as though the air conditioning had been running for hours, I was frozen solid.

"You're already shaking." The door shut behind me as I took in the room. It was clean at least, with one bed covered in blankets from this century and the chair in the corner clean and new.

That's about all I could ask for right now.

My eyes went back to the bed. "Chase, there is only one bed in here. I thought he just said there would be two."

"He did. Apparently, there was a mistake," he said with a shrug.

"Could you go ask him to fix it?"

"No. I'm tired, and it's pouring. Plus, you can handle one night next to me. I promise, I only bite if you ask me too," he said, grinning.

I only crossed my arms, glaring at him. He stared back, but didn't move.

"Go dry off and change. You're shivering."

"I didn't exactly bring pajamas or anything else to change into," I said, trying to find a way to stop the thoughts of sliding into bed naked with him, but nothing was working. There was also no stopping the sudden endless thoughts I was having about Chase giving me an orgasm.

Chase pulled off his hoodie and shirt, holding the shirt out to me. "This is still dry. Put this on and get under the covers."

"And what are you sleeping in?"

He flashed a bright smile. "Boxers, obviously."

My stomach flipped, and I snatched the shirt from his hand. "Thanks. And it's freezing in here. Feel free to crank up the heat," I said.

"Feel free to use me as your personal heater."

"You know, just for that, I'm building a pillow wall," I said, slamming the bathroom door shut behind me.

I didn't even feel bad when I pulled the shirt up to my face, taking a deep breath of the crisp, musky scent. He even smelled rich, but it was hard to complain when all I wanted to do was drown in the scent. I peeled off my wet clothes and dried my hair off before sliding the shirt on. It was long enough to cover everything, and luckily I had decided on a cute pair of green underwear today, so I didn't have to die of embarrassment if he did see anything.

I ignored him as best I could when I walked out, heading to the bed while he pulled everything from his pockets, and finished getting undressed.

I grabbed the two extra pillows, building a wall of pillows between us.

"You were serious?" He asked.

"Completely."

"What exactly do you think those two sad little pillows are going to do?"

I looked over at the two flat pillows. He was probably right. Those wouldn't stop anything, let alone a man that was currently looking at me like he wanted to eat me alive.

I really didn't know why I was protesting it. It's not like I hadn't laid awake wondering what his mouth was capable of.

He came around the bed to me, towering over me with a smile.

"Do you think that two sad little pillows are going to make me forget that you're only a foot away from me? That I could reach out and touch you."

He stepped closer, making me sit back on the bed. His eyes went heavy, and he leaned down, moving over me until I laid on my back. No part of him touched me, but my body was on fire, wishing he would.

He reached out, dragging one of the flat pillows until it was pressed between us. "Oh, you're completely right. This is doing wonders."

I closed my eyes, taking a deep breath, the heat that rolled off of him making me want to curl up and fall asleep right here.

"What are you thinking about?" he whispered. My eyes cracked open to find him leaning down closer to me, his body falling heavier on mine even with the pillow still between us, and I was resisting the urge to wrap my legs around him.

"Reese's."

"You're thinking about candy?"

"Yeah, I left it in the car and I shouldn't have."

He smiled. "I think you're a liar."

"No. I actually left them in the car."

"No, I think that you were thinking about kissing me."

"That seems absurd. If I was thinking about it, why wouldn't I do it?"

"I'm not sure. Why wouldn't you?"

"Because I don't kiss friends."

"You're the one who said we aren't friends."

"Maybe I'll head out to the car and grab my candy," I said,

my chest tightening. I did want to kiss him, and that was infuriating.

"No."

"Why not?"

"Because you're freezing and we need to go to sleep." His hand moved up my thigh, not stopping until it reached my hip. "Plus, you don't have pants on."

My breath hitched as his finger hooked under the band of my underwear.

"I'm not ready for bed," I lied. "I'm not tired."

"I don't know if it's the sweet smile you've had on your face all day or the fact that I finally get to spend an entire night with you, but I'm currently not above *making* you get into bed. I'm exhausted, and I know you are, too."

He pushed off the bed, walking around to lie down on his side. I didn't say a word as I slid under the covers, the chill in the air a harsh contrast to the warmth of him on top of me.

"Did you turn up the heat?"

"Yeah, but I think the dial is more for show than for use. If you get too cold, just come to my side."

I turned over without a word. There was no chance that I would be going to his side.

Not a damn chance.

MINUTES TICKED BY, BUT IT FELT LIKE HOURS. I WAS ALREADY freezing, and I was worried my chattering teeth were going to wake him up if I didn't get them to stop.

He had offered to keep me warm, though, and what's a little exchange of body heat between friends?

My hand moved across the bed until I found hard abs, pleasure rolling through me when I felt how deliciously warm they were.

I forced my hand back to my side, not wanting to wake him, but each part of me craved that heat now. Did his entire body feel like that? Another shiver ran over me. I could be so warm.

I finally grabbed his hand, pulling it to my side, then across my stomach, sighing at the heat.

At first he didn't move, and I almost believed he was still asleep until his thumb circled once on my hip before his fingers dug in, dragging me across the bed. He flipped over and raised himself up, moving me underneath him.

His chest rumbled with a groan as he nuzzled into my neck.

"Hey, Hellcat," he said, the deep, husky tone sending a flutter through my stomach.

"I was right about the pillows," I whispered.

"Yes you were. I should have kept them to protect myself. Now I've fallen victim to the Hellcat."

His lips found my neck again before moving to my mouth, the light kiss sending waves of heat to my core.

"I was cold."

"Then let's get you all warmed up."

His body pressed to mine as he kissed me harder. His tongue urged my mouth open as my legs wrapped around his waist. My body was suddenly on fire, the throbbing ache between my thighs making me push my hips up into him.

"Greedy girl," he murmured against my lips. "Already begging for my cock?"

I moaned, feeling how wet my underwear was already becoming. The man had barely touched me and I was ready to pull my underwear aside and take him.

Maybe I was greedy, but I don't know that I cared right at the moment.

He flipped us until I was straddled over top of him, the smile on his face making my heart flip.

He really was devastatingly handsome, the lights from outside showing me just enough of him to make me want more again.

I slammed my lips to his, taking his mouth like he'd taken mine, but he was faster. He nipped at my bottom lip as he grabbed my waist, pulling me forward until I could feel his hard cock pressing against my core.

I froze, taking in the feel of him, taking in the fact that this was for me.

"Do you like feeling how hard I am for you?"

I could only nod, trying not to rock my hips.

"Come on, let me see how you would ride me. Show me how you get off."

I moved, hesitant at first. The feeling of being on display felt strange. It's not like he could see everything clearly. The shirt hiding most of my body still, but the idea of getting off in front of him, more accurately on him, without him doing the same was different.

I lost all care when I ground down again and he matched my movement, pushing his hard cock up against me with a groan.

The pleasure built as I moved, the two thin fabrics between us only creating more friction. He flipped me onto my back next to him and laid at my side.

The sheets were cool under my legs as I let them fall open, his hand trailing down my stomach. His fingers dug into my hip before he pulled me even closer.

"I want to feel you cum on my fingers. I want to know what you sound like when your world breaks apart."

"I don't do this with my friends."

"Good thing you've been so clear that I am not your friend,

then. We can leave it here in this room. Anything that happens can stay here. Tell me to stop and I will."

He kept moving, and I stopped protesting, worried that he really would stop if I brought it up again. I didn't want him to. I wanted to know if it was different from Jesse or any other guy. I wanted to know if I would like it as much as I thought I might.

"Chase?"

"What, baby?"

"Please," I breathed, his fingers trailing lightly over my thighs until I was ready to scream for him to move higher.

He groaned, pushing harder against my side as his fingers moved through my wetness. "So wet for me."

"Yes," I breathed, pushing my hips up again.

His fingers pushed against my entrance, teasing me with the pressure for a second before he pushed into me.

I moaned, taking in the pleasure that hit every nerve. I had dated Jesse for nearly a year, and in that year, I could count on one hand how much foreplay happened.

He kissed down my jaw and neck, not stopping as he kissed down my stomach, his fingers still pushing into me at their agonizingly slow pace as his mouth came down over my clit.

"Chase!" I yelled, the sudden addition of his mouth almost making me fall apart.

"Problem?"

"No, just—" I tried to find words, tried to catch my breath, anything as I pushed my fingers into his hair and pulled him back down to me. I could feel him laughing as his tongue began its mind numbing movements.

The foreplay being nonexistent wasn't exactly all Jesse's fault. At least, not entirely, because I hated it. He was like a slobbering dog with a new bone and I hated it so much that I turned it down from ever happening again after the first time.

This wasn't like that. Chase's mouth was precise and confident. It was pushing me to the edge, and I was happy to fall.

I gripped his hair tighter, and he seemed to understand perfectly. His hand moved faster as his mouth continued until I was seeing stars, the world gone as an orgasm tore through me.

I gasped for a breath as he pulled away, the smile on his face showing just enough in the light that was coming in from the window.

He crawled up my body, kissing my stomach, chest, and lips before collapsing by my side.

I stayed quiet as I panted, coming down off the high of my orgasm as he held me.

"Hey Hellcat," he said, the word soft against my ear.

"Hmm?"

"I have an addictive personality," he whispered, wrapping an arm around my back and pulling me closer until our lips were a breath apart.

"And?"

"And I think I just found my newest addiction."

SIXTEEN

SCOUT

I WOKE up to Chase's arm wrapped around me, his head on the pillow next to mine. He hadn't been lying when he said he would be keeping me warm. I was so comfortable I barely wanted to move. The steady sound of his breath was keeping my own freak out about last night at bay, and I leaned into him, moving closer to take more heat.

For a few minutes, I didn't care what was going on between us. I loved waking up so warm and comfortable. I wiggled back again, feeling his hard length behind me as I froze.

"You can keep moving your ass around on me or we can put this to use if you're interested." His voice was so low and husky, the first words of the morning dragging from him and sending a shiver of pleasure down my spine. His hand moved to my side, caressing my hip.

"What do they say about playing with fire?"

"You get burned?" I asked, smiling.

"Exactly, and if you don't stop playing with my hard dick, you might get fucked."

"Chase!" I gasped, pushing away, but he wrapped both arms

around me, pinning me hard against his chest as he laughed. "You can't threaten me like that."

"And you can't endlessly tease me and think there wouldn't be consequences," he said, laughing as he kissed my head. "Pick a safe word because if you continue this, I promise you will absolutely find out what those consequences are."

"A safe word? Isn't that usually a whips and chains thing?"

He kissed my neck, his lips lingering there. "I'm not really a whips and chains type, but I am suddenly even harder at the thought of you tied to my bed with your ass up in the air."

I hid my surprise that he would talk to me like that. Not for how crude it was exactly, but that it was about me. Was I ever the star of someone's sexual fantasies?

"I meant pick a safe word because I inevitably push boundaries and don't want you to be uncomfortable."

"There are no boundaries to push if none of this leaves this room."

"That's not how this is going to work," he said, and I could hear the smile on his lips. "I thought you understood what I said last night." His hand trailed down my side, reaching between my legs.

"I currently can't recall anything you said," I breathed as his fingers brushed over my clit.

"I said," he paused, his fingers pushing into me, "that I was addicted. Do you think one night of this would be enough for me now?"

"It has to be," I said, the words turning into a moan as he continued.

"It won't be."

"I say it will be."

"I say you better choose your safe word fast," he said. "If all I have is right now, then I better start seeing how I can push the limits."

"Gummy worm," I said, trying to laugh, but it ended up only being more of a moan.

He laughed against my ear, his fingers still fucking me. "Fine. You say that and I stop whatever I'm doing."

I nodded, moving my hips faster as he slowed down.

"What's wrong? Are you close, or do you want to say your safe word?"

"Close," I breathed, trying to ride his hand as he held me still.

"Do you want it harder now?"

"Yes."

"Yes, what?"

"Chase," I said through gritted teeth as he slowed more.

"Say the words, Hellcat."

"Please."

He moved faster now, his fingers slamming into me hard until I was falling apart, the world blurring as an orgasm burned through me.

"I had to spend the entire night with you next to me and sinking deep into you sounds like fucking ecstasy after your little torture session."

His arms wrapped around me now, pulling me close and kissing me hard.

"Please tell me that means what I think it means."

"Nope. Time to get up and get going," I said, reaching for my phone. It was already seven, and I had planned to be on the road already. Then again, I had been planning on laying here alone and keeping a much larger distance between us.

He flipped me onto my back, crawling over top of me.

"Then you're going to have to wait until I go take care of my own problems."

"What does that mean?"

"It means I am going to be a gentleman and go get myself off in the other room."

There was no hiding my shock. My mouth fell open as I watched his face turn into a grin.

"You're just going to go do that in there? With me right here?"

"Would you rather me do it right here with you in the room because I will happily do so?"

I wanted to say yes, and that shocked me even more.

I wanted to know what he sounded like when he came, what he liked, how he looked. I didn't even know it was possible to want to see something like that.

His chest rumbled with a satisfied groan. "That's what you want, isn't it?"

I could barely move, let alone say anything. How could I admit out loud to anyone that I wanted to see them do…that?

He leaned down, kissing me hard before getting up. A lounge chair was behind him and he sat back.

"Come here," he said, that sleepy, husky tone back.

"I wasn't agreeing to a blow job. If that's suddenly what you think is happening, it's not." Sex felt new now, and not entirely in a good way. Everything I had done and gained any confidence in doing again was ruined, wrecked with the thought that I wasn't good at any of it because of Jesse.

"No, Hellcat. Just come kiss me."

I went to him, leaning down and placing a hesitant kiss on his lips.

I was kissing Chase.

And I would never admit it out loud to anybody, but I liked it. I liked it even more, knowing that he liked it.

I kept kissing him until I was moving to his neck and chest, not wanting to stop now.

His head rolled back as my lips moved lower, kissing along

the waistband of his boxers. I was never big on the blowjob thing, either. The power dynamic with Jesse always left me feeling helpless, but this wasn't like that. Somehow, he had told me what to do, but I felt in control. He was groaning at my touch, his hips involuntarily pushing up as I licked at his abs.

I sat back on the bed and watched as he pulled his hard cock out. His hand fisted it, only covering about half his length.

It was so much to take in. Watching someone do something that felt so private was one thing, but to somehow want to be involved felt foreign to me. I finally looked away, not sure what else to do.

"Eyes on me. You keep looking at me, that's the point."

"It doesn't make you uncomfortable?"

"No? This is the point. You watch me and if you want to join, I watch you. Don't overthink it, enjoy it, and if you aren't, you have your magic word."

"Join as in…be over here doing myself, or come help you?"

"Whichever you're in the mood for. You can also sit there watching, being beautiful, making me think about you coming over and sitting down right on me." His eyes grew heavier. "I can't wait to watch your greedy pussy take this all."

"All?" I asked, looking it over again.

"Every fucking inch will be buried in you."

My eyes went wide, wondering if that was even possible. Heat flooded me again, making me want to give in and touch myself. The ache grew to an almost unbearable amount. I wanted relief again, but I had spent way too many nights doing that myself. I would rather wait for him to help.

"I want to cum just from the way you're looking at me," he said.

"Then cum," I said, my eyes glued to him.

He gave a laugh that was nearly a moan and picked up his pace.

"Tell me again, baby, tell me what you want from me."

"I want you to cum," I said, hiding the nervousness in my voice.

"Do you like to boss me around now? Do you want to see how far you can push me? What you could make me do?"

My chest grew heavy as my breathing deepened. It might only last a little longer, but I liked the idea that I had any control here. It made me want to actually ask for what I wanted.

"Yes, I do. So cum."

He swore through gritted teeth, still moving his hand, the strokes shorter and faster now. If you would have asked me last week if I would be sitting here watching Chase do this, I would have died of embarrassment. Now, here I was wondering if it was worth prolonging this mess we were creating to watch him do it again.

Three more seconds, three more strokes, and then he leaned back, his body shuddering as he came.

I could barely breathe, my body tightening with need for my own orgasm again. The sight of him coming undone right in front of me sending a trail of heat down my spine.

"Fuck," he mumbled, his chest still heaving. "You are very good at that."

"I didn't actually do anything."

"That's not true." He adjusted himself, getting up with a smile. "Not even a little. You're amazing."

I don't know if it was the clarity from breaking up with Jesse, or the power that Chase seemed to hand over to me, but for the first time in a long time, I believed him.

———

I was quiet as we started the drive back home. It was too hard to find anything to say to the man I just watched get off a few hours ago.

The worst part was how much I was still thinking about it. The way his chest heaved, the muscles in his arm flexing, the way his eyes didn't leave mine.

Our eyes locked, the smirk on his face making my cheeks hot.

"Rethinking the idea that we won't be doing anything like that again?"

"No, I have no doubt that we won't be doing anything like that ever again," I said, mustering up any confidence I had to sound sure of myself.

"I would be willing to bet you a watch that it will be happening again."

"I don't have a watch to bet."

"No, but if you're so confident that it won't be happening, then you won't be losing a watch, anyway. And if you won mine, we could be considered even."

"Then you absolutely have a deal."

My phone buzzed with incoming texts, but the one that wasn't from the crew caught my eye.

UNKNOWN

Scout. I've been trying to get a hold of you for hours. I need help. The money wasn't enough. I think they are coming for me again, and if they do, you and your friends are in trouble again, too. I need more money to keep them away.

It had been sent in the middle of the night. I knew it was from my dad, but my phone had been dead and it had just occurred to me to power it back up. The man I couldn't even save as a contact was putting me in danger again. There would be no remorse, either. The only empathy the man had was for himself. In his mind, he would be the victim and I would be the problem unless I continued to help.

. We were on the edge of town now, the side of our old row of houses that the crew and I grew up in.

"Could we make a quick stop?"

"Sure. I'm in no hurry. Where to?"

I gave him directions until we were pulled up in front of my old house.

"Just stay here. Please, *stay here*." I got out and before I made it halfway up the overgrown sidewalk, Chase was by my side.

"Didn't I ask you to stay in the car?"

"You did, and I am specifically not answering because we are once again in a sketchy as fuck place. Why do you keep bringing me to these places?"

"Because this is my life?"

"You really need to start hanging out in new places."

I stopped, spinning to face him, the surge of anger in my chest overwhelming.

"*I* need to start hanging out in new places? This is where I grew up, Chase. This," I said, waving my arms around, "is not only my life but also where the guys grew up. Don't tell me I need to hang out in new places or remind me how little you think of people like me when I asked you to stay in the damn car. No actually," I said, raising my voice. "I've always asked you to stay in the car. You are the one subjecting yourself to my life, not me."

He grabbed my chin, keeping our eyes locked on each other, the hardness in his not filled with comfort or pity.

"Easy, Killer," he said, the calm tone a surprise after my outburst. "I was kidding. The warehouse, the motel, now here. We keep ending up in sketchy places. I don't care where it is.

You won't be going anywhere that looks like this alone, and you don't need to have any concerns that I am judging you. I'm in no place to judge you."

"Yeah, I'm sure you, with all your money, status, and six-pack, aren't looking down on all of us."

"Technically, I always have to look down since we have a pretty reasonable height difference. Besides that, I promise the only time I'm going to be looking down on you is when you're back on your knees kissing that six-pack," he said, the corners of his lips turning up. "But again, that's a technical necessity, and I promise I would only be thinking of you as the queen of my fucking world when you're doing that."

I took a ragged breath, knowing that I was overreacting a bit, and knowing that he was actually being nice.

I smiled, liking the way he reached up and ran my hair through his hand.

"I feel like you should think of me as the queen of your world every time you're near me," I said, trying to stare him down.

That made a full smile break across his face, and his hand tightened on my chin.

"Really?" he asked, the spark of mischief in his eyes making me fight my own smile. "In that case, consider me a loyal subject, your majesty. Should I start practicing my royal bow or are you more of a handshake type of queen?"

"I'm more of a 'crawl on your knees after me' type of queen."

"First you tell me to cum, now you tell me to crawl? If I didn't know any better, I would think you are trying to dominate me."

"I don't have any need to dominate you. I just like you listening when I tell you what to do."

"Nice try. I'll cum on demand, but I'm not going to sit in the car."

"Then at least do better this time and keep your mouth shut. That is, unless you are looking to lose another watch."

"I told you I've never been into the whips and chains, but fuck if you're not pushing me into them. If anyone ever needed to be tied up and spanked, it's you."

My hand flew out, smacking against his chest as I pulled open the door.

"One more word, and I will make sure *you* are the one tied up. Preferably in the back of my car so that you stop following me every time I have to make a stop," I said, my tone lighter now.

His arm snaked around my stomach, pulling me back hard against him with a grumble. "I promise there will not be a situation where you have that advantage over me. Now, what are we doing here?"

"My dad texted. It didn't sound good, but I missed it because my phone was dead. I wanted to check on him."

I could feel him stiffen behind me. "He needs more money?"

"I'm not sure. I thought they would be fine with the money from the watch, but I think they want more. He said that I'm in danger again, along with the crew, if I don't help him pay more."

"And what are we doing here? Asking him for money?"

"Look around. Do you think he has any money to give? I wanted to see if he was here and how much was owed, exactly. I don't want to be involved in this, and the crew still can't know what's going on."

"Do you think he will be honest?"

"No, but I also think he can't afford not to tell me how much he needs. He'll probably add a thousand or two on top for himself, though."

"Alright, then," he said, still holding me against him. "I don't normally go right from hooking up with a girl to meeting her parents, but I guess there is a first for everything."

"Lucky for us that we didn't hook up then," I said.

"Maybe not completely, but I think it's already safe to say we did hook up."

"It's not," I said, stepping inside. "I promise it's not safe for you to say we did."

"Why? Is your dad the killing type?"

"Not, but my friends are." I grinned as he shook his head. His hand rested on my lower back, bringing me a peace that I needed in the moment.

I turned the knob, shocked when it didn't turn.

"It's locked."

"Do you have a key?"

"I don't even know if there's still a key to this door."

I reached down, grabbing the switchblade from my boot and sliding into the worn lock on the wooden door. A door we could probably kick down, but this felt a bit more civilized.

"Have you had that the entire weekend?"

"I didn't stop on the way to grab it."

"How resourceful. I didn't realize we were bringing weapons."

"You should always have something on you."

"With where you take me, Hellcat, I think you're right."

I rolled my eyes, tucking the blade back and opening the door.

The house was quiet as we walked in. It wasn't big. You could literally stand in the living room and look into every room. A kitchen, a laundry room, one bedroom and one bathroom. It was nothing more than a glorified studio.

Chase didn't make a sound as we looked around.

"Dad?" I yelled. There was no response.

"Maybe he's out?" Chase asked.

I looked back at the table, the small notepad that had been there all my life, still there, on its last few pages.

Like a hundred times before, I could see the scribbling on the page.

I liked to believe I was a tough person. Even if I was emotional, I could handle a lot on my own.

This wasn't going to be one of those times.

Whatever was scribbled on that paper wasn't going to be good. He was taken, or dead, or being held against his will and would need money in exchange.

My hand slid down Chase's arm until I was gripping his hand, squeezing his fingers hard as I stepped towards the paper. He didn't protest, only stepped with me as we both read it.

> Scout - You didn't respond, so I had no choice but to leave. I had to go where they couldn't find me or they were coming after me. They still need money and I won't be able to come back until they get paid. I'll keep an eye out for when it's clear. - DAD

Dad was in all caps, as though I might forget who he was to me. I wish I could forget who he was to me.

"So what, he ran off and left his problems to you?"

"Yeah, it looks like it," I said, turning back to the room. I couldn't look at that note again without being sick. "He ran. He realized he had dangerous people after him and ran. I wasn't exactly believing I would come over here and everything would get fixed, but I was hoping that he would at least be a part of the solution."

Chase's hand tightened, and I didn't miss the way he rolled his shoulders.

I could only look over the room, hating myself for not caring to look for clues of where he went or what he could be doing. Tears rolled down my face as I grew angry, then sad, and then angry again.

Grief and guilt are a demanding mix. Should I be sad that he's gone? Guilty that I'm not sad? Guilty that I could even think that? Maybe I should be running out of the house to find him. If he had been a good person, a good father, what would my life look like?

Would I even have the crew in my life? I looked at Chase, who seemed to be taking in every inch of the living room.

"Where is your room?"

"Room? More like my corner," I said with a light laugh as I pointed to the closet in the corner. It wasn't big enough to be a room, but not small enough to consider a closet. There was also no door, there never was, and when I reached eleven or so, I had put up a curtain to try to have some privacy.

"That was your room?" He stepped inside, head swiveling, but I couldn't see his face.

"Yeah. I probably still have a few things in there, but I moved out anything of value to me."

He walked further in, disappearing as I stared at the curtain hanging to the side. There were so many days and nights I stared at that thing, cursing it. Now, I didn't know how to feel.

I hated this house. It was never a home to me, but aside from the garage and the apartments, it was the only home I knew.

Now that I lived in the apartments with the crew, this felt like someone else had lived here.

"I can't believe this," he said, stepping back out into the main living area. "I can't believe you had to live here. Live like this in general."

"No need to be rude about it. I'm obviously doing better now."

He sat back on the couch, and somehow, even in this run-down house, he looked more like the cocky rich boy that I thought he was, or at least had thought.

"I know you're some rich boy that was handed everything, but some of us weren't. Some of us clawed and clawed to get anywhere above the poverty line. If you want to rub that in, you can leave."

"I rode with you."

"Then walk, call yourself a limo, whatever it is you rich boys do."

He laughed, patting the spot next to him on the couch. "Calm the temper, Hellcat. I was sitting here more impressed by you, not less."

"No, you were just pitying me."

"I guess, but I'm also impressed that you managed such a nice life for yourself. I have been spoiled, and the thought of starting from this and having to build my way up would be terrifying. I don't know who I would be if this was the life I was handed at such a young age, and I couldn't imagine it wouldn't include crime and desperation. You managed to do it without either. All of this and you managed to be one of the happiest people around? Besides when you're talking to me, of course. How? How could you manage that? Fuck, I'm a dick about my life and I have everything I could ever need."

I shrugged, still standing in the middle of the room. "You do what you have to do. That, and find a few guys who want to give you the world." I smiled, thinking of the four guys who continually showed up for me. Now I got to add three women to that list, too.

He laughed, getting up to stand in front of me. "I think that's something you bring out in people."

"I doubt that. I'm hard to love. I think the guys didn't catch on in time, and the girls have no choice now."

"I'm surprised you could convince yourself of that when you

have more people that love you than most people will get in their entire life. I don't think it would even take one finger to count the people that would drop what they were doing to help me, who would possibly commit violence for me, and you need two hands. Crazy to think that you would have any belief that you are hard to love."

"I'm sure that you have one person in your life."

He shook his head, his eyes not leaving mine as he brushed my hair back. "Not really. One of my sisters might show up, but they are busy, so it would depend on if they could pick up their phone or not."

Chase hadn't been mean to me, at least not unprompted, and I wouldn't have considered any part of him soft, but now the sadness on his face was clear. Each edge was a little softer.

"I would say that's a lie because I know for a fact that you have a ton of friends. There had to have been over a hundred people at your party. And what about your parents?"

"My parents only care about me if I'm doing what they want, and all those other people know is my name, know that I have money, and that's about it."

"You don't have a best friend?"

"Sort of, but honestly, he probably only knows my name and that I'm rich, too."

I reached up, running a hand down his jaw, not liking the way my heart twisted at his sadness. "That seems ridiculous that he wouldn't know more."

"I prefer people not to know more."

"Why? It makes you so much more likable."

He smiled, my hand still on his face as I slid it around to the back of his neck, pulling him down to kiss me.

He listened, his lips pressing softly to mine as I leaned into him. We stayed like that before he groaned and pulled back.

"Dammit," Chase said, walking past me to the table and

messing with the notepad. He started writing something, but from where I was, I couldn't see what it said. "I told you, Scout, it's what *you* bring out in people. Getting to know me doesn't make me likable to anyone. It's why hundreds of people have hung around me for years and don't like me. The thing that makes me more likable is you. And *you* make a person want to give you everything in the fucking world."

I waited until he straightened and then looked around at the paper, reading the note he'd just written out loud. "Another down payment. Text the total. You'll get the rest, so back off." His watch sat next to the paper. "Is that another Rolex?"

"Yes, and this one was new, so I really need to stop buying them."

"Chase, no." I handed it back to him. "I already owe you for the first one. I don't want this one, too."

"You have no idea how much is owed, Scout. This could be a down payment or the entire amount. I'm guessing they will stop here first. And I mean first before they stop by the garage or the apartments. So we can leave the watch to keep them away or leave nothing and wait for them to stop by."

I looked up into dark hazel eyes that were glued to me. He was unwavering, gripping my arm and seemed one step away from running out the door with me. I guess it wouldn't be the first time.

"How am I supposed to pay my debt to you? I can only take so much from my paychecks, and it's not like I can dip into the garage's funds without everyone knowing."

"I have plenty of money, Scout. I am not hurting for anything. There's no reason to rush on ever paying me back. Although, I would love a new watch. *Again,*" he said, smirking. "There's no rush, no interest, and no threat to you or your friends. Would you rather pay me back or these guys?"

"You."

"Then come on. I would prefer to get you out of here, and you hit me when I threw you over my shoulder last time, so I can't do that again."

"Maybe because people usually don't like to be tossed around."

He laughed, holding open the front door for me as I walked out.

"Really? I've found that some people like it in the right setting. In my car, a bedroom, possibly a random hotel room."

"Chase?"

"Yes?"

"I'm taking you home, and I don't want to hear one more word."

"Well, if you're going to be so forward and demand to take me home, then you won't hear a word from me."

"I'm taking you to *your* home, and I still don't want to hear a word."

We barely spoke during the ride to his apartments besides him giving me directions. I tried to ignore exactly how expensive of a place to live it was and didn't say anything when we pulled up.

I parked at the curb as he leaned over. "Are you about to ghost me again?"

"Probably."

"Then I guess I'll just have to hunt you down again. Maybe force you in a car with me for a while. Maybe throw you over my shoulder and head to the nearest motel." He leaned in, kissing me fast before I could protest.

"Bye, Hellcat."

"Bye, rich boy."

SEVENTEEN
SCOUT

I DROPPED over the back of Fox's couch, watching as he threw on a hoodie, before coming over to hit my feet that were still kicked up in the air.

"Are you sure you girls don't want to come out with us?"

"We want to drink and watch movies without you guys bothering us," I said, kicking at him again. He grabbed my leg, twisting it until I had to flip over and shuffle away. "And this is exactly why we don't need you guys here," I shrieked as he laughed.

The rest of the guys filed in, quickly talking shit about each other before turning around and walking back out.

Quinn sighed and leaned back. "I've been dying for a girls' night."

"I still vote that we go to a once a week schedule," I said.

"With how Ransom's acting, I'm voting yes."

"Yeah, he's been acting weird. What's up with him?" I asked.

"I have no idea, and he won't tell me. He just walks around muttering and then goes for a drive."

"I tried to talk to him, but he said it would have to wait and never brought it up again," I said.

"I don't know," Quinn said. "Hopefully a break from me tonight helps because it's really getting annoying."

"I can try to talk to him again."

She only nodded. "What about you? Are you doing okay since Jesse?"

"I've been alright," I said, trying not to give any sign that I might be more than alright.

Ash smiled. "Does that mean you might be ready to date? I'm dying to set you up with someone."

I wasn't going to ask at first, but curiosity got the best of me, wondering if she would say Chase.

"Who?"

"I don't know. We will go out and find some hot, racer guy. Holt is swarming with them. We could set up with a coffee in the lobby and probably have you a date before we were even finished."

"As much fun as it sounds to sit around looking at all the hot racers, I know most of the people at Holt already and I can't say any of them are on the top contenders' list exactly. Considering most of them are already in relationships, or 15 or more years older than me, the pickings get slim fast."

She waved me off. "We can find someone. I think you should at least go on a date with somebody new. It's not like Jesse ever wanted to take you out anywhere fun, so why don't you find a guy who will? Even if he's not somebody you want to date, you might as well have fun and get yourself an orgasm."

They all burst out laughing, and I did too. When Quinn came around, girls' night quickly became something I looked forward to. After spending years being the only girl around, it was nice to finally have a group of girls to hang out with. Now Ash and

Carly were here and the time I got to spend with them were some of the best nights of my life.

Ash poured more drinks as we talked. Everything from work to relationships to any sliver of gossip that someone heard. I leaned back into the couch, enjoying listening to them all, just as much as I enjoyed chiming in.

A little over an hour later, the door flung open, a line of smiling, laughing men filing in before heading to the kitchen.

My heart dropped when Chase walked in behind Fox, laughing along with them as Ransom said something.

I was expecting to have more time avoiding him in person, but here he was, looking at me with that knowing smirk and hanging out with the guys.

"What are you guys doing back?" Quinn asked.

Kye hopped over the back of the couch next to me, a drink in his hand. "Sheriff has everyone out tonight, so it wasn't worth it."

"So you all came to crash our girls' night? Who said you were invited?" Ash said, joking with them. The guys crashed plenty of girls' nights, and all it did was give us an excuse to have another one. Fox came around, setting down his drink and spreading out on the floor next to her.

"So you didn't miss me at all? My poor heart."

The crew all chimed in, everyone bickering back and forth about how much anyone was missed. Chase sat down next to me, ignoring me completely as he looked at his phone.

CHASE

I don't even have to ask if you missed me.

SCOUT

Because you already know I didn't?

CHASE

Because I could see it all over your face when I walked in

SCOUT

Are you sure you didn't misread my glare?

CHASE

No. I think I'm getting the hang of it. Avoiding me because you're too turned on by what happened or too mad about what happened?

Every time I thought back to what happened at the motel, heat rushed over me. Even looking at him now, all I could picture was him getting off as he looked at me. Heavy eyes met mine, and I sunk back further into the couch.

Then I remembered what came after that, and how nice he had been to me at my old house. Not only nice, but sweet and supportive. For how much I didn't like the rich, asshole guy that he could be, I was surprised to find other parts of him weren't bad.

Not even a little.

SCOUT

Neither. Maybe I'm thinking of someone else.

He laughed quietly next to me, the rest of the crew bickering about movies now.

CHASE

Yeah, that's why you just looked at me with that hot glare. Want to watch me get off again? Or maybe this time you want to join in?

My thighs tightened, the heat shooting to my core, and I knew I was already getting wet. I couldn't believe how much the thought of it was already turning me on.

CHASE

Do you want to sneak out of here and let me taste you? I could put you up against that hallway and get you off on my mouth again.

SCOUT

No, I want to watch this movie.

Is this honestly what you're thinking about?

CHASE

Constantly. You taste so fucking good. I'm a starving man over here.

I knew my lips parted, mostly from the shock that this was what he was thinking about me, and that he was so open to saying it.

CHASE

Are you rethinking the hallway yet?

SCOUT

We are not doing anything tonight.

CHASE

Fine, my hands won't touch you at all tonight...unless you request it

SCOUT

Thank you.

CHASE

Should I also stop texting you my dirty thoughts?

I read the text and set my phone back down, trying to concentrate on the movie again, and not think about the disappointment of him not touching me. It was my choice, of course, but it didn't mean I wasn't disappointed in it not happening.

But I knew it couldn't. Not really.

Whatever happened with Chase would be short-lived, and

then being forced to hang around each other would just be awkward.

> **SCOUT**
> Can you at least not send them now?

CHASE
Why? Getting too turned on?

> **SCOUT**
> Maybe I'm just trying to concentrate on the movie.

CHASE
I think the movie is boring. Want to give me a tour of your apartment?

> **SCOUT**
> You are terrible.

CHASE
That's not what you were saying the other night.

I rolled my eyes and made a dramatic show of throwing my phone down while looking right at him.

He only smiled and kept his eyes on the TV.

"Hey, Chase," Ash said. "Are you coming to the races with us tomorrow?"

"Yeah, I was planning on it."

"Are you bringing anyone with you?" Ash asked. It wasn't that Ash was wondering on my account. She didn't know anything had gone on between us. It was just that Ash liked to know everything about everyone's love life, and the moment she thought she could help set someone up, she would.

Chase's hand twitched, but he didn't give any other indication that the question bothered him. "I wasn't planning on it. Should I be?"

She shook her head. "No, not if you weren't planning on it. I was just checking."

"Why?" I asked, keeping my tone as neutral as possible.

She gave a sly smile, but shrugged. "No reason, just asking." I wanted to ask more, but I worried that any question I had would make it seem like I was invested in Chase's love life.

And I wasn't.

My phone vibrated, Chase's name across the screen.

CHASE

Am I going to be set up?

SCOUT

It sounds like it.

CHASE

If I tell her no, is she going to listen?

SCOUT

Have you met Ash?

CHASE

Yeah, good point.

Is this going to cause a problem? I can try to figure a way out of it, if you want.

SCOUT

Why would I care? If she wants to set you up, she can.

CHASE

You don't care at all?

SCOUT

I told you, whatever happened ended the minute we left the motel room. It's fine.

CHASE

I feel like that makes this a hard no about fooling around in the hallway.

Very hard no.

I could hear the small groan escape him, but he didn't move. Instead, we watched the movie in silence, both of us holding our phones, but not texting more.

It was good. Not letting this go any further was the right thing to do, and after all the wrong choices I had made lately, I needed to make the right choice on this.

I couldn't let the crew down, and fooling around would cause us all issues when it inevitably went bad. My emotions were all over the place, and the last thing I needed was Chase hanging around with the crew, and me getting feelings for him.

It was the right decision.

If I cut it off now, I could save myself the heartache.

EIGHTEEN

CHASE

THE RACES TONIGHT were already packed as I pulled in with my new car and angled through the crowd. I was already on edge and only had one thing on my mind. More specifically, one girl who hadn't texted me back *again*.

By the time I found a place to park next to their cars, I had to text Fox, and he let me know they were walking around on the other side of the makeshift track.

A pretty blonde woman walked past me, smiling as she went, but I was only looking for red.

Red hair that felt like silk around my hand, and hazel eyes that got wide when she watched me get off, and a perfect face that couldn't hide any emotion.

Addicted might have been an understatement.

I've been chasing any feeling for months and coming up short, but now I managed to find every single emotion wrapped up in one adorable, feisty package.

I saw the crew gathered around a car, but no sign of Scout. For a minute, I wondered if she would flake out on race night just to avoid me more. If she really thought she was going to hide from me forever, she was wrong. I don't know if I could let her now.

Fox nodded to me, and Kye followed his gaze.

"Hey, I didn't know you were coming tonight," Kye said.

"He's coming with us later, too," Ransom said.

Later, where they had invited me to go out with them. I wasn't sure where we were going, but I didn't honestly care.

"You're hanging out with us later?" Scout's voice broke through the crowd, and she stepped closer to the group. My stomach flipped, and I clenched my abs, trying to make it stop.

"Yep. Mad that you're stuck with me again?"

"Oh no, not at *all*." Scout turned, rolling her eyes as she said something to Quinn that I couldn't hear, but Fox interrupted.

"Did you tell Chase about your trip yet?" Fox asked. Her eyes went wide a bit, and I realized they didn't know I went with her.

How fun.

"Trip? Where did you go?" I asked, probably overplaying the innocent act, but I didn't care. She said she didn't want anything else to happen between us, so what did it matter how I acted?

"She had a part for your car to get. Only dealerships had it and they were absolute assholes about shipping it," Ransom said. "Quinn tried for an hour before giving up. Scout ended up driving up there."

"I'm surprised she didn't demand payment or something," Fox said, messing with something on his car.

"I did find her digging in my wallet. I just assumed she was a thief."

Scout smacked my stomach. "You can assume it was an expensive trip, and I wasn't doing it out of pure kindness."

"No? And here I thought you treated all your customers with such...warmth and affection."

"Nope, that's all reserved for you," she said, trying to make light of it with a laugh, but I could see the red bloom across her cheeks and nose.

Damn right it was all reserved for me.

The need to drag her away and kiss her was getting to me. The restless ache not being soothed by anything other than her.

It had been exactly three days since we had been sitting in that motel room together, which made three days since I've had any other thought in my mind besides her coming undone underneath me. Even seeing her yesterday wasn't enough. I hadn't been able to kiss or touch her and that only made this gnawing ache worse.

The crew was talking about something to do with the races tonight, and I moved closer to Scout's side.

"I'm so glad to know that I'm the only one getting special treatment."

"You *were* the only one getting special treatment. Past tense because it is no longer happening."

My hand moved down her back, sliding over her ass. The car hid us from the crew enough that I tried not to make it too obvious, but I was caring less and less as the need to touch her grew.

I squeezed once, and she smacked at my hand. "We are in public," she hissed, as she stepped farther away.

"Does that mean we can go do these things in private?"

"It means keep a two-foot distance from me at all times."

"I can't when you are threatening me," I said.

"How am I threatening you?"

"You're implying that I was the only one getting special treatment, and now I won't be. I would like to know what other men you are taking to that motel room and making them perform dirty acts for you."

"Several. I wouldn't even be able to remember their names," she said, her lips pursed like she was fighting a smile.

I knew she was kidding, but jealousy still ripped through me.

I grabbed her arm, pulling her closer as I turned us. Hopefully, the crew would only think we were looking at the car.

"I would like to be the only guy you are demanding to cum in motel rooms. In any room, actually."

"Chase!" Ash yelled. Apparently she had been trying to get my attention because she was nearly frantic trying to wave me over.

I groaned. "This conversation isn't over."

"I think you've said plenty. You better hurry. Ash has the love of your life waiting over there."

I looked again, seeing the tall brunette girl standing next to Ash now.

"She seriously set me up?"

"Yep. I told you she would."

"What if I told you I'm not into tall brunettes in low cut tops? That I'm actually more into short redheads that bully me and race cars."

"She knows Ash. Maybe she does race cars," she said, crossing her arms with a glare.

"Doesn't matter. Do you really want me to go over there and talk to her?"

"If you want to, go ahead."

I grinned, the strain of anger in her tone giving her away. "You know, you are really bad at hiding those emotions. It's cute when you try, though."

"I'm not hiding anything."

"No? So you're not even a little mad at the thought of me going over there? Not upset at all with the idea of me being set up?"

"Nope."

"All you have to do is say what you're thinking."

Her foot tapped, her body jumping as she fidgeted. She looked ready to explode, and I was ready for it. I wanted her to admit that she might actually enjoy me turning this down and hanging around with her tonight.

"There is only one girl here that I would like to kiss again, and if she feels even a sliver of wanting to kiss me back, then I won't be going to talk to this blind date at all."

"Just like that?"

"Yeah. Just like that."

"Then fine. Don't."

The heavy weight of anxiety finally lifted off my chest. I had been hoping she would actually say it out loud, but part of me didn't think she would do it, though.

"Fine. I won't," I teased back. "It kind of sounds like we might be coming to a deal."

"What kind of deal?"

"A deal where we are exclusively taking out our sexual frustrations on each other."

She looked up at me with wide eyes, taking in my words before her hands went to her hips, the defiant stance letting her feel in charge.

"Are you trying to ask me to be exclusive in a friends with benefits type mess?"

I stepped a little closer to her, trying to remind myself that we were still in public. This would be a mess, but nothing that I couldn't handle. Plus, the thought of someone else touching her when I wanted to was infuriating.

"If that's what it takes to be the only one touching you, then yes."

"Does that same rule apply to other girls touching you?"

"My body will be exclusively yours whenever you want it."

"What about her?"

"Two rules. We are not telling the crew, there is no way they would let me hear the end of this, and two, no relationship stuff. I don't want this to get confusing."

"Fine," I said, not liking how hard my teeth gritted together. She was agreeing to exactly what I offered, but somehow I wasn't as happy about it as I hoped.

The crew motioned for us as they started to walk around. We followed for a while in silence until I finally broke us away from them, heading the opposite direction back to our cars.

"So does that mean holding hands is off limits?" I asked, not missing the way guys' eyes seemed to trail her way. How they didn't leave her as we passed. It felt like I could read their minds and hated every thought, even if I was having the same ones. My hands flexed, each ring feeling more like a brass knuckle on my hand than an accessory.

She rolled her eyes, but smiled. "You want to hold hands? In public? Doesn't that go against your rich playboy appearance?"

"It absolutely does, but I figured I could be holding your hand here and still keep up appearances in my circles." I leaned down, noticing how her shoulders straightened as I got close. "It could be one more addition to our dirty little secret, and damn, it is fucking dirty." I laughed as she shot me a glare.

"Alright, I think that's enough. Please keep in mind we are in my circle and I need to keep up my own appearances."

"A lone little wolf who likes to kick guys' asses in racing?"

The need to kiss her again was taking over my life, and I was currently weighing the risk of doing it right here.

"Could I be a lone wolf when I have several friends that I go everywhere with?"

"Probably not, but appearances don't always have to be true," I said.

I knew mine sure as hell wasn't. I woke up today looking forward to the day. I wasn't trying to get through it, besides wanting time to go faster before I could be here tonight with her. Not even that I was looking forward to after. Apparently, it was another night of the guys going out while the girls had their night, and I was invited. I was invited to go to plenty of parties, but a group of people who actually liked hanging out beyond getting trashed together was new to me.

I angled her along the line of cars, heading towards mine. I had parked next to the crew, but I came with a new car tonight and none of them were going to know it was me next to them.

"You seem in a weirdly good mood tonight. Something I should know about?" she asked.

"Not at all. Just enjoying myself and looking forward to the races."

We came around the last car, and I watched as she saw it. Her eyes went wide and mouth dropped open, silent as her pace picked up the slightest bit.

The neon green Hellcat sat next to Fox's Supra. I knew Scout's car broke down again, and had already planned on letting her race it, but the look on her face when she saw it was unmatched by any experience I've ever had giving someone a gift, and she didn't even know it would be hers yet.

"Oh my god," she said, walking over and stepping around it. "This wasn't here when we pulled in."

"No? It would be hard to miss."

"Hard to miss? It would be impossible. This is my dream car currently."

"Really? I wouldn't have guessed. You should sit in it." She had only spent an hour of our road trip talking about it. I hadn't even added to the conversation, just listened as she told me damn near every detail in it. My friend's dad owned all the car dealerships in town and was more than happy to order me one when I texted him.

She gave a harsh laugh with an eye roll. "I know you're fairly new here, rich boy, but you absolutely don't sit in people's cars uninvited."

I hid my groan at the nickname.

There were so many useless things I have learned being around my dad, but one of the more useful things was paying attention to people and their subtle actions.

I wasn't missing the way she was calling me 'rich boy' more often again instead of Chase, and now she was barely meeting my eye. For a girl who just agreed to be exclusively friends with benefits, she seemed more than happy to ignore me.

"No? Even hot girls like you? You don't think the owner would be mad to find you in the driver's seat." I pulled the driver's door open with a cocky grin, and she stomped forward, immediately slamming it shut.

"Chase, you are going to get us in a fight if the owner sees you messing with the car."

"Sit in it," I said, leaning down. "You like being bad, so do something bad."

"I like not getting my ass kicked."

I moved her around to the open driver's door and sat inside, pulling her onto my lap. She fought against me, trying to climb out as she yelled.

"I'm the only one going to be touching this ass tonight. Promise."

"Chase, I swear I'm going to kick your ass." I moved her back far enough to kiss her, pulling her legs in until I could shut the door. Every inch of windows on the car was tinted, even the front windshield was covered in a reflective tint, making it almost impossible for anyone to see us.

"Come on, Hellcat. I just want to get you off in a Hellcat. Consider it a bucket list item that I need to check off."

I pulled her back against me, grabbing her bottom lip between my teeth as she leaned into me.

It kept her occupied for two more seconds before she ripped herself away, kicking the door open and getting out.

"No, no, no. Not a chance. Get out."

"Fine," I groaned. "But I want to clarify that the only reason I am getting out is because you are up next for the races. I had them save you a spot."

"I don't have my car, so I don't know why you did that," she said, the little hint of attitude disintegrating.

I dug out the keys. The little Hellcat keychain was hard to miss.

"But you do have a car here tonight, and while I appreciate you helping to break it in a bit, that barely scratched the surface of what filthy things I need to do to you in that car so please hurry up on the racing part of the night. Also, I checked, the backseat *is* big enough."

Her mouth dropped open.

"It's yours?"

I shrugged, looking back over the car. The neon green stuck out even in the lineup of beautiful cars.

"Honestly, I only bought it because you mentioned it, so we can just call it yours. Although, I'm already down a car, so I'll need it until mine is fixed."

Her head was already shaking before I finished my sentence. "You bought a car because I mentioned it?"

"Scout, you went on for almost an hour about how much you wanted this exact car. Do you really think I bought it because you said it once in passing? I've never heard anyone talk about one car so much."

"That doesn't mean you had to go out and buy it."

"But I did, and while it doesn't have the long list of modifications that you require, since I assume that's something you would want to take care of, it is fast, and I would like to see exactly how fast, so get to it."

"Does that mean what I think it means?"

I set the keys in her hand. "Go get 'em, Hellcat."

NINETEEN

SCOUT

THE RACE WENT by in a blur, the car moving down the road so easily that I barely took a breath and it was done. My hands gripped the wheel as I pulled the car into the lineup behind the crew and parked. I was already in love with this car, and wondering how much I should fight Chase to let me drive it a little longer because I wasn't actually going to keep it.

I groaned, dropping my head onto the steering wheel.

What had I been thinking? Agreeing to keep doing *anything* with Chase was a bad choice, but agreeing to secretly fool around with him with no strings attached was a horrible idea. Not only was hiding that from the crew a ticking time bomb, but I wasn't exactly experienced in the world of friends with benefits. Could I even handle doing all of those things without falling for someone?

I looked at Chase, who leaned over Kye's engine with him as we waited for Ash to race Fox next. He was wearing jeans and a hoodie tonight, which made me laugh. A little more dressed down than the last time I saw him here. Even in regular clothes, though, I could still see the differences. The way he stood a little straighter, the confidence, the arrogance. It was all still there, even in jeans and a hoodie.

Maybe that was the reason I *could* do this, though. Chase wasn't anyone I could fall for. He wasn't the type I should end up with at all. I needed someone like us. A guy that knew cars, and racing, and the struggle of coming from nothing. I needed someone that could understand me, and I don't think that would be Chase.

He had shown over and over that he was a rich playboy type. He didn't have relationships and even admitted that he didn't even have close friends.

Elias, a guy we've all come to know at the races, came over, interrupting my thoughts.

"Hey, Scout. Everyone here tonight?"

I nodded, pointing to the crew who were all gathered around Kye's car now.

Chase met my eye, looking over Elias before turning back to Jax, who was apparently talking to him. For a second, I wondered if Chase would be jealous, but then Elias started talking about the new intake he put on his car and I knew there wouldn't be many reasons to be jealous. Most guys here thought of me as either one of the guys or their little sister. I never had a long line of men waiting to take me on dates, and the few that seemed to have any interest would run the other way when they saw who my friends were. The crew was all lovable–from the inside.

From the outside, we were heathens with an endless list of accusations and rumors about us. From running drugs, to stealing cars, to a thousand other terrible things. People liked to gossip, and we never corrected them.

Ransom always preferred the route of being scary to the world so they didn't mess with us, and all of us were on board. Better to be feared than walked all over.

It was great for business, but not as great for my dating life.

It never seemed fair. The girls might love a successful, tattooed, possibly dangerous man. On the other side of that, men did not like a short, possibly dangerous girl that came with four tattooed, scary, possibly dangerous men behind her.

Elias was still talking about the new modifications to his car, and I fell into an easy conversation with him. He was cute, closer to my age than the guys, and I always wondered if he had liked me at one point, but there was nothing there now.

Nope. Now I was one of the guys.

I could feel the frustration of my love life growing, and it was only compounded when Chase slid onto the hood of the car next to me.

"Hey," he said to Elias. "Do I know you?"

I don't know if it was that confidence or the arrogance, but Chase had a way of controlling conversations with new people. It was five words, but somehow, each one made it clear that Chase was now running the conversation.

"I don't think so," Elias said. "I'm Elias. And you?"

"Chase."

"Elias was just telling me about his car and the new mods," I said, turning back to him. "I'll have to stop over later this week, and see what you did to it."

"Yeah," he said, eyeing Chase a few more seconds before turning back to me. "That would be cool. Just text me."

I nodded, and he walked away, not looking back as Chase watched him.

"So, I might not be the *only* one you give that special treatment to after all."

"Yeah, that's exactly what that conversation was. We were right in the middle of sexual negotiations before you rudely interrupted."

"I know you're kidding, but I'm also ready to go punch him."

"He was telling me about his new car and the mods. I promise, as much as I hate to admit it, that men here are not waiting around to ask me into back seats." I didn't miss the smirk on his face. "Besides you, apparently."

"I might be the only one actually asking, but I promise, I'm not the only one *wanting* to ask."

"I think you are overestimating how men think about me. I'm one of the guys, not a girl they might actually like."

"What does that mean?"

I shrugged. "I don't know. Sometimes I hate being 'one of the guys.' We have come to race night for what feels like most of my life. The guys are 4 years older than me, so as soon as we could get rides out here, we came. We all lived on that street together. If one of us had a car, everyone did. Then when they got cars, we never missed a night. Ten years of my life, and every time I'm just one of the guys."

"And that's bad?" He asked, the question genuine.

"It is when you get crushes. When you like one of them and they don't see you as anything more than a little sister or 'one of the guys.' Sometimes I just want to scream that those things aren't the only thing about me. That I do like this stuff, but I'm also a girl, and I like being treated like a girl."

He laughed, and I scowled. "Wow, thanks for laughing at me. Do you know the first time I wore a dress to school I was made fun of by the guy I liked? And you know what? That's who you remind me of right now."

"I remind you of a crush you had? Interesting." His hand moved along the car until it was moving up my shirt to my lower back. "I like to know that I actually am your type."

"You know what? Forget it. There's no point in talking to you about this."

I went to get up, but he grabbed my waist, pulling me back against the car next to him.

"I was laughing because I don't think you understand the role you are playing in all of this happening to you."

"Oh, so it's my fault."

"Not exactly, but who you are when you walk around here is different from who you are when you're calm and safe, with the crew at home or at the garage."

"Okay, what does *that* mean?"

"You walk around here like a queen, Scout. Strong and head held high. I mean, fuck, the night we met you looked ready to fist fight me without a second thought. It was obviously adorable, but also intimidating. There was no part of you that worried about going toe to toe with me. And then, your army was quick to your side. I think most men are going to run from that. Your edges are not soft here. Your guard is up and you are ready for a challenge, not a date. And as for one of the guys, I would assume that they are either intimidated, scared of your army of brothers, or worried you aren't interested."

"I feel like this is a long-winded speech all to tell me that I'm great, but that I am one of the guys, and it's my fault."

"No, I just think you need to see yourself in your environment. And it's not a fault, it's who you want to be. When we're hanging out at the apartments or garage, you aren't on guard. You are *mostly* all sweet, funny, and relaxed, at least to everyone else. You know you are safe and it shows. Men would approach that girl in seconds, and I doubt you would like that here at the races. This isn't a problem of you being feminine enough or not. This is a girl who is determined to race and win when she's here, not worry about men hitting on her. It's okay to be like that, but if you wanted to come get a date, you could."

"And what about the guy I liked who made fun of me in my dress all those years ago?"

Chase shrugged. "You're talking about a young high school boy with a pretty girl in front of him, I highly doubt you were the only girl he fumbled a chance on."

"Hmm."

"Also, do you know that every single one of your brothers has told me to stay away from you? I know that I'm not good enough in their eyes, but I'm assuming they give those threats to most men who have an interest in you."

"Which is just rude."

"Sure, but it also sorts out the ones who are going to do anything for you. Which, I assume, after being around four men who would die for you, you would be looking for that sort of thing in a man."

I smirked, looking over at the crew, who were circled around talking to a few other people that were racing tonight. "It wasn't exactly something I had on a checklist for someone to date, but yeah, I guess something like that would be preferred, although I'm not out trying to get someone killed. Interesting how kind and smart you are when you want to be."

"It can be our secret."

"Why? You're cocky and rude and quiet with everyone. Why not act this way?"

"The same reason you are not sweet and soft to everyone. I don't want to be."

"I guess you are a bit nicer when you're hanging out with the crew."

"A bit? Compare that side of me to the one you met at my party. I'm a hell of a lot nicer."

"Why?"

"The exact reason I've been explaining to you. We are different people in different environments sometimes. It can be a good thing like it is for you or a bad thing like it is for me."

"You know," I said, waiting as his hazel eyes turned back to me. "You're pretty easy to get along with when you're not being a cocky rich boy."

He laughed, the low sound making a heat flood through me. "Really? I guess I could say the same to you when you're not running around biting ankles."

I didn't even respond, just reached over and pushed until he was sliding off the car.

"I'm going to start kicking your ankles every time you say that name."

"Then I'm going to start buying you something every time you call me a rich boy," he said, coming up in front of me.

"I feel like you think that's a threat, but telling someone you are going to buy them gifts really isn't as mean as you seem to think it is."

I watched as his shoulders straightened and hands flexed. He stepped closer, putting his hands on my knees and spreading my legs until he could step between them.

"I just bought you a car, and had a conversation where I was apparently not a dick, so I think I at least deserve more attention than him."

"I will give you that. Is he still looking?"

Chases nodded, his eyes darkening as a small smirk came across his lips. "You kind of look like you want to kiss me," he said.

"I kind of look that way because I kind of do, but I can't."

As if the world wanted to remind me one more time that this was a bad idea, and I shouldn't have agreed, the crew came over.

"What would you guys think about getting out of here and going to grab something to eat all together instead tonight?" Fox asked.

Ash smiled. "I think that's a great idea." She came up, throwing an arm around Chase. "You disappeared. Your date already left."

He laughed and started walking to Fox's car with her. "I think I'll survive. Not my type, anyway."

"Really? Alright then, you're going to have to tell me your type, so next time you at least talk to the girl."

"Or you could give me a hundred question questionnaire," Jax said. "Really, you should just do a full interview."

"That's not a terrible idea. There has to be some sort of online quiz."

Chase groaned, and she laughed. "Or you can let me stay single and I'll let you know if I suddenly need a girlfriend."

"Fine, I guess that's fair," Ash said, shaking her head. "Are you coming with us?"

He smirked as he threw an arm around her and looked at me. "Yeah, I think I'll survive a few more hours with you guys."

"We will see about that. Come on. I'm starving and we need to get to the diner before I faint," Ash said.

I rolled my eyes, but my growling stomach seemed to agree.

Chase smiled, falling back until he was walking next to the guys, but I didn't miss when his eyes met mine.

Messy feelings and complicated agreement aside, I was already looking forward to whatever plans he had for his tongue tonight.

TWENTY

SCOUT

TWENTY MINUTES LATER, we walked into the diner, the entire crew already in such a good mood and I was feeling it, too.

Chase didn't hesitate to sit down next to me, his confidence shining through on everything he did, including this, and leaving no one to question him.

We ordered, neither of us saying a word to each other, and I was currently preferring it that way. My mind was still going over what he wanted to do and my own surprise at how much I wanted it to happen. Or at least wanted to know if it would happen.

His arm brushed against mine and I jumped, remembering what he said about the car, and needing to break it in before I leaned in.

"Did you mean what you said about the filthy things in the car?" I whispered as everyone's attention turned to Jax and a problem he was having with his car.

Chase gave a sharp nod, the only indication that he heard me as he laughed along with everyone.

Then I felt it, a large, warm hand moving along my thigh under the table, the calm look on his face making it appear like nothing was happening. Fingers trailed up my leg before moving back down, the slow movement sending a line of heat down my spine to my core.

He repeated the movement, squeezing my thigh once before his hand fell away.

The cocky grin on his face made me angry and excited. How did he manage to do these things without anyone noticing?

I figured I might as well try it, too. I moved my hand to his leg, brushing up his thigh, until I felt the rigidness of his cock.

The crew talked around us, and I leaned in, keeping a safe distance. A distance I would keep with any of them.

"Are you that turned on just from touching my thigh?"

"Do you think I would be for someone else here? And if you say yes, I will drag you to the bathroom in front of everyone and make sure it's clear what we will be doing."

"Shhh," I said, trying to keep my face calm as I looked around. The crew was not listening at all, lost in their own conversations. "You can't say things like that."

"And you can't accuse me of getting hard touching you while I'm thinking of someone else." He leaned in a little farther. "And just to make it clear, that's all for you. There will be no more comparing me to him, because I know that pretty little head is trying to."

He wasn't wrong. I was on full alert now, trying to see if there was any sign he was like Jesse in any way. So far, though, I couldn't see any comparison.

"Even if you come out on top?"

His hand flexed on my thigh. "I could be on top or bottom. Both have their advantages."

I moved my hand a little harder against him, liking the way

the calm exterior broke the smallest amount as he leaned back, closing his eyes for only a second before sitting back up.

I finally let my hand drop when we ordered, talking to the crew and getting our food. I brushed my hand over his thigh again, moving it along his length one more time.

"Alright," he said, pushing his chair back. "I think I'm going to head out."

The crew all nodded, apparently in agreement, as they gathered up their things and got up.

"Hey wait, do I get to drive the Hellcat?" I asked, trying to sound more interested in the car than him. But that was hard to do when he stretched, the hoodie moving up to show off a sliver of abs and waist. My face flushed, embarrassment and heat covering me when I remembered I had basically licked that part of him.

"You're trying to be all sweet and use me for my car now, aren't you?"

Fox laughed. "You bought her dream car. She's suddenly going to be a little angel, so she gets to drive it all the time."

The crew laughed, and I smiled. At least they knew me well enough to know it was my dream car, so there would be no question of why I was suddenly so interested in it.

Or more accurately, Chase's plans for what we were going to do *in* it.

"Fine, *Hellcat*. I'll let you drive it to the apartments, and then I will take it home."

"Fine, but just for the ankle biter comment, I'm taking the long way there."

He winked as the crew walked out.

"We are not taking the long way because I am tired and would like to get to my bed as fast as possible," Quinn said. Carly and Ash quickly agreed.

"Lucky for you girls, we can accommodate that request," Ransom said, pulling Quinn close to his side.

Something pulled at my heart. The care and love Ransom had for Quinn, the love they all had for the girls, filling me with a stab of jealousy. Sometimes, I just wanted to know what that felt like. There seemed to be no end to what they would do for each other, and I wasn't sure how they came to love each other so unconditionally. With Jesse, there were always conditions to how much he cared, or seemed to love me each day. There was a limit to what he would do for me, depending on the day.

Chase fell behind everyone, including me, until his hand moved to my lower back, a strange gesture that I was starting to find comfort in.

"You do know that we are making a stop, right?"

"Really? For what?"

He leaned down, his lips against my ear. "So I can get you off with my mouth and taste you on my lips all fucking night."

Pleasure rolled through me, and for a second I worried that my legs might give out. Luckily, I made it to the car, and slid into the driver's seat without an incident.

The car roared to life, the engine rumbling as Chase said something to the guys before getting in.

"Ready?" I asked, the calm tone of my voice not matching my stomach that was currently flipping around.

"I've been ready for two hours. Please show me how fast you can drive."

I didn't hesitate to listen, tearing out of the parking lot and taking a right as the rest of the crew went left. They were going back to the apartments. I was heading into the hills. Nervous energy filled me to the point even shifting through the gears wasn't enough to calm me. The car sped up with ease, pushing over 100 before I realized it. Chase didn't seem to mind, so I hit the gas, pushing the car as both of us were quiet.

I slowed as I hit the curves, gasping hard as Chase leaned over, his lips finding the side of my neck as his hand wrapped around it, holding me in place as teeth and lips moved up to my ear. Then his hand slid down, moving between my thighs.

"What are you doing? That makes it a little hard to focus on driving."

"I trust that you can figure it out. I thought we would be pulled over by now. I didn't want to wait any longer."

His tongue ran up my neck as I pulled off the side of the road with a small moan. The overlook at the top of the hill was just big enough to park the car, and before I did, Chase was moving to the backseat.

"I told you the backseat was big enough. Get your ass back here."

I was already climbing back, straddling him as his lips found mine in the dark.

My hands slipped under his hoodie, moving over his stomach and up to his chest. The frantic feeling that I needed to touch every inch of him was almost overwhelming. At least I wasn't alone. His hands roamed over me at a fevered pace until they slipped under my shirt, cupping my breasts with a groan.

"Lay back, these need off," he said, as his hands slid down to the waistband of my leggings.

He laid me over the console, pulling me back until I was near the edge before leaning down and kissing along my hip.

"I want to hear how bad you want me to get you off."

"What do you mean? Of course, I want you to get me off. Do you think I would be in this position if I didn't?"

He laughed against me, the vibration sending a bolt of heat to my core.

"That's almost convincing enough, but I think you can do better."

He kissed along my hip, moving down until his tongue

pressed against my clit. The sudden contact made my hips buck up with a gasp, but then he broke away.

"That's all you get until I'm completely clear about what you want me to do."

"Chase," I groaned, trying to reach for him, but he sat up.

"What, baby?"

"I like what you did at the motel. I want you to get me off with your mouth again."

"That's a little better." His finger pushed against my entrance as his mouth moved over my clit again. The two combined made my pussy tighten, the aching need to come growing painful.

He teased me, each swipe of his tongue making me want more until I was nearly crawling off the console.

"Chase, *please* stop teasing me."

"Then make me stop," he said, going right back to what he was doing.

"How am I supposed to make you stop?"

He pulled back with a groan, his fingers still pushing harder against me and I tried to move down onto them more.

"Don't fucking ask, Scout. I'm already between your legs and will spend hours here teasing you. When you want more, demand it."

"How?"

He grabbed my hands as he leaned back down to me, forcing both hands into his hair and curling my fingers into it.

As though I wasn't turned on enough, this nearly sent me over the edge.

He put his fingers back at my entrance, his tongue going back to the lighter pressure that was breaking me. One hand was still over mine and he pushed on it.

"Oh," I finally said, realizing what was happening. "Are you sure?"

"Demand whatever you want. You fucking deserve it and I love it."

Heat pooled and as his tongue moved down further to my entrance and back up, my orgasm built. I needed more, and I needed it now.

I curled my fingers back into his hair and pulled his head harder between my legs. The change was immediate, his fingers pushing into me hard as his mouth moved harder and faster over my clit.

A moan slipped from my lips, filling the car with my cries. I pulled him harder against me, moving my hips as white stars filled my eyes and my fingers tightened in his hair. Heat burned through me, and the pleasure felt endless as he continued through my orgasm. The world spun as my head fell back onto his hoodie that he so carefully left on the shifter.

My chest heaved as I finally let him go.

"Wow," Chase said, pulling me back onto his lap. "That was even better the second time. You taking control like that is *hot*."

He kissed me hard, the taste of me still on his lips somehow turning me on all over again.

"I thought the first time might have been a fluke. I didn't realize I liked that so much."

"I'm glad you enjoyed yourself. If you like it so much, I'd like to be clear in saying you can have that anytime and anywhere you want."

"The time," I said, wondering how long we had been parked there. "We should head back. They might start to notice how long I've been gone now."

"I currently don't care. And I'm basically a lawyer. Do you think I can't lie on the spot?"

Maybe it was my emotions getting too out of control, but I was suddenly worrying about *why* he was doing this.

"Did you want Jesse and I to break up because you wanted to sleep with me?"

He pulled back fast. "Excuse me?"

"I didn't know if you were hoping for this. You were kind of a jerk about it at your party, and you have seemed like you wanted us to break up since the moment you found out we were together."

"You think I'm such an ass that I would purposefully break you and your boyfriend up just to sleep with you? If I'm such an asshole, why wouldn't I have just slept with you before you broke up?"

"I mean, you did seem to want to kiss me at that point. I assume if I made that an option, you would have slept with me."

"I guess, yeah, but it shouldn't be an issue that I'm attracted to you. I'm not a terrible person because I thought you deserved better. Hell, you knew you deserved better. For one second of my damn life, I thought you were actually starting to think I was a decent person."

"No, I don't think you're terrible. I just—" I paused. "I don't know what to think."

"You *should* think that while I may be an ass, I at least saw your worth from the second I met you."

"It's just that Jesse was so good at getting into my head, and now I feel like I'm on guard all the time. I'm…I'm just confused."

"Well, there's nothing else to say then. If you really think I broke you up with your shitty boyfriend, I can just assume that you think I'm worse than him. And if you think he deserved even a second of your time, then there is nothing I can say at this point to convince you otherwise."

I was quiet, trying to sort through every emotion that rushed through me. It had been a dumb question, one that I already knew was stupid the moment it came out. Chase was right. If he was so determined to have sex with me that he helped break Jesse and me up, then he would already be trying to sleep with me, not giving me orgasms and expecting nothing in return.

"I think I get too in my head sometimes, and I'm not sure what to believe."

"Drive to the apartments," he said, not looking at me.

"That's it?"

"That's it. Go. I won't be pushing this any further when you feel that confused."

"Chase, I —"

"*I* would like my car back, and there is no point trying to navigate this 'friendship' if you think I have some evil fucking plan behind it. Drive to the apartments so I can drop you off."

I pulled out, quiet as I headed back to the apartment. I wasn't even sure what to say. Even if it wasn't right of me to say, I couldn't hold it in. I couldn't hold anything in.

He still didn't say anything as I parked out front of our building, or when he came over and opened my door, or even when I got out.

Finally, I stepped back and out of his way.

"Goodnight, *Hellcat,*" he said, the nickname more like a curse than a term of affection tonight. I stared at the collar of his hoodie, the same one I had just had my hands under, as he got in the car.

"Goodnight," I whispered, watching as the door shut and he pulled away.

A wave of longing washed over me, wishing that I could let myself invite him up to stay the night instead of watching him go.

TWENTY-ONE
CHASE

ONCE AGAIN, Scout was ignoring me. I texted her twice this week, and got nothing in return.

It wasn't even on me to apologize, yet I was texting her asking for car updates, like when we were finishing my car.

And she was ignoring me.

For six damn days.

I wanted to be drunk, stoned, and maybe start a fight. I wanted a raging party with people who wanted my attention.

I wanted something that would make me forget about the girl who didn't want me.

It shouldn't even feel like this. I shouldn't be this pissed off that my brand new friends-with-benefits said those things. I should only be in it to get laid, and now here I was about to show up at the garage again.

I picked up a joint, lighting it as I paced back and forth. Whatever was uncoiling inside me was leaving me ready to spring, and I hated it.

There were too many emotions when I was used to having none.

All I needed was one deep inhale, and then maybe a second before I could remember to not worry about Scout.

The smoke went to my head immediately, the light, easy feeling moving through my veins like fire. The burning calm finally subsided after a few seconds until I could take a deep breath.

It would probably be better to take a night off of all these bullshit emotions and worry anyway. Maybe it would help reset whatever hole I had fallen into, and get me back to my normal life.

The one that I hated.

The life where I got drunk, and high, and tried to feel anything.

Now I felt everything, and I was ready to go back.

So I would.

I WAS TOO DRUNK.

I couldn't remember if I drove my car here.

And if I didn't drive my car, I couldn't for the life of me find a memory of how I did get here.

I pushed through the crowd, pulling out my phone and finding Scout's name.

CHASE

I'm pretty mad at you

I had texted her four times now and I knew it was getting desperate.

I thought of her back in her apartment, the idea that Jesse could be there making me grab another beer. Someone yelled about shots and I reached out, thrilled when one was put in my hand.

It didn't matter. I couldn't drink until I blacked out and Scout seemed to be the only coherent thought I had.

I sat back on a couch, letting my head roll back as I closed my eyes. The girl next to me said something in my ear and my hazy brain thought I could hear Scout's voice. I couldn't even figure out what she was saying, but when it sounded like Scout, it didn't matter.

Then my phone buzzed, my heart racing at her name.

SCOUT

Why do you think I haven't responded?

CHASE

So you're ignoring me because you're what? Scared of me because Im mad?

SCOUT

No, I just don't know what to say to make up for what I said. This is usually something I would go talk to the girls about and I can't so...

CHASE

Then talk to me.

SCOUT

That's not the same.

CHASE

I know but it sounds like your only option unless you are ready to come clean about what happened.

Nothing came through for five minutes as I watched my phone.

SCOUT

I'm just not sure how to apologize. I didn't mean to sound like such a jerk. I don't know if I'm good at this friends with benefits thing if I'm going to get so far in my head about things.

Why did you agree to do this with me?

CHASE

Because I like you and it's all I have to offer. You're not wrong. I'm an asshole. I just don't want to be one to you.

I'm not out to get you. And I doubt I could ruin a good relationship just by coming around so I had nothing to do with you and Jesse breaking up.

And we've barely touched on the benefits of this friendship so you can't judge it yet.

SCOUT

I guess that's all true. I wasn't trying to blame you for us breaking up, if anything I should thank you for helping. I guess I just don't know what to believe about people, and I'm a little nervous about trusting anyone, even myself, anymore.

Where are you?

The words on the screen were becoming a blurry mess as I tried to type.

CHASE

I'm at a party wondering if you went back to Jesse because you realized I'm an asshole. I'm not even dating you and I'm more of a mess at losing you than that prick. And fine, don't pick me, but you sure as hell shouldn't pick him either.

SCOUT
Are you drunk?

CHASE
A bit

SCOUT
Are you driving?

CHASE
I'm about 90% sure my car is at home so no?

SCOUT
Are you serious? How are you getting home?

CHASE
I don't know, maybe walk? Maybe sleep on the roof. We will see.

SCOUT
I wish you wouldn't have told me that. Send me your location.

CHASE
Are you coming to a party?

I smiled, wondering if she would come right in and sit on my lap.

SCOUT
I'm coming to get you

I sent her my location, and then waited. I had expected a text back, but there was nothing. It wouldn't be hard to leave me here. It wouldn't be hard to never talk to me again. I was putting all my hope into one girl, maybe seeing that I wasn't just a useless rich boy. That I wasn't always an asshole.

Because for once, I really wanted someone to see past that.

At some point, I think I fell asleep, but when my eyes cracked open again, Scout was in front of me. Angry with her hands on her hips as she looked me over.

"This is ridiculous, even for you."

I pushed off the couch, already groaning. "What do you mean? I'm obviously doing a *great* job showing you that I'm not an asshole."

She gave a harsh laugh. "Yeah, a great job. Come on, I was in bed and I'm exhausted."

I suddenly couldn't remember why I thought this was a good idea. Did I think this was going to help my case?

Then again, I wasn't actually expecting her to even text me back, let alone come get me.

"You came to get me."

"Yes."

"Why?"

She shrugged as she pulled out onto the main road. "I don't like worrying about my friends. I would rather know you were safe than worry all night."

"Are you bringing me home?"

"I'm just bringing you back with me."

"Awww," I said, trying to sit up straighter. "You want me to go home with you?"

"Can we not make this out to be a big thing? I just want to make sure you're okay, but I also like my bed."

"You might like my bed."

"I doubt it."

My drunken thoughts took off. I had been thinking she should be the one that's sorry because I was mad, but I quickly flipped the table on that. Now she should be mad, and I should be apologizing.

Scout helped me up the steps. I thought I was fine, but the curse word at every other step was making me rethink that.

"Can you please be quiet?" She hissed. "I wasn't trying to make this a walking advertisement for you coming to my apartment drunk."

By the time we made it upstairs and she dumped me onto the couch, I could barely think straight, let alone walk straight.

"Goodnight, Chase," she said, the unfriendly tone matching the slamming door.

I groaned as I rolled over, waiting as I heard her shuffle out into the bathroom and slam her bedroom door again.

"Scout," I yelled.

"Go to sleep," she hissed through the shut door.

I didn't want to be out here, and I tried telling myself it was because I didn't want *her* alone, but I was pretty sure it was me who didn't want to be alone.

I stumbled through the dark, reaching for my phone and dropping it in the darkroom.

"Shit."

"Chase, what are you doing?"

By the time I finally reached the bedroom door and pushed inside, I was more than ready to lie down again, the spinning room moving faster and faster.

I fell hard into the bed, bouncing her against me.

"What are you doing in here?"

"Coming to stay with you. You brought me to your apartment. I assumed you didn't want to be alone as much as I don't."

I rolled over, wrapping an arm around her, pleasantly surprised when she didn't jump away from me.

"What are you doing, Chase? You aren't seriously trying to sleep with me right now, are you?"

"I'm trying to sleep *next* to you. Big difference." I pulled her harder against me, her ass uncomfortably close to my dick, but I made my drunken thoughts shut that down. "Go to sleep, you perfect human. I'll try to fix it all tomorrow."

"What's with the weird compliment?"

My head spun again as I shifted against her. "I don't remember what I said."

"You called me —"

"Shh," I said, leaning up to kiss her neck. There was no way I was going to be able to have a conversation with her that wouldn't mess things up more. "Let's sleep."

"Scout,"

"Hmm,"

"Thank you."

IT WAS DAYLIGHT WHEN I WOKE, BUT I DIDN'T CARE WHAT TIME it was. The steady rain outside giving enough darkness to not wake me up completely.

I slid out of bed, careful not to wake Scout as I went to find water and mouthwash. A few minutes later, I went back to the bedroom. I could see her roll over. Her arm flopping onto where I would have been.

Her head popped up. "Chase?"

"Right here and glad you remembered it was me next to you."

She groaned, pulling the pillow over her head. "I was actually only hoping that you left."

"No," I said, laying down and moving against her. "I just went to brush my teeth so you could stand to be in the same room as me. And don't even lie. I was drunk, but I clearly remember you coming to get me."

"You do still smell like a case of beer," she said from under the pillow.

"I'll go shower shortly." I smiled as I pulled the pillow away, moving it under her head again.

"How about now? As you can imagine, waking up to that smell does not bring back good memories."

The weight of her words hit me as I remembered the house and all the old beer cans around. "Shit, Scout, I'm sorry." I got up, pulling off my shirt. "I haven't been drinking like that. It was just a bad night."

"Yeah, whatever, just go please."

She turned over, her eyes going wide as she noticed my shirt off and watching as I pulled off my pants.

"What are you doing?"

"Showering?"

"Here? I thought you would go home!"

My smile grew. "I have no car. I left it…somewhere."

"I'm sure you have a car service that can manage to help." And then she mumbled something about spoiled rich kids.

"There is, but I would much rather stay here for a while. Who wants to travel when they are hung over?"

"Maybe I'm mad at you now."

"As you should be, *but* you didn't want to leave me there last night, so no matter how mad you are, you must like me by now."

"No, that's not what happened. I just didn't want you to get hurt."

"It's alright, Hellcat. I like you too. Now I'll shower, wash these clothes, and repay the favor today. Decide what you want to eat and I'll order it when I'm out."

"Chase, no you just need to—"

I shut the bathroom door, stripping down and getting a shower. I could only imagine she was cursing me out on the other side, but there was no way I was going to let her take care of me like that and not make up for it. I've been going on hoping that I was better than Jesse, but here I was ruining any progress I made on that being true.

By the time I got out, she was asleep again. It was noon, but I don't know that we really slept and with the rain, I didn't think we were leaving.

Scout groaned. "You're still here?"

"Do you think I was showering and running out?"

She rolled over, her eyes cracking open. "You don't have pants on."

"I have boxers on? I threw my clothes in the wash because they smelled and who wants to have a day in bed while wearing jeans?"

"A day in bed? For the last time, you're not staying."

"I just ordered like two hundred dollars' worth of food, so I'm at least staying for that."

Her mouth dropped. "You what?"

"You heard me. I am hungry."

"Two hundred dollars' worth of hungry?"

I smiled harder. "Well, this way," I said, sliding into bed next to her. "We can stay in bed all weekend and not even have to leave to find food."

"Now you're trying to stay all weekend? I thought you didn't even want to be friends anymore, let alone hang around with me for days."

"Not trying too. I am staying. I had a bad night and would prefer being here than home alone, and you have been avoiding me when you didn't need to be. And now this way, I won't make you exhaust yourself chasing after me all weekend and just stay here to keep you company."

"Me chasing you?"

"You did come get me."

"Because I was worried about you."

I laid down next to her, staring up at the ceiling.

"I might not deserve that much."

"You do, and you deserve more than me accusing you of

having bad intentions. You've never been anything but nice to me. Besides the ankle-biter comments, of course."

I laughed. "So, does that mean I can stay?"

"Yeah, I would actually like that."

I stayed there, quiet as a calm washed over me. I wasn't sure what to do with someone who worried about me so much they would come in the middle of the night to get me, but I didn't think being apart from her wasn't going to be an option.

TWENTY-TWO

SCOUT

NIGHT FELL, but I was getting more restless. I didn't want
Chase to leave me alone, but I didn't think he should stay any
longer. Something was changing. The calm he brought into my
life helped me not feel as bad about everything that happened
with Jesse and helped me make more sense of it.

He was propped up on pillows next to me with his eyes
closed, but I didn't think he was asleep yet. It made me think
about Jesse and the fact that he would never spend a day in bed
with me just because I was sad and didn't feel like doing
anything. He would be insisting on going to a party at this point.
I knew if I asked Chase to go out for a drive or go out to eat, he
would drag himself out for me, or if I did want to stay here all
weekend, he would.

I don't know which part made me do it, but I knew as soon as
it crossed my mind that I definitely wanted to.

My hand moved over his stomach, my fingers splaying out as
I took him in. His arm was thrown over his eyes, and he barely
moved a muscle. It seemed like an opening enough that I

climbed on top of him, straddling his legs as I leaned down to kiss him.

"What are you doing?" he asked before I reached him, his eyes still closed.

"Kissing you?"

"There are now only two very, very thin layers of clothes between two very important parts of us. Please, do not kiss me right this second."

"Could I kiss you if I remove both of those layers?"

That got his attention, his eyes flying open to look me over. I still had my shirt on, but he didn't seem to notice. His heavy eyes roaming over my face.

"You're beautiful," he said, the compliment surprising me when I was expecting a line of questioning or a very strong no. "I know you might not realize it, but you can have anyone you want, and you should. If you're going to choose me for this second, then you can't choose him again. The thought that you might have gone back was eating me alive. I sure as hell can't have you and then see you with him again."

"Then please touch me and make me forget that he ever did."

He stared hard, seemingly trying to decide if I was serious.

"Chase, I need this now. If you want to make sure that I never go back, then please, please, show me how much better it can be."

I could feel how hard he was beneath me now, his cock pushing hard against my already wet pussy.

"Scout," he whispered, the word almost painful.

He rolled, pinning me underneath him. "We can make you forget he ever existed. I can kiss and lick and fuck every part of you until you forget anyone else ever touched you. And you're going to be so mad when you realize how much you liked it and have to come to me for more, that I'm the only one who will soothe that ache when you want it so bad. That you will be as obsessed with me as I am with you."

I rolled my eyes, and he could see it. "I doubt that, but I am willing to see what you've got to give."

A low laugh rumbled from him as he kissed my neck. "Always trying to knock me down a peg or two, aren't you?"

"Someone has to keep that cocky attitude in line."

"How could I not be cocky when I have a beautiful naked woman underneath me trying to challenge me to give her the best orgasms of her life?"

"Half naked. I still have a shirt on."

He laughed, pulling it off with one hand as he kept himself propped up above me.

"There, now you are no longer half naked and you're even more perfect. Damn, I don't even know what I want to do first."

"How about getting right to the sex part? I'll skip the lengthy speech and say I'm all clear and on birth control, so there is no hold up on my end."

"Well same. About the clear part, not the birth control," he grinned, leaning down and kissing me harder.

"And really? You just want me to skip right to it? That seems like a waste. I think I might enjoy making you cum a few times before we get to that."

"It's okay. I mean, I don't need any of that."

"Don't need it? I don't know that anyone technically needs more orgasms. Why are you rushing through this now when you've been fine with taking our time before?"

I let out a long breath, deciding on a half truth. "I'm just a little nervous because I haven't done this in a while and I don't know how great I am at it, anyway."

He kissed down my jaw, running his teeth along my neck and kissing his way down my chest until he pulled a nipple into his mouth. A shock of pleasure shot through me, making me arch into him more as he moved to the other one, pulling it gently between his teeth.

"You are perfect, and all you need to do is enjoy it right now. It's kind of like your environment affecting who you are. Your partner affects how good you are and I promise, we are already *very* good at this together."

My smile grew as he calmed some of my nerves. "I'll try to just enjoy it, but I'm still worried."

"Fine," he said, kissing his way back up to my mouth. "If it helps you feel more relaxed, we will skip the hours of foreplay I want but only if you promise me that the next time we do this, I get to kiss and lick and suck and bite every inch of you for hours."

"I guess that depends on how good at this we are for us to have a next time," I said, laughing quietly as I finally let my hands roam over him.

His hand slid up my thigh and fingers teased along my wetness before he moved to his knees, reaching for the condom that I had plainly set out before I started this idea.

"You are terrible," he said, ripping it open and rolling it on. "You had this entire seduction planned."

I smiled harder. "Only for a few minutes."

"Sure, getting me into bed all weekend like this wasn't the plan the entire time. You've wanted me for weeks."

"I did not, I—"

"Shh, just let me believe the lie. Are you sure you want to do this? I can stop now if you want."

"No, I want to."

"Okay, but I'm not rushing through this part."

He did take his time, teasing me as his cock moved along my wetness until I was pushing my hips up.

"So ready for me," he murmured, kissing my chest and pulling a nipple back into his mouth, making me gasp again.

My body hummed, and by the time he positioned himself at my entrance, I was nearly ready to slide down until he filled me. My pussy tightened, aching as he pushed into me slowly. I couldn't take it, needing more.

"Please," I begged, trying to wiggle my hips down.

"Please what, baby?"

"All of it, please. Right now."

He groaned, but still moved at his slow pace. "I don't want to hurt you."

"I don't care. I want all of it."

"So greedy," he said, laughing quietly before slamming into me. I gasped at the sudden fullness, enjoying it more than I expected.

He picked up his pace, and I moved along with him until he came to a sudden stop.

"You okay, or is this not working for you?" he said, smiling as he pressed a soft kiss to my lips.

"No, I think it is."

"Think it is? We have to know it is." He picked up my hips, breaking his body away from me but not missing a beat as he thrust into me over and over. His fingers moved to my clit, rubbing the sensitive area, and I immediately knew what he meant.

There was no mistaking this. There was no think-it's-working in this feeling. He kept pace as my body threatened to break apart and, just as the orgasm washed over me, he moved faster. I almost wanted to pull away. The unknown feeling that I was losing control of my body with someone else wasn't familiar enough, but he didn't stop moving.

"Chase, I—" I cut myself off with a moan as he moved his position. My hands fisted into the sheets, trying to find anything to hold on to.

I couldn't say another word, falling over the edge as he thrust into me harder, letting the orgasm break me and leaving me with white spots in my eyes and a body that I could no longer feel.

I think at some point I had yelled out again, but I couldn't remember clear enough to know for sure. His rapid pace turned to lazy strokes, and he came down over top of me.

"Look at that. I'm already learning what you like."

He kissed along my neck, every part of me so sensitive that I shuddered at the touch.

I could only stare at the ceiling, not quite sure what to think. I thought I'd had orgasms during sex before. If you would have asked me this morning, I would have said, of course I have. I'd told Jesse plenty of times how great the sex was, preferring that it wasn't anything I craved because he was barely around.

I just had my first orgasm during sex and, of all the people in the world, it was with Chase.

He leaned up, kissing me. "What's wrong? Was that not good enough? Damn, okay. Flip over, we'll go again."

He moved to flip me, a smile on his face as though me not having a good time wouldn't be an insult, but a great reason to try again.

"Chase, no," I said, laughing as he tried to move my body. That was nothing but lead now. "It was good, I'm fine. I need a second."

"Then what's wrong? I know that face and that is not the face of a pleased Scout."

"Now you know what my faces mean?"

"I'm learning." He groaned. "I'm learning a lot about you, actually."

He had moved down between us, touching my clit again and making me yell out.

"Chase, stop!" I said, the area was so sensitive to his touch that I wondered if I would have another orgasm if I let him touch me for a few seconds longer.

"Sorry," he said with a laugh. "Now tell me what is going on in that pretty head. Did I not please you enough or was I just right that it hurts to realize how much you liked it? Maybe it wasn't mind-numbing enough?"

"Can you just stop being cocky for five minutes?"

His face dropped. "I wasn't trying to be cocky, Scout. I truly want to know what's going on and if you're okay."

"It's too embarrassing to talk about."

"Embarrassing? I literally just had your legs up in the air while I was fucking you. What could you possibly be not able to tell me right now?"

"Chase," I groaned.

"Please tell me," he said, leaning down to kiss my cheek before rolling to his side next to me.

I huffed but spilled it, not able to keep it in any longer. "If you make fun of me at all. I will kick you out for good." He gave a serious nod. "I did not realize that I could have an orgasm during sex and that was my first one. I mean with sex. And a real first one during sex, not what I thought was one."

"Wait, so you thought you've had one before during sex but didn't know until now that it...what? Felt that good?"

"Pretty much. What I thought was one was fine enough, but that was a lot more than fine. I was pretty much under the impression that I could have one with the foreplay type of stuff, but not much else."

"Wait, is that why you were so nervous about this?" he asked, realization dawning as soon as he said it. "You were *that* worried that it would be boring?" he asked, the confusion and surprise in his voice almost painful. "You were worried it was going to be boring, and that was somehow going to be your fault."

"Kind of. What if I was the problem, and that's why it was never that...fun."

His mouth dropped open. "So what happened before then? You would just lay there and say 'that's fine' to him and he was cool with it? And then you blamed yourself that you weren't more interested?"

"I mean, yeah, pretty much."

"And you didn't question that?"

"Chase," I warned.

"No, sorry, I'm not being an ass Scout. I mean, you didn't think it should feel better? Did he at least make you cum with the foreplay?"

"No," I said, quietly.

He rolled onto his back. "You are telling me that he never gave you an orgasm?"

"I mean, here and there before the sex started, but like I said, not during. And it's not like anyone else suddenly decided to add their hand to the mix. He was fine not doing the extra work, I guess."

"I just need a minute to process," he said, staring at the ceiling. Two seconds went by because, at the end of the day, Chase could not keep his mouth shut.

"Scout," he said, rolling back to me. "You are not the problem. Listen very clearly, you are not the problem. Promise me that you will not think that again, and promise you won't continue sleeping with someone who isn't giving you orgasms."

"Well, obviously not. Now I know that can happen for me. It would be boring without it."

"Did you just think you were broken?" he asked, exasperated at this information.

"I mean, maybe, but also, I just guessed that I was bad at it. They tell women all the time that it might not happen with just sex, and I assumed that was my issue."

"Meaning you add other things to make it happen. Hence the hand."

"No, no, no," I said, laying down and throwing a pillow back over my face, the warmth of my cheeks burning me. "We are done talking about this."

"Fuck yeah we are. Let's get you another orgasm. We apparently have a lot of lost time to make up for."

I lifted the pillow an inch. "No, I can't do that again."

"Because you didn't like it?"

"Because that was intimate," I said, my embarrassment climbing. It felt exposing, and even if I liked it. I wasn't sure what to do with being that open to someone.

He pulled off the pillow, looking down at me. "Then we will count that happening as a fucking blessing because you've done it once. There's no harm in doing it with me again. I'm going to get us water and a snack and then I will be eating you out until your legs shake and you're ready to go again."

His naked body was pressed to mine as he leaned down and kissed me.

"You're going to gloat about this, aren't you?" I asked.

"Only to you." He pushed the hair out of my face with a gentle brush of his fingers. "I wasn't planning on telling anyone else about our business. Isn't that one of the benefits of having that intimacy with someone? You can tell me anything, do anything you want to my body, tell me loud and clear what you want and it's just between us. You can have orgasm after orgasm and I'm the only one who's going to know about it. I came too, Scout. It's not like you're all alone in that. I was also there for that mind-numbing, really great sex, too," he said with a grin. "There's no embarrassment now."

"Easy for you to say."

"Not really. You know until you're more comfortable, we can do things to help. Not that I will like all of them, but if it helps."

"Like what?"

"We can turn all the lights off, I can put music on," his grin grew, "you can be blindfolded, I could be blindfolded."

"Maybe the lights off thing, or the music, but there are no blindfolds."

He laughed, walking from the room and shaking his head.

"Not yet at least," I said, quietly, laughing as I pulled the blankets back over me.

His mouth dropped open, and he rushed back to the bed, moving overtop of me and pulling me into another kiss. Suddenly, spending the entire weekend hiding in my apartment was looking better and better.

TWENTY-THREE

CHASE

IT WAS Sunday night before I finally decided that I was going to leave. I didn't particularly want to go, but staying longer felt like we would be slipping out of the friends with benefits category and into the relationship category.

A category that I wouldn't get myself involved in.

Even if it was feeling more like we were getting there every day.

After we woke up on Sunday, she had made breakfast while I assembled a shelf she had bought. I cursed the entire time and so did she until she had burnt the eggs and we decided to switch jobs.

It was all so wholesome, and a bit too relationship-like for my taste.

She didn't want the crew to know, which meant I would be keeping it from them as long as I could. I didn't particularly want to be on Fox's bad side, and I believed that they took their job of protecting Scout seriously, so I would be staying on their good side as long as I could.

By the time I made it back to my place, I was ready to fall

into bed, but that was short-lived when I saw my father's car out front. I almost debated not going in, but I wanted to go to bed, and knew he would just want to yell at me and go.

He started in before the front door was even closed behind me.

"Where have you been?"

"Have you been sitting here all day waiting to ask that?"

"I've been sitting here for nearly two hours hoping to find you coming home to study, or coming home from studying. I know you have exams this week, and I don't see any books in your hands."

"Because I wasn't studying."

"Where were you?"

I threw my keys down, grabbing a soda out of the fridge and sitting at the counter. The best thing to do was play along and let him rant out his anger, otherwise, it would just escalate.

"I was with friends."

"Which friends? Because Justin and that group were at the banquet we had tonight. The place you *should* have been unless you were studying. I believe that's the excuse you always give your mother, isn't it?"

"I have other friends."

"If you mean you were at the pitiful garage with those people, then I wouldn't be so quick to call them your friends."

"Why? And how did you know about them?"

"Because I wondered where your car was and tracked it there. I'm not stupid. You can't honestly believe they would be hanging around you for anything more than connections and money."

Apparently, I needed to text the crew and ask them how to get a tracker off my car now.

"I'm pretty sure Ashton Holt doesn't need to hang around me for connections and money. Her family is comparable to us in wealth and status. If anything, she has more connections for them in the car world than I would."

He sneered. "Yeah, I heard about her running off with them. Her father basically disowned her, but then one accident or something and he's right back to giving her everything. You need to get it out of your head that I'm anything like that. You keep hanging around them, and I'm not supporting shit."

"I wasn't asking permission to hang out with people. If I want to keep hanging out with her — them — then I will." I didn't look away, didn't give any indication that I slipped up, but it was useless. My dad was as sharp as ever and wouldn't miss such a blatant slip-up.

"Oh god, you're fucking with one of the girls there aren't you?"

"That's none of your business," I said, wanting to defend Scout, but not wanting to give my father any more information about her.

"You're in college to become a lawyer for our company. How could you think running around with burnouts who like to race cars is going to help your future? How could you think that girl is right for you to spend time with?"

Each word out of his mouth grated on my nerves, making my blood boil. I didn't want anyone to talk badly about Scout, but especially not him.

"*That* girl is named Scout."

"I don't care what her name is. You've barely been around and now I find out it's because you're chasing a girl around? You aren't a damn puppy Chase, you're a leader, a soon to be lawyer. You don't need to run after a girl who has a job working on cars."

I stifled a laugh. "Scout does work on cars. She supports her family and their business. She is also about to be sponsored and trained by Holt Racing. Which, besides Ash, will make her their second female driver. As you can imagine, that isn't easy and doesn't happen often. Is that really something to scoff at?"

He rolled his eyes. "Maybe not for her life, but for yours? Yes, it is. My company will need a good lawyer and we have worked hard to make sure you were on the path to become one."

"Yeah, you have worked so fucking hard for that, haven't you?"

"I have. And I guarantee the last thing the partner of a law firm needs is some greased up girl racing cars. Honestly, I'd be shocked if she wanted you for anything more than our money."

"Exactly. Because what value do I bring besides money?"

He almost went to agree, but stopped before the word came out. It only made me wonder if that's the only value he saw in me. Was I only meaningful to him as someone to take over the business and continue making him millions? My value was following in his footsteps so our family could keep this fucked up legacy?

I couldn't even bring myself to ask, because I already knew the answer.

I wonder what Scout's answer would be if I asked her the same thing. I didn't know what she could possibly say, but I was pretty sure any money I had wouldn't make the list of why I was worth being in her life. Then again, she also might have a longer list of why I *shouldn't* be in her life.

"I need to go," I said. "You're absolutely right. I should be out studying, but I don't think I'm going to do that here." I picked up my bag that had all of my law school books in it and grabbed my keys again. I wasn't going to study, but I sure as hell wasn't staying to listen to more of this.

"Are you serious?"

"Completely. You are right, I need to take this seriously and to do that means I need to go study. The law school library is open all night because of exams this week, so I will go there and prepare myself."

He seemed taken aback at first, but quickly recovered and nodded.

"Well, good, I'm glad to hear that."

"I figured. So why don't you get going so I can lock up and leave?"

He stared hard at me for a moment, and I almost thought he was going to break into another lecture, but he only nodded again.

"Please let me know how your exams go this week. I need to know if we need to get you a tutor or if you're going to manage to run this company on your own."

I turned away from him, rolling my eyes with a sneer. Every word out of his mouth always managed to piss me off more. I still agreed though, and it worked, getting me into my car and out of there even faster.

I waited until his car disappeared into the night before I sped away. I wasn't going to the library to study, but now I was too keyed up to go back in and sleep.

The gas station I pulled into was nearly deserted at this time of night. The only other car in the parking lot looking almost like the crew's, but it wasn't any of them.

Before I made it a foot from my car, someone stepped in front of me.

Jesse.

I gave a relaxed smile, not flinching as two more guys stepped around the car next to him.

"What's up, Chase?" Jesse asked, as he looked around. "Doesn't look like any of your new friends are here tonight."

"Surprisingly, I can make it to a gas station on my own."

"Unsurprisingly, you won't make it away from the gas station alone."

Before I could even manage a response, he threw his first punch. It hit its target, something in my face making an awful cracking sound. I swung back, managing to hit Jesse in the stomach.

It didn't matter. His two friends were on me before I could manage another hit.

I wasn't sure how long it went on, or how many times I managed to get back up, but I knew the moment I slumped against my car, the realization settling in that I wouldn't be getting up again. In one terrifying moment, the world faded to black, swallowing me whole.

TWENTY-FOUR

SCOUT

MONDAY MORNING CAME FASTER than I wanted it to. I was back at the garage today, trying to finish up another car before I went back to finish Chase's. The last of the parts had come in, meaning that my chances to work on it with Chase was closing. I kept putting it off and ignoring him to work on it alone, and now I was almost sad that I hadn't taken more opportunities to work on it with him.

The thought made me sadder than I had anticipated. It's not like we had to end everything else, but it was a reminder that this was going to be temporary and, at some point, there would be no more Chase in my life. And after this weekend, I didn't know if that's what I wanted anymore.

I had texted him earlier, but by three that afternoon, I still hadn't heard anything.

That only made me more uneasy. The one thing I had come to count on was him texting me back every single time. It might take a few minutes, but he never ignored me.

So, I texted again.

SCOUT

> Are you mad and ignoring me or just busy?

I forced myself to put the phone down and get back to work, but only made it another twenty minutes before checking again.

Nothing.

By the time four came, I was pissed.

Jax and Kye came over, their attention on the car I was working on, but Jax's eyebrows jumped up when he looked at me.

"What's going on?"

"Nothing."

"Okay, then, why so angry?"

"I'm not angry. I'm just annoyed. Chase was supposed to come work on the car tonight and I haven't heard from him all day."

Kye laughed. "I thought that would be more of a relief than a problem."

"Usually it would be, but it's pretty rude to not even let me know that he couldn't be here. I could have made plans."

"What plans? Hang out in one of our apartments tonight instead of your own? Pretty sure that won't take long to arrange," Jax said with a snorting laugh.

"No. Maybe I wanted to go out."

The rest of the crew was heading over, already chiming in to what they wanted to do that night. Finally, my phone buzzed with a text. My heart rate jumped as I saw Chase's name and hit it open.

CHASE

> Sorry, Hellcat. Bad day. I couldn't text.

SCOUT

That must have been one pretty terrible day to not even let me know you weren't coming over.

CHASE

Considering I've been in the hospital, yeah it was a bad day and my phone was broken. I had to have a new one brought to me.

My stomach dropped, the sickening wave that washed over me nearly making me puke.

SCOUT

Where are you?

He sent me the name of the hospital, and tried to tell me not to worry about coming, but I was already heading into the office to grab my keys and bag.

"What's going on?" Fox asked.

"Going to kick Chase's ass in person?" Kye joked. "Can I come?"

"Chase is in the hospital. I need to go."

Their faces fell and eyebrows raised, but no one said a word. Instead, they all grabbed for keys and started slamming the garage bay doors shut, locking up faster than I could blink.

"Lead the way." Ransom said as everyone headed to their cars.

My heart raced as I got into my car, wishing I had a new one by now to help me get there faster, but this one would do for the moment.

By the time I ran into the hospital, I was out of breath and on the verge of crying. I couldn't believe I had been sitting there all day mad at him, and he had been here.

I made it to his room, stopping short when I saw him. His face was covered in bruises, but there was no splint on his nose, which was good. A cut had been stitched across the top of his eyebrow, and his arm was wrapped in a cast.

"Chase," I breathed, somehow upset he was here and happy that he was at least alive. "What happened?"

I didn't expect him to reply, his eyes still closed, but his head rolled towards me, smiling as he finally looked at me.

"Hey, Hellcat." His voice was hoarse, and I grabbed the cup of water, helping him take a sip of it.

I leaned down, pressing one careful kiss to his lips, and he smiled.

"Wow, I like that hello."

"I personally don't when you can barely kiss me back. What happened?" I searched his face, relief still washing over me that he wasn't completely broken. "When did this happen?"

The rest of the crew was crowding in behind me now. I still held onto him as everyone looked him over, but I couldn't find it in me to let him go.

"Last night."

I couldn't say it, but I wanted to. Last night after he had left my apartment.

"Where were you?"

"The gas station is around the corner from my place. I ran into…a few people who apparently don't like me."

"Who hates you this much?" Kye asked, moving around the sit down on the chair next to the bed.

Chase looked at me, and then back at the crew. "I'm surprised all of you came."

"Scout said you're in the hospital. We are obviously going to come see what's wrong," Fox said.

"And honestly, the food here is becoming a comfort meal," Jax said. "Do they give a punch card for this place? Like 10 hospital visits and then you get a free meal or something?"

"Really? Getting sick of my cooking?" Carly asked, her eyebrows jumping up.

"I personally would prefer your food to another jello cup," Chase said, trying to grin, but the split lip wasn't letting him.

Carly smiled. "I can promise you an entire buffet once you're out of here."

I was still watching Chase, annoyed he was avoiding answering. "What happened, Chase?"

He shrugged. "Like I said, a few guys jumped me and this happened."

"A few? How many?"

"Three. I think?"

"You said you knew them. Who was it?"

He didn't answer, but kept staring at me.

"*Who was it?*" I asked again, worry setting into my gut that I already knew.

"Jesse and some of his friends."

Bile rose up as my stomach churned.

I wanted to reach out and hug him, but I couldn't when everyone was looking at us.

"Really? Of all of us that don't like the guy, why did he go after you?" Fox asked.

Chase shrugged. "I think he blames me for that night at the restaurant when they broke up, since I was the one to piss him off. Maybe it was just the right opportunity when I was alone."

My knuckles turned white as I gripped the side of the bed.

He met my eye again, finally, and the concern for me in them made me want to fall over him in tears.

"Scout," he said softly, as though everyone in the room wasn't listening. He was somehow worried about me when he was the one laying in this bed. I didn't respond, only spun on the heel of my boot, walking out of the room.

I could still hear them as I stepped into the hallway, trying to catch my breath.

"She probably just needs a minute to cool down. She's going to feel responsible for this," Fox said.

My stomach dropped, realizing he was right. It was my fault and everyone knew it.

Quiet filled the room, and I almost walked back in until I heard Chase.

"You need to stop her," he said, quieter now.

"Stop her from what?" Quinn asked, silence following.

Chase already knew what I was about to do, and now the crew was about to piece it together. I needed to go before they stopped me.

I started running, making it outside to my car, the keys already in my hand as I ripped the door open and took off.

I hit the main road and shifted into the last gear, the car still trying to rev higher. I didn't even care. I needed a new engine, anyway. Why not blow this one up in the meantime?

I navigated until I pulled onto the dead street that ran parallel to the one I grew up on. It was just as run down as mine. I almost laughed, remembering how much of a comfort that had been before. It was what I knew, and I felt closer to Jesse, knowing that he experienced the same type of life I did. I found comfort in the familiar, and looking back now, it made my stomach churn. How could I possibly find comfort in a life I had worked so hard to outrun? Why did I think I wanted what I already had? I grew up here. I had a father that was a beer drinker, a drunk, and a gambler. It was everything that Jesse was becoming.

I turned into his driveway, pulling up onto the dead grass. I wasn't wasting any time getting inside. If he was here, he probably would have heard me by now. Unless he was that drunk already.

I walked in, finding him on the couch, a girl underneath him. Not that I cared about that, but it filled me with a deeper rage. He had the nerve to go after Chase when he had already moved on.

He had sat up, the girl's eyes wide when they both looked at me. I picked up one of the glass beer bottles, throwing it hard against the wall next to them. It shattered, making Jesse jump up.

"What the fuck?"

"What the fuck is right. What the *fuck* were you doing going after Chase?"

I picked up another, throwing it hard at him, but he ducked and charged, coming at me. I went to step aside, but more bottles littered the ground, making me stumble. He grabbed my neck, pushing me back into the wall.

The great thing about growing up with four very protective men was that they taught me how to get away from men that were bigger than me. I choked, but his hold was too tight, making me swallow it before my elbow came up, swinging hard into his nose. I ignored the crunch and swung my leg out, aiming to kick him hard between the legs, but missing and kicking his shin instead. It still broke his hold on me.

"You thought you would put Chase in the hospital and I would just be fine with it? You really thought you would get away with it?" I yelled, trying to step to the side as I sucked in a hard breath. He had lost his hold, but still blocked me in.

Jesse stood back up, laughing as blood dripped from his nose. Drunks were the worst, the pain so dulled by alcohol that they could fight longer. He pushed back against me. I tried to step to the side, but ended up pressed hard between him and the wall again.

He smiled down at me, and I gagged. I kissed that mouth.

There were some days I looked forward to kissing that mouth, now I wanted to punch it.

"What's wrong? You mad that your new boyfriend couldn't fight back?"

"Coming from the guy who was too scared to fight him one on one, so you had him jumped? You think he's the weak one? You could have killed him, honestly three against one *should* have killed him. Yet all you managed to do was give a few cuts and bruises." He was fighting again, his hands climbing up my body to find my neck again, but I was trying to move my knee, positioning myself back between his legs. I needed one good hit and if there was one thing the guys taught me, life or death means you fight dirty.

His body stayed pressed flat against mine. I had one arm halfway free, but I wasn't sure if I could reach. I swung anyway, arching up around his side to his face. It landed, but it wasn't enough. His hand wound up between us, breaking past my arm and finding my neck. He squeezed harder this time, and I realized that Jesse would kill me. He would be happy too.

Fear crept through me, and I tried not to panic as I swung again. He went to step back, his hold still around my throat, but an arm snaked around his neck from behind.

Kye ripped him back and Jesse's legs were kicked out from under him. All the guys were protective, all of them fighters, but something changed in Kye when he fought, and there was never much hope for someone to be on the other end of it. Good luck to Jesse, because I don't think the guys had ever seen someone physically hurt me like this. Fox, Ransom, and Jax filled the room, blocking the door.

Kye's arm stayed around his neck as he flipped Jesse, his face slamming into the coffee table as he threw him down. Jesse yelled out something, but it was the next scream that came from the girl in the corner that grabbed all of our attention as Jax swore. Apparently, she didn't like seeing Jesse get hurt. She had been sitting there yelling before the guys came in, but quieted down enough that we all forgot about her.

"Go," he said. "Get out now." They stepped aside, giving her a clear path to run out.

Kye wasn't paying attention. Instead, he jumped up, two heavy boots landing on Jesse's back like he was no more than a bed to jump up onto. The coffee table gave out, the wooden legs falling over, making Jesse yell again.

"What's wrong Jesse? Don't like an unfair fight?" Kye asked. "That's so weird, because Chase mentioned you had a few friends, then here we come and find you beating Scout up. Which is funny because that doesn't seem like a fair fight either."

"Come on, Scout. The girls are out front. Go wait with them," Fox said, reaching out for me.

"No," I said, stepping back. "No, I'm not leaving."

"We can handle it, Scout. There's no need for you to possibly get hurt again."

"I'm not leaving yet. It was my fault that he went after Chase. It was my fault I even let him into our lives. I'm not waiting outside. I need to know what happens, and I need to know he will never bother me again."

"Oh, I can for sure make that happen," Kye said, finally getting off Jesse's back and kicking him in the side. "Get up."

Jesse rolled over, groaning, but Kye kicked again. "Get. Up. Come on. I thought you were a bigger man than Chase. How many times did he get back up? I'm guessing once at least, and here you are, flat on your back still," Kye said, kicking him again.

"Easy," Ransom said, stepping closer to them.

Kye looked up, the wild rage there making me step back. He would never turn on us, but the feral look to him still sent panic through me.

"Easy? Did you see what he did to Chase and then we walk in and he's doing the same fucking thing to her? Should we go *easy* so he can come back and put her in the hospital? I'd rather kill him."

Ransom only nodded, looking over at me. "Yes, I get that, but it's Scout's call."

Tears spilled down my face as I looked at each one of them. Each one of them would do anything I asked right now. Four big protective brothers who chose me to protect all my life, and I let this guy into their lives. All of them worried and not even a hint of being mad that I made a mess of everything. They only asked how I wanted it cleaned up.

"I'm so sorry," I said, the words hiccuped with my tears. "I should have listened. I shouldn't have brought him into our lives."

Fox shook his head. "His actions are not your fault."

"But they were this time because I let it continue." I looked at Kye. "Don't kill him," I said, only half joking because Kye looked like he would, "but please make sure this is clear that he can't bother us again. *Any* of us."

They all nodded, Kye's boot setting on Jesse's chest so he wouldn't move.

"Go outside, Scout. The girls will want to know what's going on," I nodded, walking past them without a second glance at Jesse.

"Scout," Jesse yelled. "You aren't serious, are you?"

I ignored him as I made it to the porch, the girls all standing at the bottom of the steps, waiting.

The tears came harder now, my face hot and tear-stained as I cried, heading right to them.

"What happened?" Ash asked. "Did he hurt you?"

"Not much. The guys got there," I said, trying to suck down the sobs. Quinn opened her arms, and I stepped into them, crying against her as Ash and Carly circled around my back.

"It's okay, Scout," Quinn said, holding me tight.

"It's not. I screwed up. I screwed up so bad that Chase ended up in the hospital. I screwed up so bad that I feel terrible about myself because I let Jesse walk all over me for so long. I screwed up and now the guys are having to go in there and do whatever they are going to do to make him never come near us again." I cried harder. "How did I mess up so bad? How did I not realize how big of an asshole he is? And what do I do if Chase doesn't forgive me?"

Quinn grabbed my face, making me look at her. "Chase is smart. He won't be mad at you. If you think there's anything to forgive, I'm assuming he already has based on how much he was yelling for us to stop you."

"I feel like I am taking advantage of all of you having to be here, and for making the guys do this."

"You all once ran to save me when I needed you. Do you think we would ever hesitate to help you?" Quinn said.

"You've been our best friend since day one, Scout. For each one of us," Ash said. "You've also been *their* best friend since day one. Don't forget that those guys need you just as much as you need them. This isn't a burden, babe. This is what you have told every single one of us that we do. We are there for each other, even when it's not fun."

"And there's no reason to feel guilty for what Jesse did. You don't control his actions, and you better not apologize for him," Carly said. "He's an ass, and it's not your fault he did that to Chase."

I tried to calm myself, taking deeper breaths again as I leaned against Quinn. The guys filed out, Kye slamming the door behind him.

"Do we need to call the police or something?" Ash asked.

"Maybe an ambulance?" Carly added.

"No to both. He should be fine in a few days, and he didn't exactly call one for Chase. Nothing catastrophic. Come on, let's get home," Fox said, waving us all to cars.

"I don't know that I can drive," I said, still trying to calm down and make sure the tears didn't start again.

"Come on," Ash said. "I'll drive your car back, and you ride with me."

I nodded, heading to my car, but Kye stopped me.

"Are you sure you're okay? I mean, he didn't hurt you more than what we saw, right?"

"Yeah, that was the worst of it. I'm okay now. I mean, as good as I can be."

"Alright," he said. And then he hugged me, pulling me tight and making me cry harder. Kye rarely hugged any of us. I could probably count it on two hands how many times he hugged me in our entire lives. "You did good, Scout. How about a movie night?"

"Yes, please," I said, forcing a smile as I pushed more tears away.

Five minutes later, Ash pulled out, winding her way back into town without a word.

"Where are you going?"

"You know by now that I feel responsible for Fox's scar."

"Of course, but it wasn't your fault."

"Yeah, well, I didn't think that at the time, and I don't think you do either. The one thing that kept me awake for days was not knowing how he was. I should have gone back to the hospital that day and checked in on him. I should have stayed that night with you guys, but I was scared."

Fifteen minutes later, she parked in the hospital parking lot and parked the car near the door. "Run inside and check on him. Just for peace of mind. Even if he is mad at you, do this so you can sleep tonight."

"Thank you," I said, pushing the door open and heading inside.

TWENTY-FIVE
SCOUT

CHASE WAS LYING on the hospital bed still but had changed into jeans and a t-shirt. The minute I walked through the door, he sat up and looked ready to attempt to stand.

"Don't get up. I'm already coming over to you." I made it to the bedside, and he didn't hesitate to grab my hand.

"I'm glad you came back, and in one piece. I've been trying to get a hold of one of you for what felt like hours."

"It was a little over an hour, not hours. Did you think I was going to ignore you again?"

"No, I thought you would be in jail," he said, giving me a small smile. "I was worried."

"Not in jail quite yet. You seem to know what happened, and aren't surprised."

"Fox filled me in. Said you tried to kill the man that hurt me." He gave a weak smile as he squeezed my hand. "I was a little pissed off at first, but he said they took care of it."

"I might have been more successful if I had my knife."

"The one time you forget it," he clicked his tongue before he tried to pull me closer. He glanced down and his face fell. "Why is your neck red?"

My hand flew up, covering the sore skin. "What do you mean?"

"Your neck is red. Why?"

"You said Fox filled you in," I said.

"He told me you all showed up at Jesse's, kicked his ass, and then they finished it. He didn't mention you were strangled."

"Jesse got me. Only for a second, and then Kye threw him off."

"He *got you*? I swear if they didn't fucking kill him, I'm going to." He moved to the edge of the bed, looking me over more. He pulled my hands up, looking them over, before inspecting my arms, and then moving over the rest of my body. "Where else did he hurt you?"'

"Nowhere. The guys got there and nothing else happened."

"What happened to Jesse?"

"All I know is he got kicked a few times, and then I left him in the house with the guys."

"Good. Hopefully, they did everything I'm currently wishing I could do if they saw him hurt you."

"He's not in great shape because he hurt *you*." I reached up, running a finger above the stitched cut and down his bruised jaw. I tried to be gentle, but another round of anger rolled through me that Jesse ever thought he could do this.

"Oh yeah? You all protective over me now? Why's that?"

I shrugged, trying to take a deep, calming breath. "I kind of like you hanging around, and I don't exactly want people outside of our group to mess with you."

"No? Only you?" he asked.

He sat up more, and swung his legs off the bed before moving me until I was pressed between his legs, his lips nearly against mine.

"Yeah, only me."

He reached up with his good hand, running a thumb over my bottom lip, and then down my arm. His fingers moved over the spot Jesse had bruised me from grabbing my arm so hard and I jerked my arm back.

"Are you okay?"

"Yeah, I'm better now."

"Scout, you just got into a fight with your ex for me. A physical fight. You're allowed to not be okay."

"I might not be later, but for right now, I'm okay."

"My little Hellcat. Avenging me as I'm laid up in a hospital bed." His hand cupped my face. "And while I think I appreciate it, I never want you to do that again, Scout. I don't care what is happening to me. I never want you to put yourself in harm's way because of me ever again."

My eyes roamed over his bruised face. Even turning shades of purple, it was easy to see how good looking he was. His hair was disheveled, and the stitches above his eye looked bad, but none of it took away from his smile.

I thought back to the night I met him and how badly I wanted to mess up his hair that night. I tried to hide my laugh as I pushed a hand through it now.

"I wasn't joking."

His face was hard and serious, but mine softened. "I know. I was just thinking of how perfect you kept yourself before you met me, and now here you are, probably more of a mess than you ever have been. I'm sorry he did this to you, but I will always, *always*, protect my friends. Especially when it's my fault."

"Nothing Jesse has ever done is ever your fault."

"You know what I meant."

He laid back, struggling as he took a deep breath.

"Does it hurt?" I asked, running a hand up his good arm.

"I'll survive."

"That's not what I asked."

He smiled, reaching over to me. "I don't know that I've ever had anyone who cares about me this much...not like you do."

"Of course you have people that care about you. Who brought you the clothes?"

"My sister, but she had classes today and couldn't stay. Besides that, no one."

"No one else came or cared?"

"They are the same thing. I'm not really sure what to say or do about someone caring about me."

"You're also on some drugs for the pain, so I think you can just enjoy it for now. Are you sure you're okay enough to leave?"

"I'm fine. It's just stitches and a few weeks without a hand. I'll manage."

"I know, but I hate this."

"While I am flattered that you are so worried about me, I'll be completely back to normal soon. They've been working on discharging me since nothing else came back permanently ruined besides my wrist breaking a little."

"Can you break a wrist just a little?" I said with a tight smile. "You're coming to my apartment and staying there for the week, at least. I won't be able to get through my week if you're struggling around your place."

He smiled, but groaned as he shifted. "I will not fight you on that for a second."

"Good, because we are also having a movie night tonight with the crew, so you have to come to that, too. If you think you can handle it."

"Not going home alone to my quiet, boring apartment is manageable. I think I will be able to handle it. What is the crew going to think of that, though?"

"I will tell them that I'm responsible and helping until you are a little more healed. They know my guilt eats me alive on the smallest of things. They will believe how guilty I feel for this."

"So we aren't telling them about the messing around?"

"You're already a quarter of the way to your deathbed. Why would I push you the rest of the way now?"

"You really think they are going to kick my ass if they find out?"

I sighed, the nurse coming in and interrupting us. "I'm honestly not sure what they will do." I didn't add that this fight with Jesse only made it worse. I barely knew if I trusted myself to find the right guy, and if they found out Chase and I were just messing around, they wouldn't suddenly think he was the right guy.

The nurse moved around the room in a flurry, doing a few last checks, and telling us the doctor would be just a few minutes so we could go.

Chase laid back again, closing his eyes. I could only keep looking at him, though, surprised at how hot he looked. His eyes opened, the heavy look to them only making me hotter.

"Why are you looking at me like that?" he asked.

"I don't know. It's just…"

"Just?"

"You look kind of hot."

"The first time you want to tell me I'm hot is when I'm beat up in a hospital bed?"

"I mean, it's not like I'm *enjoying* this, but it is pretty hot."

He groaned, trying to move himself to sit up more.

"Come here," he said, trying to reach out for me. I looked down to see red knuckles. Tears welled up in seconds at the thought of him trying to fight them.

"So you're really not mad at me for all of this? Like would

you still want the benefits part of this friendship, even though knowing me has brought you so much trouble?" I asked.

"The day I tell you that I no longer want to fool around with you is the day I'm dead. And no, there is not any part of me that is mad at you."

He finally caught my hand and squeezed as the doctor came in. Twenty minutes later, we were getting into Ash's car and heading out.

"Well, I wasn't expecting you to break him out, but this works too," she said, smiling as I crawled into the backseat. Chase groaned as he slid into the front seat.

"I tried to stop her, but she demanded I break out," Chase said.

"There's no stopping Scout."

"Yeah, I'm starting to see that."

"Where am I taking you?"

"Our place," I said, trying to sound as confident as Chase would have.

"Can I at least stop at my place to grab more clothes?" Chase asked, laughing.

"Fine. I'll allow it, but you have to let me help."

He laughed harder and talked with Ash, giving her directions to his place. Ten minutes later, Ash pulled up to the row of nice condos. I walked behind him, waiting as he unlocked the door.

"I've never seen inside your place before. I've seen the ridiculous house you threw your party at, but that's it."

"No, I guess not. That's one of my parents' houses. And honestly, I think that's because you call me and I come running over like a puppy dog more than demanding you come to me." He pushed open the door, letting me walk past him.

"In my defense, it is nice to have a hot guy who likes giving orgasms to show up on demand. He also orders tons of food I like. Do you really think I would put an end to that service?"

"And you call *me* spoiled?"

"Says the man walking into one of the nicest condos in town."

He set his keys down on the counter, pulling open the fridge and pulling out some cans of soda.

"Well, welcome to the place I sleep."

The walls were bare white, the kitchen area opening up to a living room, and a door to our left that I guessed was a bedroom or office. The entire place was clean…and boring. The furniture was black to match the black cabinets. There was one checkered rug that ran from the kitchen to the living room, and besides some clothes thrown over a chair, I could barely tell someone lived here.

"Is this all of it?"

"My bedroom is through there," he said, pointing to the door to our left. "And there is another room upstairs that I never use."

I walked over to the bedroom, wondering if it looked more lived in than out here, and when I pushed open the door, I wasn't surprised.

The bed was made, the black comforter clean and new, clothes were piled on a dresser, and there was a TV mounted on the wall. The closet was a normal closet, but I assumed it was filled with all his fancy lawyer clothes.

I spun back, almost running into him, but stopping short before I hurt him more. His eyes went heavy as he leaned down, his good hand moving up my neck to my jaw as he leaned in and kissed me. It was soft at first until his tongue darted out, running along my bottom lip. We moved backwards until my legs hit the bed, and I sat back. Before it could go any further, he groaned, standing back up. His chest started shaking with a pained laughter. "Alright, I can't quite do that yet."

I fell back, a wave of pleasure moving through me as I sunk

further into the bed. "Oh my god, this bed is amazing. This bed is a hundred times better than mine."

A horn honked outside, and I watched Chase shake his head as he went to his closet.

"It's the only thing in this place worth moving out when I go."

"You know, you won't need any of your fancy lawyer suits or clothes at my place."

"Yeah, but I have to figure out my law school exams now, so I better bring something nice just in case."

"The doctor did say to take the week off. I think that includes law school.

"I *have* to spend a week doing nothing but bothering you? I can't wait. Now come help me pack before I pass out from pain meds and exhaustion."

TWENTY-SIX
CHASE

SCOUT FUSSED the entire ride home and up to the apartment, treating me like I might collapse, or suddenly break another bone.

"Scout, I'm still able to walk. I think you're one step away from attempting to carry me up these steps."

"Do you need carried?" She asked, her worried eyes looking over my legs.

"You've got to be a foot shorter than me, if not more. How the hell do you think you are carrying me up two flights of stairs?"

"I can figure it out." She moved like she might actually try to put me on her back, but I threw an arm around her instead.

"You are something else, Hellcat. Relax, my legs are fine, besides a few bruises."

She nodded, but kept fussing about it more until I sat back on the couch, groaning as my back screamed once in pain before I could finally relax. Soon she was setting me up with a drink, food, and then getting herself curled up on the opposite side of the loveseat from me, all tucked in under a giant blanket.

"You don't have to wait on me, Scout. I'm functional."

Her lips pursed into a tight smile. "I know, but I can still help."

"Not if you're doing it because you feel guilty."

The door slammed open, the few filing in and spreading out around the living room with food as they put on a movie.

Scout never responded, but I think she moved the smallest amount closer to me. If anyone else noticed, they didn't say a word, and I was grateful.

I needed Scout near me tonight, and I was struggling to care if anyone else knew that.

The movie played for a while before I pulled at Scout's blanket, and the confusion on her face was cute. The furrowed brows made me take the first real breath I had since I left her apartment yesterday.

The entire time she was gone from the hospital, I worried that she would be mad at me. That somehow Jesse would spin this into a different story, and I would be the villain of it. I thought she would end up hating me somehow. But she didn't.

Instead, she defended me, and then came to take care of me.

"Come on, give me some of that. I'm cold," I whispered. No one would think twice about it besides Scout, who by now knew that I definitely didn't need a blanket.

She relented, throwing the blanket my way and moving closer so it would cover us both. She wasn't close enough to touch me, but I could feel her inches away, so close I could touch her.

My hand moved across the couch until I slid over her thigh. Her thighs stiffened under my fingers, the thin material of her pajama pants leaving little to nothing between us. Her lips parted the smallest amount until she pulled her bottom lip between her teeth.

Her eyes went wide again as she looked around the room, and then quickly back to the TV.

I moved further down, finding the edge of her underwear and following it until my hand was between her thighs. Her hips bucked up and mouth dropped open as I brushed against her clit.

She gasped a little too loud, and I laughed under my breath.

"Movie scaring you?"

"Yeah," she said, "that part was *really* a surprise."

I laughed harder, moving back over her again, teasing her with a light touch.

"I was just wondering how ready you were for me. The second we are alone, *you're mine*," I said, whispering in her ear.

She didn't dare look at me, and I had to look away, so I wasn't as tempted to lean down to kiss her. Hiding whatever was going on between us was only getting harder, and after the past twenty-four hours, I just wanted to hold her.

Instead, I ran my fingers back up her thigh, finding her hand and lacing her fingers in mine, loving the way she sighed and gripped my hand tighter.

———

AS SOON AS THE CREW LEFT AND THE DOOR SHUT BEHIND THEM, I was on edge waiting for her to come back over to me.

I thought she would hesitate somehow, or maybe tell me we shouldn't do anything, but that wasn't the case. She locked the door and came over, immediately dropping down until she was straddling me.

"I'm going to need these off," I whispered, pulling at her pajama bottoms.

She nodded, getting up and pulling them off before taking her shirt off too. I leaned forward, hooking a finger on her underwear and pulling those down.

"You are so fucking perfect. I don't even know where to start," I breathed, my heart beat almost painfully in my chest.

She reached down, pulling off my shirt, and helping me out of my jeans, then she straddled me again.

"After the day we've both had, I'd like to skip all the formalities and foreplay," she said, laughing as her hand traced my jaw and lips. A flicker of pain sliced through me as she moved over the bruises, each one a searing reminder that he put his hands on her too.

"Skip my favorite part? You're going to have to show me that you're ready for me then, baby."

She moved up onto her knees, not taking her eyes off me as she guided my cock to her, running it through her already wet pussy. The groan that escaped me was painful, knowing that I was inches from being buried in her, it was an agonizing fight to not just force my hips up and slam into her.

"Fuck, of course you're ready for me. Always so greedy with wanting my cock, aren't you?"

She nodded in agreement, biting at her lip and positioning me at her entrance. I was usually so good at controlling myself, but I could already feel the tightness in my groin. There was no way I was going to last long with her so eager for me.

For me.

Not a part of me, not the things I had, not because of who hung around me. She just wanted me.

My good hand wrapped around the back of her neck, careful as I brought her lips down to mine. She fell against me, deepening the kiss as she sunk down onto my cock.

"That's it," I groaned as she sunk down onto me more. "Fuck yes. It's all yours baby, every fucking inch, so take it all."

She listened, sinking down until there was nothing left to take. Her head fell back, the mane of red hair falling down her back as she moaned.

I had liked to hear her pleas and begs, but this time she was in control, and I was the one begging for more.

"Please," I said, trying to move with her but wincing at the pain. "Use me. Use my cock to take what you want."

I didn't move as she took over, riding me until her moans filled the room. Her hips sped up, and I reached down, pressing against her clit as she came apart. I was right there with her, my head falling back as the aching tension in my body finally released.

She finally slowed on top of me but didn't move from my lap, instead she fell against me, kissing my neck as I tried to steady my breathing.

The horrible day, the pain, the anger all washed away with her, and I didn't know how I would ever get through another bad day without her again.

TWO HOURS LATER, WE HAD SHOWERED AND NOW SHE WAS curled up against me, her hair a mane of red across my chest.

"My bed would be better," I said with a quiet laugh.

"Yeah, I'm now seeing the difference, and I have no way to fight you on this."

"I still like being here with you. Thank you for taking care of me."

"I didn't really do much."

"You fed me and got into bed next to me. That's all I needed."

I ran my hands over her. We were both still naked, but somehow it didn't feel sexual, it just felt normal.

"I needed you tonight, and you were there. Thank you."

"What are friends for?" she joked.

"I have never been jealous of your guy friends before, but if you are cuddling naked with them, we need to talk."

"Eww, gross."

"Then I am glad we are more than friends to be doing this."

"Yes, friends with benefits."

I didn't even want to respond. This may be her first time attempting a friends with benefits situation, but it wasn't mine, and I already knew we had moved way past the line of only being friends with benefits. For some reason, the moment I went to say that, though, I couldn't.

Instead, I ignored the aching in my chest and kissed her head instead. "I like these benefits. Are you really wanting me to stay the rest of the week here? I can manage fine at home."

"Yeah, I really do."

I shifted to pull her further on top of me, somehow needing her closer, even though that wasn't possible. "I have a dinner on Sunday I can't miss. It's going to be pretty funny showing up looking like this."

"Is your dad going to be pissed?"

"Oh, he already is. The hospital called him as a next of kin type thing. They knew who I was. He already called to bitch at me for a solid thirty minutes for hanging around dangerous people and getting myself in trouble."

"Dangerous people," she said with a small laugh. "Did they come to the hospital?"

"No, they are out of town. A relief for them, I'm sure."

"I doubt that."

I closed my eyes, taking a deep, shaky breath from the pain. Physical and mental. There was something weird about admitting to someone that no one cared about you, even the people that were biologically supposed to. Could anyone really see past someone's flaws if their own family couldn't?

I ran a hand up her arm to her face and then through her long hair, comforted by the fact that even though we had lived two completely different lives, she was one person who could understand that exact thing about me.

She propped herself up on an elbow, searching my face, but I wasn't sure what for.

"What are you doing, Hellcat?" I asked, my voice a tight whisper.

"Looking at you."

"Why?"

"Because I like what I am looking at."

"Hours of you being so sweet to me is absolutely breaking me. I never thought I would have you like this."

"What do you mean?"

"I mean, I knew I was getting the friends with benefits thing, I didn't know I would be getting treated like king of the fucking world. I don't know if you ever treated your ex-boyfriends like this, but I have no clue why any man would choose anything other than being in this bed with you every night if you gave him the option. I know I'm a little fucked up on pain pills, but you're fucking amazing, Scout."

She was quiet for a second, still looking at me until her face pinched. The room was almost too dark to see them, but I felt every tear drip onto my chest.

I wasn't really sure how she held it together this long. The day had almost broken me and I was pretty sure my chest was hollow. Hers somehow held a thousand hearts but she waited until now to fall apart.

I wrapped my arms around her, pulling her hard against me. She handled everything all day, She took care of me and worried over me all while she was fighting this. I should have worried about her more, but I was too busy needing her next to me.

"Hey, Hellcat," I whispered. "Not okay?"

"Not okay," she whispered back.

My arm wrapped tighter around her, holding her as close as I could.

"I'll be right here until you are."

TWENTY-SEVEN
SCOUT

NEARLY A WEEK WENT by of Chase staying with me. By the second day, he got bored and had started coming down to the garage with me most days. Surprisingly, even with one arm, he was starting to learn a lot and actually becoming helpful working on the cars.

The bruises on his face had started to fade the smallest amount, and his arm was finally feeling comfortable enough to not toss and turn all night. The ache in my chest was easing from the guilt, finally. The daily reminder that he didn't blame me seemed to help along with his healing.

I hadn't spent a night away from him, blaming it on my guilt for trying to help him heal, but I couldn't lie that I also was loving spending the time with him.

I didn't mind being warm and held every single night, either.

Was a girl supposed to be mad when a tall, gorgeous man wanted to strip down and keep her warm all night? For one that is perpetually cold, it was a dream come true.

Tonight, though, he had to go home for some important dinner with his family, and instead of staying home, I decided to get the crew out to race. Thursday races were done for the week, but we could still go out and find some people to race.

Twenty minutes later, I was already lined up at a light on a dead-end street, ready to race the guy next to me. Chase hadn't said a word about it, but I still owed him money, and I was slowly saving enough to start paying him back. The goons after my dad hadn't reached out yet, which was surprising, and I was hoping that meant my dad took care of everything. Although, he hadn't texted me back either, which was leaving a bad feeling in the pit of my stomach.

The crew was parked behind me, everyone hanging out while I raced, even though it wouldn't take long before we moved onto a new spot. We tried to move around town, a few pockets of side streets and deserted roads almost reserved for races these days.

Ransom ran up, flicking the light on, and we both took off. The race was short-lived when I looked up and immediately slammed on my brakes.

The red and blue lights lit up the dark night, blocking the path as my heart raced.

I hit at the steering wheel, watching as Kye slipped around one of the sheriff's cars and took off, cutting his lights and disappearing around a corner.

None of them went after him. Instead, they closed the gap, leaving us all stuck.

I groaned, already getting out as they swarmed the rest of the crew, handcuffs being put on everyone, and before I could blink, they were on me. Ten minutes later, I was being helped into the back of a sheriff's car and hauled to jail.

By the time I was led into the cell with the rest of the crew, I was fuming.

"Are you seriously arresting us all when we weren't doing anything?"

"You were street racing," the sheriff said. "That's illegal."

"We were not," Fox said, sitting down and kicking out his legs. "We were parked and hanging out."

"Right? Then how did we get a tip about a group causing trouble to local businesses and street racing?"

Ransom shrugged. "You can get a tip *and* it not be us. Did they have license plate numbers?"

The sheriff grinned. "I'm so glad you asked. They did. Hers." He pointed to me.

"Mine was the only one given?"

"Should there have been more?"

The shock hit me hard, but I quickly recovered from the confusion. "No. Mine shouldn't have been given. Maybe they saw my car, and assumed?"

"Or maybe you were racing and got caught."

My first thought was Jesse, but he wouldn't have been dumb enough to call only me in. I knew all the places he raced at, including any hidden spots, and he had to know I would turn him in immediately if he did this to me.

And I didn't think the goons after my dad would have any reason to turn me in. Wouldn't that just set them back further on getting money from me?

"Don't we get a phone call?" I asked, looking back at the crew. "Or several."

He nodded, pulling me back out and bringing me over to the nearby desk.

"I'm going to need my phone for the number."

He gave a sarcastic smile. "We don't do that here."

Ash laughed. "You better, because I'm going to be calling my dad."

Panic tore through me because I knew how pissed her dad would be with all of us, and at this point, I was worried he would be pissed enough not to let me have a chance on the team.

"I'll call someone!" I said quickly, holding out my hand from my phone. "But I need my phone, and then Holt doesn't have to come down here and yell at you."

The sheriff rolled his eyes, but dug out my phone, his eyes not leaving it as I pulled up my contacts, and hit Chase's number into the phone.

It rang a few times before he picked up.

"Hello?"

"Hey, it's Scout."

"Did you get a new number or something?" he asked.

"No, but I do need some help."

"Alright," he said wearily. "Where are you?"

I paused, not knowing how he would react to this. "Jail."

Silence filled the line and for a second, I thought he had hung up, but then I heard the faint sound of laughter. It grew louder and he must have pulled the phone back to his face.

"Did you say jail?"

"Yes, the crew and I are here and need some help getting out. I thought our lawyer could help."

"*Your* lawyer?"

"Yes, mine."

A deep rumble came over the phone. "Say that again and I might come help."

"Do you mean our lawyer?"

"No, the other part."

I fought my smile. "Mine."

"Yeah, that. I like that. Is everybody watching you right now?"

"Pretty much so keeping it professional would be great," I said, plastering a smile on my face.

"What are they saying you did?"

"They are accusing us of street racing."

He clicked his tongue. "A good girl like you would *never*. I am disappointed to find out that another man put you in handcuffs tonight. I still fantasize about you in handcuffs."

"Do you think that's necessary?"

He laughed. "I think so. Handcuffed to the bed, helpless to me making you come over and over. My hands, my tongue, my cock. I would be able to just keep going until you were begging me to stop."

I squirmed in the seat, heat pooling between my thighs as I tried to stop it.

"Maybe that's something we can talk further about when you get here."

"Why? I'm not the one that needs to stay professional right now?"

"I do."

"Are you managing to do that? Or are you getting wet thinking about the things I want to do to you?" He groaned. "Now I'm just sitting here fantasizing about my little criminal. Maybe I should bring my own set of handcuffs. I could add a vibrator too, hold it against you until you're in tears from endless orgasms. You love it when I do that with my hand. I bet you'll come harder than you ever have in your life."

"Okay, great!" I said, my pussy so tight it almost hurt. "Will you be coming soon, then?"

"Talk to me like that and I might come *very* soon."

"Please," I asked, gritting my teeth.

"Okay, now you're just playing into it."

I was silent, waiting for him to answer, and I worried I was going to start playing into it too much.

"Fuck, I can't wait for the day you get on your knees asking to *please* take my cock. I already dream of wrapping one of those fucking braids around my hand as you take my cock in your throat."

My face dropped, and I tried to recover as another wave of heat shot down my spine. "That would be great."

"Yeah? Would you like to try that with me?"

"Yes, I would."

He groaned. "Good, because I'm already on my way, but please know I will have to wait a few seconds for my dick to not be hard. I'll be there in about fifteen minutes."

The sheriff waved his hand, urging me to wrap it up. "*Good*, because I have run out of time. See you in a few."

The sheriff grabbed the phone, slamming it down, and walking me back to the cell.

Quinn's eyebrows jumped up. "Who did you call?"

I knew they were minutes from finding out, but telling them somehow felt like I was announcing to everyone that I was sleeping with Chase.

"I called Chase. I didn't want your dad to know what happened," I said to Ash. "And he was the only person I could think of that had the money and some legal knowledge to maybe help us get out of here tonight."

"It's ten PM. I doubt we are getting out of here tonight," Fox said.

I shrugged, trying not to smile. I couldn't exactly tell them that after that phone call, Chase might have a little more incentive to get us out of here tonight. And I *really* couldn't tell them that I was hoping to get out of here tonight to perform those incentives.

I sat back, quietly waiting and trying to keep my cool, but almost fifteen minutes later exactly, Chase walked in.

Somehow, every time I saw him, it felt a little like a punch to the gut. He was back to perfect Chase, every hair in line, a button-up shirt and suit jacket covering every part of his body that I had come to know so well. He was in jeans, but somehow on him, it looked professional. This time, it didn't bother me like it had before because this time I was too excited to be the one to mess it up.

TWO HOURS LATER, THEY OPENED THE DOOR, AND I SAW CHASE'S perfect face again, covered in a huge smile.

"Well, hello my little band of heathens. You'll be happy to know your lawyer, me, got it all brought down to warnings. But if you get caught street racing, which I *assured* them you were not doing, it's jail time." His lips pressed together with a smile as his voice dropped low enough for only us to hear. "Again."

"You seem awfully happy to be picking us up from jail," I said, stepping aside as the crew walked out.

"Oh, I am. This is being added to one of the best days of my life."

"They basically ambushed us. I would like to know how they knew where we were."

He waved to the sheriff as we walked out. "So where's Kye?"

"Spun a 180 and got the hell out of there while we all got caught," Ransom said.

"It probably helped our case," Ash said. "No one's going to let us off the hook if they see the long list of trouble Kye has been in."

"True," Ransom said. "But I wasn't hoping to sit here half the night either."

"I'm starving," Carly said. "And no, I'm not cooking anything for you now." She glared at Jax, who kissed her head.

"Listen, you knew the life you were signing up for when you started dating a bad boy."

She scoffed and rolled her eyes. "Right. *Such a bad boy.* What were you doing this time last night? Oh, that's right, taking a bubble bath." He laughed hard, pulling open the door for her as we walked outside.

"Then you shouldn't be complaining," he said.

"How about we meet up at the diner?" I asked.

"I got a hold of Kye so we met up, and he got us the keys to Quinn's car. I had my friend bring it over, but he had to head to a party. I assumed you all would need a ride since yours are all a little...locked up for the night."

Kye jumped on his car, yelling as half the crew got into his car and half got into Quinn's.

"While those look cozy," I said. "I'm making Chase drive me over. We'll see you there."

They all yelled and waved, tires screeching as they immediately started to race out of the parking lot.

Chase turned to me, laughing as we headed to the car. "You know, for a band of heathens, you guys are all pretty great."

"Yeah? You like picking us up from jail?"

He smiled, opening the passenger door for me. "It was a fun phone call to get."

I slid inside, my nerves making me feel like my entire body was buzzing. I tried to stay calm as Chase got in and pulled out of the station. The drive to the diner wasn't more than ten minutes from here, so I didn't waste any time leaning over and undoing his belt.

I could hear the harsh breath he sucked in and he grabbed my hand. "What are you doing?" he asked, a smile on his face.

"I thought I owed the lawyer a payment?"

He laughed, watching as I unbuttoned his jeans and moved them a little off his hips. "You don't have to do that. I know you don't like doing it, and I was only kidding on the phone."

"I wasn't. And I want to do this."

He groaned as I reached in and pulled out his hard cock. His hand tightened on the steering wheel and I smiled as I leaned down. He was right. I usually hated this, but I was already so turned on that I couldn't remember what part about it I hated before.

I pulled him into my mouth, liking the way he groaned again and moved his hips, pushing a little deeper into my mouth. I hollowed out my cheeks, moving faster for a few seconds before attempting to take him all.

"*Fuck,*" he hissed. I felt the car speed up, and I moved faster, liking the way he cursed and groaned. The car jerked, and I went to sit up as we came to a stop, but his hand went into my hair, keeping my lips wrapped around his cock.

"You wanted my cock, baby, so take it."

I did, dropping back down until he was buried in my throat. I could feel how wet I was already and was wishing I could do anything about it. I wasn't expecting to actually get turned on by this and I wished I would have known. There wasn't any time to do more than this, so I moved faster until his hips pushed up hard one more time as he came.

I finally sat back up, breathing hard along with him. There was no way I hated that. Based on how wet I still was, I could never say I hated that again. I just hated doing it with certain people.

Chase took three more steadying breaths before adjusting his jeans and pulling back onto the road. If it took us too long, it would bring up too many questions, and I was glad he seemed okay with that.

"You're fucking amazing, and I will be coming back to your apartment tonight to give you orgasms until you pass out," he said, his breath steady again.

I laughed, smiling as he pulled into the diner, adjusting his jeans and shirt the rest of the way as he watched me. "I mean, I can't say no to that."

"Somehow, you keep surprising me. I thought picking you up

from jail was a shock. Who would have thought that came after?"

"Like I said, we did discuss payment beforehand," I said, liking the way his hand rested on my lower back.

"I hope for my sake you have some sort of need for a lawyer again in the future."

I turned, making sure he didn't look like he had just been given a blowjob in the car and then flipping the mirror down to check myself. "I don't think that has to be the *only* time I ever do that."

"Really? Decided you don't hate it?"

"No, I don't think I do," I said, as he pulled open the door to the diner for me. "Actually, I think I could enjoy doing that again very soon."

TWENTY-EIGHT

SCOUT

THE NEXT OFFICIAL race day with Holt came before I felt ready. The Holt Racing car I've been using was more prepared than I was, but it didn't feel as much of a comfort as I hoped.

The last two weeks had been nothing but Chase, and catching up at the garage. I barely got time to practice, but I hoped it was fine. We were back at Holt's track for this race and I knew it well, so there was nothing for me to be too worried about. If I placed in the top five again, I would be guaranteed a spot at the races next week in Las Vegas. With this race being pushed back, we now had two back-to-back weeks planned.

Now, if I went and placed in the race in Vegas, Holt agreed to keep me on the team permanently, which meant I would be traveling around the country during the race season, getting to race professionally.

My anxiety spiked, the idea that my entire life goal was on the line again making me nervous. Today was only five races, which meant five races to win the entire day, and three needed to place enough to move on. Ash came over, handing me my race suit and helmet.

"Are you sure you don't want a last name on this?" she asked, holding up the race suit. "It's so much cuter with a last name."

I shook my head, looking at the back with her. "No, thanks. The name Allen can die with my dad because there is no way I am bringing any light or success to it."

"You could always use Holt," she said, shrugging. "And I'm sure any of the guys would let you use theirs."

"I think I'd rather it be blank. Those aren't mine, and I'd rather not use Holt and let everyone think he has a long lost red-headed daughter that he isn't telling people about."

She laughed harder, pulling me into a hug. "I would take you as an adopted sister any day of the week."

"Until your dad offers, I'll just be over here as Scout and nothing more."

"You know, they are going to need a name to add to the boards. Your name is already going to be posted. If you want to change it for the public, you're going to need to do it soon. Especially after you win in Vegas."

"*If* I win in Vegas."

"Nope, I said it exactly how I meant it. You'll kick ass today and in Vegas. Come on, suit up so we can get you on the track."

Everyone crowded around my car while I went into the trailer to get dressed. Before I could even shut the door, someone was tapping on it.

"Scout?"

"Yes?" I asked, pushing the door open a little to see Chase.

He was smiling, looking as good as he had the first time he came to my race, but this time, I was a little more appreciative of it. I pushed open the door, pulling him in fast. The crew was on the other side of the trailer and wouldn't see him come in, but I wasn't going to risk him standing out there too long.

As soon as the door shut, he grabbed my face, pulling me in hard and kissing me.

"You ready to win?"

"Always."

He smiled, his lip healing and bringing back the devastating smile that made my stomach flutter. He kissed me again before I stepped back.

"If we make out in here for too long, we are bound to get caught."

"They don't know I'm here yet. I'll just walk around the other side and pretend I just showed up."

"Alright. I just don't want them to know about…" My voice trailed off as I pulled my bottom lip between my teeth. It didn't feel right to call this a friends with benefits situation anymore, but I knew Chase wasn't going to give me more. I had been fighting it all week. We had basically been living together, and I had loved every second of it. But every time I went to bring up the idea of ending this arrangement and starting a new one, my stomach would churn and I would get too nervous to say a word.

Kind of like now.

He was still smiling. "Know about us?"

"Yeah, that."

"How about we talk about it later and for now, you go win some races?"

I gave a sharp nod. "I think that's a great idea."

FOR THE NEXT FEW HOURS, I DID EXACTLY THAT. I FOCUSED, I raced, I won. Each race went by with ease and before I knew it, I was lined up for the third race. I needed to win this one or the next to stay in the running for Vegas.

I took a deep breath, sitting behind the wheel as a car next to me lined up. My adrenaline spiked as the roar of engines drowned out the world around me. It wasn't long before the light changed and we both took off. It was a simple race, one straight line for a road against another car. I had done it a thousand times, and I knew as soon as the back of my car broke loose, I was in serious trouble.

The entire car started moving sideways as I tried to correct it and failed. The car turned too much, slamming into the wall. The sound of the metal smashing into concrete was nearly as bad as the impact, the crunch of metal and plastic making my eyes squeeze shut.

I let off the gas, but the car kept going, the screech of metal reverberating through me.

The car finally came to a stop, the impact still reverberating through my body, every nerve tingling with shock. I tried to calm the panic that bubbled up, knowing I could get it under control if I didn't let it get worse. I kicked my legs out, feeling that they were free enough. My hands shook as I reached for the release of my safety harness, the metal click echoing loudly in the eerie aftermath of the crash.

I pushed against the driver's door, which luckily opened with ease. It was the passenger side that was mainly ruined. My heart sank as I looked over the car. I couldn't imagine this was going to help my chances, and after losing that race and not having a car for the next, I was pretty sure my dreams of racing in Vegas next week were crushed.

By the time I turned to look down the track, the crew was already there.

"Are you okay?" Fox yelled before they even stopped.

I gave him a thumbs up, still fighting to get my helmet off.

"I'm fine," I yelled as they stopped. The track officials were right behind them, looking over the car to make sure it wasn't going to catch fire before seeing if anything was leaking. The track would be down for a while if anything spilled out.

I didn't listen as they talked to Ransom and Fox, who were quick in moving the car. Chase came over, looking me up and down and then to the car behind me.

"Are you actually okay?"

"Yeah, it didn't do any damage to me, just the car."

His eyes were wide, his jaw tight as he looked at me again. I could see how bad he wanted to reach out and check me over like he had at the hospital. He was inspecting every inch of me, the hardened look on his face not softening.

"You were just thrown into a wall at a hundred miles an hour. What do you mean it didn't do any damage to you?"

"The suit, the roll cage, the helmet. They all did their job and I'm completely fine."

He didn't look like he believed me, and it really didn't seem like that when he slammed against me, wrapping his arms around me tight and fast.

"Fuck," he mumbled, squeezing me so hard that I almost couldn't breathe.

"Come on," Fox yelled, waving at us. "Let's get her down the track and checked out."

Chase nodded, his face hardening and apparently going into business mode. He walked me to a car without a word, and once we were back down the track, he brought me right to the EMTs who checked me over.

"Was that enough?" Chase asked. "Shouldn't you check her over more than that? Doesn't she need a brain scan or something?"

The EMT's eyebrows furrowed as he looked at me. "You passed all the concussion checks, but is any part of your head or neck hurting? Did you hit it on anything?"

"No," I growled, looking at Chase. "I was perfectly strapped in and was barely jolted. I am fine."

"If you are feeling any headaches, nausea, dizziness, anything that could indicate a concussion, you need to go in immediately and get checked further, but unless that happens, everything looks good."

I hopped up, grabbing Chase's good arm and dragging him away before he ordered any more tests.

"I'm fine, Chase. I wouldn't lie about that."

"But what if you aren't?"

"Then I will go to the hospital."

He started behind one of the race trailers, dragging me along with him.

"Scout, you have to be sure."

"I'm sure. Are *you* okay?"

"No, I just watched you smash into a fucking wall. Why would I be okay?" His chest rose and fell faster now, his hand plunging into his hair. I knew he was worried, but I didn't know how else to tell him I was okay. It was the best outcome for a wreck, and I had smashed up plenty of cars in my life when learning how to race, or drift, or even more recently, how to race on dirt tracks. There were endless ways to wreck and the only thing I could do was try to correct the car as much as I could to make the wreck less damaging. At some point, though, there was nothing I could do to help.

"Because I didn't get hurt."

"But you could have. I remember Ash's crash. I remember how badly she was hurt. That could happen to you."

"Maybe, but Ash is here, and she's okay now."

He only shook his head, and the angry flex to his jaw made me step back.

"Chase, I don't know what else to say. I'm okay. This is just a part of racing sometimes."

His jaw didn't loosen, and if it was possible, I think he tightened it even more. "Yeah," he said, his eyes meeting mine. "I guess it is, but I don't think I was ready for that."

"No one ever is, but it's okay, Chase."

"I don't think it is," he said quietly. Tears threatened me, knowing that whatever he meant by that wasn't going to be good.

I looked past him to the crew, who were pushing the car up to its parking spot next to the trailer. "Come on," I said, pulling him with me. "I need to see if the car has any chance at another race today if I want to stay in the running for the races next week."

Suddenly, I was sick to my stomach for another reason, not liking the look on Chase's face, and to add to it, the look on Fox's wasn't comforting either.

I might just lose my chance to race next week, *and* this arrangement with Chase all in one day.

TWENTY-NINE
SCOUT

I HAD WAITED for two days to hear from Holt, and on Sunday, he finally called. I held my breath the entire call, waiting to hear if I would continue on in the races.

When I ended the call and turned around, the entire crew was waiting.

Finally, the smile broke on my face. "I'm going to Vegas," I said, almost too stunned to believe it. "Someone else wrecked after me and I had a few more points, so they let me move on."

Yelling and cheers broke out as they crowded around me, ready to celebrate.

"There was one condition," I yelled as they nearly piled on top of me. A round of groans broke out as everyone stepped back.

Ash sighed. "What does my dad want from us now?"

"He wants us all to go to the party that someone is having? He said you already know what it is and he would like us all there to show our support."

She groaned. "Yeah, it's a party for some guy and my dad is trying to partner with him. I guess he's hoping the party will finalize the deal. He wanted me there to play up how great the racing division is going. I don't know why, the guy is obsessed with my dad. He's obviously going to work with him."

"Well, we have to go, and if that's all it takes to keep your dad happy, I'm going."

"Do we all have to go?" Kye asked.

"No, don't even worry about it. Scout and I can go, and he will be fine," Ash said.

They all nodded, dispersing into the living room.

"Well then, I need to run out for a few things before we go."

"Scout, I have plenty of dresses. You can borrow something of mine."

"I already have a dress," I said, already knowing I was going to wear a green dress that hung in the back of my closet. "I have other errands I need to do. I'll be back with plenty of time for you to do my hair and makeup," I said, smiling as she laughed.

While I didn't need a dress, I did need shoes after I broke the last pair of heels that actually looked good with the dress, so I stopped and got those first. Then I had a few errands for the garage and a stop at the grocery store before I was finally ready to head home.

My car was parked in the middle of the parking lot, a black SUV behind it. I adjusted my grip on the bags in my hand, wishing I had a free hand to reach down and grab my knife from my boot. I went right back into the habit of carrying it around with me, and would drop the bags if the doors to the car opened.

Every move I made was hesitant as I reached the car and put the bags in. The windows were as black as the SUV and there was no way to know if it was the gambling goons or not, but I wasn't risking it. My heart rate spiked as I jumped into my car and locked the doors.

There was still no movement, but that didn't mean anything yet.

I pulled out, trying not to look back the entire time, but seeing the car pull out not far behind me. Worry settled into my gut, but I tried to ignore it and focus on driving.

Anyone could be pulling out at the same time. It's not like that didn't happen, and just because they parked behind me meant nothing.

I made a right turn, heading towards the highway, and watching as the car followed. They kept in sync, turning when I turned, going where I went.

Fear and anger flared as I thought back to the night the stupid guys had found me and pushed me into my car. I couldn't believe that my dad still hadn't paid his debts and sent them after me for more. I picked up my pace, pulling into the garage under our apartments and shutting the door fast behind me. I froze, watching as they drove past, slowing down for a second before speeding off.

At this rate, I would never have any money.

Or Chase would just never have a watch again in his life.

ASH AND I WALKED INTO THE LARGE BALLROOM ALREADY flooded with people.

"I always forget how big these things are," I said.

"It seems like they get bigger each time. Come on, let's get drinks first. That always helps." She gave me a smirk and pulled me into the crowd.

I pulled us to a stop, catching sight of the man across the room, the man I knew so well now. I knew the way his eyes brightened when he smiled, the crinkles around his eyes, and the dimples that came out when he smiled hard. I knew the way he held me, how sweet he could be, and how he really liked to give me orgasms.

I knew that guy, but this wasn't him.

Chase's eyes were a haze now, his lips pulled into a tight frown that never let up. The way he moved wasn't calm and sure, like I had grown used to. Now it looked robotic. He reached out to shake someone's hand, the stiff posture of it a harsh contrast of the relaxed way he greeted the crew.

I could barely recognize him now, the hollow look about him making him a zombie.

"Is that Chase?"

Ash looked around. "Oh yeah, I didn't know he was going to be here. I mean, he comes to some of them, but it's rare to find him anywhere but hiding out drinking in the back," she said, laughing.

She didn't know my heart was thundering, the roaring sound drowning out the party. A girl walked up next to Chase and smiled up at him. I was surprised when he gave her a half smile back. She reached up, resting a hand on his bicep as she talked. He didn't shake her off and didn't step away.

I felt like I was watching something that I wasn't supposed to be seeing.

"Come on," Ash said. "Let's go say hi first."

She moved me through the crowd, my legs following her from muscle memory more than an understanding of what was happening.

The crowd parted as we got closer and the thought of her touching him so intimately only made my stomach drop more. A strange mix of anger and jealousy making me flush, and sick.

"Hey Chase," Ash said, a smile plastered on her face, but Chase's eyes went right to mine. Dull, lifeless eyes that only widened when they saw me.

"Ashton? Is that you?" Chase's dad said, sticking out a hand to shake hers. "I haven't seen you around lately."

"I've mainly kept to my dad's parties, but he asked for my

assistance tonight," she said with a small laugh. "Said this would be a bigger party and he would need reinforcements."

That made him laugh before he turned to me. "And Scout, correct?"

"Yes, that's me." I shook his hand, not daring to look at Chase again, but I did notice the girl's hand had dropped from him.

I wanted to reach out and grab him. I wanted her hands to stay off of him.

I wanted him to be mine, and have any right to tell him not to let other girls be all over him.

Ash turned to the girl. "I feel like we may have met, but I apologize. I've been away so much my memory isn't working great."

The girl got the hint, shaking Ash's hand. "Luckily, I don't believe we've met. I'm Claire."

She was sweet, her blonde hair pulled up into a fancy bun. Her jewelry flashing in the lights, and I'm sure every single diamond on her was real. Her dress fit perfect, and I realized this was the life Chase had. Every hair in place, every piece of clothing being tailored to fit like it was made for you, everything had to be perfect.

Ash had put waves in my hair, half of it pulled into a braid that sat at the back. It was pretty, and I felt beautiful in my deep green dress, but I would never be this type of beautiful.

"Nice to meet you. Both of you." She reached her hand out to me and I took it, my stomach threatening to throw up the burger I had inhaled on the way here.

"Claire is Chase's soon to be fiancé," his dad said, smiling proudly, and I tried not to notice how he was looking at me when he said it. I would hope that was only a coincidence. He couldn't possibly know what was going on.

"Fiancé?" Ash said, nearly spitting out her drink, her shock mimicking mine.

He had a fiancé, or at the very least, his dad thought he did.

"I swear to god if you keep telling people we are going to be engaged I'll —" Now I was really going to be sick. I couldn't even look at him, but I could hear the disgust in his tone.

"You'll what, Chase? Embarrass me in front of everyone like you are threatening to do now?"

I finally looked up and was surprised that Chase's eyes were on me. The calm, hollow look was still there, as though what his dad had just said didn't even faze him.

"Excuse us," I said, grabbing onto Ash, and immediately pulling her away.

"Scout, wait," Chase said. I thought he would catch up to us, but when I looked back, his dad had his bad arm in his hand, holding him in place. If it was anyone else, I might start threatening them to let him go, but this wasn't my fight.

If he wanted to let his dad stop him, he could.

We made it to the table someone had directed us to, and we were swarmed right away. Two guys sitting down on either side of us.

Ash smiled with that fake smile she had mastered. "Can we help you?"

"Only wanted to see if you two cared for company."

"No, thanks we —" Ash started, but I cut her off.

"Yes, actually, we do."

Her eyebrows jumped up, but she didn't say a word as they sat down next to us.

They quickly introduced themselves, Justin and Josh. I wasn't sure how I was supposed to keep that straight, but I didn't think it mattered.

Justin sat by me, throwing an arm over the back of my chair. His fingers hovering near my shoulder.

They started talking about who was who, and Ash joined in. She was always pleasant in conversation no matter what was happening. Years of dealing with these types of events drilling it into her. I didn't know how she did it because I was ready to stomp out of here.

I wanted to turn around and look for Chase, but I wouldn't do that. If he didn't want to come find me and stay with his fiancé instead, then we had nothing to talk about.

Another minute went by and I realized Justin's hand had moved closer to my shoulder. I went to move forward, but froze as a head came down between Justin and I.

"If you don't take your hand off her chair, Justin, I'm going to break it."

Justin laughed, but didn't move. "Hey man, where have you been?"

"I'm pretty sure he was with his fiancé," I said, leaning back again.

"Oh yeah, Claire is here?"

I only sneered, so it was common enough knowledge that they were engaged somehow that even this guy knew about it.

"I think you thought I was kidding, but I'm not." Chase grabbed Justin's arm, pulling it back until he ripped it away.

"Ouch, what the fuck?"

"Don't fucking touch her again."

"Go away Chase. You don't need to be over here bothering us when you have a fiancé to attend to."

Justin shook his head. "She's right. You can't have a fiancé and take the other single hot girl here."

"I don't have a fiancé and she isn't single. Come on, Scout. I need to talk to you."

Ash's eyebrows jumped up and a smile spread across her face.

"Don't you dare say one word," I said, pointing at her.

"Oh babe, I don't need to say anything. I will be here enjoying every second of this, though."

"Scout, come with me."

"No."

"You don't have a choice right this second and if you don't get up right now, I'm going to throw you over my shoulder and walk you out of here like that in front of everyone."

I stared at Ash and she laughed more. "He will do it, Scout."

"Fine," I said, standing up so fast that the chair knocked into him. "You get five minutes."

He grabbed my waist, pulling me against his side, and holding onto me as though I might bolt. I tried not to look up, but failed. Everything about him wasn't him. The dull lifelessness in his eyes, the weirdly perfect posture, the cold tone. I hated it.

We rounded the corner, making it into a side room before he slammed the door shut, falling against it with a hard, deep breath.

This was the Chase I didn't like, the one that I met the night of the races.

This wasn't my Chase, and a lump formed in my throat when I realized he may never be *my* Chase again.

THIRTY
CHASE

I DON'T KNOW how long I leaned against the door. I had already been on edge, and then she had showed up, ruining any semblance of control I had over the night.

It had started off like any one of these parties, but for some reason, the way my dad bitched at me the entire ride here pissed me off more than usual.

I had already been in a bad mood. I wasn't actually sure if my heart had stopped racing since Scout's wreck. I had wanted to stay with her, but her apartment had felt suffocating. The way she looked at me kept making my stomach tighten and roll. I wanted to reach out and hold her in fear that there would be a day I wouldn't be able to, that one of those wrecks could be the end for her. And at the same time, I wanted to run and save myself before I even had the chance to lose her.

But then, two days went by and I kept getting more agitated.

I had known it from the moment I met Scout that she wasn't a girl I should mess with. Not only did I know it, but she knew it. Fox knew it. Hell, even Ash had reminded me more than once to not waste my time bothering Scout.

It hadn't mattered, though. I still pushed for more. Then, the moment she broke up with Jesse, I was nearly begging for more. I knew I was shit at relationships, so I offered everything I could, even when I knew it wasn't enough for her.

And now, I still wanted to push for more again. I had planned to talk to her at the races, but instead I watched her run into a fucking wall.

Every emotion, every feeling I had remembered these last few months was replaced with a gut-wrenching ache that it would be gone forever. That I could go home that day and never see her again.

I wasn't sure how to live a life without Scout in it now, but how was I supposed to live that life with a girl who was making a living out of cheating death? Ash almost died from her crash, the scar across her chest a reminder of how close she had come. Could I stand there and watch Scout do the same?

I had spent the entire two days away from her wondering about it all, and before I could even come close to figuring it out, she walked in and saw Claire by me.

It wasn't right, but I had even loved the way the jealousy had been all over her face.

And I had to realize it was because I loved everything about Scout.

My heart wasn't mine anymore. I thought Scout would be the one to make a mess of this and want a relationship, yet here I was, avoiding her because I didn't know what the fuck I was supposed to do next.

I opened my eyes and looked her over. I had tried to force myself to stop staring before, but in here she was all mine to look at. I could openly stare and take it all for myself.

"You look beautiful," I finally said.

I spent my life being stupid and reckless, being told I was going to marry a country club girl that liked these lawyer parties, and cooking, and maybe tennis. A girl who definitely didn't race cars, or get emotional at the drop of a hat. Not only emotional, but somehow manage to feel every emotion simultaneously.

A girl I would never be picking up from jail in the middle of the night. And while it was never specified, I assumed it included girls who weren't giving you blowjobs behind the police station.

I always guessed that I would be the reckless one in a relationship, but somehow Scout liked a lot of bad things.

"I wasn't trying to be a dick, I just didn't want everyone staring at us," I said, realizing that my time was probably running out and she had barely said a word to me still.

What I really wanted to say was that I didn't know how I was supposed to continue on with this life that had been planned for me when I knew a life existed with Scout. I would have to live every day of my pathetic life knowing that someone, somewhere, had Scout in their life and I didn't.

"Why? You don't like more eyes on you when you look like a zombie?"

"A zombie?"

"You're all scary and dead walking around down there. You look dead and hollow again."

"I guess that's how I get at these things. I didn't realize it was so noticeable," I said. I shouldn't be shocked now that I knew Scout and her ability to care so deeply about the people she cared about, but I still couldn't believe someone cared about me enough to notice those things. To see that I was struggling when everyone else carried on like normal.

"I guess it wouldn't have been to anyone else. Maybe I've just come to know you a little differently."

"I think you know me better than anyone."

"Is that why you've been avoiding me?" she asked.

"No."

"Then why?"

"Because Scout," I said, the words painful before I even got them out. "You ran into a wall. A fucking *wall*. And what? I'm supposed to hang around until you do it again? Just wait for the day I get to see you wreck and get hurt or worse? I can't fucking do that."

Her eyebrows furrowed, and her face fell. "So you're avoiding me because I wrecked a little? Are you trying to say that I should give up racing because *you* are worried?"

"No, of course not. I would never even think to ask you that, and I don't want you to. I just don't know how to sit and watch it happen again. What if you're hurt? What if there is nothing I can do to help? There would be nothing I could do but stand there. And then how do I explain that? My dad nearly had a heart attack with me showing up bruised and broke. What would happen if it were you?" I pushed a hand back into my hair again. The stress was eating me alive, making me pace the room as she stared at me.

"Are you worried about me wrecking and getting hurt or are you worried about what other people would think about who I am and what I do?"

I stopped, taking three large steps and reaching for her. "You. I'm worried about you, but the other stuff only adds to the mess. Standing there helpless and waiting to find out if you were going to get out of the car was the worst minute of my life. In ten fucking seconds, it felt like everything could be over, and I had to stand there and watch it."

She slipped out of my grip, stepping back and out of reach again. The hurt in her eyes was killing me, but I didn't even know what I should do about this, let alone what I could tell her to make it better.

"I think we have two different lifestyles," she finally said. "I think we have two completely different lives, and I don't think those two lives can survive together. I think we both knew it from the start and it's just finally showing how well it *doesn't* work together. There's no overlap, Chase, and yeah, I might wreck again. It might be tomorrow, it might be a year from now, but it doesn't mean it's going to be bad. What I won't ever be, though, is anything like the girls down there. I grew up in a very different life from them, and even if I tried, I would never be them. Whatever agreement or arrangement we had is done. It's getting too messy for both of us now." She started towards the door, but I caught her.

"Wait, Scout. It can't be done."

"If we keep going, I'm going to get hurt, and I'm sorry, but I can't do that again." She pulled open the door, making me follow her into the hallway.

"Dammit," I said as we ran right into my dad.

"What are you two doing up here? Are you two up here fucking around after I just introduced you to his fiancé?"

Scout smiled, holding her head up and facing him, which only made my chest tighten more. I didn't know who Scout would ever be scared of, but it sure as hell wasn't going to be my father.

He stared her down until she finally turned to me, rolling her eyes. "Like I said, two different worlds that will never fit together."

She walked past us, and I moved to go with her, but my dad caught my arm.

"What are you doing?"

"Fucking hell, can you just leave me alone for ten minutes?"

"Excuse you?" he asked. The way his shoulders straightened almost made me apologize, but as I watched Scout disappear down the steps, I realized how little I cared.

I didn't care about him. I didn't care about being a lawyer. I sure as hell didn't care about taking over his slimy company.

"I said leave me alone. You know exactly what you were doing when you tried to pretend Claire and I were engaged. You fucking knew what you were doing, and you thought all your manipulation tactics were going to work? Did you really think I wouldn't clear that up with her?"

"I see how well that went for you," he said, smirking as he looked over his shoulder.

My fingers flexed into a fist until I realized how badly I wanted to punch my own father.

"What do you want?" My words were strained, my throat feeling like it was ready to close up.

"I want you to get back downstairs and knock this off. I told you she wasn't worth it and then you brought her here? Even worse, you disappeared with her. Your mother is just as upset as I am, and you need to go down and apologize to her. Claire too."

"You can't be serious right now?"

But I already knew he was. This was my life, and the reason I never felt anything was because I was told I wasn't allowed to.

And all that time I had laid down and fucking listened until I wasn't even myself. Until I wasn't even sure who I was. That was never the person I wanted to be, but I let it happen over and over again until I was so disconnected that Scout would call me hollow.

Why would I fight for the life he was trying to force me into now?

Could I manage to not become him? Or would I just work a job that made me scum with a wife that didn't like anything about me but stayed for the money? My parents could say that they loved each other, but I never thought it was true. And seeing the way that the crew not only loved each other but the way those guys talked about each one of the girls only proved my point.

Even if I loved Scout, I didn't know how I was supposed to sit back and watch her crash into walls.

I pulled away from my dad and headed back downstairs, ignoring his demands for an apology, and stepping outside to take a deep breath. I wish I had anything to smoke, wished I could stay numb to the world. I wasn't sure how Scout managed all her emotions and didn't collapse under the weight of them all. She opened up whatever heart I had left and unleashed every pent up emotion I'd been holding back for years.

It didn't matter. No matter what happened now, Scout was right. I couldn't have this life and have her.

THIRTY-ONE

CHASE

MY BAG WAS ALREADY PACKED for Vegas when I picked up my phone and called Ash.

"If you're calling to explain what the hell happened the other night, I'm listening, because Scout is not talking. If you're calling because you think I'm somehow going to make Scout not hate you again, you might as well hang up now, because there is no use," Ash said, but I could almost hear the smile in her voice.

I laughed. "At least you picked up the phone, so I might still have a chance. I was calling because I need a favor."

"Alright, what is it?"

"I know you are all going to Vegas, and I want to get a ride with you."

"You think showing up unannounced on her race week is the best option to not piss her off? Maybe if you tell me what exactly happened, I could be more helpful."

"I can't wait another day waiting to hear back from her, so this is currently my only option. And no, I won't be saying what happened, but let's leave it at—she saw me being an asshole and called me out for it."

"As she should. I really want to demand for you to tell me more, but I think the less I know, the better. The plane takes off in an hour, so hurry up. My dad got a private plane for the teams, and I think we have an extra spot. I'll text you the address. A quick heads up, if she doesn't want you on the plane and sends the guys to take you off of it, there will be no putting up a fight. This is my dad's business, and some of his partners are coming. We can't have a fight going on."

I grabbed my keys and bag and was already heading out the door. "That's all fair. I'll be there shortly. And thank you, Ash. I owe you."

"And I will be holding you to that. Just try to get yourself on the plane before you promise anything more."

I laughed and thanked her again before heading out. My Porsche had been mysteriously delivered yesterday. The last way Scout cut our ties. I had been mad when I first saw it, but it didn't matter. I didn't need her around to fix my car.

I sped up. The address Ash gave me was about thirty minutes away, and I would need to get there with plenty of time to get on and stay on.

It was clear where I could park when I got there. Two of the crew's cars were parked in the small parking lot. My heart rate picked up when I got out and grabbed my bag. I wanted to think I could be relaxed about this, but if Scout tried to tell me to leave, I didn't know if I could go as easily as Ash told me I would have to.

I stepped onto the plane, Kye and Jax greeted me immediately, and the rest of the crew turned to chime in. Everyone seemed fine with me coming, but when I turned around, I came face-to-face with my beautiful little ankle-biter.

And she looked ready to fucking bite.

"What are you doing here?" she asked, her eyes wide as I set my bag down.

"Going to Vegas."

"Why?"

"Because I wanted to see you race."

Her eyes rolled hard, and her hand flew to her hips, the stance only helping her angry glare. "I think you made it clear that you don't want to do that."

"Do you want to talk outside for a second?" I asked, leaning down to whisper the rest. "Because some of the things I want to say will make what's happening between us very clear."

"No. I don't, and there is nothing between us now," she hissed. Her foot tapped a few times before she looked up at me, her face not giving away even a hint of emotion. "You're seriously trying to come with us?"

"Bags packed, and I'm here, so yes."

She stared at me for a few more seconds before turning on her heel and going to sit down. The plan was set up in clusters of seats, and she sat off on her own, the rest of the crew packed around with Holt.

They were shutting the doors, and she didn't kick me off, so I took that as one win. I wasn't sure how fast I could push it, but I was going to see. I needed to know how upset she was before I could figure out how to fix this.

I headed over, sitting in the seat next to her. Her headphones were in, and she still wasn't smiling. I knew I couldn't expect it from her, but it felt like I put us right back at square one. My arm pressed against hers, and I leaned back, closing my eyes. After days of chaos, that calm feeling she always brought into my life finally returned, and I leaned in more to revel in it.

"Gummy worm," she said, making me sit back up.

"What?"

She pulled out her headphones and looked at me, the hint of a cocky grin on her face making me smile.

"I said, gummy worm."

I finally laughed, realizing what she meant. "That is not the way it's supposed to be used."

"It's my word. I can use it however I want."

"Fine," I said, laughing as I moved. "Can I at least sit across from you?"

"*Fine,* but no staring."

There was no way I wasn't going to stare. Her hair was back into two long braids, and today, she had makeup on, the sparkling brown making the hazel of her eyes stand out more. She also had a little ring in her nose, which was new.

"Is that a new piercing?"

"Chase, I don't want to talk right now." She looked around at the crew quickly. "Maybe later, but definitely not now. And no, it's fake. I just thought it was cute."

"I'll take later if that's the only option I have. And you're right. It's very cute."

Her cheeks turned the lightest shade of red as she put her headphones back in and looked down at her phone.

Later.

Later was a hell of a lot better than never.

IT WAS ALREADY DARK OUT WHEN THE PLANE LANDED, AND WE settled into the hotel. I was sharing a room with Kye, which I didn't mind, and Scout was happy because that meant she got her own room.

After spending a few hours on the strip, everyone headed to a club Ash found to celebrate Scout's races, along with Ransom and Quinn.

We walked in, and I tried to stop Scout again, but she was brushing me off for the hundredth time today.

"Scout, please, I need to talk to you."

She spun to face me, her eyes narrowed, and lips pulled into a frown. "Why?"

"Because we need to fix this, and I don't want to keep going through this weekend pretending nothing happened."

"We aren't pretending nothing happened. We are doing exactly what we should be doing after *many* things happened, and we agreed not to let them happen anymore."

The crew had disappeared into the club, and she looked ready to bolt inside, too.

"But I want them to happen more. I don't want this to be over just because of that fucking party."

"It wasn't that party," she said, nearly yelling. "It's that this won't go anywhere else. I don't want it to, and neither do you. We aren't together, Chase. You can do whatever or whoever you want."

"There is no one else."

"I was recently introduced to your *fiancé,* so I beg to differ."

"You know that was all bullshit from my dad."

"Either way. My point still stands."

"So that's it? You aren't even going to give me a chance to talk about what happened or tell you."

"We have nothing to talk about. Just go do whatever. There's a club full of girls here. Plenty of them will blend into your life better than I would."

"Dammit, Scout. Fine. I'll do whatever or *whoever* I want since you won't even hear me out."

She broke away, storming into the club. By the time I made it inside, I had lost her to the crowd, but it didn't take me long to find the rest of the crew, half of them filling one of the booths that Ash had apparently reserved. I forced a smile as she waved me over.

"Hey," Ransom said. "Drink?"

I nodded, but was already searching for the red hair that was braided onto her head like a crown tonight. She wasn't here, though. I looked at Ash who sucked in her bottom lip before pointing out towards the dance floor.

Scout was out on the floor dancing to the beat, some guy moving closer and closer, and she wasn't stopping it.

Red-hot anger burned through me. I didn't want anyone else, and I didn't want anyone touching her.

I pushed through the crowd, heading right toward her. I didn't care about the crew seeing. I didn't care about them knowing I wanted her. If the only other option was burning every bridge with them to stop her going home with someone else, and at least attempt to listen to me, I would.

She glared up at me when I got closer, but backed up into the guy. A random girl spun, facing me with a smile as her hands shot out to run up my arm and chest.

I was still looking out at Scout, her lip curling as she watched the girl's hands on me. I didn't flinch, but part of me was filled with relief. If she didn't want this girl touching me, at least there still might be a chance of being with her.

I pushed around the girl as nicely as possible to reach Scout, the guy at her back still moving in.

"What are you doing?" Scout said, yelling over the music.

"I'm trying to talk to you."

"Here?"

"I will talk anywhere if you would just give me five damn minutes and listen."

"We are not talking here."

The guy behind her stepped forward. "If she wants to dance and not talk to you, why don't you leave?"

"Get the fuck out of here," I said, brushing the guy off and looking back down at Scout.

"That's not your decision," Scout said, getting angrier.

"Tonight, it is my fucking decision. I will give you a thousand other nights to call the shots, but tonight I am."

"No, you aren't."

I looked back up at the guy. There was no fucking way she was leaving with any other guy tonight. "Listen, you don't want this one. She has a literal switchblade in her boot, and I can almost guarantee she will use it once before the night is over."

The guy looked down at her feet, but it was too dark to see it. His eyebrows shot up, but he backed up, finally putting some space between them. "Have a good night, you two," he said, and then he was gone.

"Chase!"

"Scout!"

"Fine!" she yelled. "You only get five minutes, or you are right—I *will* use that switchblade tonight. It will just be on you."

THIRTY-TWO

SCOUT

AS I PULLED Chase through the narrow hallway, my fingers squeezed his as hard as I could, trying to show him exactly how annoyed I was about this. Him showing up on the plane had immediately made me angry until I could feel the relief that coursed through me when he sat down by me.

I wanted him there. I wanted him here tonight, and I really wanted him at my races tomorrow. I knew we couldn't have anything more than this stupid friends with benefits thing, and I knew I had to stick to that, but I was struggling not to turn around and kiss him.

The crowd pushed together for a second, everyone trying to get into the hallway for the bathrooms. The sudden stop made Chase push against me. His arms wrapped around me, and before I knew what was happening, he was lifting me up, carrying me through the crowd. He kept moving until he found a less crowded hallway. By the time he set me down and I turned to face him, my body was on fire.

It didn't matter how mad I wanted to be, or how upset I could be because of the party. I wanted to kiss him more than I wanted to yell or fight.

I moved up onto my toes, and he was quick to understand what I wanted. His lips found mine, kissing me hard as he backed us into a small alcove.

My back hit the wall and held me there against it while I wrapped my arms around him, trying to pull him closer.

"I fucking missed you," he said, his hands moving down my body until they dug into my hips. "I really fucking missed you."

He kissed me again, his tongue moving against my lips until I parted them. I wanted more, and the thought of that made my stomach flutter.

My chest tightened, and I pushed him back, the weight of my own conflicting emotions pressing on my chest like a weight. I couldn't do this. I couldn't let myself keep getting myself wrapped up in Chase when I knew the outcome was heartbreak. I couldn't ignore that, no matter how much I wanted to. Reluctantly, I stepped back and tried to take in the painful truth that Chase didn't want a relationship, and I did.

"Scout, please."

"I need air," I said, stepping around him and not stopping until I was back outside on the sidewalk. Our hotel was a two-block walk, and I had already started on it when he caught up to me.

"Scout, stop. You aren't listening and I need you, too. You said I got five minutes."

"And you wasted them kissing me instead."

"That was not a waste."

The fear that he was only going to tell me that we couldn't have more than this was eating at me. I knew it already, but hearing it out loud from him was still going to hurt and I had been trying to avoid it. I didn't need him hunting me down just to reiterate that we could keep this friends with benefits arrangement even if we had nothing else. I couldn't admit to him that I had already fallen for him and ruined any chance that this would ever be a casual agreement again.

"You were right," he said, apparently taking his five minutes now.

"About what?"

"I can't have the life that I've had and have you. I would have to keep half of myself in that world and half in yours. I wouldn't be able to bring you to all the places I had to go, not only because you would hate it, but my dad would try to ruin you at every chance. He would never be okay with this, and as long as I worked for him, he would have the control he wanted, even over my relationships. Not only that, but I would have to watch you die every fucking time we went to those things. You would be miserable having to do that once or even twice a week sometimes."

"I could tolerate some of them," I said, hating how small my voice sounded, and wishing this didn't hurt so bad. "It's not like I asked to be this way. I'm sorry I'm not some fancy, perfect robot like you and those people. I like messy. I like not worrying if my hair is perfectly in place, or if I'm acting how other people want me to. I can't control my emotions and sometimes, they get the best of me."

"I know," he said softer now, stepping closer. "You feel everything, Scout. Every small emotion cracks through you until it's a damn volcano. The night we met at the races, you could barely contain yourself. Every second those emotions grew until you looked wild, you were so mad at me. And I fucking wanted it. I wanted to feel a second of anything the way you felt it. I could barely manage to feel depressed before you. I'm not telling you this because there is anything wrong with you."

"Well, some people have said I feel too much."

"Those people are jealous. *I* was jealous. I don't think I ever understood how people felt things so strongly until I met you. I knew anger, jealousy, endless defeat, but all the others? I didn't know it could feel like this."

"I'm not sure what you're trying to tell me. Did you actually come all the way here to tell me that I was right and this wouldn't work? Or you finally agree our lives can't work together?"

"Kind of. I came to tell you that if I can't have both, then I will choose one. I don't care what life is being offered to me. I would choose a life with you a thousand times in a thousand lifetimes. There is no life that I could want if you weren't in it. You were right that I couldn't have both, so I won't. I'll take the life with you and leave the other one behind."

My face fell, the shock of what he was saying making my stomach sink. He tried to step closer, but I stepped back. "What do you mean? You're giving up working with your dad?"

"I'm giving up law school, working with my dad, probably my place to live since there is no way I'm going to pay for that stupid place. Don't worry, I'm securing the Hellcat and Porsche for us before I tell my dad all of this," he said with a smirk. "Just in case that persuades you at all."

"You think I'm worried about the *cars*? Chase, you are talking about giving up your entire life."

"I'm talking about giving up the life I've had. I'll build a new life."

"Just like that? You think you are going to go from being rich and having everything in life to nothing?"

"I'm hoping to at least have you, so it won't be nothing."

"Even if I did agree to that, you don't understand how hard it is to start from nothing, Chase. No place to live, no job. I don't even know if you would even qualify for a job."

"I know you think I'm useless and rich," he said, his smile growing. "I can figure it out, and no, it doesn't have to be your job to figure that out for me. I'm pretty sure I have some skills I can put to use. All I need from you is you."

I grabbed my chest, trying not to cry, or maybe just not pass out.

What were you supposed to say to someone who is telling you they are giving up their life because they want to be with you?

Even worse, how could I tell him that I wasn't willing to do the same thing? Even if he was willing to give up the life I didn't want to be a part of, I couldn't give up racing even if it did scare him.

"I can't," I finally said.

His face fell, and he stepped closer. "Why? Am I alone in wanting more than just hiding this and messing around? I want you, Scout, and I don't want to hide it. I want to openly date you and not have to worry about the crew not finding out or my dad interfering."

The tears were welling in my eyes and I wished for one second I wasn't emotional. Chase didn't seem to mind, wiping them away as he waited for me to respond.

"It's not that. I can't give up my racing, even for this. I could never stop racing and you've already made it clear you would rather me not."

"I don't want you to," he said quickly. "I never really wanted you to. But I was dealing with the fact that I had already fallen for you and learning not to handle that while watching you wreck was less than ideal. It was selfish, and I'm sorry, but no. I fully expect to be your biggest fan at every damn race you go to."

"But I'm telling you that I won't give up anything for you when you're giving up everything. I can't stop racing. I can't be with you if my family doesn't like you. I'm not moving out of my apartment like you would be. I'm not leaving the garage. I can't give any of it up, Chase. That's not even fair of me and I know it, but I like my life."

"I don't want you to give any of that up," he said, reaching for my hands. "I want to be a part of it. You have worked hard to build that life, and I am asking to have a place in it. I will give up my life that I've had because I don't want it, but you want yours. There isn't a requirement on how much we each need to give up to be together," he said, smiling. "I think I'll give up enough for the both of us."

"Even if all of that was okay with me, the crew still has to agree to this. I know it sounds dumb saying they get to choose who I date, but I can't go through them not liking my boyfriend again. My life is tangled in theirs and I don't know that I could ever, or would ever want to, unravel it."

"I know. You're a package deal. But what if they are okay with this?"

I sucked in a shaky breath, trying not to cry again. "Then yes. I think we could try this *dating for real* thing out."

He smiled harder and leaned down to kiss me.

"What about tonight?" he asked, not letting me go. "Do I get to share that room with you?"

I smiled as his hands moved over me like he couldn't touch me enough. I felt the same way. The thought that this had been over was leaving me more desperate for him than before.

"The crew is all still inside. If we go now, we will barely have to sneak in."

"Even if they tell you that they don't want this?"

"I have a big day tomorrow with the races. Maybe we keep this to ourselves for the weekend and talk to them when we get back?"

He smiled as his arm snaked around me, angling us back towards the hotel. "What happens in Vegas can stay here if we need it to, right? Let's go. I like the idea of not waiting until Kye is asleep to sneak into your room."

The weight on my chest had lightened, but it still lingered, a constant reminder of the mess I was inside. Despite my efforts not to, I had fallen for Chase. But actually being able to be with him felt out of my hands, even if it shouldn't be. I knew the crew would want what makes me happy, but I could never face them being at odds with any boyfriend I had. Desperation surged in me as I held onto him tighter, hoping that my heart had led me to the right person this time.

THIRTY-THREE

SCOUT

IF I THOUGHT I was already setting myself up to get hurt before, it was nothing compared to waking up next to Chase when I knew he actually wanted a relationship with me.

It still felt surreal, like the entire night had never happened, and I would lose it all again. I rolled to face him, and his lips immediately found mine. Before I could worry more, he was making me forget everything for a while.

By the time we dressed and made it downstairs, I nearly felt invincible, which was good considering I had to race in a few hours. There were only two rounds for me today, and if I lost either of them, Holt had every reason not to let me on his team. Ash tried to assure me a thousand times that this wasn't the end, even if I lost both, but I knew losing today would only make climbing back up this high even harder. Holt had already given me every opportunity to succeed. I just had to prove that I was a reliable driver. I had no excuses and wouldn't start going easy on myself today.

We weaved through the casino to find where the crew told us to meet for breakfast.

SCOUT   289

"I'm suddenly pissed that I can't be touching you right now,"
he said.

"Why? We just did *a lot* of touching."

"And I'm already deprived."

Chase stepped in front of me, smiling as he pulled me to a
stop.

"Scout?"

My name caught both of our attention, my heart rate spiking
because I knew how obvious it would be that Chase had been
about to kiss me.

"Dad?"

This was even worse than one of the crew catching us.

"Scout! I've been looking all over for you," he said, the
smile plastered on his face as fake as the gold chain around his
neck. If it had been real gold at one point, it had been pawned off
since then and replaced with a fake.

Chase's hand tightened on my arm, and I let him pull me in,
moving as close to him as I could. I didn't think my dad would
make a big scene in public, but having Chase here was
comforting.

"What do you mean you've been looking all over for me?
How did you know where I was?"

"Your races. I saw your name on the list back at Holt and that
you made it here," he said, his smile growing, but it wasn't a
comfort.

"And?" My fingers dug into Chase's side, unease settling in
my gut.

"And I wanted to come to cheer you on, of course."

"But you didn't bother to come to my other races back
home?"

He was shaking his head before I even finished my sentence.
"No. No, between these guys finding out where I lived, and
having some trouble with the Sheriff there, I didn't want to risk

going back. I'm so happy you made it here now. At least now I can watch you today."

"I believe those are called debts and warrants," I said, knowing damn well that if the Sheriff was looking for him, it was because of a warrant. It wouldn't be his first, or his last. "Did you really get tickets to come today?"

"Well, no. I assumed I could get in with you to watch."

That was the first thing he would want, free tickets, which would turn into a food and drink tab.

"No. My team is full. I don't have any free tickets." Chase was still quiet next to me, but I could see my dad looking at his arm over my shoulder.

"Don't I know you?" my dad asked, his eyes lingering a little too long on the new watch Chase was wearing. It was probably another ridiculously expensive watch, one my dad would want, not knowing that Chase had already given up two for him.

"Probably," Chase said.

My dad's eyes narrowed before he started nodding. "That's right. You're the lawyer's kid. Jake Parker's son, right? Your dad sure is a big deal back home."

"Yeah, so I've heard."

"Interesting that you are here with her, then."

"Why?" Chase asked.

My dad looked me over with a scrutinizing gaze and then looked at Chase. "I don't think I need to explain why that would be strange. I know your dad well enough. I can't imagine your dad knows about this? Or if he does, he sure as hell isn't happy about it."

"What I do is none of my dad's business."

"Isn't it? Aren't you set to inherit everything, including his law firm?"

"You seem to know an awful lot about my dad."

My dad smirked. The small joy he was getting out of this

was setting me further on edge. "I do, don't I? Interesting how people come to know each other in smaller towns. Here, I'm invisible, but back at home? Everyone starts to know each other. It's both a curse," he said, his smile growing, "and a blessing."

Chase didn't reply, but his arm tightened around me. If my dad noticed the sudden shift in us, he didn't dwell on it more.

"There's really no way to get me in? I'd love to see my only kid win a few races," my dad said.

"Would you like to help me spend the prize money, too?"

He laughed, the deep hearty laugh I knew well. This was all a show. He was currently on his best behavior and would keep that up until he got what he wanted. "Would I complain? Of course not, but I'm not expecting it. I just want to watch you do what you were born to do."

"Really? Now, this is what I'm born to do? I thought before I was being a slut hanging around all the guys all the time." Chase stiffened beside me but didn't say anything yet.

"I know you were just working on learning to drive so well."

"How much do you want?" Chase asked, making my eyes jump to him.

"Excuse me?" my dad asked.

"You heard me. How much do you want? What is the amount that is going to make this pathetic show of pretending you care about her stop?"

My dad's eyes flicked between us, but I didn't miss the way they landed on Chase's watch for a few extra seconds.

I almost laughed. This seriously couldn't be happening a third time.

"About ten grand," my dad finally said. I wanted to be surprised. I wanted to feel shock reverberate through me that there had been a number in his head all along, but none of that happened. Instead, I just nodded, anger burning through me. My dad had cost me more money this year than my damn car. I wasn't even sure if I spent thirty grand on myself this year, even if I made enough at the garage. But here he was, living a lavish life without having to work for anything.

"No," I said as Chase pulled his arm off me. "You are not doing this again. It's getting ridiculous."

"Do you want him to go, or do you want to play this stupid game with him all day just to find out he wants the money later?"

"Of course I want this done, but not like this. He doesn't deserve the money. *Again*."

"It's okay," he said, pulling off the watch and holding it out in his hand. "I'm not sure how much this will get you at a pawn shop, but I'm sure you can shop around in this town." My dad looked it over, smiling, when he slipped it and saw the brand name on the back. "Will that cover whatever you wanted today?"

"That should do it. What a good guy. I don't know how you trap a guy like this into a relationship with you, Scout, but you've got good taste. Maybe now I can stop by and see you race."

Chase's face fell, his eyes narrowing on my dad. "This comes with the stipulation that you don't set foot near that fucking track today, and you don't 'run into her' again this weekend."

He gave a dramatic eye roll, but nodded. "Fine, fine. That's fair. Well," he said, his fingers rubbing the watch. "I guess this is it. Good luck today, and maybe I'll see you around back home one day."

"Chase," I hissed as he pulled me away. "You can't do this. Please let me go get it back." He didn't stop until we were at the door, but I could feel him shaking next to me.

It wasn't until we were out on the street that I could see the shaking was from laughter, not anger. "What's so funny? How is anything that just happened funny?"

"Because that wasn't a real Rolex. You learn real fast as a

rich boy that you don't travel with the real stuff. That watch is maybe worth a hundred dollars on a good day. For him at a pawn shop? He might get ten dollars if he's lucky."

"Are you serious?"

"Yeah, and we're going to have to let the track help us make sure he doesn't have a chance of getting in today."

"You know, as soon as he finds out, he's going to freak out."

"I know. Hopefully by then we are at the track, and then heading home."

"And what about when he finds us back at home?"

"I'm not sure," Chase said, turning to face me. "But we will figure it out either way. I've given up everything because I want to be with you. I'm not going to let him get in the way now."

I nodded, knowing that my dad would try to bother me as much as he could until we left. I should have guessed this was where a gambler would run off to, but it never occurred to me that he might actually look for me.

He never cared to look for me when I wasn't around at home, but I guess this was different. He knew I was making more of my life and that more money would come with that. He didn't care about me, and never did. He cared about the money.

"I think there's something I can give up in my life to help this work."

He cocked his head and reached out for me again, running a hand down my jaw. "I told you, there's nothing you have to give up."

"But I have to make sure you get to keep your watches." I smiled, taking a deep breath. "I need to do what I can to stop this, and now I at least know how I can."

I dialed the number, Chase watching me the entire time.

"Hi, I need to talk to Sheriff Wells," I said, waiting as they transferred me.

"What are you doing?" Chase asked, grabbing my hand.

"I'm taking care of the problem that I have. If he keeps popping up, we will never stop having to pay him or the people after him. I'll give him up. I should have done it before, but never knew what I could do."

"Hello?"

"Hey, Sheriff. It's your best friend, Scout Allen."

He sighed. "Are you calling to confess to the street racing?"

"No," I said, smiling as I looked at Chase. "But I am calling because I heard you have a warrant out for my dad."

"Yeah. I'm one of many that does now. You should come forward and tell me if you know where he is."

I rolled my eyes. "Do you think I'm calling just to check up on my dad's warrants? No. I ran into him when I was racing in Vegas, and I would be willing to give you his exact location."

He was quiet for a minute and then gave a long huff. "I'm waiting for the *but* that I'm assuming goes along with this."

"Wow, you are right. There is one thing I'm asking in return."

"If you think I'm going to back off all of you street racing, you're wrong."

"No, *but* could you please stop patrolling the old road outside town? We like practicing there, and you've had a patrol car there every time lately."

"Because even if it's unused, it's still technically a road."

"Barely. That's all I want in return."

"Fine, tell me where your dad is, and I'll back off. Only if we actually get your dad."

I gave him the hotel and area before hanging up.

Chase was still staring, his eyebrows raised as he watched me.

"You okay?"

The warm breeze washed over me, and for the first time in a really long time, I didn't feel the weight on my shoulders crushing me. Every problem I had months ago was gone, and even if I had a few new ones, the problems that had been drowning me weren't a problem anymore.

He was still waiting for a response, the concern in his eyes only making me smile more. I threw my arms around him, and he pulled me hard into his arms.

"I'm okay," I said, taking in a shaky breath. "I'm okay, and it feels nice knowing he might not be a problem for us anymore."

He kissed my head and turned us back inside. "Well, all we need to do now is go meet the crew for breakfast, win you a few races, and see if we actually get a relationship after this."

I thought he would be mad, but when I looked up, he was smiling.

"You're not upset about that?"

"No, Hellcat. Not upset at all."

"Why not?" I didn't know how it couldn't be fazing him when I had barely slept because of it. What if the crew came out and said they hated him for me? Or me for him? He had grown close to them all, and it's not like we made a habit of dating other people in the group. It had never happened, and while he wasn't exactly as close to everyone yet, it still felt like Fox had decided he was in now.

He dropped my hand as we made it to the restaurant the crew was at, but he still smiled down at me. "Because, Scout, I'll do whatever it takes to make sure they are all okay with it. I mean, that and I still have great fucking negotiation skills, so I might be able to convince them that I am not the worst thing in the entire world."

We were already heading to the table, but I stepped next to him so he could hear me. "Not even close, Chase. You might be the best thing in the world right now."

He smiled but didn't say anything else as he sat across from me, jumping right into the conversation with the crew.

THE RACES STARTED A FEW HOURS LATER, AND WHEN I WALKED out of the trailer, I came face to face with eight people wearing eerily similar shirts.

"Is that my face on your shirt?"

"It is," Ash said with a smile.

"Why?"

"Obviously, we're your biggest fans and need to let that be known. I want to add that while everyone got one. Mine was first."

I looked around, the black shirts printed with a picture of me next to my car. Others might not know it was me exactly, but I did, and I could already feel my face turning red. "Oh my god, we're the embarrassing family that wears matching shirts now?"

"We're adorable," Ash said. "So yes."

I looked everyone over, scoffing when I got to Jax. "You vandalized my face! You put a mustache on me?"

He was laughing, Carly smacking his stomach.

"Listen, at least I didn't put devil horns on you," he said, pointing to Kye, who proudly showed his shirt.

"You two are the worst."

"Yeah, yeah. And while we are here for you, we don't want to be embarrassed wearing the shirt of a loser, so you better get out there and win," Kye said.

"Wow, what a pep talk." I gave him a thumbs up before flipping them off as Chase pulled me away. The trailer blocked us from view as he pulled me into his arms, kissing me hard.

"What are you doing?" I asked, needing to get back and get in my car.

"I needed to give you a private good luck before you went out there."

I looked past him, making sure the crew hadn't come around

the corner, as he kissed me again. His hand wrapped around one of my braids, worrying filling his gaze as his eyes met mine.

"Please be careful."

"You know I'm not going out there *trying* to wreck, right?"

"Yeah, I know that, but it isn't stopping me from picturing every terrible scenario in my mind. And I swear if you pick the front end of that car off the ground, I'm going to lose my mind."

"If you really think I'm going to take my time getting off the line, you have already lost your mind."

He leaned down, kissing me once, his lips lingering on mine.

"How the fuck did Jesse not cower at your feet?"

"I'm starting to wonder that myself."

"You should. You're the Queen of my entire fucking world, and I don't know how anyone could think anything different of you."

"While sitting back here to talk about how much you worship me sounds like a good time. I do have to go race, and someone will walk back here looking for me soon."

He groaned, kissing me once more before stepping away. "Fine, go kick some ass and make everyone here fall in love with you."

I only smiled, trying to hide how much my heart jumped at the word love. Chase offered to give up his entire world, but hadn't said he loved me. I preferred it that way for now, at least until we told the crew, but it was starting to make me wonder how serious this would be.

I started to head back out, and Chase followed behind me

"What are you doing?" I asked with a smile.

"Going to sit with the crew?"

"You said I was the Queen of your world? Did you already forget you're supposed to be crawling after me on your knees?"

I laughed as his hand wrapped around my braid again, yanking my head back. "I think people might get a little suspicious if I do that, but I will happily oblige if you would like. Or we can wait until later when I can get on my knees and beg to get a taste of you."

My head was still tilted back, looking up at him as he held me there.

"I'm obviously going with the second choice," I said, heat flooding me.

"I think that's an excellent choice. Now, go win your races. I'm running out of time in Vegas, and now I have big plans I will need to attend to before we leave."

THIRTY-FOUR
SCOUT

YESTERDAY HAD FELT like one of the biggest days of my life. I won my races and Holt was already making plans for me to join their team. There were huge things happening, and everything I ever wanted was finally coming true. Technically, it was one of the biggest days of my life.

That was until I woke today and realized it was time to face the crew about Chase. For everything I had been hiding from them, I was nervous to hear what they had to say, not only about Chase, but about me keeping it from them.

I was strict about not sleeping together once we were back home and when he stomped in the next morning, I could tell he was as happy as I felt about it.

"You couldn't have even let me stay on the couch? Even if I behaved?" He leaned down to kiss me, but I swerved out of the way.

"Nope, no kissing either. And the last time I let you sleep on my couch, you snuck into my bedroom and cuddled me to death, among other things."

"And? Are you saying you weren't cold and lonely last night at *all*?"

"It was a little colder than normal, and I have grown a little used to you next to me."

He lifted me onto the counter, his hands running up my thighs as he drew in a ragged breath. He moved higher until the small pajama shorts I had were going up with them.

"I missed you," he said, leaning down to kiss my inner thigh before moving higher. "Can I kiss here?"

"You are not helping my self control," I said, groaning as my legs fell open the smallest amount.

He got up, laughing as he went to his bag. "You're going to be so happy to learn that I got you a present, and I think this is the perfect time to use it."

My eyebrows jumped when I saw what was in his hand.

"You bought a *vibrator*?"

"I did. I told you when you were locked up, all horny and in jail, that this will really be useful in making you cum."

"And you're totally good with that?"

"I didn't buy it because I wasn't?"

"And why would this be the perfect time to use it?"

His low grumble of a laugh made me nervous. "Because this way," he said, running the vibrator up my thigh until he was using it to push my bottoms aside. I hadn't put on underwear and he noticed, immediately pushing it against my entrance. "I can fuck you without even touching you." He pushed it further in, clicking it on as I yelled out.

"Wait!" I yelled, making him turn it back off, but he still held it in place.

"Why?"

"Because you're right, you could use this to fuck me without touching me, *or*..." My words trailed off, nearly losing my confidence until he moved it deeper, making me moan.

"Or what?"

"Or you can take me to the bedroom and you can watch me while…while I watch you."

The smile that grew on his face was blinding as he picked me up, one arm wrapped hard around me while the other held the vibrator in place. He turned it on as he lifted me. I yelled out again, my legs tightening around him as I threw my head back.

In seconds he had me laid back on the bed, and I watched as he pulled out his cock.

"Fuck yourself for me," he said. "Get yourself off while you watch me."

I could only nod, my mouth watering at the sight of him. The second he moved his hand down his cock, I started moving the vibrator, keeping in sync with every stroke he made.

He stayed kneeled on the end of the bed, not taking his eyes off me.

It was even better than the last time I watched since I was a part of now. I let the orgasm build, every part of me tightening.

"You're close now?"

I nodded, suddenly desperate for him. As fun as this was, I needed him, not a toy.

I was seconds from begging for it when he crawled over top of me.

"Am I really supposed to watch this without burying myself in you?" He asked, the words strained as his hand still stroked his cock. "Take my cock, baby. I'm too jealous to watch this and not get to fill you."

I could only nod, a whimper escaping me as I reached down, knocking his hand out of the way and moving his cock to my entrance. His teeth ground together, his head resting back as he sunk into me. Three hard thrusts and I was falling off the cliff I had pushed myself to until I was clinging to him.

"Sorry I broke your rules," he said, quietly laughing as he fell harder against me.

"At this point, I would have been more disappointed if you *didn't* break that rule."

"The good girl that needs to break all the rules, huh?"

"Exactly."

He pulled me up with him, carrying me into the bathroom to clean us up.

"I think we have to go see if I'm getting kicked out of your life now, don't we?"

"I'm sorry," I whispered as he handed me my shirt.

"It's okay. Come on, we need to see what they think about this before we worry about it any longer."

* * *

"Do you want to walk in all over me, or do you think that would be too much of a shock?"

"Let's keep the hands off of each other and you let me do the talking. Please." My hands were nearly shaking as I pushed the door to Fox's apartment open. I had texted them all to get down there a few minutes ago and knew everyone was already inside.

"What's up?" Fox asked. "Did she make you come to this, too?"

"Yeah. I was forced into it," Chase said.

"Interesting how fast you got here, or maybe she just texted you earlier," Ash said, the cocky smile on her face not helping my nerves.

"Uh, yeah," I said, trying to figure out where to start. All eyes were on me and Chase even turned to look down at me. "So I needed to talk to everyone, and this seemed like the easiest way. Although, it's not as easy as I thought it was going to be."

"Do you want some help?" Chase asked with a smile.

"No, I mean, I should be able to do this. I wanted you all here because I needed to ask about Chase."

"What about Chase?" Fox asked, looking more confused than before.

My nose crinkled as I tried to find my next words. I wasn't sure if I could see the disappointment on their faces like they had when I told them I was dating Jesse.

Chase put a hand on my back, catching my attention. "I got it. What Scout is trying to say is that she would like to know if you all think I'm not a huge asshole or not, and if you would all accept me dating her. She would like permission to date me before I can even ask her out because she will just tell me no until you are all on board. After Jesse, she doesn't want to disappoint you all again, and there seems to be a pretty decent concern that I am a disappointment."

My eyes flew up to him as I grabbed his arm. "I don't think you're a disappointment."

He was laughing now. "I know, but I thought a joke might soften the blow a little."

The last thing I needed to add into this mess was him believing that I thought anything bad about him. Especially when it seemed everyone in his life seemed to tell him they thought little of him. I stepped a little closer, liking that we were doing this together.

"I'm sorry, you guys. I wasn't trying to hide it, but I didn't know how to talk about it after what happened with Jesse."

"I thought we all kind of knew what was going on?" Quinn asked, looking around. "I mean, I hadn't said anything, but I already knew after the hospital."

"I knew," Ash said. "The night of the party kind of solidified that for me for a while now."

"And I knew," Carly said. "But that's because I actually pay attention and you two make it *pretty* obvious." She smiled hard as she wrapped an arm around Jax.

"I didn't know," Fox said, his eyebrows high.

"I didn't know either," Ransom said.

"I mean, I hoped for your sake, dude. You looked a little pathetic looking at her, but I didn't know," Jax said.

They all looked at Kye, who was currently downing a glass of strawberry milk. Seconds went by before he finally noticed. "If you love sick puppies didn't know, how the fuck would I? I've barely had a girlfriend and don't understand how you all do."

Ash rolled her eyes. "Do you think she was running to his side in the hospital because she *didn't* like him?"

"I just thought she felt responsible for it, so was trying to make up for that," Fox said. They all shook their heads, looking between us.

The guys were quiet as they looked around at one another. Suddenly, their faces fell, and they came around to us, pushing Chase towards the door as Kye opened it.

"Go. Get fucking going," Fox said, pushing him out.

"Hey, wait, you can't just kick him out!" I yelled, trailing after them. The barricade of tall, muscled bodies stopped me from getting close to Chase again, though. Jax stopped me, Kye and Ransom trailing after Fox and Chase.

"Well, that didn't go nearly as good as I planned," Chase said, his voice echoing as he was forced down the stairs.

"Yeah, well. You literally just came in asking to date our little sister. How the fuck should we feel about that?" Ransom said.

"Stay here," Jax said to me, "And don't you even *think* about coming after us."

The door slammed shut, and I turned to the girls. All of our mouths dropped open.

"Wow," Ash said. "I thought we were all on board that we liked Chase."

"I mean, I was on board," Quinn said. "I think you two are cute."

"Even I liked him, and I don't like many people. I mean, I really, *really* hated Jesse," Carly said.

"That seemed to be the common theme here," I said, shaking my head at her. "Well, I liked Chase too, but what the hell was that about? What am I supposed to do now?"

Ash shrugged. "Hang out with us until they get back?"

"But I didn't even get to make my speech that I liked him, and that he's giving it all up for me, and that I liked that you were all friends with him already," I said, feeling more defeated than I had in months.

"What do you mean, *giving it all up for me*?" Ash asked.

"I mean, his dad hates me and we weren't going to continue even talking, but Chase decided that he would give that all up with working with his dad, and being a lawyer, and all that."

"Wow," Quinn said, her eyes wide.

"Damn," Carly said. "That seems extreme."

"Well, now I feel a little worse about the guys taking him like that. Maybe I should text Fox and let him know to go a little easier on the guy?"

"*Please,*" I begged, as she pulled out her phone.

"Aww," Quinn said, coming over to hug me. "You really do like him and I'm so happy because this is so cute."

"It's not going to be very cute if he's dead or beat up. *Again.*"

"I doubt they will be that rough on him."

"Hopefully," Quinn whispered. "I don't know what they are doing because they are already friends. With Jesse, they just tried to become friends, and bitched when he was rude."

"Honestly, it would have saved me a lot of time if they would have been more drastic."

"But you would have been just as pissed," Ash said.

"Which is why I currently don't trust my own judgment and wanted you all to approve first. I felt so bad telling Chase that, but I couldn't handle making the wrong choice again."

They all gave a tight smile, and Carly came over to hug me. "Come on. It's never too early to start in on mimosa's, and you can catch us up on everything to do with Chase."

———

THREE HOURS LATER, THE DOOR BURST OPEN. THE GUYS walked in laughing as I searched their faces for Chase. Finally, I saw him walk in, smiling and laughing as Fox came in behind him.

"What the hell is going on?" I yelled as they fanned out, each of them going to the girls besides Kye, who went for the mimosa still sitting on the counter.

Chase came over, leaning down and kissing my cheek as I clung to him.

"What happened? Did they punch you? Are you hurt?"

Fox laughed, his arms around Ash. "Relax, Scout. We were completely messing with you. He's fine."

"And technically, we aren't the ones who hurt him," Kye said, his grin widening.

"What does that mean?" I asked, turning back to Chase. My eyes searched for him for any sign of an injury.

"It means they were messing around thinking it would be funny to make you panic, and before you get mad at me, I left my phone in your apartment so I couldn't say a word," Chase said, smiling. "They didn't do anything to me, and they didn't make me do anything, but they did want to know how serious I felt about this."

"Oh," I said, wishing I could ask the same thing. "And?"

"And we dared him to show us how serious he was," Kye said, not controlling how hard he was laughing now.

"What does that mean?"

Chase laughed, pulling off his hoodie.

I could see the wrap over a tattoo on the inside of his arm, right above the inside of his elbow.

"They dared me to get a tattoo, and I was happy to agree," he said, holding his arm out so I could see the black and neon green in the tattoo. It was a knife going across his arm, the top half of my name above the knife and the bottom half reflected in the blade.

"You have a tattoo of my name," I said, the shock obvious.

"Yes, and I think it turned out pretty great."

He wasn't wrong at all. I loved it, but he had my name on his body.

"And that's all you guys made him do?"

"We didn't make him. He basically offered," Jax said. "And before you get all mad, we would have been fine even if he didn't do it."

"Why would you be so worried about telling us, Scout?" Fox asked, almost sounding hurt.

Tears welled in my eyes as I stared at the tattoo a little longer, trying to find the courage to face them all. I did turn, but the tears were nearly dripping down my cheek now.

"Because after everything with Jesse, I couldn't mess up again with the wrong person and I knew you guys would jump down my throat if I *did* pick the wrong guy. You guys never screwed up like that, so how could I possibly do it multiple times? Then what if I did mess up and ruin your friendship?"

"Scout, we didn't *not* screw up relationships in our life. Just because you didn't always know what happened, doesn't mean it didn't happen," Fox said. "Then we all just got stupidly lucky. If your stupidly lucky story is with Chase, then we don't care. We didn't like Jesse because Jesse was a fucking asshole. If you chose another shitty guy, then yeah, of course, we wouldn't like him. If we brought a girl around who was an ass to you, would you be nice about it? I mean fuck, we would be out with Jesse and he would be openly hitting on other girls. God, hitting him the other week was a dream come true after the number of times we all wanted to. The night we left him at the races, and you were mad about it, it's because he got a girl's number. Chase can be a dick, but we all can. I can't tell you how it will work out for you, but you didn't mess up. And Jesse wasn't your fault, either. We're older than you, so your mistakes might be a little more obvious to us, but that's because we made mistakes. You were younger, which made it easier to hide them from you. No one here is expecting you to be perfect."

I couldn't even respond, instead heading across the room to hug him. He pulled me into a hard hug before I moved down the line, hugging each one of them, even forcing Kye into a hug.

"I look up to all of you. I just didn't want to make the same mistake twice."

"You're not," Fox said. "If you want to try out dating him, we are all good."

"And good luck," Kye said, shaking his head with a laugh. "I hear he's about to be broke."

"Yeah, I heard that, too. As long as the Hellcat stays, so do I," I said, walking back to wrap my arms around his waist. He groaned, pulling me against his side.

"Don't even remind me. I have to get a job? Ridiculous."

"How about we all go out and grab some food," Fox said, already grabbing his keys and pulling Ash along with him.

"And don't worry, we'll pay this time."

"Ha ha, very funny," Chase said, staying back until they all walked out. "Well, one more thing is out of our way, Hellcat, just one more to go."

"Which is?"

"Telling my dad might even show him my new tattoo and give him a heart attack."

"Want to wait until tomorrow for all that?"

"Tomorrow," he said, leaning down to kiss me once before we headed out with the crew.

THIRTY-FIVE
CHASE

IF THERE WAS any concern left for Scout that we couldn't be together, it seemed to have disappeared last night.

We went out with the crew, and I could see how worried she was at first. In every lull of conversation, she tried to support my case that we could date, even if I didn't need it. Each one of the guys acted the same way as always towards me, and the girls were too busy telling Scout how happy they were to talk to me much. It wasn't until the end of dinner that she finally relaxed, her entire demeanor shifting until she was smiling and genuinely enjoying herself.

Now she was here at my condo, sprawled out on the bed talking to me while I went through my things, and packed. I knew as soon as I told my dad I wasn't following in his footsteps that he would kick me out of here, so I figured getting a head start would help me.

"I love this bed. This is amazing," she said, rolling over and burying herself in the pillows.

"If I bring it with me, could I stay at your place for a little while?" I tried to make a joke of it, but was suddenly worrying about where I would go next. I wouldn't have a job after I told my dad, and I wouldn't have money to rent anything fancy.

"A little presumptuous to think you're going to move in with me," she replied with a smirk.

"You could have said the same thing two months ago about sleeping together, but now you're here on my bed looking like you want me again after only an hour."

"I will admit that you do look very good right now."

I smiled, letting the towel drop before coming down over her.

"Good enough to have sex with again?"

"Yes, definitely good enough for that."

She was already wrapping her legs around me, but I slowed. "I really wouldn't mind having you in my bed every night. What would you think about me moving in temporarily? Just until I find a new place."

"I guess that wouldn't be the *worst* and I do kind of feel bad that you are giving all of this up for me. Honestly, this bed is so comfortable. I think you moving in for a little while might benefit me a lot."

"Is that a yes, then? I am going to have to start packing, and actually having a place to take some stuff would be great."

A door slammed, making us both freeze.

"Were you expecting someone?"

I shook my head, already knowing that there was only one person who would let himself in to my place unannounced.

"Chase?" a man's voice rang out.

"Shit," I whispered. "Get dressed and I'm going to apologize in advance for this. I was hoping to deal with this without you here. Get dressed, and please don't be mad at me for any of this."

"What is happening? Who is that?"

I pulled on a pair of shorts and grabbed a t-shirt. "My dad."

By the time I walked out into the kitchen, I was seething.

"What are you doing here?" I asked, heading to grab my cup of coffee and trying to draw any attention away from the bedroom. It's not that I didn't want him to know I was with Scout now, I was about to tell him that exactly, but more that I didn't want to subject her to the horrible things my dad would say right to her face.

"I came to see why you haven't responded to me in days," he said, looking over the living room. He always checked on things and snooped through my stuff when he was here.

"Because I've been busy?"

"Too busy running around with that girl? Too busy with school? What are you so focused on? Because I have a pretty good suspicion that it's with her and not on what it should be."

"And it should only be on school so I can become a lawyer and help your slimy ass company win horrible cases?"

"Chase," he warned as I grabbed a drink.

"*Father,*" I said back.

"Have you been to your classes?"

"Not in two weeks or so. I've needed some time to think."

"What is there to think about? The schooling that I'm paying for, the apartment that I'm paying for, the cars?"

"Technically, the cars came out of my trust fund, so those are mine," I snapped back. I already made sure they were in my name, so besides the cars and a few boxes from the apartment, I was fine to take all my stuff and never speak to him again.

"Those cars won't be yours for long after you get into gambling debt with her," he said, cocking an eyebrow. My heart sank, but I tried to not let it show. "Did you think I wouldn't find out about that? That she's running around with gambling brokers, in debt to them, and let me guess, she wants you to pay them off?"

I didn't respond, knowing that anything I said would just be twisted to help him win his case.

"Oh god, don't tell me that you've already paid them off for her. How much?"

"They aren't her debts, and it's none of your business. How did you know about that, anyway?"

"I heard everything about her father's case. That news travels fast in my circles. Did you think I wouldn't be asking around about her and that group she hangs around with? I know everything about them, and I know damn well they are not good for you to be around." He shook his head, but froze when he looked at my arm. I had completely forgotten about the tattoo. "What the hell is on your arm? Is that a goddamn tattoo with a car name in it? What the fuck would you want a tattoo for?"

I smiled, looking down at the knife. I'd hadn't made such a good decision in months, if not years. I loved seeing it there, and I loved that it reminded me of her every single time.

"I will not have you throwing away law school because of one fucking girl who isn't keeping her legs closed and likes cars. That's the stupidest thing you can do."

The room went silent, the tension heavy as we stared each other down. This was it, a few more words, and I would be done with this forever. The thin rope of restraint I was holding onto snapped, and apparently, I wasn't the only one.

The bedroom door swung open, and Scout stepped out, her face etched in defiance. Somehow, it only spurred me on further.

"Is that how you talk about all women? Your wife, too?" she asked. "Do you think we all just spread our legs to force men out of law school? Watch out Chase, next time I 'spread my legs' I might force you into the kitchen to make me a sandwich after."

I smiled. There was no part of me that didn't love her. She walked out to face him, and there was no fear on her face when he did look at her, the blatant hate on his face obvious.

"I would gladly. Do you want one now?"

"No," she pursed her lips, happy to play along. "You'll need an apron first. Wouldn't want you to ruin those expensive clothes."

"Always thinking of me, thank you."

"Enough!" he yelled. "Whatever joke you think this is, is over. This relationship you think you two have *is over*. You are not going to be throwing your money at some girl who thinks working on cars and sleeping with nice rich guys is going to support her lifestyle. If you continue this, you will no longer have this condo. Do you think she's going to want you when you don't have these nice things?"

"Yes, we were actually just talking about moving into *her* apartment. She would never live here."

"Is that what she says? And what about a week later when she starts looking for bigger and more expensive places? What do you think she's going to do if you don't have a fancy, high-paying job?"

"You can't be serious," Scout mumbled, moving to my side.

"Of course I'm serious. And at no point in his life is Chase going to be ruined by a girl like you. Chase, you are going to school, you are getting your degree and you're working for my company. That's it. If you don't do that, you have none of this."

Scout's eyes went wide, and she looked at the floor, staring hard at nothing.

"See, she finds out all this will be gone and she's immediately rethinking all of this."

"Yeah, I am actually," she said, making my heart stop.

Scout wanted to call me unpredictable, but the girl was wild. Her thoughts and emotions moving too fast for me to keep up with. I was starting to worry she was taking all this in and finding more things to not like about me.

Then she turned, walking over and reaching up to put her

arms around my neck. I leaned down, every movement from her scaring me more. I didn't want to lose her and definitely not like this. I knew she wouldn't just give me an innocent hug.

Her lips stopped by my ear.

"I'm so sorry. I knew my dad was a shitty person, but yours hides it better. You are a good person, Chase. And regardless of my attitude, you have always been there for me and treated me amazing. You do not need him to be who you want to be. And yes, even without the money or fancy things, I will treat you just the same, rich boy. You've been there for me at every turn. Make the choice you want to and I'll be here."

She kissed my cheek and stepped back, but I grabbed her hand, pulling her neck to me. Her hand wrapped around mine and she immediately began spinning the rings on my fingers.

Scout when she was fighting me was beautiful, but this Scout made me weak. She was strong, kind, and everything I could only wish for in a person.

I knew she meant it. She truly didn't care what I was doing or how much money I had, as long as I was doing what I wanted to be doing with my life.

Now she was offering me everything I needed.

"So, is this shit done? Are we on track and moving forward again?" my dad asked.

I was quiet, trying to make a thousand life decisions. Talking about cutting my life off from my dad was one thing, but standing here doing it felt a lot bigger. When I looked at Scout, there was no question though. She made an amazing life for herself, starting at the bottom. I was a full grown man and could create one for myself. One that she was included in now.

"I'm back on track, yes, but not with your plan. I have never wanted to be a lawyer. I have never wanted to work for your crooked ass company and I have never wanted to work around you at all, honestly. Spending holidays with you is a nightmare, but being around you every day, working for you, that would be torture."

I knew he was seeing red. His plans crumbling right in front of him.

Years of ordering me around and deciding my life for him falling apart in weeks because of one strong willed, beautiful woman.

I almost laughed but didn't want this to get anymore out of hand with her here.

"You would quit everything we worked for because of her? To what? Become her bitch? Clean and cook and be a good wife to her?"

"I guess if that's how things work out, then fine, but I would like to find a job that I enjoy doing."

His lip curled. "Pathetic. This is pathetic. How the fuck did my son become such a pathetic excuse for a man? You think a woman is going to want that? After your money is gone and days go by, she will drop you like trash. Do not come crawling back to me to fix your fucking life. And you better be out of this apartment by tomorrow or the cops will be escorting you out."

He turned, cursing, as he stormed out and slammed the door.

I stared at the door before finally turning back to Scout.

Her mouth was open and eyes wide.

"Chase, you just blew up your entire life."

"Wasn't that the plan?"

"Yeah, but someone telling you they are going to blow up their entire life for you and actually watching it happen was different."

"For you, with you, same difference."

Her hands moved around my waist as I closed her in a hug.

"You still have your abs. There's always that."

"What a relief." I leaned down, kissing her, pleased when she moved in closer.

"Are you okay, though? You just lost everything."

"Not everything. You're still here. I was a little worried for a second there that you changed your mind."

"I didn't even waver," she said, smiling, "But just having me is not enough."

"I'm fine, Scout. I want you more than anything he has to offer and even if I had nothing, I would prefer to live my life how I want. You just made that decision a lot easier."

"And you're going to move out of this place?"

"Yes, by tomorrow apparently. And hopefully, you know of a pretty redhead that would still let me stay with her while I look for a place?"

"Move that bed to my apartment and you can move in."

"Done. Absolutely done."

"Why don't we grab some stuff and head back over there for the night and come get the rest tomorrow?"

I nodded, grabbing a few things, and heading out. I somehow managed to drive us back to her place and make it upstairs, but every part of me was suddenly bone tired. The day's events were too much to grasp.

But I had her, and when we got into bed, she wrapped herself around me, and I was never so sure of my decisions in life. I was on the right track. I wasn't sure what I was doing next, but it didn't matter.

I had her.

THIRTY-SIX

CHASE

SCOUT HAD BEEN RIGHT about a lot of things, including the fact that my condo looked like no one had ever lived there. Aside from my clothes and two boxes of random items, I had nothing. The sad reality that I had never really built a life, even though I had worked hard every damn day, hit me hard. At least this time, all the work I did would have a better outcome and I could make sure of it.

For the first time in a long time, I was excited about what came next, even when I didn't know what that was.

I checked my phone, expecting some sort of update from Scout, but there was nothing. She had left two hours ago to grab food, insisting I stay to finish all of this today. The diner was twenty minutes from here on a bad day, and Scout could probably get there and back in twenty minutes.

I called her again, her voicemail picking up again.

I'd assumed we were meeting back here to eat and finish up, but maybe I was supposed to meet at her place. It's where I was going next anyway, since Scout was letting me stay with her until I found a new place.

I had promised her that I wouldn't permanently move in until she asked me. I wasn't going to push her to make a decision, but I was already hoping she would decide soon because there was no part of me that wanted to be anywhere else. She walked such a fine line between being independent and needing others and I knew I couldn't rush her decision in this. At least for now, I would temporarily live here as long as she would let me.

I shoved the last box into the Hellcat and headed to her place. The Porsche wasn't out front or in the apartment garages, so I ran one of the boxes up before going back out. The only other place we could have agreed to meet was the garage, so I headed there next.

My stomach dropped a little more when I pulled in and didn't see the Porsche. The garage bay doors were open and I could see most of the crew was here. Maybe someone just borrowed the Porsche. It's not like they hadn't all asked to drive it once or twice already.

"Hey," I said, heading inside. "Is Scout here?"

Fox stood up as Ash smiled at me. "Lose your little love bird already? I thought you two were moving you in?"

"We were, but she left a bit ago to pick up food. I thought she was coming right back, but that was almost three hours ago now."

"Not at her place?" Fox asked.

"No, I just came from there. I mean, if she was picking us up food, there's only so many places she is going after."

Kye headed over, sitting on one of the cars next to Ash. "Maybe she took the Porsche out on a drive. It's not like we all wouldn't take the opportunity."

"But there would be no reason for her to take it out on a drive and not answer any call or text within the last three fucking hours." I started pacing, my heart rate picking up as I pictured her wreck, the car slamming into the wall over and over in my mind. It only made me worry what that would look like out on the winding forest roads outside of town.

"What do you guys do if you wreck when you're out on your own?"

They all looked at each other, Ransom and Quinn coming out of the office with Jax and Carly not far behind them.

"In our cars we set up radios, which help with the wrecking usually," Fox said, a little more serious now. "But your car doesn't have one."

"If we wrecked without that and can't reach our phones, you have to just walk somewhere or hope someone stops to help."

I pushed a hand into my hair, the panic setting it. "Okay, is there somewhere else she would be that I wouldn't know about?"

Quinn shook her head. "No where that I could think of that one of us wouldn't know about too. She's probably just out for a drive. There's a lot going on lately and maybe she needed a little break."

I didn't stop pacing, though. There had been a lot going on, but all of it was good... at least I thought it was. If she really didn't want me to move in, couldn't she just call me back and tell me that? Or even just break the news to me face-to-face?

But no, she had kissed me and left for food, seemingly excited that we were all going to Jax's tonight to have the buffet of food Carly had promised me in the hospital. I even told her we could skip lunch, but she had fussed that I was technically still healing and more food was necessary.

"Dammit," I said, grabbing my phone and hitting her name again. The call rang and rang until it went to voicemail again. At least it was still on, but that didn't do as much as I hoped to calm my nerves.

I hadn't wanted to spill Scout's secrets, but there was one thing she still wasn't telling them about and I was worried that it was coming back to bite us.

I finally stopped and faced them all.

"The first night I actually hung out with Scout, without all of you, obviously, was when Jesse left her at a restaurant on her birthday. She was in a rush to get somewhere and I gave her a ride. That somewhere was a run down warehouse where she was meeting what I now know was some sort of gambling mob broker guy to give him money. A good bit of money, actually. All to go towards her dad's gambling debts. He fucking told them that she would pay, and she did. Then it happened a second time. When we went to Vegas, her dad found her and Scout called him in to the Sheriff. As far as we understand, he was arrested, but now I'm worried that he had more debts waiting for him, and they went after her."

Their faces had fallen more and more throughout the story, until the worry turned to anger.

"And neither of you thought to tell us? What the fuck is wrong with both of you?" Fox asked.

"It wasn't my place to tell, and I handled it as best I could to help her. I even gave them two of my damn watches just so she didn't have to keep killing herself trying to get money without you all noticing."

"Why couldn't we notice?" Ransom asked. "We would have helped."

"From what she said, she felt like you all had been doing things for her all her life, and thought this was on her to handle herself. I don't think she felt she was doing the right thing, and thought you all would disapprove."

"So you think they came back after her?" Kye asked.

"I have no idea, but now I'm worried they have. She told me the first time they found her, they had waited until she was alone and cornered her. Maybe they found her alone again and took the opportunity."

"If that's what happened, wouldn't the Porsche be parked at the diner?" Carly asked.

They were already pulling out keys and jumping up to go, but Carly threw up her hands.

"Everybody freeze!" she yelled. "Before you run all over town, let me just call the diner and ask if there is a ridiculously expensive Porsche in the parking lot or if they saw Scout. It's not like anyone there is going to forget either of those."

"Fine, I'm going to call Scout again while you do that."

My call went to voicemail and I hung back up as Carly was talking.

"Okay, thank you," she said, laughing. "Yeah, we will all stop in this week. Promise." She hung up and looked right at me. "They saw Scout there a few hours ago, and she did leave the parking lot because their cook commented about the car. And we all have to stop in and see Ella this week because we missed last week."

"Fine, but I'm pretty sure we need to figure out where Scout is first," I said, gritting my teeth. We were running out of options on where to look and my nerves were starting to eat me alive. "The Porsche," I said, everyone's eyes on me again. "My dad put a tracker on the Porsche and with everything that happened, I forgot to ask you guys to help me take it off. It's still on there."

Everyone stood back up. "Alright, how do we track it?" Fox asked.

"I don't have access to it, but my dad's computer would. Come on, I need you all to come with me."

"Where?" Ransom asked.

"My parents' house. I don't know if they are going to let me in, but if you are all there, there won't be much of a choice. Will you guys come?"

Kye got up, laughing as he grabbed his hoodie and threw it

on. "If you told us to burn the fucking place down to help Scout, we would. Come on, this will be a breeze. Parents *love* me."

"Then let's go," I said, already heading back out to the cars.

In seconds, everyone was in their car and following me to my parents' house. Kye, Jax, and Carly rode with me, with Ash, Fox, Ransom, and Quinn in another car. The driveway to my parents' house wasn't long, but it was obnoxiously fancy.

I hit the gate code and parked in front of the house. All the cars were in garages, so I couldn't tell who was home, and who wasn't, but the sinking feeling in my stomach had me feeling pretty confident that my dad wasn't going to be inside.

I led the way to the oversized front door, my heart pounding with each step. The crew stepped inside the luxurious foyer, and I almost laughed. The pristine marble floors and chandeliers were a harsh contrast to the crew's darker attire and tattoos.

My mother appeared in the doorway of the living room, her eyes wide in alarm as she took in the sight of them all. "Chase? Who are all these people?" she asked, her voice nearly trembling as she held onto the door frame.

"My friends. We need to use Dad's office, and then we will be out of your way again."

She didn't move, her eyes glued to the crew. "Your father doesn't like anyone in there. He has sensitive information on his computer."

"And I don't care about any of that. I need to see where my car is. If he has an issue with it, he can call me."

"Chase," she said with a shriek of fear in her voice as Kye stepped forward.

"He's just introducing himself. Calm down. Come on, let's just get to the computer," I said.

They all moved at once to follow me, and she yelled again, backing up into the living room to put more distance between her and my scary friends. I could only shake my head as we headed to the familiar oak door of my father's office. She was always the first to judge people based on what they looked like, and I never realized how horrible she was about it.

The computer was on, but locked. The crew looked through the place while I attempted to get it unlocked. Thankfully, my dad used all of three passwords in his life and ended up telling me all three when he would inevitably forget them. My knee shook in anticipation as the app loaded and finally brought up the homepage. Each of the cars had a link, the Porsche's sitting at the top, making me wonder if he had looked at it recently.

The crew crowded around me. I didn't hear anything else from my mom and wondered if she was calling my dad, the police, or maybe both.

The map loaded, the small red dot making my heart rate pick up again.

I kicked back the chair, moving around the desk. I never thought I would want to hurt my own parents, but red coated my vision and it was taking everything I had not to shake her.

My stomach churned as I headed downstairs. My mother sat on one of the couches, not even glancing at me or the crew as they crowded around behind me.

"What is going on?" I asked.

"What do you mean?" Ransom asked.

I glanced back at seven worried faces before I turned back to my mother.

"Why the *fuck* is my car showing that it's here on this property?"

THIRTY-SEVEN
SCOUT

<u>EARLIER THAT DAY</u>

My phone started ringing the second I set the bags of food down on the seat, and I fumbled to grab it.

I assumed it would be Chase, but an unknown number popped up. My stomach dropped. The gambling goons were back and wanting more money. I had to face it, though. I was starting over with my problems, and I couldn't let this one keep following me around.

I connected the call and tried to find any ounce of strength I had left to deal with them.

"What do you want now?" I asked, the firm tone making me happier. I could do this.

I could handle the situation and not involve the crew, or Chase and his watches, anymore.

"Excuse me?" a woman's voice asked. "I'm not sure if I have the right number, but I was looking for...Scout?"

"Oh," I said, surprised that it was a woman, and from the sound of it, an older woman, but I couldn't place the voice. "That's me. Who is this?"

"Oh good. This is Mrs. Parker. Chase's mother."

My mouth dropped open, the words barely processing. I had met her at the party, but besides a strained smile, she hadn't spoken to me. I didn't really know where she stood on Chase and me together, or him changing his whole life, but if she was willingly calling me, I guess I was about to find out.

"Um, of course," I said. "Is there something I could help you with?"

"There is actually. As you know, Chase and his dad had a bit of a falling out over all these changes, and now it seems Chase isn't answering my calls either. I was wondering if you would be willing to stop by and talk with me? Maybe us girls could help to get this all straightened out. As you can imagine, I really don't want to lose Chase in my life, and with the way his dad is running things, that's exactly where this is headed."

My body was frozen, trying to listen for anything in her tone that gave her away, but all I heard was a worried mother.

Not that I had much experience with a worried mother, but I could imagine any mother wouldn't want her son estranged from her just because he and his dad were fighting.

"What would me coming over help, though? I can't exactly change Chase's mind on anything."

"Of course not, but it may make him see that I don't want to be the bad guy here. That maybe there is a chance we could talk this out in a more civil manner. I don't want to take up too much of your time, but it would really mean a lot if we could start working on this."

I looked over at the bag of food, and the beautiful interior of the Porsche grabbed my attention.

If there was any way that Chase could keep his fancy life and be with me, I would try to help him do it. He didn't deserve to give up everything just because he wanted to be with me.

"I don't have a lot of time, but I could stop by for a few minutes."

"Ahh," she said, and I could hear the smile on her face. "Perfect! I wouldn't want to keep you so head over and I will have some tea ready for us."

Ten minutes later, I was perched on a ridiculously fancy couch being handed a small teacup, and feeling like I fell into someone else's life.

A couch just for politely sitting, not sprawling out on with eight other people to watch a movie, or fall asleep on. I bounced a bit, the cushion underneath me so thin I could feel the wood beneath it.

"I'm so glad you could stop over," his mom said, handing me a small plate with a few cookies on it. "I really don't want Chase to think he has to run off like this."

"I don't think he's running off. He is staying with me right across town."

"He's staying with you?" she asked, her eyebrows shooting up. His mom was pretty in a way, but the way she dressed and did her makeup seemed to age her even more. I couldn't stop staring at the dried, cracked, pink hue of her lipstick. Something about it making me uneasy.

"He is. Temporarily, but after his dad told him to leave the condo, it was the fastest option for a place to live for now."

"He has a room here that he could have stayed in," she said with a huff. "This is exactly what I'm talking about. He should be running *to* his parents, not from them." The grimace of her thin lips quickly turned into a broad smile. "Would you like to see his old room?"

I set down the cup, already nodding. No part of me liked his dad, but his mom seemed pleasant enough. Maybe she felt a little more open when his dad wasn't around. Not that I would blame her.

We headed up the wide staircase as she told me more about their house and Chase growing up there. It was clear she loved him, and each kind word was making me wonder if it would be possible to have a bit of a relationship with his parents.

His mom, at least.

"Right here, dear. This door."

She pointed to a door on the left and I pushed open the door to step inside. The room was a deep blue color, and my eyes immediately began to roam over every inch.

"Now!" she yelled.

Two huge arms wrapped around me, squeezing me hard and lifting me off the floor. I yelled and kicked, but adjusted his grip and put one giant, sweaty hand over my mouth.

"Take her downstairs, and one of you go hide the car."

"And our money?"

"Oh shut up and do the job before you even think about getting paid."

The chilling demand echoed through the room. I tried to breathe in fresh air, but his huge palm covered my mouth and most of my nose.

The lack of air was making me dizzy, my mind screamed with a single, chilling realization—I had been lured into a trap, and now I was at her mercy with no one knowing where I was, and no one ever thinking to look for me here.

THIRTY-EIGHT
SCOUT

THE BLOOD that trickled down my neck was starting to tickle, the slow drips making me twitch to touch it, but my hands were tied behind me to a chair, so there was nothing I could do but rub my cheek against my shoulder. A scarf was tied around my face, gagging me and keeping me quiet.

The room was chilly as when I finally looked up, I realized why.

She put me in a wine cellar.

Apparently, wine cellars were the new dungeons for rich people.

I was alone still, but I didn't think that would last long. I could faintly hear people talking, but I couldn't make out a word, let alone who was saying it.

Another minute went by before the door slammed open. Chase's mom stepped inside. The brute who grabbed me, stepping in next to her, and I recognized him immediately. One of them came over, ripping the scarf down along with a clump of hair.

"You asked for help from those guys?" I asked, looking each of the gambling goons over.

She gave a soft smile and turned to them. "I was told that you owed them some money, and they were happy to help me in return for that debt being paid. Sorry dear, it seems they were a little rough getting you down here."

"You paid off my dad's debts in return for them tying me up? That seems like an incredibly unfair trade," I said, still fighting at the ties on my wrists. My knife was in my boot and there was no way I could get to it until one hand was free.

"When you add in the fact that I will be getting you away from my son, it seems like a perfectly reasonable trade." She turned back to them, handing over one big envelope. "I see you tied her up well, so you two are free to go. I will take it from here."

They smiled and waved before heading back out. She stood unmoving, looking me over and seemingly coming to some sort of conclusion.

"I wondered for hours if this was the right choice, but here now, looking you over. I think it was exactly the right decision. You are not fit for my son."

"So you are just like his father, then? Making his choices for him and telling him exactly what to do with his life?"

"His *father*? You mean the man I have been telling for weeks to take care of this issue and can't seem to get a handle on it? The one who said he *tried* to take care of it, but Chase was being difficult? Of course, the boy is going to be difficult when he thinks he's in love."

"Have you thought about the fact that he actually is in love with me?"

She gave a deep laugh, her chest shaking. "He might think he is, but I assure you, my son is not in love with any whore mechanic girl. Just because you have sex with him does not mean he is in love. And then you think you're going to tell him to ruin his life, and let you move into his condo together? Did you forget that we won't be paying the bills when he's acting like this? That he will come to resent you when he looks back on his life, and realizes he settled for someone like you instead of pursuing a career as a lawyer?"

"Do you know *anything* about him? Besides the stupid lawyer shit you all rant on about constantly."

"I know it's hard for you to understand, but some people have more ambition in life than working on cars and driving them around in circles."

Chase hadn't talked about his mom much, making me think she wasn't as bad as his father. It didn't take me long now, though, to realize that it was because she was, in fact, worse.

My chest tightened. I missed Chase. I wasn't sure how long it had been, maybe a few hours, but I would imagine he was already looking for me.

The diner was close enough to him that when I wasn't back within an hour, he should have started to wonder.

"So what's all this for? What happens now?"

"You're the problem. If you are no longer around," she said, waving a hand at me. "Then there is no more problem."

I had always wanted a mother in my life, but this was starting to make me wonder if I had been lucky.

"So then what now? You kill me? You keep me down here forever?"

"I buy you out of his life. I've seen your garage, your apartments, even your car. I know extra money would help you."

"You've been stalking me?"

"Checking up on you. I've been trying to determine what exactly my son was doing with you and your friends."

"And?"

"And the only conclusion is that he likes that you are easy, and different, from the girls he usually hangs around, but that is just a phase. A phase that has quickly gotten out of hand because my stupid husband can't handle a situation no matter what help I give him. I even had you arrested and instead of my husband stepping in to finish the job, he gives you plenty of time to call my son to help you. He's an idiot. How he runs that business is beyond me."

"*You* got us arrested for racing?"

"Of course. I thought my son would see how worthless you are after that and drop you, but no, Chase got to play the hero, and that only helped push you two together. That's why I have taken the matter fully into my own hands this time, and left no room for mistakes."

"But why? Is Chase happy and living a life he wants that bad?"

"It is when it doesn't follow our family's plan. His father's business will need someone to take over, and while one of my daughters went to law school, there is no way I am going to support a woman taking over that company. Especially one who thinks she is too good for this world we live in, and would ruin all the clients my husband has worked with for the last twenty years. No one but Chase is going to be able to run that business while keeping their mouth shut and doing what they are told. Chase is loyal, and besides this hiccup, he is loyal to his family. That loyalty will go far in that company, but then you come along and convince him he doesn't need to finish law school. You're so upset about your pathetic life, you want to drag him down to your level."

I curled my lips in, trying to hide my smile.

"You think it's amusing?"

"I think it's interesting that you feel so threatened by me. You're concerned that he's more loyal to me now."

"Don't get too cocky. I think he's loyal to you right this

second. The moment you leave him, though, he will see his mistake and come back to me. There is love and there is infatuation. I think we both know which one this is."

"But I'm not leaving him," I said, my stomach churning at his words. It's not like Chase and I had told each other we loved each other, but that was where we were headed.

Wasn't it?

His actions spoke enough for themselves, and I had to remind myself that his mom was doing this out of desperation, not because she knew Chase better than I did. Nothing she said was true.

"Technically, you will be leaving. He just won't know why."

There were so many flaws in her plan that I couldn't even start to name them, but I tried. It would at least buy me some time. "Do you honestly think my friends are going to be fine with me disappearing?"

"No, I've seen how you all are, and I'm even sure that Holt girl will get involved, but I have my plan laid out. You will stay down here until tonight. From there, you will either take the money and break up with my son for good, or find out that I am much, *much,* worse for you and your friends compared to those gambling broker idiots. My lifestyle depends on my son taking over his father's business and continuing to make the money. I wouldn't be dumb enough to let that go because of one good-for-nothing slut of a girl."

I tried not to let it, but the comment stung. I knew so much about me, and my life wasn't good for Chase. At least not in comparison to the life he could have, but what he did with his life wasn't exactly my choice.

Part of me wanted to agree, to force him back into this life that would give him all the money he could ever want. The other part of me remembered how miserable he looked in that life, though, and I wasn't going to be the one to force him back into it. If he wanted it, he could go back on his own, not by me breaking up with him.

"I won't do either of those things," I said. "I won't break up with Chase. If you are really that desperate for his loyalty, then you can earn it. And I won't be staying down here all night. My friends will be looking for me, and at some point, they are going to find me."

I knew the crew would do anything to find me, but I wasn't sure where I was or how they would even begin to know who took me. Chase would probably have the same idea that I did and expect it to be the goons going after my dad, but hunting them down could take hours only to come to a dead end.

As much as Chase had come to hate his dad, I wasn't sure that it would even cross his mind to think his mom would be involved in any of this. It never crossed mine.

Which meant it could be days, not even hours, before they found me, and I was under the impression that I had minutes left.

I groaned, a headache starting to throb incessantly. I needed to get my hands untied, and I needed to get out of this room. There were plenty of times we had dealt with fighting and dangerous situations, but I was never alone in them. I always had the crew there with me, and it made me stronger. I could do this, though. I wasn't weak, I wasn't timid, and if I got to my knife, I could get out of here.

She was still staring me down, her gaze unwavering, but I could see the anger that simmered beneath the surface. She came to some decision, and in three strides, she reached me. Her hand flew back and swung forward. The sting of her open palm on my cheek made me hiss, the burning sensation lingering.

"Are you serious?" I yelled, but she ignored me.

An alarm buzzed on her phone and she clicked it open. Her eyes went wide, and those creepy lips pressed together hard. She looked at me, and back at the phone before coming over and shoving the scarf back into my mouth.

"Keep your damn mouth shut, or this is going to get a lot worse for you. I have something to take care of."

She turned and walked out, shutting the heavy door. The click of a lock echoed in the eerie silence of the dark wine cellar. A shiver ran down my spine, the reality of my situation sinking in. I was alone, and unless a miracle happened, I wasn't sure if anyone would ever find me.

THIRTY-NINE
CHASE

"WHY THE HELL is the car Scout was driving showing that it's here at the house?" I asked again. She wasn't answering, her shoulders back and her face giving nothing away.

"How do you know that it's here?"

"Because my father put a damn GPS on my car and thought I wouldn't notice."

Her eyes went wide, and my heart dropped.

She knew something which meant that Scout very well might be here along with the car.

"She might be here on the property," I said. "The car is in one of the old barns out back. Let's start there."

They all nodded, and headed outside, no one hesitating to start around the back of the house. My mother yelled something, but I ignored it. The car might give us some clue as to where she was, and I didn't think any questions I had for my mother were about to be answered now.

I pointed out the barn ahead where the car pinged, and was surprised when the girls broke out in a run. We all picked up the pace to catch up to them, but they were faster.

"I think we have a problem," Jax said.

"Obviously," Ransom said, rolling his eyes.

"No, I think we…I think we created a girl gang," Jax said, pointing to where the girls were pulling hard on the doors. None of them looked happy, and as pissed as the guys were, they all looked deadly.

"Their little leader might be inside," Fox said. "Pretty sure we need them to be a girl gang right this second. We will worry about the consequences of that later, and how they might turn on us one day, but we shouldn't be surprised."

Kye laughed as we reached the doors, all of us grabbing on to pull the old wood doors open. "I'm all for it. Sending a group of rabid women after people is amazing. And luckily, they love me since they don't have to date me, so they aren't turning on me."

The wooden latch inside was fighting to break loose.

"There's two windows on the side," I said to the girls. "See if you can see inside at all."

They nodded, all of them disappearing around the corner as we all pulled again.

Finally, the wood broke loose, the doors swinging open, and the Porsche was on the other side. Everyone fanned out, but the whine of an engine caught my attention. From here, I could only see part of the driveway, but I didn't miss the black SUV that pulled up to the front of the house.

I took off running back towards the house. I knew that SUV.

It was the same blacked out one that had pulled up that first night with Scout at the warehouses. The gambling broker who took my watch and changed my life forever.

If Scout hadn't been meeting them that night, she might not have ended her date with Jesse, and I may have never had a chance with her.

By the time I made it around the front, the car was shut off and no one was inside it.

I slammed the front door open. "Scout!" I yelled, running back upstairs and opening doors. I hadn't seen any sign of my dad yet, but that didn't mean he hadn't come with them.

He was using her father and the money he needed against her. Those guys would take her, or worse, hurt her.

There was no one upstairs, and the crew had come back in the front.

"She's not out there," Fox said. "I don't see any sign that she was at all."

"There's a guest house out back that he might have her in," I said, pointing to a side door. Ransom and Kye took off, but I stopped them. "Listen, if you run into my dad, do what you need to do to get to Scout. I don't think he deserves any mercy after this, and I need her back more."

They nodded and headed out the back door to the guest house while I turned back to the crew. "There's this level, and the garage." I kept pointing out directions. Jax and Fox went to the garage, the girls insisting they would check this floor together.

That left me with checking downstairs.

I nearly jumped down the stairs, yelling her name as I went. I still hadn't seen anyone, which meant they were with her, wherever she was.

I knew my dad, and I had to think about what he would have done. He would feel safer if he put her somewhere more enclosed, somewhere safer and more contained. He would think he was smart for it, he would think he was far enough away from the threat that he could do anything he wanted.

But I was the threat this time. *I* was the one coming for him this time, and I was currently ready to rip him apart. There did not need to be any mercy from whoever found him, but I hoped it was me.

I was opening more doors, even checking the closets, when I heard it. The cry was faint at first, but clear. I knew exactly where they were, and I couldn't believe it hadn't been my first thought.

The wine cellar was old now, but my dad had been having it redone months ago. I hadn't been in it since, but it would be nearly soundproof.

"Scout," I breathed, already running down the hall towards the sound. She was here, and I would have her in my arms in seconds.

I would get to him before he hurt her more.

More.

I pulled the heavy door, the creaking of it impossible to miss. The sight in front of me nearly made me sick. Anger burned through me as I watched the larger of the stupid gambling guys lift her up and the other work to tie her legs.

It wasn't just that, though.

It was my own mother stepping closer to Scout and slapping her. A line of red cut across Scout's cheek where my mother's ring had snagged against her skin.

Scout looked at me, eyes wide, with a scarf wrapped around her mouth.

"Mom?" I asked, making her freeze and turn to me. "You did this?"

I had been ready to face my father. I was angry and ready to fist fight him if it came to it. There was nothing preparing me for finding my own mother on the other side of this door, though. At most, I thought she knew about it, but I didn't think she would be the one running it.

"Chase?" she asked. "What do you think you're doing down here?"

The goons set Scout back on the chair, flanking my mother as though she was their leader.

"How many times did you hit her?" I asked, stalking towards her.

She stepped back, keeping a distance between us, the fear clear on her face.

"Enough to keep her quiet," she said, her words cold and careless.

My vision blurred with rage. I had been ready to hit my father, but my mother? What was I supposed to do about that?

"It had to be done, Chase. She's ruining your life and neither of you are ending this. I care about you enough to give you a better life than what she is trying to convince you to settle for."

"If this was about me having a better life, you would be happy for me."

"Why would I be happy to watch my only son throw away everything we worked for? Everything we have given you? What part of that should I be happy about?"

"The part where *I'm* actually happy for once. The part where I found someone I love who loves me. This has nothing to do with me having a better life. This is about you keeping your money and wanting more. I'm a part of your plan and without me, you lose out. I don't know everything that you lose out on, but it has to be something big enough to hurt her."

"You can be happy in a different life with a different person. Not one who tells you to drop it all and run off with her. Not one who can't even make it through one dinner party without embarrassing us all. You need to decide right now, Chase. You need to decide who it's going to be so I can take care of this," my mother said. She didn't look sad or scared anymore. She was trying to scold me, to talk down to me as a son so I would hang my head and listen. Honestly, I didn't even blame her for trying. It had worked so many times before, but things were different now.

"Who is it, Chase? Who is it going to be?"

"Who it's going to be for what?" I tried to step around her and closer to Scout, but the two guys still crowded around her. The cold, calculating look in her eyes made me finally see what Scout had seen in me that night of the party. It was dead, and hollow just like she said. It was all a plan of greed and my mother didn't care who she took down in the process.

"She wants to know who you're loyal to." Scout's quiet voice filled the room as she tried to push the scarf out of her mouth more.

"What?"

"She thinks that you are only temporarily loyal to me and wants that to be over. She wants your loyalty back, and that's what he wants to know right now, if you are loyal," she said, her legs still tied together.

"Shut her up!" my mother yelled. "Get her upstairs and get her the hell out of here."

They looked at each other and shook their heads. "Kidnapping is going to cost you," one of them said.

"I don't care about the price, just go."

"We need to be paid first if we are risking the cops following us."

My mother sighed and looked them over. "Does it look like I have a checkbook or cash on me right this second?"

"No, it doesn't," the bigger one said, stepping around me and heading towards the door. "Feel free to give us a call when you do."

I stepped closer to Scout now, careful to not spook my mother and encourage her to call them back in.

"My boot, Chase," she said, moving her left boot. I nearly smiled. Of course my girl had her knife in her boot.

I dug into her boot, the ties keeping her ankles tight together. She hissed, and I pulled back, not wanting to hurt her any more.

"Get it. I don't care, just hurry and get it."

"Stop, Chase," my mother said. "You two need to stop him!" she yelled out the door to the goons. "Chase, I can't lose you." I could hear the panic in her voice this time, but I knew it wasn't for me. It was for herself. For money, status, and power.

The plans her and my father had set up for me all those years ago were crumbling around her all because of one girl.

One girl who showed up and wrecked my entire world, and I was more thankful for that every day that I knew her. The knife finally came out, and I reached back to cut through the ties on her hand.

"I'm sorry," I said to her. "I am so fucking sorry, and I really hope you still love me after this."

"You love me?"

"Of course I love you."

"Well, I wasn't sure. You never said it, but of course I'll still love you after this."

I smiled, the tension in my chest finally loosening since I found out she was missing. It wasn't a far jump to assume that she wouldn't want any connection to me after this. I should have known Scout wouldn't be fazed nearly as much. She was a fighter, and nothing was going to stop her until we were out of here and back home. She might fall apart then, but for now, we were okay.

"Cut that and run. The crew is here and will be upstairs somewhere."

Before I could get her completely untied, a full bottle of wine flew across the room, smashing against the rock wall behind me.

"Stop it right now!" my mother screamed.

Scout reached down, sawing at the ties around her ankles, as my mother screamed and threw another bottle. It was fine. As long as her attention stayed on me, Scout could get out of here without any incident.

The ties broke free and Scout stood. As though my mother could hear my fears, she screamed, taking off with a wine bottle raised up as she ran at Scout.

I reached out, grabbing Scout and but she fell back into the chair, covering her head with her arms.

My mother made it two feet before she was tackled to the ground with a thud. She yelled as she fell. Immediately screaming about them getting off of her, and when I looked over, I was surprised to see the girls.

And they were not being kind to the woman who just hurt Scout.

"I've never been so happy to see an angry girl gang."

"A what?" Scout asked, as I helped her up again.

"Jax called them your girl gang, and I see why." I stepped closer, keeping Scout next to me. "Alright, come on, let's get her upstairs." They all glared at me but agreed, getting her up and walking out.

"I would offer to help make sure she gets upstairs, but I think they have it covered."

"They will handle it," she said, leaning against me harder.

"Good, because I need a minute," I said, grabbing her waist and pulling her to face me. "I'm sorry, Scout, so fucking sorry, and I promise I'm going to make sure neither of them ever bother us again."

She smiled, reaching up to run a hand down my jaw. "I know. We can worry about that later. For right now, I would like to go home."

"Not until we stop at a hospital and make sure you are okay."

She groaned, but nodded. "Fine. They didn't hurt me too much. Just some scrapes and bruises."

I reached up, wiping at the blood dripping down her neck. "You think this isn't much? You have a head injury."

She shrugged. "Just a scratch."

"No need," Kye said, stepping inside and taking in the damage. "We already called the police, and an ambulance. The goons are sitting upstairs with the guys who stopped them at the door, and your mother is sitting *peacefully* with the girls."

I could only laugh. "It's not even a girl gang. You have your own damn army."

"Is that a problem?"

"Not even a little. Come on, let's go get this part over with."

HOURS WENT BY AS WE WAITED. SCOUT HAD BEEN CHECKED OUT first. As she was being checked by the EMT's, my mother and her two helpers were being arrested.

My dad pulled up, his eyes frantic as he searched the crowd for her.

Not me.

Her.

And I knew right then that even if he didn't have anything to do with today, he was just as guilty.

When he finally made it to her side, he looked for me. Our eyes met, and even from across the driveway, I could see the anger and disgust.

"Do you like what you did?" he yelled. "Do you feel better about your life trying to ruin your mothers? They were in our home stealing officers," he yelled. "They should all be locked up immediately."

I shook my head, winding around the ambulance to find Scout and the crew. Her hair was still in the two long braids, but was a mess now. Her cheek was red and the fresh cut on her neck wrapped up and over her jaw a little. It wasn't bad, but I hated seeing her in any pain.

Those big, hazel eyes still lit up when they met mine, and

before I could worry anymore, she was wrapping herself around me. My chest felt ready to burst. The love she had seemed never ending and somehow, some of that love was mine now.

I was going to deal with my dad. I was going to ruin his life the way that he tried to ruin mine, but for now, all I was going to do was take my girl home.

FORTY

CHASE

<u>TWO WEEKS later</u>

They always say revenge is bad.

That hitting back won't be satisfying, but they were lying.

I've never felt better than when I walked into my father's office surrounded by FBI agents.

It hadn't even taken long for them to organize it, and with his own son as the leading witness, they couldn't ignore it.

I started pointing to filing cabinets, already knowing which one held the documents that had been tampered with. He didn't fill all of them, knowing that if they looked through documents that had merit first, they might not keep digging.

He thought he could get away with it all. He thought he was nothing short of a genius, and for years that worked out for him.

And maybe it would have kept working out, but he tried to ruin the one thing I loved. After my mother was arrested for kidnapping, and he immediately bailed her out, they went after all of us. He began throwing every accusation and lawsuit against us that I could barely keep up.

Scout was doing fine now, mainly just cuts and bruises left, but it didn't matter because they had both wanted to do worse.

They wanted Scout gone from my life, and had only been growing more desperate to ruin her.

So now I was taking away everything that he ever loved, which was his power and success. His success that had been built on the backs of others, and power that was nothing more than his image. An image that was currently being ruined on national news stations right this minute. The news crews outside the building were stopping other partners that were being walked out in handcuffs, and any employee that would stop to gossip, which was a surprisingly large amount.

Apparently, on top of being an asshole for clients, he was an asshole to his employees. It shouldn't be a surprise, but it was strange to let go of every shred of respect you have for someone who was supposed to be the most respected person in your life.

My mother had already had everything taken from her, the rumors swirling so fast that her reputation was being drug through the mud, the downfall of her husband not helping the rumors calm down at all.

I stayed for another two hours, doing everything I could to get every drawer, cabinet, and locked box opened until they finally said I could go for the day.

Scout was downstairs, lounged across one of the oversized chairs in the waiting room. Her head was tilted back to the ceiling, eyes closed, and she looked so relaxed. I leaned over the back of the chair, brushing a stray lock of red hair off her forehead as her eyes fluttered open.

"You seem relaxed," I said, nearly laughing.

"Not relaxed, just thinking."

"About?"

"You."

"What about me?"

She got up and wrapped her arms around me. "I was wondering if you wanted to make this living together thing *not* temporary."

"Scout, are you finally asking me to move in with you?"

"Yes, I am, but only if you are agreeing."

I laughed, leaning down to kiss her. "Do you think I would want to live anywhere else? I've been trying not to rush you, but damn, I've given hints."

"Well, I was just a little unsure how you felt about me."

I laughed harder. "Was it the giving up of my life to be with you, or the tattoo of the nickname that made you question it?"

She held me harder as she laughed. "None of the above, just my anxious brain making me doubt that someone could love me that much."

"Better start believing it, Hellcat, because I'm here to stay, and now you have to live with me, too."

She groaned but kissed me again.

"Well, I have a whole new life to build now, and I'm done here, so what do you want to do first?"

I leaned down, kissing her hard as she pressed hard against me.

"You know, I have this really fast car now," she said.

"Oh really?"

"Yeah, do you want to see how fast I can get us back home and into bed?"

I smiled, already pulling her to the front door. "Absolutely yes. You have ten minutes before I start undressing you and it doesn't matter to me if that starts in the car or in the apartment."

She revved the engine, the vibration sending a shot of adrenaline through me, but it wasn't just from the car or knowing she was about to take off at a ridiculous speed.

It was the realization that I finally found where I belong in my life. In all the chaos, I found my home, and to my surprise, it was never a place.

It was her.

EPILOGUE

SCOUT

THE SUN DIPPED low on the horizon, casting the entire track in a warm glow. Chase stood by my car, waiting for me.

It was all so familiar. The roar of engines, the smell of gasoline, the electrifying atmosphere of a race night.

But tonight was different.

Tonight was the first night of my official race season as one of Holt Racing's drivers. It was the start of my career as a racer. I knew tonight's race would, hopefully, be the start of hundreds of races around the country, and maybe around the world, if Holt let me do any other type of racing for him.

My career had taken off, and somehow, in the mess of getting to this point, I found Chase.

Chase, who had been there every second of every race day, training day, and everything in between. Who proudly told everyone he could that his girlfriend races cars for a living, and was most recently learning everything he could about engines so he could be more involved on race days. The crew was happy to teach him, too. He still went out with them on their guys' nights.

Somehow that rich, rude, perfect man from the first night at the races was the perfect guy for me all along.

He waved me over to the trailer, the box in his hand sparking my curiosity as I headed his way.

"Is that for me?" I asked, the neon green bow on top matching the Hellcat's color perfectly.

"It is."

"And what is it for?"

He chewed on his bottom lip, his cheeks turning the slightest shade of red. I had never seen Chase nervous, but the sudden uncertainty on his face made my heart melt.

"I thought you might want some options, so I had this made. If you don't want it, that's okay. I won't be offended at all, but I just...wanted you to know it was an option."

My eyebrows furrowed as I opened the box.

The black racing suit was folded up neatly, all my sponsorship patches clearly on the sleeve. I pulled it out further, seeing my name on the front in the same neon green color as the bow.

"A new racing suit? I mean, I always love to have more, but I do have one right now. I'm not sure what you mean by options."

He grabbed it, turning it around and showing me the back. My stomach flipped as I saw the last name 'Parker' in neon green block letters across the back. Unlike the current one I wore, where that space stayed blank.

"It has your name on it."

"It does," he said, and I could still hear the uncertainty in his tone.

"Is this some type of proposal?"

He laughed. "Not quite. I'd like to do that the traditional way, with a ring, not a racing suit. I didn't think you would love me asking you to marry me quite yet, but there's no doubt in my mind that I want to. I don't think either of our last names brings the best family history, but I was thinking that maybe we could start over and try to make this one better. My sister has done a lot of good with it. Maybe we could, too. Like I said, though, you don't have to wear it unless it's something you want."

He looked at me with a soft smile, and I knew he meant it. He wouldn't push me if I wasn't ready, just like he hadn't when we were thinking about moving in together. He was always there to remind me that he wanted to, though, and I appreciated every reassuring comment.

Tears welled up in my eyes as I traced the name on the back. It wasn't my name, but the last name attached to me felt gross now. It felt full of betrayal and deceit. It felt like a brand of every terrible thing my father did that I now had to carry, and the weight of it was too much. Allen was my last name, but I wanted a new one. I wanted a fresh start and a life that matched it. Scout Allen was the little girl who grew up in that terrible place with a father who hated her. Now, I could be Scout Parker. A professional driver, a girl who had a family that loved her, and a guy who seemed willing to do anything for her.

That's who I wanted to be.

I grabbed the suit from him and headed inside the trailer to change. Maybe it was a little soon since we weren't married, but for once, I was willing to take that chance on someone.

When I stepped out, Chase's smile grew, and when I spun around, he picked me up.

"You made a good choice showing up with a racing suit and not a ring," I said, laughing.

"Oh yeah? Was I right about it being a little too soon?"

"A little, but I want you to know that I definitely want that."

His face broke into a wide grin, relief flooding his features as he kissed me.

"I like this, though. It kind of makes me feel like we're in this together," I said.

"We are in this together," he said. "I like knowing we have

each other. Hell, I even like knowing we have the whole crew with us. It's nice not feeling like you have to face everything alone."

Without another word, I wrapped myself around him, kissing him hard as he walked us towards the trailer. He deepened the kiss, his mouth growing demanding as his hands slid over my ass to hold me up.

"You know, I have to go race. I don't think we have enough time for this."

He laughed and turned. "I really want to convince you that we do have enough time, but I think watching you race and then getting you all to myself tonight sounds better."

I groaned as he set me down and almost changed my mind until the crew started yelling for us.

Just like every race, everything turned to chaos, with people running in every direction and yelling out things that needed done. For once, though, I stopped and looked around, Chase coming to my side and grabbing my hand.

It had been hard getting to this point, but we were here now. And now I knew no matter what the future held, we would face it together. With Chase and the crew by my side, there was nothing we couldn't overcome.

And I had been right that night I met Chase. He was perfect, just not in any of the ways I first thought.

"Chase?"

"Yes, Hellcat."

"I love you."

"I love you, too. With every damn part of me, I love you, too."

THANK YOU!

Thank you so much for reading Scout and Chase's story!

You can jump into **Kye's story Reckless Fate** coming this June!

If you enjoyed Love Collided, please consider leaving a review!
Support from readers like you means so much to me!

If you loved the crew, don't miss:
    Ransom and Quinn's story in Heart Wrenched
    Fox and Ash's story in Wrecked Love
    Jax and Carly's story in Racing Hearts

Printed by Amazon Italia Logistica S.r.l.
Torrazza Piemonte (TO), Italy